AMAZING STORIES OF CYPRIOT MIGRATION

CONSTANTINOS EMMANUELLE

ISBN 978-0-646-86446-4

THE CORSICA: Amazing stories of Cypriot migration

Printed in Australia

First Printing, 2022

ISBN 978-0-646-86446-4

A catalogue record for this
book is available from the
National Library of Australia

Written by Constantinos Emmanuelle
Book design by Constantinos Emmanuelle
Photography of interviewees by Constantinos Emmanuelle

www.talesofcyprus.com

THE CORSICA

AMAZING STORIES OF CYPRIOT MIGRATION

> *Of course we are happy that we came to Australia. It's the first time in our lives that our stomachs were full. If life was good in Cyprus we would have stayed.*

KYRIACOS CHRISTODOULOU

DEDICATION

This book is dedicated to those remarkable Cypriot migrants who took a leap of faith after the Second World War to migrate to a foreign land in search of a better life. Their gutsy determination and resilience helped to ensure that my generation and my children's generation would prosper and succeed. Their unwavering sacrifices and selfless acts have not been in vain. I am forever grateful and have the deepest respect for this incredible group of people. I am certain that we shall never see their kind again.

Illustration titled *Homesick* by Costas Emmanuelle © 2021. Digital and traditional media.

ACKNOWLEDGEMENTS

I would like to begin by thanking all of the
wonderful Cypriots who allowed me to interview
them for this book, especially the passengers
who travelled on the Corsica and migrated to
Australia in 1952.

I would also like to acknowledge those kind
individuals who have taken the time to help me
in my quest to learn more about immigration
and migration, ocean liners and other related
topics. They include; Nick Cree, Paul Woods, Keith
Stodden, Andrekos Varnavas, Nick Henderson,
Maria Shialis, Peter Yiannoudes, Peter Plowman,
Michael Protopapa, Anthony Pezzano, Con
Pagonis, Lella Cariddi and Costa Nicola.

Of course, this book would not have been possible
without the help and support of my family,
especially my beautiful wife Christina Pavlides and
her father Andreas Pavlides. Christina has always
inspired me to follow my dream and do whatever
it takes to preserve and promote our Cypriot
cultural heritage. Without her unwavering love
and support, I don't think I would have gained the
confidence to produce this book.

Lastly, I would like to thank all my friends and
family, including my loyal online community.
Your words of encouragement and praise over the
years have fuelled my desire to document
and preserve the stories of this incredible
generation of migrants.

DISCLAIMER

The names of people mentioned in this book
are spelt in accordance with the wishes of the
storytellers. Location names are spelt as they
appear on maps pre-1950. In addition, all of the
vintage photographs have been scanned in their
original state and have not been digitally altered
or enhanced in any way. Photographs that
appear blurry or out of focus are authetic to
the original copy.

[Form M. 27.]

COMMONWEALTH OF AUSTRALIA

APPLICATION FOR PERMIT TO ENTER AUSTRALIA.

(Immigration Act, 1901–1935).

Notes.—(1) If the applicant is residing in the British Isles or Europe this form should be forwarded to—

The Official Secretary,
Australia House,
Strand,
London,
England.

If the applicant resides elsewhere the form should be forwarded to—
The Secretary,
Department of Immigration,
Canberra,
Australia.

(2) This Application must be filled up in the English language, and the Certificate from a qualified medical practitioner, police officer or other public official, if not in English, must be accompanied by a certified translation in that language.

Full Name—Surname to be stated in block letters. Address. — I, *Ibrahim Rifat*

of *Mennoyia Larnaca Cyprus* ....do hereby make application for permission to enter Australia, and in support of the application submit the following information, which I declare to be true :—

(1) Full name *IBRAHIM RIFAT*

(2) Nationality *British by birth*

(3) Race *Moslem Turk* (State also whether Jewish or not) *not Jewish*

(4) I was born at *Mennoyia Larnaca Cyprus* on the day of *3rd day of March*, 19*23*

(5) Marital status (single, married, widowed or divorced) *Single*

(6) I shall be accompanied by the following members of my family :—

If unaccom...

2

DESCRIPTION
SIGNALEMENT   Wife-Femme

Profession }
Profession } *Farmer*

Place and date }
of birth }
Lieu et date } *Menoyia, Cyprus*
de naissance } *3. March, 1923*

Residence }
Résidence } *Cyprus*

Height }
Taille } *5* ft. *5* in.   ft. in.

Colour of eyes }
Couleur des yeux } *Brown*

Colour of hair }
Couleur des cheveux } *Chestnut*

Special peculiarities }
Signes particuliers } *Nil*

ENFANTS

3

PHOTOGRAPH OF BEARER

WIFE   FEMME

SIGNATURE OF BEARER. SIGNATURE DU TITULAIRE.

Ibrahim Rifat

Et de sa Femme.

person to whom
...ional Archives of
...wer under sub-
...1983, certify that
...document that is
...ives of Australia.

...7

...Cyprus

P.T.O.

CONTENTS

84 Loukia Papaharalambous

89 Andreas Tryphonos

96 Eleftherios Charalambides

102 Haralambos Theophanous

107 Phokion Pavlides

110 Eleni Savva

117 Eleni and Maria Christodoulou

120 Chrysi Georgiou

125 Iacovos Christodoulou

128 Andreas Savva

133 Christodoulos Apeitos

136 Nicos Jonis

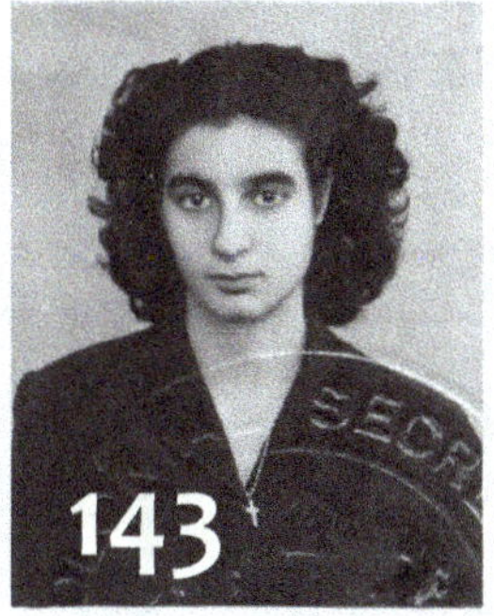

143 Olga Angellis

146 Loizos Panaouris

151 Andreas Charalambou

156 Chrysanthos Theodosiou

CONTENTS

228

Costa Leonidas

233

Stavros Symeon

238

Michalis Mavrogenis

243

Georghia Kefala

246

Christos Georgallis

250

Pieris Loizou Piera

255

George Christofi

260

Sevil Haki Abdurazak

265

Angeliki Demetriou

268

Evdokia Nikiforou

271

Demetrious Georgiou

274

Evdokia Haralambous

281

Kyriacos Christodoulou

285

Anastasia Ioannou

288

Other Passengers

295

**A Quick Look at
Maltese Migrants**

Ephemera from the author's personal collection
TRAVELLERS' GUIDE TO
PERTH
KANGAROO PAW
— a native flower.
With Compliments
A.N.Z.
A.N.Z. BANK
AUSTRALIA AND NEW ZEALAND BANK LIMITED
AUSTRALIA AND NEW ZEALAND SAVINGS BANK LIMITED
AUSTRALIA SAYS "WELCOME!"
A Message for the Migrant and the Visitor from Overseas
GOVERNMENT OF NEW SOUTH WALES
DEPARTMENT OF PUBLIC HEALTH
X-RAY EXAMINATION OF THE CHEST
Australia
in brie

Facts about
YOUR VOYAGE
to Australia

Edition No. 9   **August 1960**

IF you have arranged to go to Australia under the Assisted Passages Scheme for British migrants you will soon be setting off on the sea voyage to your new life, and this pamphlet is designed to help you to prepare for the trip.

You will travel either in an all-migrant ship specially chartered for the voyage, or you will be an ordinary tourist class passenger in one of the liners on the England/Australia run. A limited number of migrants will fly to Australia, but separate instructions will be issued to them.

When you reach Australia, Commonwealth and State immigration officers are available to help newcomers with their problems on baggage, temporary accommodation and other matters.

Entry into Australia

As a general rule, no restrictions are placed on the entry into Australia of British subjects of pure European descent, providing they are of good character and in sound health and have a valid British passport or equivalent. The term "sound health" means freedom from...

Off to Australia . . . it's a wonderful trip, with plenty of time for relaxation.

BERTH NO.
NAME
MEAL TICKET
ESSEN SCHEIN
POTRAVINOVE LISTKY
TESSERA DI GENERI
ALIMENTARI

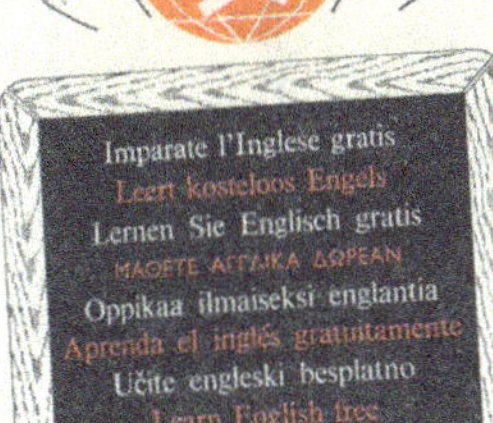

Know
AUSTRALIA!

MAP OF
MELBOURNE
AND SUBURBS

TRAVELLERS' GUIDE TO
TASMANIA

AMUSEMENTS

CINEMAS AND NEWS REELS		Telephone
...any (News Reels)	232 Collins Street (near Swanston St.)	Cen. 6251
...enaeum	188 Collins Street (near Swanston St.)	MF 3831
...tralia Theatre	270 Collins Street (bet. Elizabeth & Swanston Sts.)	Cen. 4387
...itol	118 Swanston Street (bet. Collins & Lt. Collins Sts.)	Cen. 1141
...tury (News Reels)	Cnr. Swanston & Little Collins Streets	Cen. 1001
...uire	238 Bourke Street (bet. Swanston & Russell Sts.)	FB 2636
...osvenor	203 Little Collins Street (near Swanston St.)	MF 1111
...g's	135 Russell Street (bet. Lt. Collins & Bourke Sts.)	MF 3031
...eum	237 Bourke Street (bet. Swanston & Russell Sts.)	MF 1556
...estic	179 Flinders Street (bet. Swanston & Russell Sts.)	MF 3741
...tro	167 Collins Street (near Russell St.)	MF 3131
...tro	20 Bourke Street (bet. Exhibition & Spring Sts.)	FB 3401
...eon	293 Bourke Street (near Swanston St.)	Cen. 4321
...ia	191 Collins Street (bet. Swanston & Russell Sts.)	MF 8383
...gent	191 Collins Street (bet. Swanston & Russell Sts.)	MF 8131
...oy	172 Russell Street (bet. Bourke & Lonsdale Sts.)	FB 3366
...r (News Reels)	Cnr. Elizabeth Street & Flinders Lane	MF 8796
...ce	154 Flinders Street (cnr. Russell & Flinders Sts.)	MF 8656
...ler (News Reels)	266 Collins Street (bet. Swanston & Elizabeth Sts.)	Cen. 3626
...os (News Reels)	283 Bourke Street (next Odeon Theatre)	Cen. 4323

THEATRES		
...nedy	244 Exhibition Street (cnr. Exhibition & Lonsdale Sts.)	FB 3211
...' Majesty's	205 Exhibition Street (cnr. Exhibition & Lt. Bourke Sts.)	FB 3211
...ncess	163 Spring Street (cnr. Lt. Bourke & Spring Sts.)	FB 1211
...oli	249 Bourke Street (bet. Swanston & Russell Sts.)	MF 2111

CITY SWIMMING BATHS		
...y Baths	Swanston Street (Open throughout the year)	FJ 3940
...mpic Pool	Batman Avenue (opp. River Yarra, east of Princes Bridge)	MF 8239
...C.A.	City Road, South Melbourne (south of Princes Bridge)	MB 4153
...mming Stadium (Olympic Park) Batman Avenue.		BM 3894

SKATING RINKS		
...darium (Ice)	16 City Road, South Melbourne (opp. Y.M.C.A.)	MB 4405
...Moritz (Ice)	Upper Esplanade, St. Kilda	LA 9837
...rth's Park and Olympia (Roller), Princes Bridge.		MB 4443

DANCING		
...o's Cabaret	57 Collins Place (bet. Flinders Lane & Collins St.)	MF 5448
...io's Restaurant	Cnr. Exhibition & Lt. Bourke Sts.	FB 2555
...ale Ballroom	Exhibition Buildings (Saturday nights only)	FJ 1097
...cadero Palais	Princes Bridge	MB 4552
...gett's Ballroom	Greville Street (opp. Prahran Railway Station)	LA 3176
...son de Luxe	(Cabaret) Broadway, Elwood	LF 8260
...is De Danse	The Esplanade, St. Kilda	LA 7878
...n Grove	The Esplanade, St. Kilda	LA 7900
...ridge's Restaurant	53 Toorak Road, South Yarra	Win. 7298
...eman's Dances	25 Collins Street	MF 4270

SPORTING—VARIOUS		
...letics—Cinder track and sports ground, Olympic Park, Batman Avenue		—
...ck Cycling—Board Cycling Track, Strathmore (formerly North Essendon)		FX 1793
—Velodrome, Batman Avenue		BM 2079
...rse Racing—Flemington, Caulfield, Moonee Valley.		
...ght Trotting (in season)—Showgrounds, Flemington.		
...g Racing—Sandown Park.		

Published July, 1957, by the Victorian Railways Public Relations and Betterment Board by direction of the Commissioners.

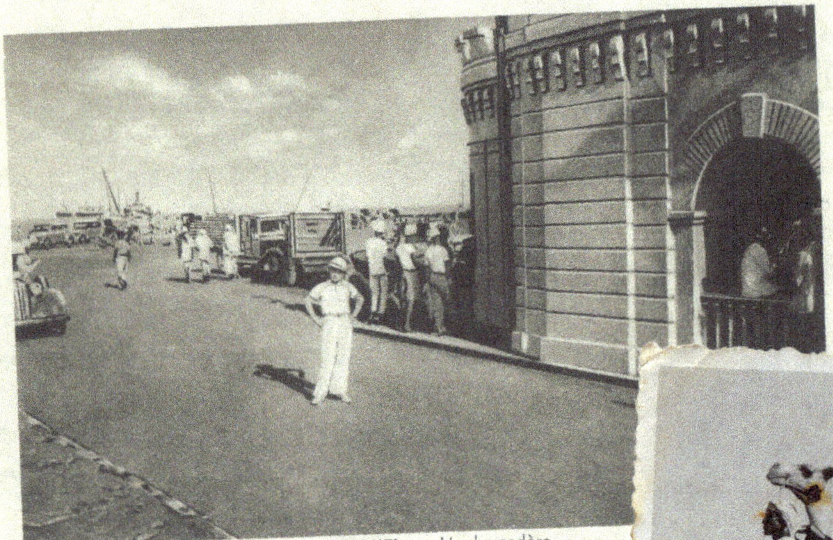

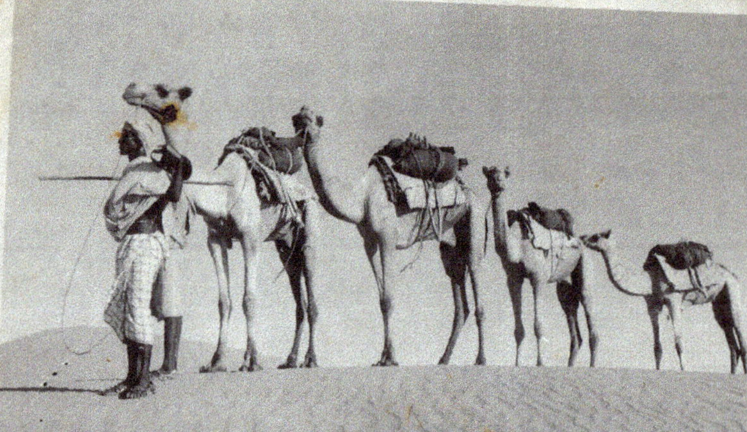

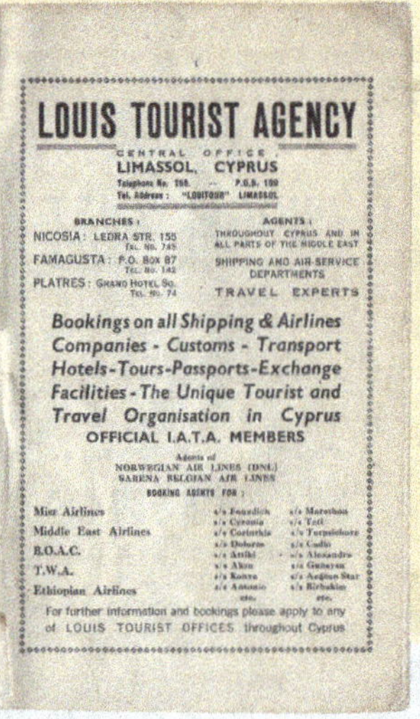

DJIBOUTI — L'embarcadère

NWEALTH OF AUSTRALIA

RTMENT OF IMMIGRATION
NEW SOUTH WALES BRANCH)

PLEASE ADDRESS REPLY TO
COMMONWEALTH MIGRATI
BOX 3914 G.P.O., SYDNE

AND QUOTE: N50/3/

18-20 YORK STREET
SYDNEY

13th April, 1951.

CAMEL TRAIN IN MASSAWA, 1951

The issue of a document does no
holder to any special or preferential
gards the grant of a visa for, or a passa
nd in view of the number of persons wishi
stralia, a considerable period may elapse
possession of a document can embark. Th
clear to the grantee.

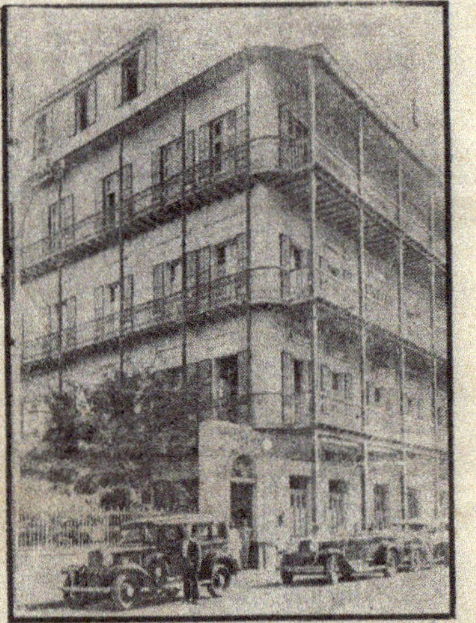

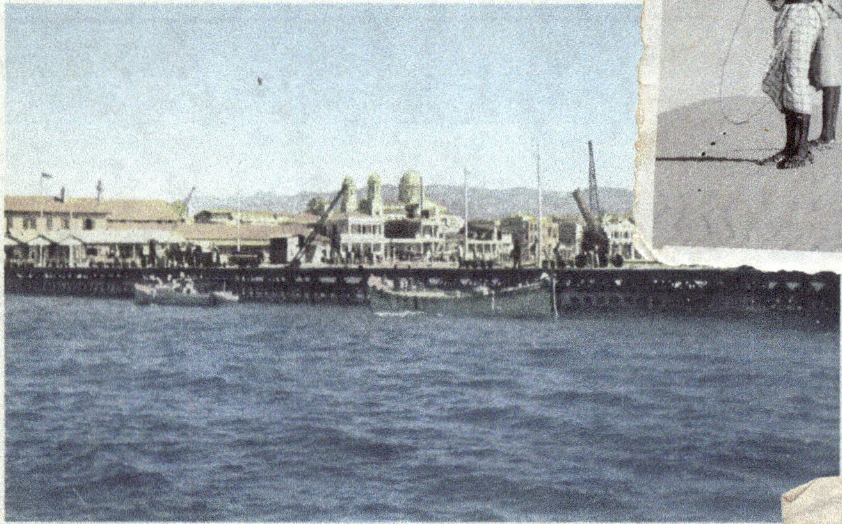

23 SEA FRONT. LIMASSOL. CYPRUS

plant origi

COPY

LR.

COMMONWEALTH OF AUSTRALIA

No. V46/

DEPARTMENT OF IMMIG

28th July, 1950.

Dear Sir,

I refer to your application for the ad
Australia of Christoforos Yianni Kikkides and des
that the application has been approved sub
the usual

A document authorizing the admission
Kikkides has been forwarded to the
foros Yianni Cyprus, and provided there is no
Secretary ation, facilities to enable him to
Australia will be made available by the Colonial

Yours faithfully,

Sgd. H. Feilby

for Commonwealth Migratio

Mr. George Tsindos,
Monte Vista,
Portsea Rd.,
SORRENTO, Vic.

لوكاندة سميراميس - بور سعيد

SEMIRAMIS HOTEL

Proprietor: GEORGE LAHANAS - Manager L. SINIGAGLIA
Nº 2 Constantinieh Street
Phone 2812 — P.O.B. 295 — R.C. Canal 8996 ex 137
PORT-SAID

LOUIS TOURIST AGENCY

CENTRAL OFFICE:
LIMASSOL, CYPRUS
Telephone No. 188. — P.O.B. 199
Tel. Address: "LOUITOUR" LIMASSOL

BRANCHES:
NICOSIA: LEDRA STR. 155 Tel. No. 745
FAMAGUSTA: P.O. BOX 87 Tel. No. 142
PLATRES: GRAND HOTEL SQ. Tel. No. 74

AGENTS:
THROUGHOUT CYPRUS AND IN ALL PARTS OF THE MIDDLE EAST
SHIPPING AND AIR-SERVICE DEPARTMENTS
TRAVEL EXPERTS

Bookings on all Shipping & Airlines Companies - Customs - Transport Hotels-Tours-Passports-Exchange Facilities - The Unique Tourist and Travel Organisation in Cyprus

OFFICIAL I.A.T.A. MEMBERS

Agents of
NORWEGIAN AIR LINES (DNL)
SABENA BELGIAN AIR LINES

BOOKING AGENTS FOR:

Misr Airlines
Middle East Airlines
B.O.A.C.
T.W.A.
Ethiopian Airlines

s/s Foundich, s/s Cyronia, s/s Corinthia, s/s Dolores, s/s Attiki, s/s Akra, s/s Konya, s/s Antonio etc.

s/s Marathon, s/s Tell, s/s Terpsichore, s/s Cadio, s/s Alexandra, s/s Gunaran, s/s Aegean Star, s/s Birbakim etc.

For further information and bookings please apply to any of LOUIS TOURIST OFFICES throughout Cyprus

INTRODUCTION

The majority of my interviews for Tales of Cyprus have been with Cypriots who left their homes and migrated to other countries. These were desperate people, escaping poverty and financial hardship after the Second World War. They left to seek their fortune and perhaps a better life in foreign countries like Australia. Most of these people were born in the 1920s and 30s so by the time I got to meet them and record their stories, they were aged in their eighties and nineties.

During the course of my interviews, a ship called the Corsica kept popping up. I soon discovered that this was no ordinary migrant ship and no ordinary migrant journey. Of course, there were other ships mentioned such as the Cyrenia, Hellenic Prince, Misr, Ana Salen, Surriento and Castel Felice - but no other ship seemed to stir as much emotion in my interviewees as the Corsica. This may have been because it was so dilapidated and unsuitable for passenger travel. As one person stated, "it was the ship from hell."

In January 1951, the Corsica, (then known as the Liguria), broke down near Fremantle and had to be towed to port where it was arrested and held by the Australian authorities for repairs. It is therefore astonishing, that ten months later, renamed as the Corsica, she was commissioned to bring over 780 unsuspecting Cypriot passengers to Australia. This was the largest group of Cypriot migrants ever to leave the island by ship at any one time. This was also the Corsica's only voyage from Cyprus to Australia. By comparison the Surriento made twenty-eight voyages and the Cyrenia made twenty-six.

In 2019, I decided to investigate the Corsica further by re-interviewing the Cypriots who had first brought this ship to my attention. Cypriots such as Christos Apeitos, Nicos Jonis, Sevil Abdurazak, Takis Ioannou and Loizos Kyriacou. I then posted a 'call-out' on my Facebook page for other passengers of the Corsica to come forward. The response was swift and overwhelming. I spent many, many hours in 2019, travelling and intervewing people who had journeyed on the Corsica. When the pandemic began in 2020, Melbourne went into one of the strictest and longest lockdowns in the world. Thankfully, I was still able to complete many interviews via Zoom or by telephone.

In total I managed to track down seventy-eight passengers who travelled to Australia on the Corsica, of which, fifty-six where selected for this book.

With each story of migration I have tried to include some background information about the passenger, such as their family life, upbringing and schooling. I have also recorded their reasons for leaving Cyprus, their recollections of the journey and some details about their life in Australia soon after migration.

I had always planned to publish this book about the Corsica in 2022 to mark the seventieth anniversary of her journey to Australia. I am so grateful that I have been able to meet and interview so many of the passengers of this voyage before it was too late. The youngest Cypriot I interviewed was seventy-one years old and the oldest was almost one hundred.

Given the passage of time since the Corsica docked at Port Melbourne back in February 1952, I had anticipated that my interviewees might struggle to remember details or facts about the journey. However, this was not the case. All of the passengers I interviewed, remembered the rotten potatoes and onions and the stench on the ship. Most recalled a slow and uncertain journey. They also recalled the poor quality of the food and the absence of fresh drinking water.

Given the fallacy of memory, I was careful not to edit the comments made by the passengers. If they said the trip took three months (when it took seven weeks), I left their comment unchanged. If they recalled eating only spaghetti every day – so be it. More than anything, I wanted to preserve their living memories, even though at times, they were at odds with the facts. After all, they are trying to recall events that occurred seventy years ago. Moreso, some of my interviewees had not really discussed or shared their story of migration with anyone, until I came knocking on their door.

Like most of my Tales of Cyprus endeavours, researching the Corsica has been a real eye-opener for me – a real education. I always knew that my parent's generation were special, but I can now fully appreciate the guts, determination and hope that was shared by these early migrants as they ventured into the unknown. Can you imagine going into debt, just to pay for your ship fare. Or deciding to leave your family and friends, to seek a better life on the other side of the world not knowing if you would ever see each other again? Imagine not knowing the language or the culture of the new country and arriving penniless with no guarantee of finding accommodation or work. One might say it was sheer madness or perhaps, just extraordinary faith and resolve. One thing is for sure – they were a resilient generation.

Throughout my interviews for this book, the word *philoxenia* was mentioned over and over. This word means friendship towards others and hospitality. There are many stories in this book of Cypriots reaching out to help one another. The earlier migrants jumped at the opportunity to welcome the new arrivals, to ensure that they felt safe and secure in what must have seemed like an alien landscape.

Metal travel case belonging to Elefterios Charalambides.

I hope you enjoy reading these amazing stories of migration as much as I have enjoyed bringing them out of the shadows of a forgotten past and into our present consciousness.

I am sure that you will agree that the sacrifices made by these early Cypriot migrants have ensured that their descendants will be able to live a richer and better life.

They are my heroes.

ABOUT THE CORSICA

Length	441.8 feet
Width	55.8 feet
Beam	55.8 feet
Weight	7475 gross tons
Speed	14 knots

1914	Launched as Hilda Woermann.
1917	Renamed Wahehe
1918	Surrendered to the British
1920	Renamed Marella
1946	Renamed Captain Marcos
1949	Renamed Liguria
1951	Renamed Corsica
1954	Sold to Belgium shipbreakers

The Marella. Photo by Allan Green, circa 1930s.

The Italian ship Ravello, left Limassol a few days before the Corsica, with 150 Cypriots on board and arrived in Melbourne on the 14th of January, 1952 - three weeks before the Corsica. The Ravello weighed 8,452 gross tons and had a service speed of thirteen knots.

The Ravello. May, 1951.

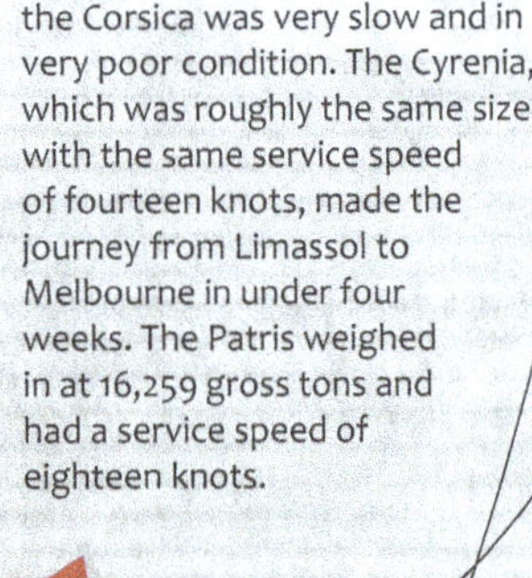

The Liguria in Dublin, Ireland, 1950.

Compared to other migrant ships, the Corsica was very slow and in very poor condition. The Cyrenia, which was roughly the same size with the same service speed of fourteen knots, made the journey from Limassol to Melbourne in under four weeks. The Patris weighed in at 16,259 gross tons and had a service speed of eighteen knots.

Illustration by Wilhelm Angelo Gallon.

Kaiser Wilhelm II, 1902.

In 1917, the Kaiser's luxury liner was named 'Wahehe' and converted into a troopship and sent into service during the First World War. She was claimed as a prize of the war by the British in 1918 and thereafter was used for repatriating Australian troops and for trade between Britain and Australia.

In October 1920 she was purchased by the Australian-owned shipping firm, Burns Philp and renamed the 'Marella'. The ship was refitted to carry first and second class passengers, along with cargo. She operated routes from Melbourne and Sydney to Singapore for twenty years until the outbreak of the Second World War. She became a troopship once again, operating mainly in the South Pacific.

In 1946, after the war, the Marella was returned to Burns Philp where she resumed her trade between Australia and Singapore.

In 1948, she was sold to a Panamanian shipping firm named Cia Nav Buru S.A., Panama and renamed 'Captain Marcos'.

Initially when the Corsica was known as the Wahehe, she operated with four 2-cylinder quadruple expansion engines driving twin screws, coal fire boilers and travelled at a speed of fourteen knots.

In 1948, (as the Captain Marcos) the ship was converted to oil fuel.

In 1949, she was renamed 'Liguria' and used to transport pilgrims from New York, America to Europe and the Holy Land.

In 1950, the Liguria was commissioned to transport 950 persons from Europe to Australia however she broke down 200 miles from Fremantle with engine failure and had to be towed to port. This was the beginning of the end for this tired old ship. She spent eight months being repaired in Fremantle before she was renamed Corsica and sent to Cyprus to collect 784 passengers bound for Australia. The Corsica left Limassol on the 17th of December, 1951 and arrived at Port Melbourne on the 4th of February, 1952. This was her maiden and only voyage.

Two weeks later, she left Melbourne for Adelaide and departed for Europe on the 24th of February. Sadly, she broke down in the Atlantic Ocean and was towed to Casablanca where she remained for two years. She was eventually sold to Belgium ship-breakers and towed to their Ghent shipyard in November 1954.
This was her final resting place.

The Corsica has a long and interesting history dating back to 1914 when she was built by Reiherstag Schiffsw in Hamburg as a luxury liner for the King of Prussia and the last emperor of Germany, Kaiser Wilhelm II (1859-1941).

According to some reports, the Kaiser's guests sat on period furniture and dined off silver plates in saloons that were fitted with marble.

ABOUT THE PASSENGERS QUICK STATS.

TOTAL

863 passengers

784	-	from Cyprus (653 male 131 female)
62	-	Greece
12	-	Egypt
5	-	Other

GENDER

706	-	males
157	-	females

MARITAL STATUS

523	-	single
335	-	married
4	-	widowed
1	-	divorced.

RELIGION;

755	-	Orthodox,
56	-	Muslims
52	-	Other

AGES

2	under 1*
37	aged between 1 - 5
25	aged between 6 - 10
19	aged between 11 - 15
139	aged between 16 - 20
249	aged between 21 - 25
157	aged between 26 - 30
84	aged between 31 - 35
66	aged between 36 - 40
71	aged between 41 - 50
10	aged between 51 - 60
3	aged between 61 - 70
1	over 70

* The youngest passengers were twin babies aged ten months and the oldest was a 71 year old male.

Source: National Archives of Australia

LISTED OCCUPATION

126	Unspecified	2	Accountants
221	Farmers	1	Wireman
51	Carpenters	1	Workman
48	Mechanics	1	Wine grower
41	Masons	1	Watchmaker
38	Housewives	1	Tractor Driver
36	Tailors	1	Tinsmith
35	Shoemakers	1	Tinker
33	Labourers	1	Tanner
32	Seamstresses	1	Shop assistant
25	Students	1	Shepherd
24	Clerks	1	Sculptor
17	Barbers	1	Saddler
16	Drivers	1	Printer
14	Waiters	1	Policeman
11	Cooks	1	Oxyg. Welder
8	Electricians	1	Mosaic craftsman
8	Blacksmiths	1	Hawker
6	Gardeners	1	Hairdresser
5	Miners	1	Gov't employee
5	Shop keepers	1	Fitter
4	Engineers	1	Embroider
4	Bakers	1	Driller
3	Merchants	1	Dressmaker
3	Grocers	1	Digger
3	Employees	1	Board writer
3	Confectioners	1	Bike repairer
2	Sailors	1	Bee keeper
2	Plumbers	1	Bar keeper
2	Painters	1	Architect
2	Kitchen boys	1	Telephone repairman
2	Butchers	1	Goldsmith

INTENDED DESTINATION

430	-	Victoria*
302	-	New South Wales
56	-	South Australia
31	-	Queensland
22	-	New Zealand
11	-	Western Australia
6	-	Northern Territory
4	-	Tasmania
1	-	Australian Capital Territory

* Some passengers did not go to their intended or listed destination. For example: Christodoulos Apeitos had Darwin as his listed destination but stayed in Melbourne.

PASSENGER LIST—INCOMING

Nav. (Passengers) Recs.

Return of Passengers Brought to the Port of ....FREMANTLE
(To be furnished in Triplicate)

Name of Ship.	Official Number.	(a) Port of Registry. (b) Steamship Line.	Master's Name.
C O R S I C A		(a) PANAMA COMPANGIA DE NAVI- (b) GATION "BAKU"	SCOUFOPOULOS Costas

NAMES AND DESCRIPTIONS OF PASSENGERS

(2) Class	(3) Port of Embarkation.	(4) Surname and Initials. (Separate line to be used for each Passenger.)	(5) Nationality. (As shown on Passport.)	(6) Racial Origin	(7) Sex (M. or F.)	(8) Age last Birthday	(9) Conjugal Condition	Occupation
III								
142	Limassol ✓	CALLUS Mary	British	E	F	45	W	Nil
143	Limassol ✓	CALLUS Joseph	British	E	M	20	S	Student
144	Limassol ✓	CALLUS Andre	British	E	M	19	S	Student
193	Limassol	DEMOSTHENOUS Sava	British	E	M	28	M	Mechanic
284	Limassol ✓	GALDIES Paul	British	E	M	52	M	Clerk
285	Limassol ✓	GALDIES George	British	E	M	14	S	Nil
286	Limassol ✓	GALDIES Jeanne	British	E	F	49	M	Nil
287								
357								
382								
419								
420								
421								
422								
611								
612								

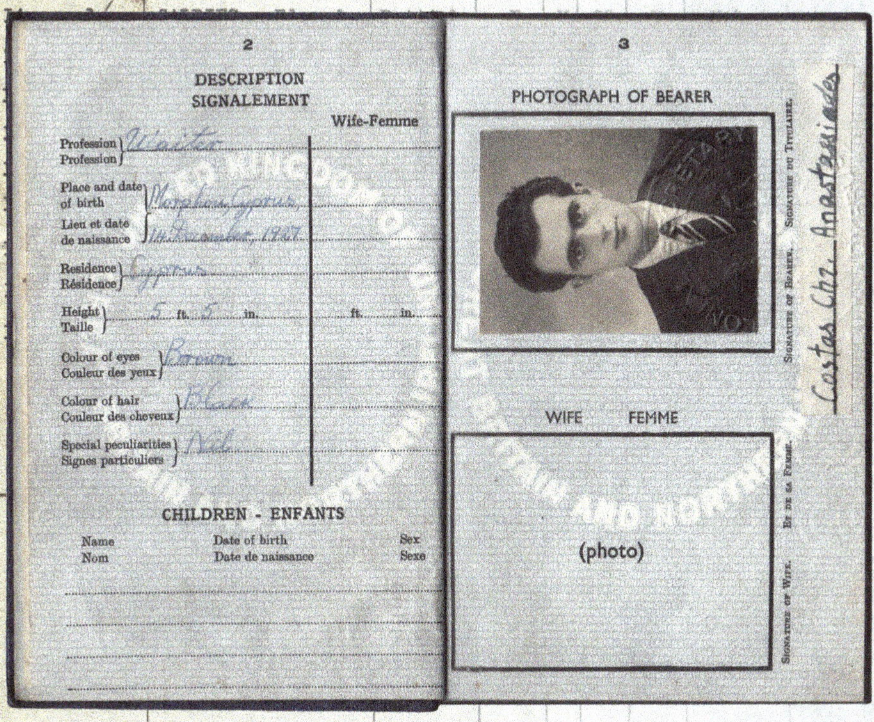

a) Permanent Residence means residence for one year or longer.   (b) Indicate whether "New Settler" (N.S.)," Australian Resident Returning"...   as shown in brackets.

The fact that the Corsica made her maiden and only voyage from Cyprus to Australia over seventy years ago has limited my access to passengers. Many passengers have since passed away or now have dementia or Alzheimer's disease.

The majority of the people I met and interviewed for this book were Greek Cypriots. That is not surprising since ninety-six per cent of the passengers on the Corsica were Greek Cypriot. I did however record the stories of a few Turkish Cypriots and Greek passengers.

All of the passengers had to borrow money or sell assets to afford the passage to Australia. On average, the ship fare cost 120 pounds one way. Their decision to emigrate to Australia was largely based on economic reasons such as unemployment or a poor and diminishing quality of life. The phrase, 'I left to seek a better life,' was uttered many times.

Interestingly, many of the male passengers interviewed stated that they had always intended to return to Cyprus after working in Australia for a few years. They believed, at the time, that there would be plenty of jobs, paying good money (even double what they would be earning in Cyprus), so if they could save a few hundred pounds they would be able to return to the island and live a better life.

When the civil unrest of the mid-1950s threatened peace on the island, most passengers decided to stay in Australia and began making arrangements to help their own families emigrate. Many of the single young migrant men even sent telegrams back home asking their mothers (or siblings) to find them a wife.

Of the 131 female Cypriot passengers on the Corsica, half were already married and either travelling with their husbands or on their way to be reunited with their husbands in Australia. Those travelling with young children experienced an even more harrowing and difficult journey.

Some female passengers who were listed as single, were actually engaged and travelling to Australia to meet their fiancés for the first time.

VILLAGES OF ORIGIN

This map shows the villages and districts of my interviewees.

PAPHOS DISTRICT *

Choli - 1 person
Droushia - 1 person
Kathikas - 1 person
Kato Paphos - 1 person
Ktima - 5 people
Lysos - 1 person
Neo Chorio - 1 person
Peyia - 2 people
Polis - 3 people
Prodromi - 1 person
Stroumbi - 1 person
Tsada - 1 person

NICOSIA DISTRICT

Kaimakli - 1 person
Lagoudera - 1 person
Meniko - 1 person
Morphou - 1 person
Nicosia - 3 people
Geri - 1 person

KYRENIA DISTRICT

Larnakas tis Lapithou

- 1 person

LARNACA DISTRICT

Agios Theodoros - 1 person

Aradippou - 1 person

Arsos - 1 person

Kalavaso - 1 person

Kornos - 1 person

Menoyia - 1 person

Pyrga - 1 person

Troulloi - 1 person

LIMASSOL DISTRICT

Agios Therapon - 1 person

Agros - 2 people

Germasogeia - 3 people

Kato Platres - 1 person

Kellaki - 1 person

Limassol - 1 person

Vasa - 1 person

FAMAGUSTA DISTRICT

Agios Ilias - 1 person

Agios Memnon - 1 person

Agios Sergios - 1 person

Koma tou Gialou - 1 person

Komi Kebir - 2 people

Rizokarpaso - 2 people

Varosi - 2 people

* Location names are spelt as they appear on maps pre-1950.

THE JOURNEY

The journey of the Corsica is written here based on eye witness accounts and written journals.

I was very fortunate to meet and interview a few passengers who had the foresight to write down their thoughts about their journey. These small notebooks, purchased before departure, contain key dates and times as well as great details about each stop-over. Had it not been for these notebooks, I would know very little about the journey.

So what did I discover? Sometime in early December, 1951 the Corsica left the Port of Piraeus in Greece and made her way to Limassol, Cyprus to collect over 780 Cypriot passengers. This is the largest number of Cypriots to ever leave Cyprus by ship at one time.

The Corsica was meant to arrive on the 12th of December, 1951 and leave Cyprus on the 13th of December, but the ship did not depart until the 17th of December. Hundreds of anxious passengers crowded at the Port of Limassol that morning with their loved ones but were told to find accommodation in the town. Many actually managed to board the vessel but she remained anchored out to sea for four days. No one knew why the ship was not moving or what was causing the delay. It was only later that some passengers discovered that the delay was due to the loading and placement of a large consignment of potatoes and onions in the cargo hold. It was common for migrant ships and ocean liners at that time to carry both passengers and cargo. It was winter in Cyprus and the sacks of vegetables got wet in the rain as they were being loaded. This would cause them to rot in the hold and dissolve into a stinking black sludge later in the journey.

As it happened, another ship named the Ravello left Limassol on the 14th of December, 1951 with 150 Cypriots on board and reached Fremantle, Australia on the 10th of January, 1952. Two weeks before the Corsica arrived.

At approximately 8pm on Monday the 17th of December, 1951, the Corsica sounded her horn and departed from Limassol bound for Australia. She travelled through choppy seas arriving at Port Said, Egypt at 1.30pm on Wednesday the 19th of December, 1951.

From Port Said the Corsica travelled slowly down the Suez Canal until she reached the port town of Suez (approximately ninety miles away) at 11pm. There, the Corsica is halted until the bridge that connects Egypt to Palestine is raised to allow the ship through. The ship remained at Suez for two days. It departed at 8.30pm on Friday the 21st of December after refuelling and replenishing its fresh water tanks. She made her way along the banks of the Red Sea for the Italian colony of Eritrea in Africa.

The Corsica reached the Port of Massawa, Eritrea around 8pm on the 26th of December, remaining there for two days and two nights before departing at 11.30am on the 28th of December for Djibouti. According to some reports, the locals in Massawa were very poor but nice and friendly and the port town was very clean. In Massawa, some passengers spoke about buying chickens and baby goats which were slaughtered and prepared by the locals at the port-side markets. The passengers brought the meat onto the ship and a Cypriot from Aradippou cooked the meat in the kitchen using his own pots and pans.

After two days and two nights the Corsica arrived at the Port of Djibouti, Ethiopia (French Colony) at 5am (some say it was 7am) on Sunday the 30th of December, 1951. It departed at 9pm that same day. Once again, the ship was refuelled.

The most outstanding revelation in Djibouti was the discovery of a Greek Orthodox Church (Saints Konstantinos and Eleni). During this stop-over the local Greek priest performed a special service for his grateful congregation of Corsica passengers.

After leaving Djibouti, the Corsica slowly zigzagged her way across the Indian Ocean towards Ceylon (British Colony), arriving after nine days at the Port of Colombo on the 8th of January, 1952 at 9am.

It was at Colombo that the cargo of rotten potatoes and onions was dumped into the ocean. Apparently, many passengers stayed in hotels in Colombo while the ship's hull was being cleaned. Many of the passengers enjoyed their stay in Colombo, visiting places like the markets, Zoological Garden and the Botanical Park. Once again the ship was refuelled and her fresh water tanks replenished.

On Sunday the 13th of January, 1952 the Corsica departed crossing the equator at approximately 7pm on Tuesday the 15th of January, 1952. Thereafter, a celebration between the crew and the passengers took place on the decks of the ship. One passenger recalls how the Captain was dressed as King Neptune and the crew began spraying everyone with champagne (another passenger claimed it was water). Ice-cream was also handed out to all those present.

At approximately 7pm on the 26th of January, 1952 the Corsica reached Australia and docked at the Port of Fremantle. The next day at 2am in the morning, the Corsica left Fremantle and made her way across the Great Southern Ocean towards Melbourne, dropping anchor in the bay at Port Melbourne on the 3rd of February at approximately 7pm.

The Corsica remained in the bay overnight and the next day on the 4th of February, 1952 she was towed to a berth at Station Pier. At approximately 6pm the passengers were allowed to disembark and make their way through customs and finally into Melbourne. Many had friends and relatives awaiting them.

Melbourne was not meant to be the final stop for the Corsica. The ship was originally booked to travel to Sydney but because she was in such a dilapidated state, the local authorities arrested the vessel at Port Melbourne and around 300 passengers, who were meant to travel on to Adelaide and Sydney, were sent there by train instead.

WHAT THE NEWSPAPERS SAID

Even before the Corsica reached Melbourne, reports about the conditions on board the ship began to filter through to the Australian press. By the time she was berthed at Station Pier, many Australian newspapers had run stories and articles, with some even making the front pages. What follows are reproductions of some newspaper articles reported at the time. These are listed in chronological order.

The Maryborough Chronicle - Qld.
(Monday 15th of November, 1948, page 3)
The Australian vessel Marella, 34-year-old veteran of the Australia-Singapore service, has been sold to a South American company for £80.000 sterling, reports the newspaper Free Press. The ship will be handed over at Singapore on November 23rd placed under the Panama flag and renamed Captain Marcos. Under her new registry the Marella will go to Shanghai early next month to pick up several hundred wartime Italian refugees and take them back to Italy.

The Cairns Post - Qld.
(Saturday 15th of December, 1951, page 1)
A Reuters correspondent at Limassol says that the largest single batch of Cypriot emigrants ever to leave the island, embarked for Australia in two ships today. The migrants, numbering nearly 1000, are all young bachelors. They are travelling on the Greek ship Corsica and the Italian vessel Ravello, and will be employed in Australia as farmers, builders, drivers and artisans.

The Sunday Times - Perth, WA.
(Sunday 27th of January, 1952, page 5)
You could smell the old ship Corsica when she was berthing at Fremantle yesterday. Corsica spent months at North Wharf last year for repairs--when her name was Liguria. She berthed with a list which was later corrected. Repainted since she last saw Fremantle, the white paint was already cracked and rusted. Sleek lines of the Italian liner Australia which also berthed yesterday morning were in sharp contrast to Corsica. Smell of bad potatoes--not surprising, as a large cargo of potatoes for Ceylon had been loaded wet in Cyprus and rotted before reaching their destination. Three holds were being cleaned yesterday. Corsica was once well known on the Australian coast as Marella. She had been designed as a royal yacht for the Kaiser. Corsica carried 863 migrants.

The Daily Telegraph – Sydney, NSW.
(Tuesday 5th of February, 1952, page 5)
Cypriot migrants who arrived in Melbourne today said that they had had a voyage of 'thirst, hunger, and filth.' The migrants came from Cyprus in the 7000-tons Panamanian ship Corsica. The ship had: seven stewards to care for the 900 passengers. Passengers said that the ship's officers rationed drinking water for the last three days of the six-weeks voyage." The ration was three short periods a day from one tap. One passenger said: "Only the toughest got near the tap. The others had to buy mineral water from the ship's bar for 3/ a bottle. Before rationing began petrol-stained water came irregularly, out of cabin taps."
A reporter who inspected dormitories below decks said: "Stench from uncleaned latrines permeated the 'whole' place. Mrs. M. Mavris, British wife of a Cypriot; said: "We were treated like savages. I begged, from the galley the only food my children ate." George Stant, 31-year-old Cypriot, said. "A tourist agency in Cyprus advertised the ship as a 32,000-tons liner with two swimming pools. When we made complaints, an officer threatened to send us back to Cyprus." The ship's master, Captain C. Scoufopoulos, said: "The food was good, and the water was scarce only because passengers left faucets open." Lowest fare on the ship was £120 sterling, against £70 sterling from Britain on P.&O. and Orient liners. When the ship berthed the migrants threw watches, cigarettes, and other dutiable goods to friends on the wharf. Police and Customs officers confiscated the goods!

The Herald - Melbourne, Vic.
(Tuesday 5th of February, 1952, page 8)
About 300 Cypriots from the Corsica were to have left Melbourne by special train at 1.15 p.m. today for Sydney. But because of Customs search delays, their departure was postponed to 6.40pm. And later they were told they would not leave until tomorrow. The reason given was 'completion of Customs and feeding arrangements.' Contraband valued at hundreds of pounds was smuggled from Station Pier after the migrant ship Corsica berthed late yesterday, Customs men claimed today. A shortage of barriers and no overhead gangway direct to the Customs inspecting room had helped the smuggling, they said. Customs inspectors said they were prepared for a thorough search of passengers from the 7000-ton Panamanian-registered ship. But as soon as the Corsica berthed migrants leapt from a deck at wharf level and mixed with friends. In this way much contraband could have quickly changed hands. This would not have occurred if enough barriers had been available, said the Customs officers. A Navigation supervisor will inspect the Corsica for seaworthiness while she is at Station Pier.

The Courier-Mail - Brisbane, Qld.
(Tuesday 5th of February, 1952, page 3)
'Hell ship conditions', with insufficient water, food, and filthy accommodation, were alleged against the migrant ship, Corsica, by many of the passengers today. The master, former Rear Admiral of the Greek Navy (Captain C. Scoufopoulos) denied all the charges. He said that the ship was built in 1915 to be the Kaiser's luxury yacht, and was 'a fine vessel.' Mr. H. C. Pash, 50 a passenger, said the chief trouble aboard was caused by migrant passengers, who he described as 'practically uncivilised: people who had never seen a toilet before coming aboard: amazing people to import into your country.'

The Age - Melbourne, Vic.
(Tuesday 5th of February, 1952, page 3)
Migrants who arrived in the Panamanian ship yesterday angrily alleged that they were filthy, hungry and thirsty after a 50-day voyage in a 'floating slum.' As the crowded vessel drew in to Station Pier with a 15-degree list to starboard, passengers crowded along her rail and

shouted bitter comments on the voyage. Customs officers cordoned off the wharf to prevent more than a thousand relatives and friends' ashore from rushing aboard. Two men were questioned by Customs officials after watches wrapped in handkerchiefs had been thrown from the ship to the wharf. The Corsica had not, representatives or agents ashore, and lay in the Bay for two days before action was taken to get her a berth. Her master came ashore early yesterday to act as agent. Water 3/-Passengers claimed the Corsica had been without drinking water for three days. They had been forced to buy' bottled water at 3/ a bottle. The only water available for toilet use throughout the voyage had been putrid. Women and children had kept clean by sponging themselves with methylated spirit. Mrs. A. M. Mavris, an Englishwoman, said there had been petrol in the drinking water for several weeks, It had been an ordeal to keep her young family clean and reasonably healthy. "It has been a hell trip on a floating slum," she said. "The food was uneatable and there were only eight stewards on the entire vessel to attend to the wants of 900." Medical attention had been most inadequate. George Stelot, 21, a Cypriot, said everybody aboard with the exception of the officers and one family had been hungry, and thirsty since leaving Cyprus. They had been unable to bath or wash from Colombo to Fremantle. A young Cairo journalist, Miss Jacqueline Kleimann, said she had spent £30 on water during the voyage. The only water tap, had been on for only three brief periods daily for most of the trip and had run dry three days out of Melbourne. All passengers had paid at least £125 sterling for their passage. The ship had been advertised In Cyprus as a "22,000 tons luxury liner with two swimming pools." The Corsica is of 7475 tons and its one swimming pool was empty throughout the voyage. Yesterday it was filled with rubbish. A young Italian, Romeo Alberti, claimed the ship had been swept only- three times since embarkation— the day before calling at Port Said, Colombo and Fremantle. Master of the Corsica, Captain C. Scoufopoulos, denied all the migrants' claims. He said there had been a troublesome element aboard who, had come from the slums of Cyprus and had no cause for complaint." Captain Scoufopoulos was supported by a Cyprus Government official, Mr. H. C.

Pash, who said the bulk of passengers had never seen a cabin or wash basin before. "I have eaten with the captain throughout the voyage, but I understand we ate the same meals as the passengers," he added. "They were quite satisfactory." The Corsica was built in 1914 as a luxury yacht for Kaiser Walhelm II. She was claimed, as war reparations in 1918, and later, traded off the Australian coast as the Marella. She was sold several years ago to Greek owner, who registered her in Panama and renamed her the Liguria. Last year she was 'arrested' for non-payment of wharfage dues in Fremantle after a seven-month stay. She has since been renamed Corsica.

The Argus - Melbourne, Vic.
(Friday 5th of February, 1954, page 9)
Judge Mitchell said in the County Court yesterday he was glad an Australian firm was not responsible for the 'very hard bargain' a migrant had entered to bring his family from Cyprus in the Panamanian ship Corsica. The judge said he was satisfied that the Corsica's voyage - for which the migrant was charged £630 for himself, wife, and three children - had been filthy. "This man has to pay a sum out of all proportion to the value he received," said Judge Mitchell. "The food, sanitary arrangements, organisation of the vessel, and standard of cleanliness were very bad indeed. I do not see why his whole future in this country should be spoiled because of this very hard bargain." The migrant Andreas Anastasiou, of Tramoo Street, Thomastown, was sued by Louis Pareskeva Loizou, of the Louis Shipping Agency, Collins St., Melbourne, for £380 owing on promissory notes. Judge Mitchell said he had to give judgment against Anastasiou because there was no evidence that Loizou had made any false or fraudulent misrepresentations. But his order against Anastasiou, now a State Electricity Commission employee, allowed repayment of the £380 at £4 a month. Judge Mitchell said he believed Anastasiou's claim that he had worked from 6a.m. to 8p.m. to raise the £250 he had already paid. Anastasiou said water was severely rationed on the 53-day voyage, and the food was poor. Fresh sheets were not provided, and passengers frequently slept on deck because the cabins were too stuffy. Mr. S. Wilson (for Anastasiou) said a P. and O. passage from Port Said would have cost about £85 a

passage. A fare from Cyprus would have been about £6 more. An advertisement in a Greek newspaper, published after Anastasiou had signed the promissory notes, had described Corsica as a luxury liner, with library smoke rooms, and swimming pools.

The Advertiser - Adelaide, SA
(Tuesday 5th of February, 1952, page 3)
'Hell ship' conditions, with insufficient water and food, and filthy accommodation, were alleged against the foreign migrant ship Corsica by many of the passengers who arrived here today. The skipper, a former rear admiral of the Greek Navy (Capt. C. Scoufopoulos) denied all the charges. He said that the ship was built in 1915 to be the Kaiser's luxury yacht, and was 'a fine vessel'. Passengers alleged that: Water came out of the taps black and evil smelling. Water was sold in the ship for 3/ a bottle. Sewerage overflowed during the voyage, flooding bathrooms and lavatories. Dormitories were filthy and had a strong stench. The ship was advertised as a 22,000-ton liner but actually was only 7,475 tons gross. Mr. H. C. Pash, 50. a passenger, said the chief trouble aboard was caused by migrant passengers whom he described as 'practically uncivilised; people who had never seen a toilet before coming aboard: amazing people to import into your country.'

The Daily Telegraph - Sydney, NSW.
(Wednesday 6th of February, 1952, page 7)
Cypriot migrants who reached Melbourne yesterday brought about 1500 bottles of brandy with them. The migrants today paid more than £1000 Customs duty on the brandy. They paid 15/ duty a bottle on brandy which they bought in Cyprus for 6/ a bottle. One migrant had 300 bottles. About 900 migrants reached Melbourne in the Panamanian ship Corsica. Four hundred of them, who were to have left for Sydney by train today, will now leave tomorrow. The Victorian Railways Department could not make available a special train for them today.

The Argus - Melbourne, Vic.
(Wednesday 6th of February, 1952, page 5)
A migrant brought 300 bottles of brandy when he arrived with 900 other Cypriots in the Corsica Monday. He and others who brought brandy with them paid more than £1,000 Customs duty on the

The Age

N THE | Unhappy Bunch of Migrants

WHEN THE PANAMANIAN chartered ship Corsica arrived in Melbourne, last evening, 900 Italian and mid-European migrants complained bitterly about the conditions on the voyage. They were loud in their condemnation of the food and lack of entertainment. Left: Passengers waving from the two decks. Right: The Corsica berthing with a considerable list. (See story on Page 3).

"Rest" at Royal Lodge Proving Strenuous

From a Reuters Correspondent

Labor's Important Move

"The Age" Correspondent.
LONDON, Feb. 4.
It now appears almost

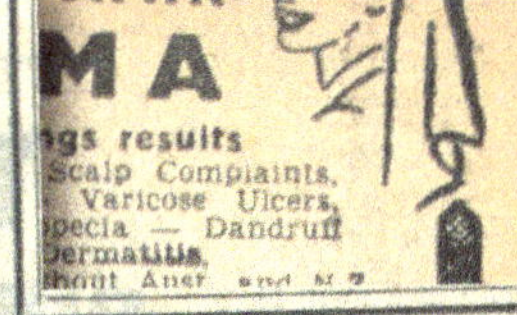

She was no luxury liner

THE CORSICA ends her unhappy six-weeks' voyage from Cyprus to Melbourne with 900 migrants—

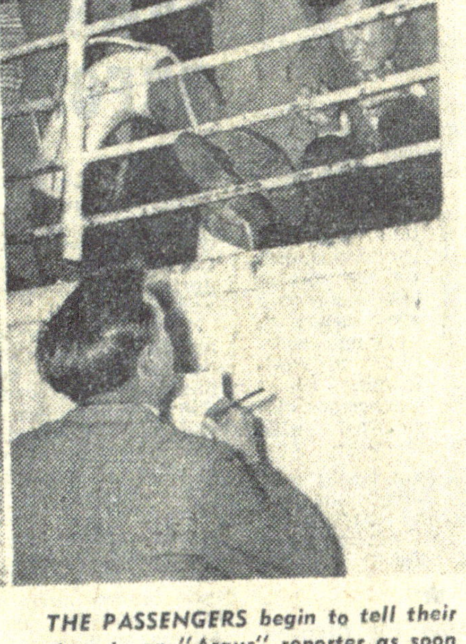

THE PASSENGERS begin to tell their story to an "Argus" reporter as soon as she comes alongside—

Immigrants tell story of hardship

A story of thirst, hunger, and filth was told by Cypriot migrants who reached Melbourne in the Corsica yesterday.

Nine hundred migrants arrived in the 7,000-ton, Panama-registered, ship after a six-weeks voyage from Cyprus.

The Corsica is the ship that broke down in the Indian Ocean last year with a full load of migrants and had to be towed to Fremantle. She was then named Liguria.

Passengers who arrived in her yesterday said that drinking water had been rationed for the last three days to three short periods a day from one tap.

Those who missed in the wild scramble to get to the tap had to buy mineral water from the ship's bar at 3/ a bottle.

Before rationing, they claimed, salty, petrol-stained water came irregularly out of the cabin taps.

Passengers alleged that food was scarce and sometimes bad, and that

WATCHES, cigarettes and other dutiable goods are flung to compatriots waiting on the wharf, but—

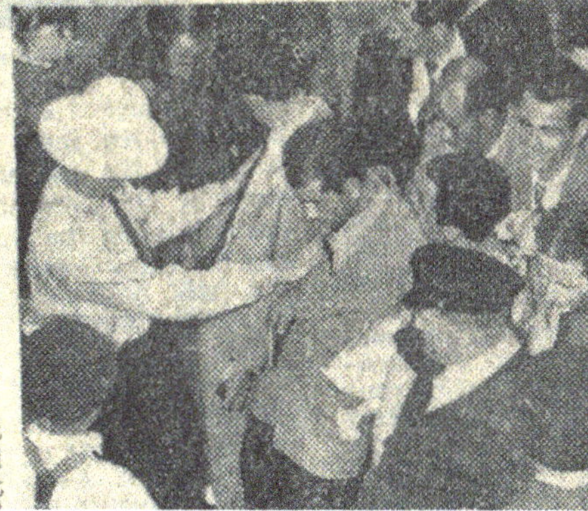

CHARGE
RANT SHIP

ints of Wat
et, Hunger

rrived in the Panamanian ship rily alleged that they were after a 50-day voyage in a "fla

vessel drew in to Station Pier starboard, passengers cro nd shouted bitter comment:

rdoned off the wharf to prevent and friends from rushing aboard.

let use throughout the voyage had been putrid. Women children had kept clean by nging themselves with thylated spirits.

Mrs. A. M. Mavris, an nglishwoman, said there d been petrol in the drinking water for several weeks. had been an ordeal to keep r young family clean and asonably healthy.

t has been a hell trip on a ting slum," she said. "The was uneatable and there only eight stewards on the re vessel to attend to the ts of 900."

edical attention had been inadequate.

ngry, Thirsty

eorge Stelot, 21, a Cypriot, everybody aboard with exception of the officers one family had been ry and thirsty since ng Cyprus.

ey had been unable to or wash from Colombo to antle.

young Cairo journalist, Jacqueline Kleimann, she had spent £30 on r during the voyage.

only water tap—it had on for only three brief s daily for most of the had run dry three days f Melbourne.

25 Fare

ngers had paid at

same meals as the p he added. "They satisfactory."

The Corsica was 1914 as a luxury Kaiser Wilhelm II. claimed as war repa 1918, and later trad Australian coast Marella.

She was sold sev ago to Greek ow registered her in Pa renamed her the Li

Last year she rested" for non-pa wharfage dues in after a seven-month She has since bee Corsica.

Rebel Ship Plot Thic

DARWIN, Mond mystery of an allege by three foreigners rebellion in Ceram Darwin as their "ju port deepened to doubt about the of a launch.

One story is that was going to Wynd load of beer to brin Darwin.

The launch left or day, but has not Wyndham—a three at the most.

There is no official

bottles. Duty was 15/ a bottle on brandy bought in Cyprus for 6/. But Customs men said hundreds of pounds worth of other dutiable goods had been thrown from the ship's deck to relatives waiting on the wharf. There were no barriers to keep visitors away until the passengers had passed the customs. Four hundred Cypriots who are bound for Sydney spent last night on the Corsica which they alleged was a 'hell ship'. A special train to take them to Sydney will leave this afternoon. Mr A. Priest said the Immigration Department had no control over migrants on the Corsica apart from screening them and ensuring that they had proper landing permits.

The Courier-Mail - Brisbane, Qld
(Wednesday 6th of February, 1952, page 1)
The Greek migrant ship Corsica was 'deliberately sabotaged' during its 53 day voyage to Australia, a passenger and members of the crew said today. The passenger Mr. Romeo Aliberti, who travelled in the ship with his wife and son said water in the ship's 14 tanks was polluted 'mysteriously.' A day after 1200 tons of fresh water was taken aboard at Colombo, it tasted of bad potatoes. Later it tasted of petrol, and later still of salt.

The News - Adelaide, SA
(Wednesday 6th of February, 1952, page 2)
The smell in the holds of the migrant ship Corsica was so bad today that watersiders removing passengers' baggage became violently ill. Because of the 'dirty and obnoxious conditions' among passengers' baggage in the holds, a board awarded the men extra money for handling it. Men working in the holds received an extra 1/ an hour, those on the deck 6d., and hatchmen an extra 3d. an hour.

The Advertiser - Adelaide, SA.
(Wednesday 6th of February, 1952, page 3)
The Greek migrant ship Corsica was 'deliberately sabotaged' during a 53 day voyage to Australia, a passenger and members of .the crew said today. The passenger is Mr. Romeo Aliberti, a former canteen manager in Egypt, who travelled in the ship with his wife and son. He said water in the ship's 14 tanks was polluted 'very mysteriously.' A day after 1,2M tons of fresh water had been taken aboard at Colombo it tasted of bad potatoes. Later it tasted of petrol, and later still of salt.

He added that there had been enmity between certain nationalities aboard; and he believed this had resulted in someone 'getting at the water.'

The Advocate - Burnie, Tas.
(Thursday 7th of February, 1952, page 5)
The appalling stench from passengers' luggage being unloaded from holds of the migrant vessel Corsica yesterday caused many watersiders working in the holds to become violently. Some of the men said that baggage in dormitories showed signs of human filth. The watersiders sought a board of reference, which was granted immediately, and they were awarded 'dirt money' for handling the luggage. Later, it was stated that a cargo of potatoes and onions had rotted in the holds between Cyprus and Colombo, causing a dreadful smell to permeate the vessel, but this had been accentuated by the filthy habits of some of the migrants.

The West Australian - Perth, WA
(Thursday 7th of February, 1952, page 16)
Because of the 'dirty and obnoxious conditions' among passengers' baggage in the holds of the migrant ship Corsica, a board of reference today awarded waterside workers extra money for handling it. The stench in the holds of the ship was so bad that some of the workers became violently ill. The men said that there was evidence of human filth on baggage below decks and in dormitories.

The Age - Melbourne, Vic.
(Thursday 7th of February, 1952, page 6)
The Federal Government has no control over accommodation or amenities on ships bringing migrants not under assisted passage schemes. The Minister for Immigration (Mr. H. E. Holt) said, the migrant ship Corsica brought migrants from Cyprus who were screened in the ordinary way after nomination by friends and relations in Australia. The Government was deeply interested in conditions on migrant ships, but could not control them unless the migrants came under schemes of assistance.

The Herald - Melbourne, Vic.
(Monday 8th of February, 1954, page 9)
The Commonwealth Immigration Department is making some inquiries about the Louis Shipping Company — a Cyprian concern which has acted as travel agency for thousands of Cypriot migrants to Australia. The company is owned and managed by Mr Louis Pareskeva Loizou, who was given judgment by Judge Mitchell in the County Court on Thursday when he claimed £380 unpaid fare from a Cypriot migrant whose wife and three children travelled to Melbourne in the Corsica in 1951. But the judge said he would rather have given judgment for the migrant, because he was satisfied that the man "had to pay a sum out of all proportion to the value he received, and that the food; sanitary arrangements and organisation of the vessel were very poor indeed."

The Sydney Morning Herald - NSW
(Friday 8th of February, 1952, page 6)
The Greek ship Corsica was arrested at its berth at Port Melbourne today following the issue of a High Court writ by a passenger, Vladimiros Petrou. The writ alleged non-payment for work done by Petrou between January 7 and February 2 and claimed unspecified damages. When the ship berthed earlier this week it was described by passengers as a 'hell-ship.' Watersiders demanded extra money for working in what they described as 'dirty and obnoxious conditions aboard.'

The Townsville Daily Bulletin - Qld.
(Friday 8th of February, 1952, page 1)
The Greek ship, Corsica, was arrested at its berth at Port Melbourne today. When the ship arrived this week, it was described by passengers as a 'hell-ship'— a black stowaway was taken off, and then watersiders demanded extra money for working in what they described as 'dirty and obnoxious conditions aboard.' Today, law officers boarded the ship at Princes Pier and tied a Supreme Court writ to the mast. As reporters began to read it, crew men tore it down. The pressmen were then requested to leave the ship, and guards were placed at the gangway. The writ, taken out by a passenger named Vladimiros Petrou, alleged non-payment for work carried out between January 7 and February 2, and claimed unspecified damages. The writ may delay the ship's departure from Melbourne. In any case it could not sail immediately. When it was moved from the Station Pier to Princes Pier for bunkering today, a towrope fouled the propeller. Officers who tried to free it said it could only be cleared by a diver.

The Daily Commercial News and Shipping List - Sydney, NSW.

(Wednesday 13th of February, 1952, page 1)
Renamed the Corsica, a ship which was a familiar sight in Fremantle harbour last year, arrived there recently with more than 800 migrants from Cyprus. She is the 35-year-old former Liguria, ex the Burns Philp steamer Marella, which broke down in the Indian Ocean last January and was towed to Fremantle by the British freighter Chandpara. Well known at Melbourne and Sydney, the Marella traded to Singapore for many years, firstly, with the Montoro and later the Merkur.

The News - Adelaide, SA.

(Saturday 1st of March, 1952, page 2)
The German-built, 7,475ton freighter Corsica, now loading bagged oats at Port Adelaide for the Continent, began its varied career as the Kaiser's yacht in 1914. The Corsica came to Sydney after World War One as the Wahehe, was bought by an Australian company, and renamed the Marella. Before World War II it traded between Melbourne and Malaya, but was switched to the interstate liner service during the war. Afterwards it was sold to an overseas company, and this is its first trip to Port Adelaide under its present name.

The Advertiser - Adelaide, SA.

(Saturday 8th of March, 1952, page 5)
The Panamanian freighter Corsica, reported to have been built in 1914 as the Kaiser's yacht, is due to leave Port Adelaide today for the Continent with a cargo of bagged oats. The Corsica, which brought 900 migrants from Cyprus to Melbourne, is sailing back to Europe without passengers.

The Newcastle Sun – NSW

(Wednesday 13th of August, 1952, page 2)
Moroccan authorities yesterday seized the 7475-ton Panamanian ship Corsica, specially chartered to carry 795 Moslem pilgrims to Mecca, but declared unseaworthy by Casablanca port, officials. It was decided to fly the pilgrims to Mecca in a special air lift.

The Herald - Melbourne, Vic.

(Saturday 25th of September 1954, page 4)
Reuters' Paris correspondent in his story "Kaisers' Yachts Rot in Ports" (Herald, 23/9/54), makes the Corsica a "luxury yacht, formerly the pride of Kaiser Wilhelm II." The Corsica is the ancient Burns Philp steamer Marella. In her day she was one of the most comfortable ships on the Singapore-Australia run. Despite her comforts she was no yacht. She was a passenger and freight ship laid down in the First World War for the Germans' Woermann Line, in the East Africa trade. Since Burns Philp sold her, about 1948, the Marella has been the Captain Marcos, the Liguria and now the Corsica. Her present plight in Casablanca sounds similar to that in Perth in 1951. Then, as the Liguria, she was towed into port after breaking down in the Indian Ocean. To get pay for the crew sold even the bath mats.

The Newcastle Morning Herald and Miners' Advocate - NSW

(Saturday 30th of October, 1954, page 10)
The 7475-ton Corsica, seized by the port authorities when the present owners failed to pay harbour dues, is rusting at Casablanca (Morocco) a helpless hulk. The crew of this ship, in which the Kaiser's guests once dined off silver plates, were reduced to begging to feed themselves. The Corsica, 325 feet long, was built in Hamburg in 1915 and called Wahehe. Its saloons were fitted with marble and guests sat round on period furniture at sumptuous parties given on board. After World War I, the Wahehe was sold. She changed her name several times and sailed on the Cherbourg-New York and the Greece-Australia routes; The once-proud vessel's decline became a downfall in 1952. Now called the Corsica and sailing under the Panamanian flag, she was chartered to take Moslem pilgrims from Morocco to Mecca. On August 10, 1952, 800 Moslems lined up on the quays at Casablanca with their clothes, baskets and umbrellas to wait for the pilgrim ship. She turned up four days later, after two months undergoing repairs in Cadiz. But Casablanca port authorities said that she was not fit to sail. An air lift was organised to take the pilgrims to Mecca and the Corsica with her Greek captain, 36-year-old Stavros Lemos, from the Isle of Chios, and her crew, remained in Casablanca. Port authorities seized the vessel and put her up for auction when the owners, 'Baru of Panama,' failed to pay harbour dues. These had been increased considerably when storms blew the Corsica of her moorings last autumn and tugs had to rescue the powerless ship. The auction took place last December but no bids reached the reserve price. Meanwhile, the Corsica's crew of 14 Italians, Spaniards and Greeks lived as best they could. They sold all tile fittings they could remove to buy food and finally, before they and the captain were repatriated, were reduced to begging on the harbour quays. The Corsica stayed in Casablanca with an Italian chief engineer keeping an eye on her. The engineer, Antonio Semini, of Genoa, declares that the ship could he made seaworthy again with only five days' work on her boilers. But the future of the Kaiser's ship rests with the Casablanca port authorities, whose main hope seems to be to sell her for scrap.

Hungry, Thirsty

George Stelot, 21, a Cypriot, said everybody aboard with the exception of the officers and one family had been hungry and thirsty since leaving Cyprus.

They had been unable to bath or wash from Colombo to Fremantle.

A young Cairo journalist, Miss Jacqueline Kleimann, said she had spent £30 on water during the voyage.

The only water tap—it had been on for only three brief periods daily for most of the trip—had run dry three days out of Melbourne.

£125 Fare

All passengers had paid at least £125 sterling for their passage. The ship had been advertised in Cyprus as a "22,000 tons luxury liner with two swimming pools."

The Corsica is of 7475 tons and its one swimming pool was empty throughout the voyage. Yesterday it was filled with rubbish.

A young Italian, Romeo Alberti, claimed the ship had been swept only three times since embarkation — the days before calling at Port Said, Colombo and Fremantle.

Master's Denial

Master of the Corsica, Captain C. Scoufopoulos, denied all the migrants' claims.

He said there had been a troublesome element aboard who had come "from the slums of Cyprus and had no cause for complaint."

Captain Scoufopoulos was supported by a Cyprus Government official, Mr. H. C.

THE IMMIGRATION DEPARTMENT

Keith Stodden in the 1970s.

This short summary of early Australian immigration is largely based on information gathered from my interviews with Keith Stodden, a highly intelligent public servant who worked for the Department of Immigration during the 1950s, 60s and 70s. This is supplemented by other interviews he recorded for SBS Television and National Library of Australia. Although Keith did not have direct interactions with migrants coming from Cyprus, he was able to explain in some detail how he dealt with migrants who arrived under the Assisted Passage Scheme.

I first learned about Keith after watching a documentary series titled 'Tales from a Suitcase'. It has taken me two years to finally track him down to a nursing home in Elsternwick, Victoria. At ninety years of age, he was still able to recall some important details about his job as an Immigration Officer.

During Keith's time as an Immigration Officer, the 'White Australia' policy with regards to migrant selection and assistance was being implemented by the Australian Government. The aim of this law was to limit non-white (particularly Asian) immigration to Australia, to help keep Australia 'British'.

Between 1945 and 1952, almost half a million migrants arrived in Australia. Directly after the Second World War, anyone wishing to migrate to Australia under the Assisted Passage Scheme had to be white, healthy and if not British, prepared to work under contract for two years before being offered 'alien' residency. Arthur Caldwell was the very first Commonwealth Minister for Immigration to promote the idea of 'populate or perish'. During the war, Australia faced the threat of Japanese invasion. This created an anxiety and fear that, unless the country's population was boosted dramatically, the threat of being overrun by the so-called 'yellow peril' was ever present and real.

Britain after the Second World War was over-populated and only too happy to select and send thousands of their best men and women, to come to Australia. Likewise, the European countries which were ravished and decimated by the war agreed for their citizens to migrate in large numbers. At the time, there were shortages of factory workers and unskilled labourers in Australia. So, the doors of immigration were cast wide open by Australia for countries such as Italy, Greece, Malta and Yugoslavia. Numerous members of minority groups, who were persecuted one way or another or displaced because of the war and who wanted to get as far away as possible from the horror they had endured, came to Australia through the Assisted Passage Scheme.

The Australian Government officials were initially very selective in choosing the right sort of Europeans to come to Australia. Individuals who were white, fit and healthy and resembled the British in appearance, manner and culture were thought to be better candidates for assimilation into Australian society. Based on this there was a preference for fairer looking Europeans to be selected for immigration in the post war years. In particular people from Eastern Europe or Nordic countries or perhaps people from Northern Greece as opposed to people from Southern Greece or the Greek Islands were preferred. People from Eastern Mediterranean countries such as Cyprus, Lebanon, Syria and Egypt were not particularly sought after.

Keith Stodden, with a love for languages and other cultures, became an Immigration Officer in 1949. In the early years of his employment, his main duty was to see that all assisted migrants were carefully processed through customs at Station Pier before being placed on a train

to the Bonegilla camp outside Albury.

Keith would be flown from Melbourne to Perth where he would go to the Port of Fremantle to meet the ships and the incoming passengers. "I would stay at the Murray Hotel, and board the ship the following week," he explains. "After

Keith Stodden in June, 2022.

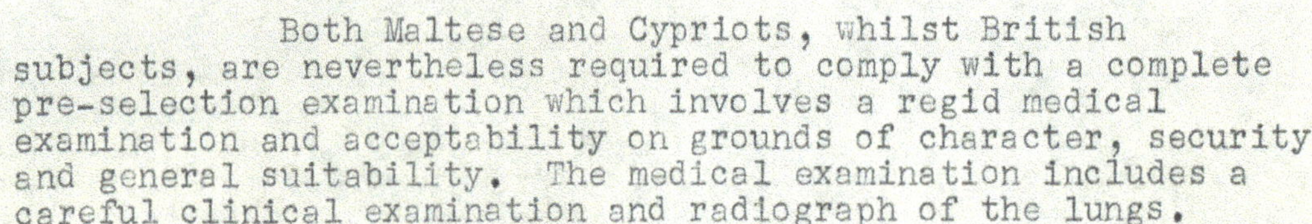

ABOVE
A Lloyd Triestino liner arrives at Port Melbourne in the 1950s. Photo courtesy of Nick Cree.

RIGHT
Booklets produced by the Australian Government to attract migrants, 1950s.

eating in the Officer's Mess Hall with the Captain, I would go to the main hall and begin registering all the 'aliens' under the Alien Registration Act and welcoming the Assisted Passage migrants." Keith would board the migrant ships in Fremantle

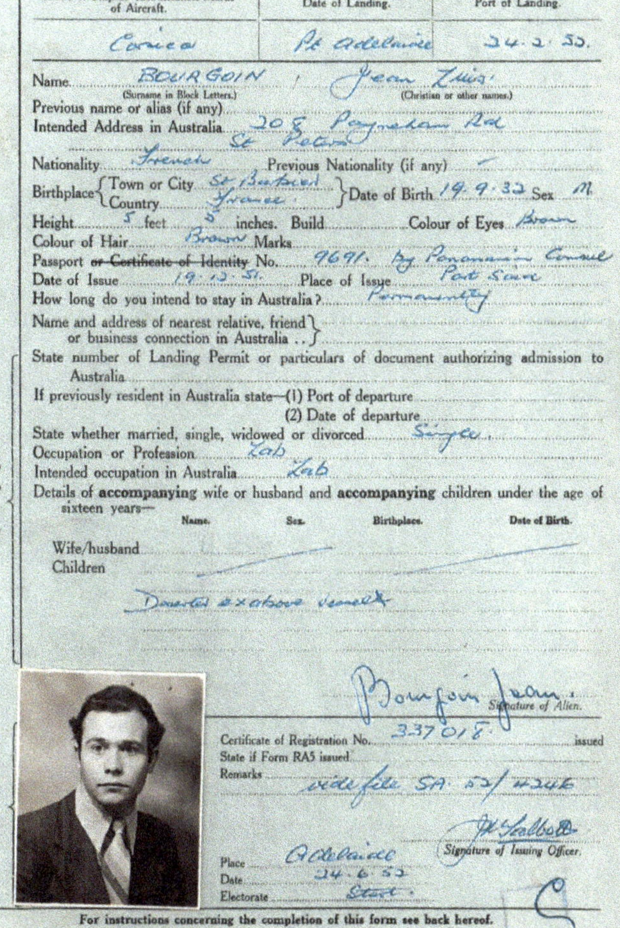

COMMONWEALTH OF AUSTRALIA.

Form RA.

Aliens Act 1947.

e information to be given is required in accordance with the Aliens t and Regulations, from aliens (non-British persons) over sixteen years of age entering the Commonwealth.

Name of Ship or Identification Marks of Aircraft.	Date of Landing.	Port of Landing.
Corsica	Pt Adelaide	24.2.53.

Name. BOURGOIN, Jean Luis
(Surname in Block Letters.) (Christian or other names.)
Previous name or alias (if any)
Intended Address in Australia 20 § Payneham Rd St Peters
Nationality French Previous Nationality (if any)
Birthplace { Town or City St Barberel Country France } Date of Birth 19.9.32 Sex M
Height 5 feet 5 inches. Build Colour of Eyes Brown
Colour of Hair Brown Marks
Passport or Certificate of Identity No. 9691. by Panama in Consul
Date of Issue 19.12.51. Place of Issue Port Said
How long do you intend to stay in Australia? Permanently
Name and address of nearest relative, friend or business connection in Australia ..
State number of Landing Permit or particulars of document authorizing admission to Australia
If previously resident in Australia state—(1) Port of departure
(2) Date of departure
State whether married, single, widowed or divorced Single
Occupation or Profession Lab
Intended occupation in Australia Lab
Details of **accompanying** wife or husband and **accompanying** children under the age of sixteen years—

Name.	Sex.	Birthplace.	Date of Birth.
Wife/husband			
Children			

Deserted ex above vessel

Bourfoin Jean.
Signature of Alien.
Certificate of Registration No. 3-37 018. issued
State if Form RA5 issued
Remarks vide file SA. 52/4246
Signature of Issuing Officer.
Place Adelaide
Date 24.6.53
Electorate Sturt.

For instructions concerning the completion of this form see back hereof.

and sail to Melbourne with them. "For refugees in particular, who came out on a crowded ship that was blown around and they got seasick, how glad they were to finally land in Fremantle and to have somebody like me explain to them what was going to happen when we got to Melbourne. What they were entitled to and so on."

Keith dealt mainly with European migrants. "My job was to explain to them about the Commonwealth Immigration Reception Centres and the migrant hostels such as Bonegilla. The first week at Bonegilla was free. Free meals, free rooms, free laundry, everything."

When the ships arrived at Port Melbourne, Keith would assist the migrants through customs, checking the migrant alert lists, checking who was going to Bonegilla and giving them a yellow button to wear. "If the migrants already had a nominated sponsor and accommodation provided, they were given a blue button and sent on their way. If they were going to Tasmania I gave them a purple button and a pink button if they were going to Adelaide."

According to Keith, the migrants who were given yellow buttons were placed on a special train at Station Pier and taken to Bonegilla. "I did quite a few train trips from Port Melbourne to Bonegilla," says Keith. "When the train arrived at Seymour, the station master Alf Birmingham would be there to greet the new arrivals offering them fresh fruit, an orange, bread rolls, soup, whatever and there was always plenty of food for them. That man deserved an Order of Australia Medal for arranging such wonderful receptions for these poor people who had endured four weeks on a ship and then a four-hour train-ride." Keith would notify his colleagues at Bonegilla to let them know who was coming and who to expect so they could allot them their accommodation and make sure they had a meal upon their arrival, even if it was late at night.

"Whenever I registered aliens," he says, "you had to know their name, their address, their parent's names, their date of birth, when they married, who they married, their children's details, their occupation or status, you know, a dozen points of information. The British migrants of course, didn't have to be registered because they weren't regarded as aliens."

Many of the skilled migrants and refugees resented the Australian immigration policy, especially when they received their work contracts. The males were listed as labourers and the females were listed as domestics (housekeepers). Of course, these highly skilled migrants felt deprived of their lifetime achievements and careers because they were nominated as either labourers or domestics despite their skill level or qualifications. By comparison, British assisted migrants did not need to sign a work contract at all.

Keith Stodden recalls that men and women had separate sleeping quarters in the migrant camps like Bonegilla. Even married couples were kept apart. However, they could certainly mix and be together in the dining hall or in the recreational hall while they watched films or during English language classes or go for walks together at the camp. "Australia was just the thing these poor migrants needed after the horrors of war and occupation and then a long and crowded voyage through the hot tropics in stuffy and smelly ships. What a peaceful and wonderful experience Bonegilla must have been for them."

Most assisted migrants tolerated this situation since their travel to Australia was free and they felt lucky and grateful - so they put up with some discomfort for the chance of a new life. "I found myself telling many migrants that they might find it difficult to assimilate into Australia society," Keith remarks. "I would tell them that there will be temporary separations and disappointments and frustrations; there will be language problems, you won't understand what people are saying and you'll have to get used to pointing at things and it might be rather humiliating and difficult at times. Australian citizens themselves had a strong claim on the government for support, especially returned servicemen who were looking for jobs and accommodation. The last thing the government wanted was to be seen to be treating migrants or refugees better than ordinary Australians. Their priority I think, was to getting migrants working into useful productive work, especially where there were shortages of labour, often in the most menial, dirty, dangerous and unpleasant types of jobs. I imagine they consoled themselves with the thought, well at least we'll have an income, we'll be getting some cash."

Looking back, Keith agrees that Australia should have made more of an effort to ensure that every ship coming to Australia had doctors and nurses on board, as well as interpreters, chaplains, teachers and other professionals to help and assist the migrants prepare for their destination and indeed a new life in Australia. He exclaims, "it was all a matter of too little – too late I'm afraid."

It was not until 1972, when the Australian government saw fit to abolish their 'White Australian' policy, that the complete removal of any criteria for entry that was based on race, colour or health status was enacted.

ACKNOWLEDGEMENTS

I would like to thank Keith Stodden for allowing me to publish his valuable insight into post-war migration and the Australian immigration process at that time. Special thanks to his nephew Paul Woods and also to Nick Henderson for their kind help and support.

```
        There is no evidence available to suggest, on
the grounds of health, that Maltese and Cypriot migrants are of
a lower standard than other classes of migrants or the community
generally.  Unlike statistics of social behaviour, those relating
to the health of migrants remain fragmentary but because of the
precautions taken, it is reasonable to infer that the incidence
of serious ill-health (such as tuberculosis) among migrants is
relatively small.
```

HMAS Kanimbla and the train to Bonegilla, 1947.

Station Pier, Port Melbourne, 7th of August, 1950. Photo by Allan Green.

COMMONWEALTH
OF AUSTRALIA

ALIENS ACT
1947—1966

Annual notification by Aliens

Important for aliens

All aliens 16 years of age or over living in Australia—Must notify the Department of Immigration during SEPTEMBER each year of their address, occupation and marital status.

An alien is a person who is not an Australian citizen, a British subject, an Irish citizen, or a British or Australian protected person.

Visitors to Australia for a period of 12 months or less are exempt from this requirement.

Belangrijk voor buitenlanders

Alle vreemdelingen van 16 jaar en ouder die in Australie wonen—

Moeten ieder jaar in September het Departement van Immigratie kennisgeven van hun adres, beroep en echtelijke staat.

Een buitenlander is een ieder die niet Australisch staatsburger of Brits onderdaan is, of een staatsburger van Ierland, of een Brits of Australisch 'protected person' (Beschermd Persoon).

De bepaling is niet van toepassing op buitenlanders die Australie bezoeken voor een periode van ten hoogste 12 maanden.

ΠΡΟΣΟΧΗ ΔΙΑ ΤΟΥΣ ΑΛΛΟΔΑΠΟΥΣ

Άπαντες οἱ ἀλλοδαποί, ἡλικίας 16 ἐτῶν καὶ ἄνω, διαμένοντες εἰς Ἀυστραλίαν, ὀφείλουν ὅπως εἰδοποιῶσι τὸ Ὑπουργεῖον Μεταναστεύσεως κατὰ μῆνα Σεπτέμβριον ἑκάστου ἔτους περὶ τῆς διευθύνσεως τῆς κατοικίας των, τοῦ ἐπαγγέλματός των καὶ τῆς οἰκογενειακῆς των καταστάσεως (ἐὰν δηλαδὴ εἶναι ἔγγαμοι, ἄγαμοι, χωρισμένοι ἢ διατελοῦν ἐν χηρείᾳ).

ΑΛΛΟΔΑΠΟΣ εἶναι τὸ ἄτομον ποὺ ΔΕΝ ΕΙΝΑΙ ΑΥΣΤΡΑΛΟΣ ΠΟΛΙΤΗΣ, ἢ ΒΡΕΤΤΑΝΟΣ ΥΠΗΚΟΟΣ, ἢ ΙΡΛΑΝΔΟΣ ΠΟΛΙΤΗΣ, ἢ ΠΡΟΣΩΠΟΝ ΥΠΟ ΒΡΕΤΤΑΝΙΚΗΝ ἢ ΑΥΣΤΡΑΛΙΑΝΗΝ ΠΡΟΣΤΑΣΙΑΝ. Οἱ ἐπισκεπτόμενοι τὴν Ἀυστραλίαν διὰ περίοδον 12 μηνῶν ἢ ὀλιγώτερον ἐξαιροῦνται αὐτῆς τῆς ὑποχρεώσεως.

P. R. Heydon

(P. R. HEYDON) Secretary

Forms are available at . . . . . . **ANY MONEY ORDER POST OFFICE**

or the

DEPARTMENT OF IMMIGRATION,
COMMONWEALTH CENTRE,
Cnr. LATROBE and SPRING STREETS, MELBOURNE, VIC. 3000

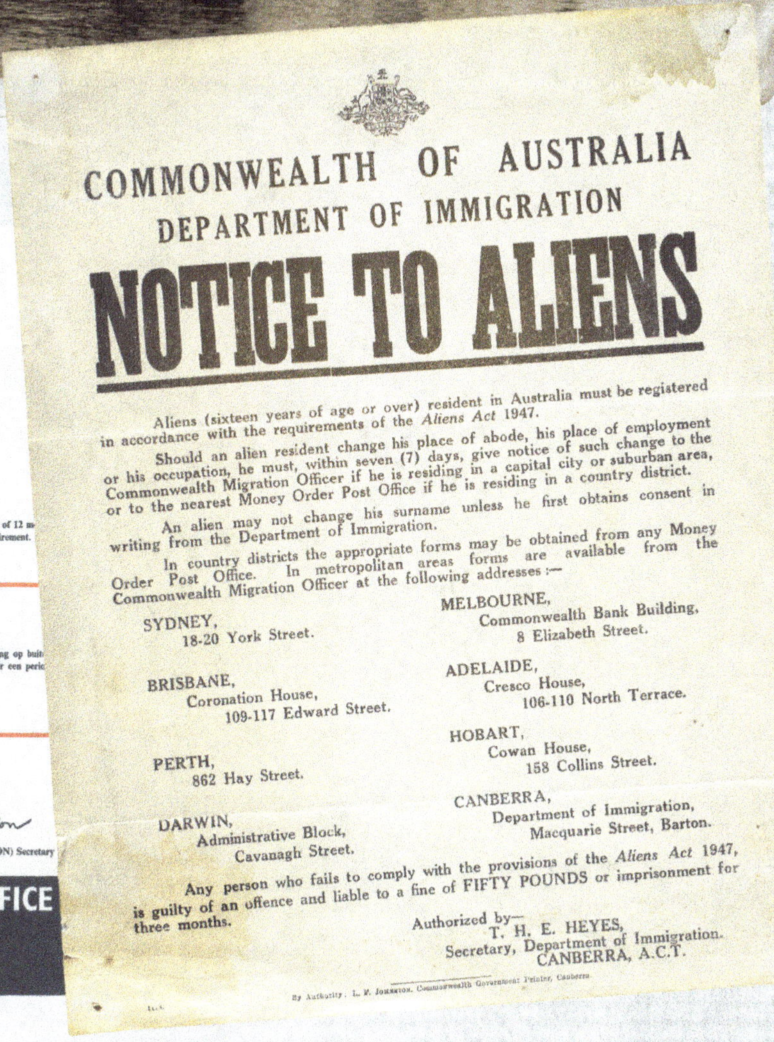

COMMONWEALTH OF AUSTRALIA
DEPARTMENT OF IMMIGRATION

NOTICE TO ALIENS

Aliens (sixteen years of age or over) resident in Australia must be registered in accordance with the requirements of the *Aliens Act 1947*.

Should an alien resident change his place of abode, his place of employment or his occupation, he must, within seven (7) days, give notice of such change to the Commonwealth Migration Officer if he is residing in a capital city or suburban area, or to the nearest Money Order Post Office if he is residing in a country district.

An alien may not change his surname unless he first obtains consent in writing from the Department of Immigration.

In country districts the appropriate forms may be obtained from any Money Order Post Office. In metropolitan areas forms are available from the Commonwealth Migration Officer at the following addresses :—

SYDNEY,
18-20 York Street.

MELBOURNE,
Commonwealth Bank Building,
8 Elizabeth Street.

BRISBANE,
Coronation House,
109-117 Edward Street.

ADELAIDE,
Cresco House,
106-110 North Terrace.

PERTH,
862 Hay Street.

HOBART,
Cowan House,
158 Collins Street.

DARWIN,
Administrative Block,
Cavanagh Street.

CANBERRA,
Department of Immigration,
Macquarie Street, Barton.

Any person who fails to comply with the provisions of the *Aliens Act 1947*, is guilty of an offence and liable to a fine of FIFTY POUNDS or imprisonment for three months.

Authorized by—
T. H. E. HEYES,
Secretary, Department of Immigration.
CANBERRA, A.C.T.

By Authority: L. F. Johnston, Commonwealth Government Printer, Canberra

Colombo Zoological Gardens in Colombo, Ceylon, January 1952.
Back row from left to right: Stavros Shaili (barber), Haralambos Stylianou (stone mason), Georgios (cook) and unknown.
Front row: Nicos Savva, Yiangos Stylianou and Philippos Ioannou (brother of Haralambos Stylianou).
All men were from Neo Chorio, Paphos except for Georgios who was from Polis Chrysochous.
Photograph from the album of fellow passenger Andreas Charalambous, also from Neo Chorio.

THE INTERVIEWS

STORIES OF MIGRATION

PHILIPPOS IOANNOU

Name **PHILIPPOS IOANNOU**

Date of birth / Age **7.3.1926 / 25**

Occupation **MASON**

Place of origin **NEO CHORIO, PAPHOS**

Port of departure **LIMASSOL**

Date of departure **17 DEC 1951**

Date of arrival **4 FEB 1952**

Philippos (left) with two friends and his brother Harry (playing the banjo) soon after he arrived in Wollongong, 1952.

Philippos Ioannou was born on the 7th of March 1926 in the village of Neo Chorio in Paphos. His parents were Ioanniou Styllianou and Elizaveth Ioannou and they had eight children (seven sons and one daughter) of which Philippos was the second youngest.

Philippos did not like school. He preferred to roam around his village, exploring the countryside and catching little birds to bring home for his dinner. In the summer, he would play on the beach with other children from his village. By the age of seven, he had become quite a confident swimmer and could dive and stay underwater for four minutes. A local fisherman named Giorgios Frangos, was impressed with young Philippos and offered to teach him how to fish.

For five years Philippos was taught how to repair nets, find and catch fish and how to scale and prepare the fish for sale at the markets in Ktima. "I was working seven days a week and practically lived on the boat with Master Frangos," he tells me. "For all my time and labour, I was paid three pounds a year. Our nets were always full. There was plenty of fish in those days. I was even taught how to smoke by all the other fishermen."

At the age of twelve, Philippos left the sea and returned to dry land. He found work looking after a large herd of goats that belonged to a wealthy landowner from Neo Chorio. "I was expected to take the herd to pasture at 5am each morning and return them back to the village by sunset. That was twelve hours a day, seven days a week. Once again, I was paid only three pounds a year."

In 1942, Philippos joined the British army as a volunteer to assist the Allied war effort. He was only seventeen. Perhaps it was the lure of getting paid two shillings a day, or maybe it was the promise of free cigarettes that enticed him. After he joined the Cypriot Volunteer Regiment (CVR), Philippos was sent to Syria, then to Palestine, Egypt, and finally, to the battlefront in Italy.

Philippos was not afraid of the horrors of war, and was often the first to volunteer to lead his two mules to the front line. One day however, one of his mules stepped on a land mine and was instantly ripped to shreds. The shrapnel from the blast wounded a number of other animals and soldiers, including Philippos.

Medical officers quickly bandaged his wound and after a few days rest, he was sent back to the front line.

After the war, Philippos returned to Cyprus and back to the familiar world of fishing. With the money he saved from the CVR, he bought himself a fishing boat.

Sometime in 1946, the wife of the village *mukhtar* (headman) introduced Philippos to a girl named Vasilia Chrysanthou Mene. She was a self-taught weaver who was able to produce the most beautiful and intricate rugs and bed spreads on her *voufa* (loom). Philippos and Vasilia were married on the 25th of October, 1946. "Some of our Turkish Cypriot friends from Androlikou brought seven slaughtered lambs to be served at our wedding feast. The Christians and Muslims in our community were always friends and with one another."

In September 1949, Philippos and Vasilia welcomed the birth of their son Savakki. Their daughter Panayiota was born in November 1951. Less than a month later, Philippos boarded the Corsica to travel to Australia, leaving his wife and two young children in the village. "My plan was to go there and work a few years and then come back to Cyprus with enough money to give my family a good life. Australia was the only country that could offer me a visa at that time."

As soon Philippos boarded the Corsica in Limassol harbour he knew that it was a tired old ship. "This ship was very slow and had to stop at many ports along the way for fuel and repairs. I had heard that the captain didn't want to travel on this ship to Australia. He knew the engines were broken so he tried to take the shortest route possible."

Philippos was initially placed down below in the steerage section of the ship, where the cargo was stored. "As soon as I saw the area, I said to my friends from my village, wait here, I will go upstairs and try and find us a cabin to stay in. We can't stay here. There were nine of us from Neo Chorio. My friend Nicolas Mavros came with me. We found a room and we all moved in. I remember one man had to sleep on the floor because there weren't enough beds. The crew tried to make us leave but I told them, if you don't give us this cabin, you can take us back to Cyprus. I told them that we had paid 125 pounds each for a cabin, not to sleep at the bottom of the ship like animals. My mother-in-law paid for my ticket and after I found work in Australia, I eventually paid her back little by little. My nephew Yiangos Stylianou (my brother's son), was travelling with us and he found work in the ship's kitchen. He was nineteen years old, five years younger than me and he would fry potatoes for us and give us extra food. The food on the ship was okay. The only food that we didn't like was the steak. It was like rubber. You couldn't eat it."

Philippos would pass the hours of the day on the deck with his friends playing croquet or cards. "We would also sit together and tell each other stories. Of course, after so many days at sea we got very bored, but what could we do. It was a very long trip and the ship was too slow. My friends and I didn't get seasick at all because we were used to the ocean."

When asked about the cargo of potatoes and onions, Philippos said he believed they were destined for Ceylon. "Unfortunately, by the time we reached Colombo they had turned to mush and were ruined. The smell was awful and many passengers became quite sick. We had to all stay on the deck for fresh air. I remember the ship's captain had

to ask some of the male passengers to help empty the potatoes and onions overboard. I'm not sure if they got paid"

When the Corsica arrived at Fremantle, Philippos and a few friends went ashore to try and buy some food. "I knew a few words of English so when we walked into a grocery store I said to the man, 'I want two bully beef.' He looked at me confused. 'Bully beef, bully beef,' I kept repeating. He eventually understood that I meant 'corned beef' and he sold me a few tins."

Despite his lack of education, Philippos was a quick learner and was able to acquire skills in many areas after he reached Australia. During his first few years in Sydney, he found work in a number of factories, learning multiple trades without any prior experience. "I heard that after the Corsica left Australia, it sank. That's what we all heard. We all left Cyprus thinking that when we come to Australia we would be picking up coins on the streets. But it wasn't like that at all. We had to look for work and many migrants struggled in those first few years."

Philippos moved to Wollongong, NSW where he worked on a fishing trawler at nearby Port Kembla. Because he had learned Italian in Italy during the war, he was able to communicate with the Italian trawler owner. Unfortunately, his lack of schooling meant that he was unable to send any letters to his wife and family back in Cyprus. Frustrated, he bought a Greek and English dictionary and taught himself how to read and write in both languages."

Two and a half years after arriving in Australia, Philippos had made enough money to bring his wife and two young children from Cyprus to join him in Wollongong. In 1954 he bought a house for four thousand pounds and taught himself how to cook.

In 1961, Philippos and Vasilia welcomed the arrival of twin daughters, Anna and Eleni (Helene).

Eventually, Philippos and Vasilia opened their first fish and chip shop in Figtree, Wollongong. It was an instant success and regarded by many of the locals as the best fish and chips in the region. In 1968, they move to Melbourne with their twin daughters Anna and Helene to be reunited with their married children Panayiota (Donna) and Savvaki. They opened a fish and chip shop in West Sunshine which they ran for four years. Vasilia was in charge of the grill and hamburgers. She developed a special gravy that was a real winner with the customers who would come from near and far to buy the hamburger with the special sauce.

ACKNOWLEDGEMENTS

I would like to thank Philippos Ioannou for allowing me to publish his story of migration. Special thanks to his daughter Helene Polydorou for all her support along the way.

Philippos and Vasilia with their children Savvaki, Panayiota (Donna) and twins, Anna and Eleni (Helene). Wollongong, 1964.

LELLA NEARCHOU

Standing L-R: Lella's Aunt Mirianthi, her father Fotis Nicolaides and her mother Thalia Nicolaides. Seated L-R: Mirianthi's husband (name unknown) and Lella's maternal grandparents Polycarpos and Eleni. The baby is Lella's sister Erasmia. Ktima, Paphos. Circa 1923.

Lella's mother Thalia Polycarpou.
Paphos, Cyprus. Circa 1920.

Lella Nearchou (nee Nicolaidou) was born in Ktima, Paphos on the 23rd of December, 1929. Her mother Thalia was a primary school teacher and her father Fotis owned and operated a restaurant called 'George Bar Restaurant' which was located on the ground floor of their house on Leoforos Athinon Street. Lella is the third eldest of six children: Erasmia, Socrates, Nikos, Georgios and Polycarpos.

As a young girl, Lella remembers playing with other children in a field near her house which was located in the Turkish quarter. "We all played together, Christian and Muslims together," she says proudly. "There was never a problem."

Life in Ktima was mostly wonderful for Lella and her family. While most people in the surrounding villages still used paraffin lamps, Lella's house had electric lights. "Many houses in Ktima had electric lights when I was growing up," she tells me. "We had a good life. I remember there was always plenty of food to eat. No one starved in Ktima. My mother made us everything: *spanakopita*, *bourekia* with meat, and many different sweets. When my mother wanted to make bread or *flaounes*, or a Sunday roast she would prepare the dish at home and I would take the tray to one of the bakeries in our neighbourhood. I would pay the baker half a shilling to cook our meal. Everything was prepared and cooked fresh on the day. It was wonderful."

In 1949, Lella met Neophytos Nearchou. He was from Yeroskipou and lived with his widowed mother Eliatha after his father Nearchos had died from Tuberculosis when he was six years old.

When Lella met Neophytos, he was working as a waiter at the 'Olympus Hotel' in Ktima. "I was told that while he was riding to work, he would past my house and see me standing on the balcony. He eventually mustered the courage to tell my Aunt Mirianthi that he wanted to marry me. I thought he was good looking but I still took my time giving him my answer."

Lella and Neophytos were married on the 20th of June, 1950. Less than a month after their wedding, Neophytos left Cyprus bound for Australia. "We had both agreed before we got married to leave Cyprus and immigrate to Australia," Lella tells me. "Neophytos was reluctant at first but I kept insisting that we should go. I had heard many stories about how much better life was in Australia and I wanted to go and see for myself. Besides, after the war there was great unemployment in Cyprus. There were very few jobs and the wages were low. Neophytos did have his job at the hotel but that was only paying around twelve pounds a week. He left Cyprus to go and find a job and a house in Australia before arranging for me to join him. That was the way it was done back then. We were married only twenty-two days and then he left."

Neophytos left Cyprus on the 5th of August, 1950 on the ship SS Cyrenia. "When he left for Australia, I stayed at my parents' house," says Lella softly. "There

was a lot of sadness and heartache at that time. What could I do? We had both agreed that Australia could offer us a better life. We kept hearing good stories about Australia and how much better things were over there. People who had migrated earlier were sending letters back home to their loved ones stating how much money they were making. They said that if you didn't gamble or squander your money at the races, you could live a decent life in Australia. We heard all these good stories so we decided to try our luck abroad."

Four months after her husband left, Lella boarded the ship Corsica together with her older brother, Socrates (Takis) Nicolaides. She was twenty-one years old. "I remember we arrived in Limassol on the 13th of December and we were taken in small boats out to the ship which was anchored some distance off-shore. In those days the ships couldn't come close to the pier because the water was too shallow."

Lella shared a cabin with some young girls from Rizokarpasos. "There were

around seven or eight of us and we all slept in bunk beds. Some of these girls were engaged and on their way to meet their fiancées. There were quite a few passengers from Rizokarpasos and Paphos on the Corsica. My brother Takis shared a cabin with his work friends from Ktima. Takis and I paid 125 pounds each for a cabin but I did meet one woman and her husband who paid 150 pounds each for a slightly better cabin. They must have been in First Class. His name was Evagoras Papadakis and his wife was Olga. Evagoras had a camera and was taking photographs on the ship. The majority of the passengers, perhaps 900 passengers were from Cyprus. There was a poor Cypriot woman with four children travelling on her own to meet her husband. We tried to help her out. I think she had twin baby daughters. There were also some Greeks and Macedonian migrants and some Jewish refugees on their way to New Zealand. At Port Said, some Slavic and Jewish people boarded the ship."

Lella recalls that every time the Corsica would arrive at a destination, the

dergarten school photograph. *Parthenagoiou Dimitriou*. Lella Nicolaidou is standing second from left in the back row, Ktima, Paphos. Circa 1935.

passengers would get excited and rush to the port side of the ship for a better view. "The crew kept shouting at us to move back. They were scared the ship might tip over. The food on the Corsica was not good. I remember they served us sardines, macaroni spaghetti, olives and salads. The fridges in the kitchen must have been broken because when they served us the food, there was a funny smell. No one wanted to eat it because of that smell. Whoever had money in their pockets would wait until the ship docked somewhere and they would go ashore to buy supplies and fresh food. Many Cypriots would eat the food they brought with them from Cyprus. Thankfully the weather was okay. Only in the Indian Ocean did we encounter bad weather and large waves and that's when we got dizzy."

Lella preferred to stay in her cabin at night rather than attend any festivities in the main hall. "Sometimes there were dances in the main hall but I didn't attend any. During the day, I would sit on the deck with my friends talking and getting to know one another. Quite often we would see dolphins swimming alongside the ship.

Lots of dolphins. To tell you the truth, no one bothered us on the ship. The men were well behaved and good-hearted. Let me tell you, the men in those times were decent and God fearing. Everyone respected one another and behaved like decent Christians. It's not like it is today. The men back then left you alone and did not bother you. I remember somewhere in Africa, Ethiopia I think it was, a Greek priest came on board the ship and blessed us all. It was the *Fota* (the Epiphany) and we celebrated this on the ship. I remember all the Cypriots who were gathered together on the balconies were singing Christmas Carols and chanting religious hymns. It was very emotional."

When Lella and her brother Socrates arrived at Port Melbourne, Neophytos was there to greet them. "We were so relieved that we finally made it safely. I can never understand who decided to commission this ship and allow people to travel on it over such a long distance. Which company gave the licence for this ship to travel, I'll never know. It was emotional to finally arrive and see my husband again. So many people became emotional on that pier in Port Melbourne. Neophytos and I caught

Lella and Neophytos' engagement photograph. Paphos, 1949.

a bus back to his rental property in Clifton Hill but without my luggage. They kept that on the ship and told us to return the next day to collect it. We went back the next day but the luggage was still on the ship so we had to return the following day.

Lella and Neophytos' wedding outside the church of Agios Nicholas in Chlorakas, Paphos. 20th of June, 1950.

En route to Australia. Back row, from left to right: Socrates (Takis) Nicolaides, Avraam Christofi, Michalis Thesalos and Evagoras Papadakis. Middle row: Demetris Parlan, Andreas (Rikos) Artemis, Andreas Tryphonos, Georgoula Achileos and Olga Papadakis. Front row: Lella Nearchou, and Loukia Papastylianou. Takis appears to be holding a bottle of whiskey or brandy. January, 1952.

I can't remember how many days we had to go back but it was after many days before I was finally allowed to collect my luggage. Apart from my suitcase, I had brought a large *paoullo* (dowry box) with me from Cyprus."

Reunited, Neophytos and Lella spent many days together getting to know Melbourne. "We went everywhere in those early years," she says. "We would socialise with other migrant couples and go on picnics or visit the beach at Mornington and Anglesea."

In 1953, Lella and Neophytos welcomed their first child. "Our son Andrew was born in January, 1953 and then every eighteen months (or so) another baby was born."

Lella and Neophytos were blessed with six children. Andrew (1953), Thalia (1954) Leah (1956), George (1957) Mario (1961) and Christine (1966).

ACKNOWLEDGEMENTS

I would like to thank Lella Nearchou and her family for allowing me to publish her story of migration.
Special thanks to her daughter Christine for all her support over the last few years.

Lella's certificate of vaccination (Small Pox). Ktima, Paphos, 1951.

CLOCKWISE:
- Lella Nearchou in a rickshaw, Colombo, Ceylon. January, 1952.
- Lella Nearchou with her brother Socrates Nicolaides (centre) and Olga Papadakis (on Lella's right) surrounded by some of the locals in Colombo, Ceylon. January, 1952.
- Neophytos and Lella Nearchou in Melbourne, Australia, 1952.
- On the way to the Melbourne Zoo. From left to right: Lella Nearchou, Neophytos Nearchou, Olga Papadakis, Socratis (Takis) Nicolaides and Michael Neofytou (holding his box brownie camera). This photograph was probably taken by Olga's husband Evagoras Papadakis. On the left is the door to the room where Lella and her husband Neophytos were staying. Location: North Melbourne near Victoria Market. 11th of May, 1952.
- Lella Nearchou (left), with Loukia Papastylianou, Georgoulla Artemis and Olga Papadakis on the top deck of the Corsica. Christmas Day, 1951.

PAPHOS

YILDIZ EYIAM

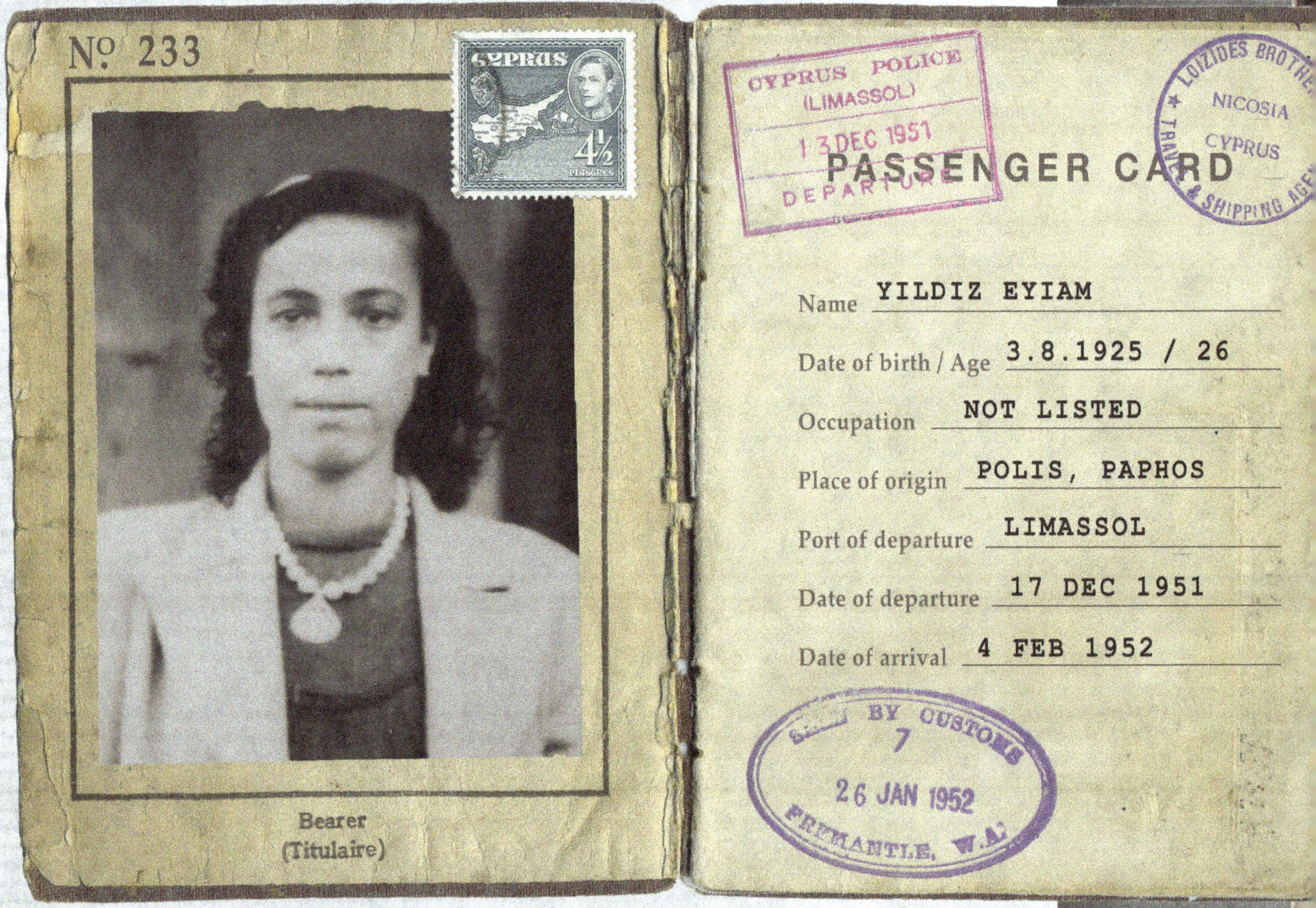

PASSENGER CARD

Name **YILDIZ EYIAM**

Date of birth / Age **3.8.1925 / 26**

Occupation **NOT LISTED**

Place of origin **POLIS, PAPHOS**

Port of departure **LIMASSOL**

Date of departure **17 DEC 1951**

Date of arrival **4 FEB 1952**

Yildiz outside her family home in Polis, Paphos on the day she left Cyprus. December, 1951.

Yildiz's family in Polis, Paphos. Circa 1935.

Back row from left to right: Older sisters, Heniye, Remziye, Vahibe, Refika, Hayriye. Seated: Sherif (mother of Yildiz), Ahmet (son of Remziye), Heniye, (Grandmother of Yildiz), Dervish (father of Yildiz). Front row: Younger sisters, and Museref, Naime, Yildiz.

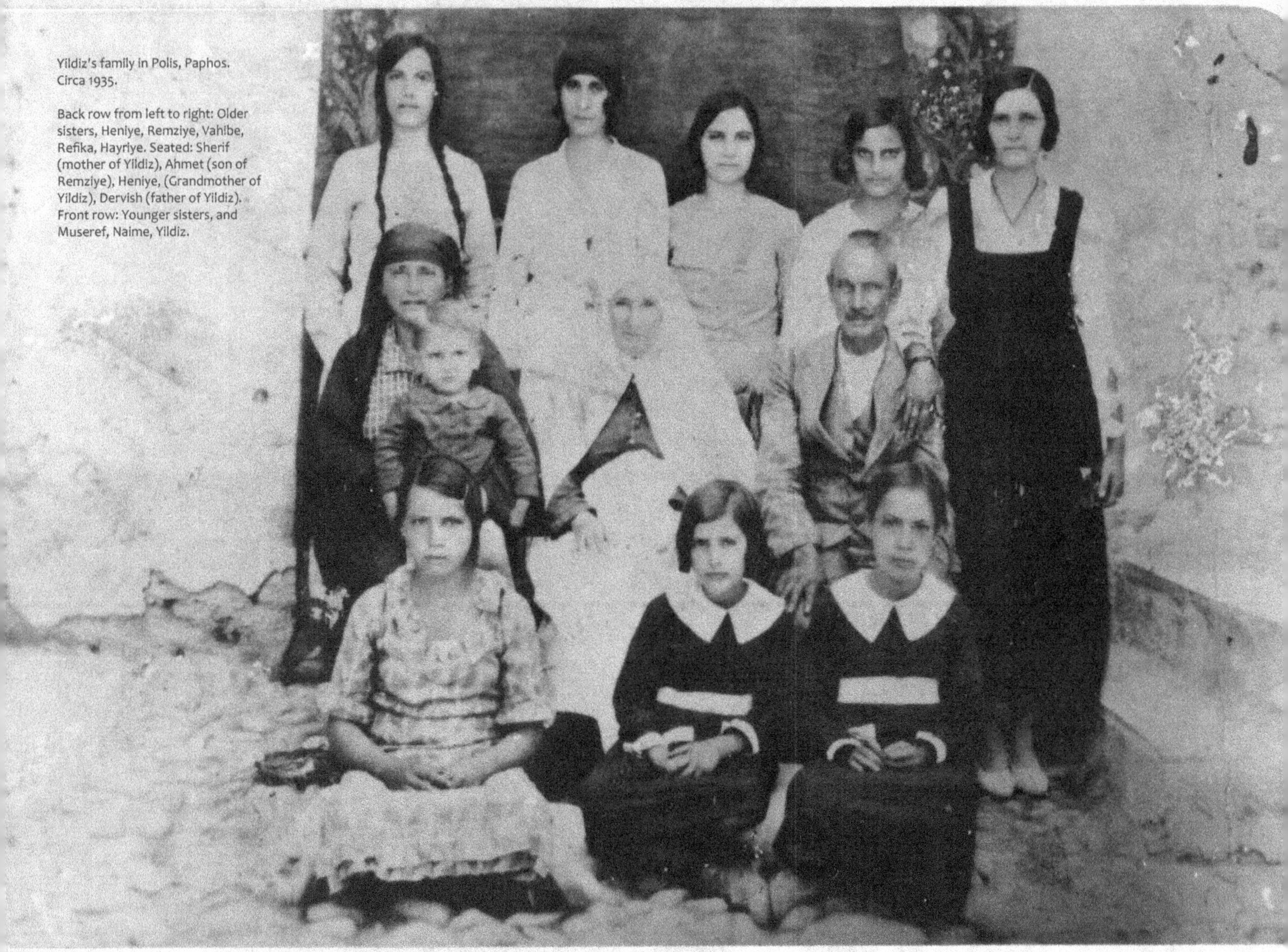

Yildiz Dervish was born in the mixed village of Polis, Paphos on the 3rd of August, 1925. She was the second youngest child of Dervish Hassan and Sherif Naim. Her sisters were; Remziye, Heniye, Hayriye, Vahibe, Refika, Museref, Naime and her brother was Cevdet.

Yildiz's parents were wealthy land owners and involved in agriculture. Apparently, when Yildiz's great grandfather Hassan Aga came from Egypt to Cyprus sometime in the 19th century, he had brought a bag of gold with him and was able to purchase many parcels of land in Polis.

Yildiz's sister Heniye was married to a Palestinian man during the 1930s. Many Turkish Cypriot girls were married to Arab suitors at that time. Some did not fare well and were taken to Palestine and Jordan, never to see their families again. Fortunately, Heniye had a good marriage. Her husband agreed to live in Cyprus for a while and four of their five children were born on the island. Yildiz had taught Heniye's son Marwan how to read.

In 1950, Yildiz's parents received an offer of marriage from Redjeb Eyyam who was living in Melbourne, Australia. When her parents asked her if she wanted to marry Redjeb, she did not hesitate to say 'yes' and agreed to travel to Australia to meet him. She was a determined young woman who did not want to live in her village and marry a farmer or shepherd. Yildiz was educated in the 1930s. She wanted to seek a better life for herself.

Redjeb was born in Chrysochou on the 1st of January, 1922. He was a boot maker by trade and had served in the Cypriot Volunteer Regiment (CRV) during and after the Second World War. He served in the CVR for seven years. It is said that after he was discharged from the Regiment he returned to his village with chocolate and a toothbrush. It was the first time the locals had tasted chocolate and the first time they had seen a man brush his teeth with a toothbrush."

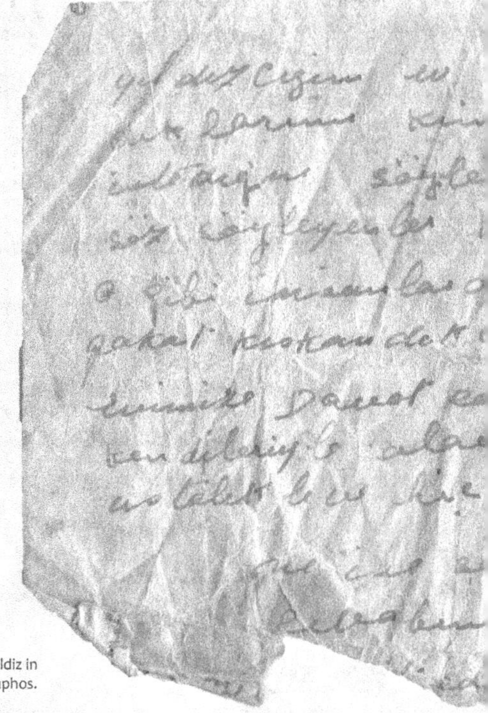

A letter written by Redjeb Eyyam to his wife Yildiz in September 1951 and addressed to her in Paphos.

Yildiz's sons, Aly (aged four) in the toy car and Eshref (aged two) on the tricycle outside their house in Austin Street, Seddon, 1957. In 1958, the family moved to Burns Street, Yarraville.

In 1949, Redjeb migrated to Melbourne in search of a better life. He travelled on the ship Misr. When he arrived, he was unable to find work as a bootmaker so he went to work at the Preservene Soap Factory in Richmond and then at ColGas in Yarraville as a stoker. His job involved placing coal in hot ovens to produce gas. "Dad was an avid reader of books and newspapers," his daughter Sheri tells me. "When he migrated to Australia, he would buy the 'Herald' newspaper every day and that's how he taught himself to read English."

Yildiz and Redjeb were married by proxy in February, 1951. Because he was in Melbourne, a relative stepped in to take his place as groom at the wedding ceremony in Polis. In December that year Yildiz farewelled her family and set sail for Australia on board the Corsica. Her recollection of the journey differs from other passengers on the ship. When retelling the story to her children, she would state that the journey took two and a half months to get to Australia and the ship was carrying a cargo of onions. "Mum didn't really talk much about the Corsica," says her daughter Sheri. "She told us that she was so sea sick that she didn't leave her cabin. According to mum, by the time they reached Australia, the onions had rotted in the hull and that's why the ship was prevented from docking at Station Pier until they could clean up the mess."

Redjeb was at Station Pier waiting for his new bride. Apparently, when he saw the ship anchored in the bay, he hired a row boat and rowed out to find his bride. He called out her name and when he saw her standing against the rails, he threw chocolates up to her. It was only after the ship cleared quarantine and was allowed to berth at the pier, when Yildiz and Redjeb finally met in person. She was twenty-six and he was twenty-nine.

Yildiz was among only a small number of Turkish Cypriot migrants to come out to Australia at that time. She spoke no English and knew no-one, not even her husband. By the time Yildiz arrived, Redjeb had saved enough money to buy their first small house on Bayview Street in Prahran before moving to Footscray. They rented rooms in their house and had many boarders over the years (at both houses) to help them pay their mortgage. Their first child (a son) Ali was born in 1953, followed by Eshref in 1955, Sheri in 1957 and Rebiye in 1961.

My mother never worked in Australia," says Sheri. "And my father never had a car. He owned a bike and he would ride that bike to his work."

Over the years, Yildiz managed to sponsor some of her nieces and nephews to come to Australia. In fact, Redjeb and Yildiz helped many Turkish Cypriots to migrate during the 1960s and 70s. They also encouraged their children to go to university. To them, education was the foundation of a secure and successful life.

Yildiz returned to Cyprus in 1971. Redjeb never went back. He had stated that because his parents had passed away, he did not see a reason to return. He became very involved with the local Turkish Cypriot community.

Sadly, Redjeb passed away in February, 2011 and Yildiz died nine months later, in November.

ACKNOWLEDGEMENTS

I would like to thank Sheri Seyit and Rebiye Eyiam for allowing me to publish their mother's story of migration and for their ongoing help and support.

SOCRATES NICOLAIDES

Takis (Socrates) Nicolaides was born in Paphos on the 23rd of August, 1926. His parents Fotis and Thalia had six children; Erasmia, Takis, Lella, Nikos, Georgios and Polycarpos. His mother was a primary school teacher and his father owned a restaurant called 'George Bar Restaurant' which was located on the ground floor of their house on Leoforos Athinon Street in Ktima. Takis would sometimes help his father at his restaurant serving the English soldiers who would come there to eat.

After finishing primary school in Ktima, Takis found work at the Power Station. "The Power Station was owned by the Paphos municipality," Takis explains. "Back then, each district had its own power station. I used to do shift work working with both Greek and Turkish Cypriots.

In 1951, Takis was asked to escort his sister Lella to Australia so she could be reunited with her husband Neofytos. Two friends from the Power Station, Andreas (Rikos) Artemis and Andreas Tryphonas agreed to travel with him. "My friends and I agreed that after I delivered my sister to Neofytos, we would stay in Australia for a holiday. Our boss at the Power Station had given us six months leave."

Takis recalls seeing an advertisement about the Corsica in one of the local newspapers. "The travel agency in Limassol had advertised the Corsica as a very big ship. The best ship. I remember reading that it had swimming pools and fancy rooms. We each paid 130 pounds for

Kindergarten photograph. Takis is seated in the front row (far left) in front of Olga Papadakis who has the bob-style haircut. Ktima, Paphos, 1931.

our tickets. That was a lot of money back then. Then after we boarded the ship, we each paid an extra twenty pounds to this Italian crew member so he can give us a cabin. No one wanted to sleep in the lower deck of the ship. This arrangement with the crew member was done in secret."

After leaving Port Said, Takis noticed that the Corsica was making regular stops for repairs. "This ship kept breaking down. It was leaning over and not going straight. When we reached Ceylon, a passenger named Frixos, who worked for the British Government in Cyprus, went to the High Commission in Colombo to complain about the condition of the Corsica. The officials there ordered the captain of the ship, who was a Greek man from Samos, to empty the rotten potatoes into the ocean before we could proceed to Australia."

Takis remembers arriving in Djibouti on a Sunday. "As we were walking down the main street towards the town, we hear the sounds of a Greek church. We managed to find the church and we went in to kiss the icons and light candles. After church, we met a Cypriot man who owned a soft drink company in Djibouti. He warned us about the local people and to watch out for thieves. As it happened, I was walking down the street with some of the other passengers from the ship. One man, who was from Arsos, was wearing sunglasses. Suddenly, out of nowhere, this man grabs his sunglasses and runs off before we could do anything about it. After that, we were extra cautious."

According to Takis many migrants did not know how to react to the conditions on the ship. "Most of us have never travelled in our life. We didn't know what to expect. We didn't know if the conditions on the Corsica were the same as other ships. Was this normal? On the other hand, we didn't know if the food they served us was normal. The *macaronia* was not too bad, but the chicken was terrible."

The worst part of the journey for Takis was between Fremantle and Melbourne. "The seas were so rough. One of the passengers told me that he repaired a hole in the ship. He was a plumber and he told everyone that he helped to save the ship from sinking. I'm not sure if that was true."

When the Corsica finally docked at Port Melbourne, Takis remembers walking along the pier with his friends when someone noticed a ten shilling note on the ground. "It was so funny," laughs Takis. "We came to Australia to make money and straight away we find money on the ground. I remember one man joked, 'I'm not ready to make money today,' so another man picked up the note and put it in his pocket. After that, we all split up and went our separate ways."

Takis stayed with his two friends from Ktima. They rented a room in a house in Carlton, near the City Baths. "We used to go to the baths to have a shower because the house where we rented a room didn't have one. I think we paid three shillings each. I'll never forget the first time we went in the city; the streets were pretty empty. I remember there was a Salvation Army band playing on one corner. One day, my friends and I caught a tram to St. Kilda. We were sitting opposite these two older Australian men. They were dressed up and wearing army boots on their feet. We were all wearing these fashionable shoes from Cyprus that were two colours – white and brown. One of the Aussies began pointing at our shoes and saying, 'look at these bloody wogs. Look at the shoes they are wearing.' They were big Aussie men so we were too scared to say anything."

Unlike Ktima, Melbourne became a ghost town in the evenings. "Everything closed at 6pm. Not just the pubs, but all the shops. We used to go to these underground wine bars. I remember we would pay six pence (half a shilling) for a glass of wine and some peanuts. We used to also go to the Acropoli club on the corner of Russell and Lonsdale. There was a lot of gambling amongst the migrants back then. A lot of money was lost at those Greek clubs."

Takis' first job was at General Motors Holden (GMH) in Fishermans Bend. "My brother-in-law Neofytos worked there.

Takis going on rickshaw ride in Colombo. January, 1952.

Takis with his sister Lella in Djibouti. December 30th, 1951.

I remember I had to pay this Greek man two pounds to let me work there. I started on the production line and then moved on to the foundry. I helped to build the first Holden. It was very fast work. I had to produce sixty parts a day and I was getting around eleven pounds a week."

After GMH, Takis found work at a printing company where he was trained in offset printing and lithography. First at a placed named Jack Savage and then at Victory Publicity.

In 1955, Takis returned to Cyprus. "I knew this fisherman in Melbourne named Sam Savvas who arranged for me to meet his niece back to Cyprus. Her name was Despina Savidou. Her father Haralambos liked me but did not want me to take his daughter to Australia. Apparently, when he came to Melbourne a few years earlier he saw young girls kissing men on the street and that disgusted him. Can you imagine the shock, coming from Cyprus? 'I like you Takis but if you marry my daughter, you must stay here in Cyprus'. I was thirty years old and Despina was around twenty-two. My mother-in-law on the other hand disagreed with her husband. 'Let him marry our daughter and go to Australia,' she said. 'They can work for a few years and then come back.' And so, we got married in Limassol in July 1955. We left Cyprus for Australia on the P&O Stratheden which was a luxury liner compared to the Corsica."

Takis and Despina did not go back to Cyprus to live. They settled in Melbourne and eventually welcomed two sons into their family. Forde was born in 1965 and Harry in 1967.

ACKNOWLEDGEMENTS

I would like to thank Takis Nicolaides for allowing me to publish his story of migration. Special thanks to his son Forde for his help and support along the way.

The Corsica at the port in Massawa, December 27th, 1951. From left to right: Evagoras and Olga Papadakis, Michalis Thesalos and Loukia Papastylianou.

ACHILLEAS DEMETRIOU

A chilleas Demetriou was born in the town of Polis Chrysochous on the 2nd of February, 1928. His parents Demetrios and Anastasia Haralambos were humble people who struggled to make a living against a backdrop of poverty, economic depression and an unfair government taxation system. Achilleas was the eldest of six children (George, Mihali, Savvas, Yiannaki and Ellie).

From a young age Achilleas worked with his father making furniture for customers in Polis and the surrounding villages. When he turned eighteen, he decided to abandon the life of a travelling carpenter and opened his own workshop in Polis. "All our furniture was made by hand back then," he explains. "We used ancient techniques. Even our woodworking tools were traditional."

Despite owning his own business, Achilleas struggled to earn a living. "Many of my customers were unable to pay me. They would come to my shop to collect their furniture with a bag of wheat as payment. Some customers never paid me at all."

Achilleas and Eleni Demetriou. Polis, Paphos. Circa 1949.

In 1948, Achilleas met Eleni Alexiou. She was born in Neo Chorio on the 10th of January, 1925. Her parents Michalis and Marika Alexiou had commissioned Achilleas and his father to build some furniture for them. When the two fathers met to discuss the making of the furniture they also discussed and arranged a marriage between Achilleas and Eleni. The wedding took place the following year in October, 1949.

By 1951 Achilleas could see that his business was not improving and that he simply was not earning enough money to raise his family. His daughter Maroulla (Mary) was born in 1950 and his wife Eleni was expecting their second child (Stasoulla, born in 1952). As their financial situation became more desperate, Achilleas responded to a notice that he spotted in a newspaper from the Australian government seeking qualified tradesmen and craftsmen from Cyprus. He decided to take a chance and try his luck in the so-called lucky country.

"When I got to Limassol, there was a delay at the port," recalls Achilleas. "I was with a friend from Polis named Kemal. He said to me, 'don't worry I have relatives in Limassol and we can stay with them until the ship is ready to leave.' I'm not sure why there was a delay with the Corsica but thanks to Kemal, at least I had somewhere to stay."

Achilleas was travelling with five or six young men from his village. "We slept at the bottom of the ship in beds that were like army hammocks. The smell was terrible down there. As soon as we would wake up, we would all rush upstairs onto the deck for fresh air. That's where we stayed all day. We'd pass the time by telling each other stories or playing games. There was a Turkish woman with us on the ship. Her name was Yildiz. I knew her parents. When her father found out that I was travelling to Australia he said to me, 'son, please take our Yildiz with you. Please take her to meet her husband Redjeb in Melbourne. We looked after her on the ship. She stayed in separate quarters of course. She could speak perfect Greek. Most of the Turks in Polis could speak Greek."

A popular game that Achilleas and his friends would play on the ship was called *ziziros*. A person named the *ziziros* (cicada) would stand in the middle of a group and cover his eyes with his right hand, whilst placing his left hand under his right arm showing an open palm. The other players would then take turns hitting his open hand, sometimes softly, sometimes harder! The *ziriros*, has to guess who hit him and if he is correct, that person takes his place.

When the Corsica arrived at the other ports Achilleas was fascinated to see that, unlike Cyprus, large passenger ships were able to dock at the pier. "I remember when we docked at Djibouti, the harbour was different to Limassol. The ship was able to come close to the land. When we went for a walk we discovered all kinds of shops, Greek shops near the pier and even a Greek church. I remember we were having conversations with the Greek shopkeepers. Most of us had a few shillings in our pockets so we could buy a few things. Most people bought fresh food to eat on the ship. I didn't really like the food they were feeding us on the ship. I remember they fed us *bakalaos* (cod-fish). Who knows how long it was stored in their refrigerator."

At some point between Colombo and Fremantle, Achilleas was informed that seawater was entering the hull of the ship. "Whatever happened, there was a hole on the side of the ship and they had to fix it quickly. I remember thinking, if something bad happens I might have to jump into the sea. The captain asked for men who knew a trade to come forward to help fix the hole. Thankfully, there were many builders and carpenters on the ship. I remember this man Stelios. He travelled for free because he was employed from Limassol to work as a mechanic on the ship. Anyway, that ship was in a terrible condition. It was leaning so much on one side. I mean, it was leaning for most of the journey. The poor captain kept shouting at the passengers to stay away from the side that was leaning. He was scared the ship would tip over. There must have been something wrong with the ship's engine."

Achilleas remembers all too fondly the moment he stepped off the Corsica onto the sturdy wooden pier at Port Melbourne. "I made the sign of the cross and thanked God for my good fortune in bringing me to such a country. Can you imagine, coming from a village with mud brick houses with no electricity, to this wonderful place full of grand buildings, big green parks, footpaths, trams and trains and wide asphalt roads."

Upon his arrival, Achilleas went to live with a Cypriot acquaintance named

En route to Australia on the Corsica. Achilleas Demetriou is standing bottom left. His friend Philippos Ioannou from Neo Chorio is top right behind his brother Haralambos (Harry) Stylianou. January, 1952.

Andreas Ioannou who was from the village of Peristerona. "Andreas came to greet me at the pier when I arrived. In fact, he rented a small boat and would come out to where the ship was anchored in Port Phillip Bay." After three months the two men travelled together to the Victorian country town of Winchelsea located about thirty miles from Melbourne to work as 'rough carpenters' for a coal mining company called Roach Bros.

Achilleas enjoyed living and working in country Victoria. At Roach Bros he was earning around nine pounds a week and receiving three square meals a day, as well as room and board. He had heard that some migrants became sidetracked once they arrived and were swept away with delusions of grandeur or seduced by their newfound freedom. Some married men ran off and had affairs with local Australian women, conveniently forgetting about

their wives or fiancés waiting for them back in Cyprus.

Achilleas had planned to earn enough money in Winchelsea to return to Cyprus to live a more comfortable life with his wife and two daughters in Polis. However, one day he received a stern letter from his father-in-law warning him not to return to Cyprus because the political and economic situation on the island had deteriorated. "Stay where you are," his father-in-law warned. "Stay and arrange to bring your wife and children to live with you over there." Achilleas agreed and prepared the immigration papers for his family.

In 1953, Achilleas returned to Melbourne where he purchased two blocks of land for four hundred pounds in the leafy suburb of Essendon. By the time his wife and daughters arrived in 1954, he had just finished building his first home on one of those properties.

Achilleas and Eleni would soon adopt what would become a lifelong practice of welcoming and inviting many new arrivals from Cyprus to stay at their home until they could be resettled. They also welcomed the arrival of two more children, Chrysa and Pheodon (Fred).

In the late 1950s Achilleas sold his house in Essendon and moved his family to a new home he had built in Sunshine. For the next decade he would build many homes in the area. In 1977, he was employed by the Ministry of Housing, where he stayed and worked for sixteen years. He was also actively involved with the Greek Cypriot community in Sunshine and helped with the building of a Greek Orthodox Church dedicated to Apostolos Andreas, as well a community hall and Greek school.

Achilleas was forever grateful for what Australia had given him. If any foreigners dared to criticise Australia, he would retort. "Listen mate, this country gave us our livelihood. It gave us food to eat. It made us wealthy and helped us to raise and educate our children. What more do you want?"

ACKNOWLEDGEMENTS

I would like to thank Achilleas Demetriou for allowing me to publish his story of migration. Special thanks to his daughter Mary and granddaughter Helen for their help and support along the way.

EVAGORAS & OLGA
PAPADAKIS

Evagoras Christou Papadakis and Olga Theodoulou left their three-month-old son Andrew in Ktima with Olga's parents to travel to Australia on the Corsica.

"My father was born on the 17th of March, 1929 in the village of Polis in Paphos," their son Andrew tells me. "His father, my grandfather, was a policeman which meant that the family moved around the district quite a lot. My mother Olga, was born on the 1st of November, 1926 in the town of Ktima. I'm not entirely sure how they met but they were married in May or June 1950 and I was born in September 1951. My father was twenty-two and my mother was twenty-five when they left Cyprus."

According to some reports, Evagoras (who was a keen amateur photographer) converted his cabin on the ship into a makeshift darkroom. Perhaps he was keen to take photographs of the passengers and provide them with prints.

Andrew admits that his parents did not say much about the Corsica to him. "My parents never really spoke about their trip to me. To tell you the truth, I didn't show any interest in any stories of the old days. I know that they went to Australia to see if it was a suitable place to raise a family. I know that they had always planned to return to Cyprus to fetch me and their belongings and move there for good. They stayed longer than they intended and tried many times to bring me over, but it never happened. I didn't end up leaving Cyprus and seeing them again until I was eight. In fact, a friend of my parents came over to get me. My grandparents didn't want me to leave Cyprus. They always wanted my parents to come back."

Andrew was finally reunited with his parents in 1958. "I came across on a plane. When I saw my parents at Essendon airport, I didn't know who they were. Remember, I was a baby when they left. My grandparents, my mum's parents were heartbroken when I left Cyprus. It must have been around Christmas when I arrived because I remember there was a fibreglass Santa Claus at the airport. Of course, I didn't know English, but I picked it up within three months after attending primary school."

Evagoras worked at General Motors Holden (GMH), then later he became a cinema projectionist. "He loved that job," says Andrew. "Dad always had an interest in photography and the cinema. I remember in the early days, watching him develop his photos in a makeshift dark room that he had set up in our garage." Olga worked as a seamstress for a factory on Victoria Street, near the market.

According to Andrew, his parents knew English when they came to Australia. They had learnt the language at school in Paphos. Andrew believes his parents found life in Australia to be better for them than in Cyprus so they decided to stay for good.

"I know that when they first arrived in Melbourne they lived in rented accommodation in Collingwood and Brunswick. Eventually, they saved enough money to purchase their first house in the suburb of Fawkner, which is where I grew up. My father was mechanically minded. I think his first car was an FJ Holden but he bought and owned many, many cars."

After Andrew turned seventeen, his family moved to Brighton. "I had finished school by then and started to work at my father's service station. That's where my interest in cars and mechanics really took off. I was rather spoilt by my parents, especially by dad. As far as cars are concerned, I could have bought any car I wanted at the time."

Andrew remembers his dad pulling apart engines and putting them back together. "He was self-taught. He tried to teach me a few times but I just couldn't get it. He just had a mechanical brain. He could try his hand at anything and somehow managed to do it."

Andrew visited Cyprus in 1973 where he met his first wife. "I worked at the Apolonia Hotel in Limassol which was owned by the British. I got the job because of my English language skills. I managed the bar and the nightclub at the hotel. I returned to Melbourne with my wife just before the invasion in 1974. Our son Evan was born soon after."

Olga was once Treasurer for the Greek Cypriot Community of Melbourne and an active member of the local Cypriot diaspora.

Evagoras died in 2010 aged eighty-one. Olga died in 2019 aged ninety-three.

ACKNOWLEDGEMENTS

Thank you to Andreas Papadakis for allowing me to publish his parent's story of migration.

Various photographs of Evagoras and Olga Papadakis taken in Paphos before they departed for Australia on the Corsica.

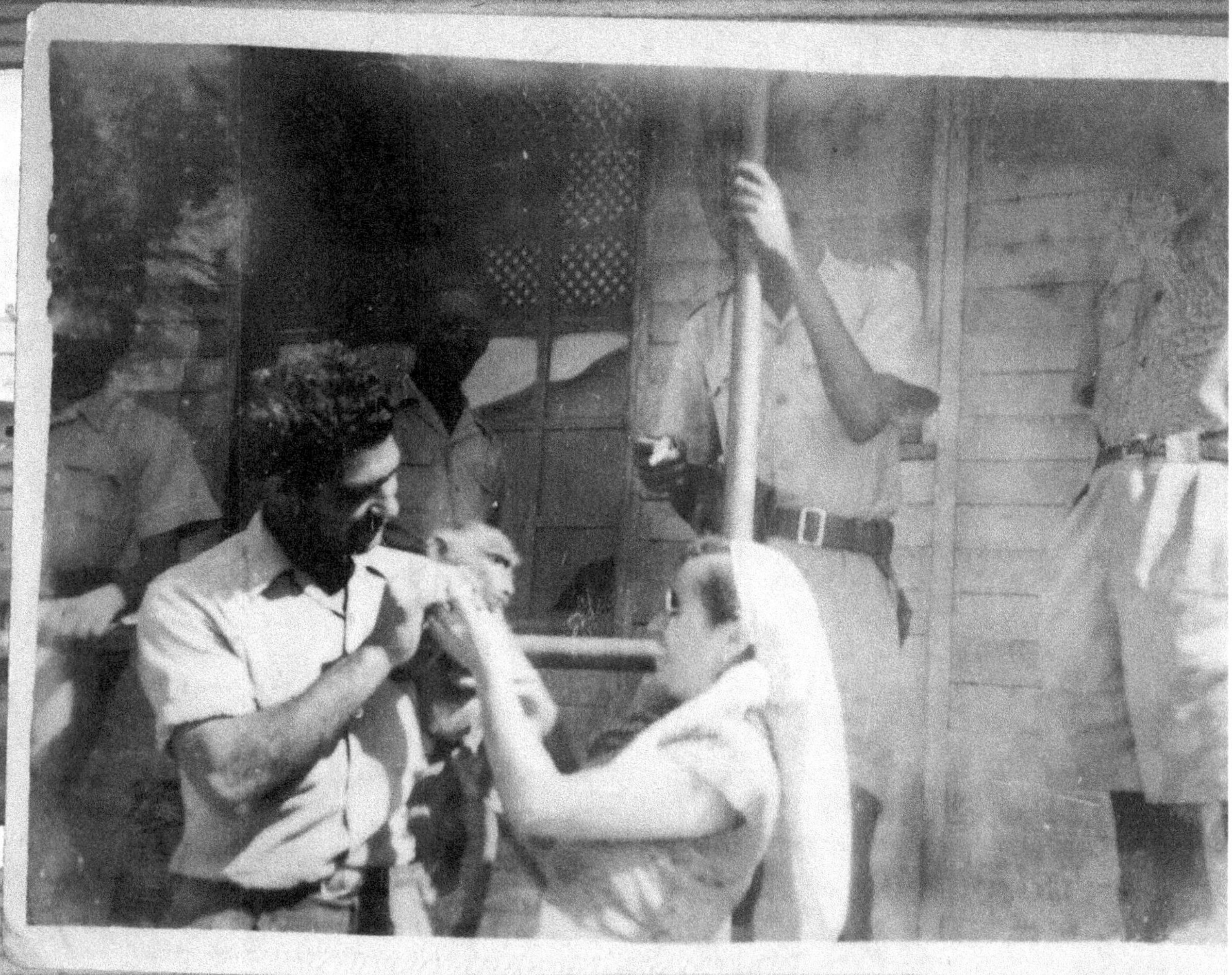

A selection of photographs from Evagoras and Olga's family album.

These photographs were taken en route to Australia in places such as Massawa, Djibouti and Colombo except for the photograph on the left showing Evagoras and Olga with family and friends at a gathering in Melbourne, Australia.

NESTORAS EFSTATHIOU

PASSENGER CARD

Name   **NESTORAS EFSTATHIOU**

Date of birth / Age   **16.1.1930 / 21**

Occupation   **BARBER**

Place of origin   **LYSO, PAPHOS**

Port of departure   **LIMASSOL**

Date of departure   **17 DEC 1951**

Date of arrival   **4 FEB 1952**

From left to right: Charalambos Christodoulou, Nestoras Efstathiou, Maria Aggelidis with her baby Androula, Odyseas Ioannou (Nestoras' cousin who arrived on same ship) and Theoylanis Georgiou (Nestoras' best man). Melbourne, 1952.

Nestoras was born in the village of Lysos (Lyso), Paphos on the 16th of January, 1930. His parents were Efstahios Panayiotou and Katerina Papasavvas and his siblings were Harilaos and Alekos.

From a young age Nestoras was fascinated by music, especially the traditional folk songs that were unique to Cyprus. After an apprenticeship that lasted four years, he became a talented and highly sought after violinist in Paphos and made a decent living playing at weddings and other family celebrations. "I was taught by a man named Alvero who played in the European manner," he explains. "I was twelve years old when I was sent to him to learn the violin. Originally, I was apprenticed to a barber so I could learn the trade, but I only lasted six months. I remember one day, I saw this old gypsy woman holding an old violin. I went up to her and asked her if she would sell it to me. I found out it was a Stradivarius violin

from 1813. I bought it for eighty pounds. Back then you could buy a block of land for eighty pounds. When my master saw this violin, he wanted to buy it from me but I wouldn't part with it."

When asked how he could afford to buy such an expensive violin, Nestoras stated that his father was relatively wealthy and had quite a lot of assets and property in Paphos. "The gypsy woman had come to Cyprus from Turkey but I don't know how she came across this old violin. Perhaps she stole it from someone."

Nestoras was apprenticed to three different violinists in Paphos from the ages of twelve to fourteen. "My mother paid sixty pounds in total for my tuition and apprenticeship. Each master violinist taught me different tunes and songs."

From the age of fifteen onwards, Nestoras was fully trained and he performed for money at numerous events in the region. "A typical Cypriot wedding

will last for four days – from Friday until Monday evening," he tells me. "I would play violin together with a lutist for three days and we would get paid five pounds each. Some days, we might receive forty pounds in tips. Eventually, I went to Ktima to live and work."

In 1949, when Nestoras turned seventeen, he met and married Elpida Philipou from the nearby village of Filousa. Together they had two daughters, Maria (Maroulla), born in April 1950 and Athinoulla (Athena) born in April 1951. "I first met Elpida at a function organised by her father where I was commissioned to play my violin. She was only fifteen or sixteen years old at the time."

Nestoras was almost twenty-one by the time he left Cyprus for Australia. "It was my wife's first cousin who convinced me to leave. He had left in 1948 and settled in Melbourne. I had a *kafenion-taverna* (coffee house-restaurant) and grocery store in Philousa and I was quite content to stay there. I was doing okay. Besides I just got married. This cousin kept insisting that I should join him in Australia, so finally I agreed to go. I paid 150 pounds for the fare. The agent in Limassol took my money six months before the ship arrived."

Initially, like so many other migrants, Nestoras had intended to stay in Australia for a short while, work hard, make good money and then return to Cyprus. "I left my wife and daughters in the village and came to Australia. I remember that I stayed on the second level of the ship. I had my violin with me and so I spent my time entertaining the other passengers. What little money they had, they would toss their coins at me. I played in the main dining hall and people would come and sing and dance. From Cyprus to Ceylon I made around fifty pounds in tips. I went to the post office in Colombo and I sent the fifty pounds to my wife in Cyprus. After Colombo, I made a further twenty-six pounds however, I gave most of it away because people didn't have any money to buy water and basic supplies. Every port that we stopped, we were delayed for a few days; we stopped for six days in Massawa, another six in Djibouti, another twelve in Colombo. So many delays. I even entertained the kitchen staff and waiters with my violin. They would dance and toss what little money they had at me. I remember the cook, he was a Greek man named Kyriacos. I used to get seasick quite a lot on the ship. When the ship was stationary I was fine but as soon as it started moving I became quite ill. Kyriacos the cook would bring me bread to eat to settle my stomach."

Before long, Nestoras became friends with the entire crew on the Corsica. "I knew them all. After their shift, we would all sit together. 'Come and join us', they would say to me. They would be drinking whiskey. We would sit together and eat and drink whiskey. Jimmy the cook would give us fresh bread with Kashkaval cheese to eat. I became very good friends with Mitso, a Greek who was second-in-command on the ship. As I was returning to my cabin many of the passengers would follow me because they knew I was carrying fresh bread and cheese. People were hungry. The food they served on the Corsica was not very good. The meat was over-cooked and so dry and hard to eat. I was looked after, because I made friends with the cooks."

Upon his arrival to Melbourne, Nestoras was met by Andreas Diamantis, a compatriot who had emigrated in 1948. "He brought me to his house in Sunshine where he was renting out rooms and beds to new arrivals. I paid him two pounds a week to stay there. After three days I found a job in an automotive factory in a neighbouring suburb called Tottenham. Later I went to work at a flour mill in Sunshine. There I was earning twelve pounds a week."

When he wasn't working at the factory or flour mill, Nestoras would go and visit various Greek owned cafes in the city. Many of the passengers from the Corsica would also meet there. "They all knew me because I entertained them on the ship with my violin. Most migrants went to the Cyprus Club on Russell Street which was managed by Christos Morphitis and a man named Jimmy. One day, someone told Jimmy about the Corsica and how I had saved everyone from boredom by playing my violin on the ship. Jimmy then invited me to play at the club, which I did. He put a tray on a chair in front of me and I began to play while everyone got up to dance. People put money on the tray as I played. One Saturday I made 120 pounds. From then on, I was invited every weekend to play at the club. Initially, Jimmy would pay me twenty pounds to play there. I could eat and drink as I liked and I got to keep all the tips."

According to Nestoras, at the end of 1952, Jimmy made him an offer which was too good to refuse. "He offered to pay me fifty pounds a week and let me sleep in a small room which had a bed at the club. I did this for about a month but I didn't end up living at the club. During the week I would stay in Sunshine and on the weekends I would play my violin at the club. Eventually I started to play at engagements and weddings. At one wedding I made 166 pounds. I sent a lot of money back to my wife. She couldn't believe it."

By the end of 1953, it was clear that Nestoras was not returning to Cyprus. He had steady factory work during the week, a regular music spot at the Cyprus Club on weekends and even managed to purchase a block of land in Sunshine for 160 pounds. The following year, he arranged for his wife and two young daughters to immigrate to Melbourne. They arrived in March 1954 on the ship Fairsea. Sometime later, Elpida gave birth to sons, Andrew and George.

Around 1963, Nestoras bought himself a cafe (with accommodation attached) and even joined a professional Greek band with whom he continued to play at Greek functions for many years. It is clear that music has played an integral part in Nestoras' life. "The violin has helped me to achieve so much," he says proudly. "My music has helped to sustain me in Cyprus, on the Corsica and now here in Australia."

ACKNOWLEDGEMENTS

I would like to thank Nestoras for allowing me to publish his story of migration. Special thanks to his daughter Athinoula and her husband Michael Yiallouros for their help and support.

Studio photograph of Elpida with her two daughters Maria (left) and Athinoulla. Cyprus, 1952.

ANDREAS NICOLAOU

PASSENGER CARD

Name **ANDREAS NICOLAOU**

Date of birth / Age **9.10.1932 / 19**

Occupation **SHOEMAKER**

Place of origin **KATO PAPHOS**

Port of departure **LIMASSOL**

Date of departure **17 DEC 1951**

Date of arrival **4 FEB 1952**

Andreas Nicolaou was born in Kato Paphos on the 9th of October, 1932. His father was Nicos Konstantinos (Macheropios) and his mother was Evdokia Demetriou.

"The Turks would refer to my father as *Pikshashis* (knifemaker)," Andreas tells me. "During the day, he would make knives at his shop for the local butchers in Ktima. At night, he would play his violin. My father was a very generous man. I remember he was always inviting our neighbours in Kato Paphos to dinner, Turkish Cypriots, Greek Cypriots, it didn't matter. We would all sit at the table and eat, drink and sing all together. When my father was seventeen, he went to serve in the First World War. He was up in the mountains near Turkey pulling cannons with mules. One day his unit was caught in an explosion of gunfire and his companion was shot dead. My father escaped by hiding in a wheat field until the English rescued him. Oh yes, this is a big story. He was over there for three years. He came back to Cyprus aged twenty-one and he married my mother when he turned twenty-two."

Andreas was the second youngest of eight children born between 1919 and 1934. "I'm the only one alive now. My siblings were Maria, Kostas, Dimitris, Georgios, Yiannis, Theodoros and Polyxeni. My brother Yiannis died from Meningitis when he was nine and my sister Maria was born deformed and crippled from birth. The doctor told my mother that she will only live for twenty-two years and that's exactly what happened. My mother had other children who sadly died after they were born. That was common in those days."

From a young age, Andreas trained to be a shoemaker in Ktima. He also dreamed of travel. "I always wanted to go to Australia," he says proudly. "I remember we used to study history and geography at school and I would look at the map of Australia and say to myself, one day when I am older, I will go to this faraway land. When I turned eighteen, my neighbour Christodoulos Theofilou said to me, 'when I go to Australia, I will send you an invitation to join me.' And that's what he did. In fact, he arranged for eight Cypriots from Paphos to go to Australia."

Andreas paid 130 pounds for his ship fare. "My older brother Kostas was a chauffeur in Nicosia and he loaned me forty pounds. I had to borrow the other ninety by mortgaging a block of land."

On board the Corsica, Andreas shared a cabin on the lower deck of the ship with five other men. "There was Mustafa Houssein, a carpenter and four other men I knew from Paphos. I can't remember their names but Mustafa was my childhood friend. The cabin had bunk beds on both sides, three beds on each bunk. We would climb onto our beds with ladders."

Andreas also knew a female passenger who was travelling to Australia. "Her name was Loukia Papastylianou. She was thirty-one and the daughter of a priest who I knew from Kato Paphos. His name was Papa Stylianou. We were meant to look after her, but she ended up looking after us."

Apparently, the journey on the Corsica was not too bad for Andreas. "Plenty of people got sick, but I didn't," he says. "The sick passengers would give me money to go and fetch them food from the kitchen. We were 850 Cypriots on that ship and perhaps another 200 from Greece. I was only nineteen years old and full of life. If you were over the age of twenty-five back then, they used to say you were old."

In terms of entertainment on the ship, Andreas recalls two Cypriot passengers who had musical instruments. "We would go up to the top deck, outside on the veranda, and Nestoras would play his violin and we would dance. A man named Vassos Katsiamis played the accordion. That's how we passed the time."

When the Corsica docked at Massawa, Andreas went to explore the town with his friends. "I remember in Massawa, we bought a large bunch of bananas for one shilling. When we got to Djibouti, we found a Greek Orthodox Church. It was Sunday morning and the church was soon full of passengers from the ship, so was the church courtyard. I remember the priest was so happy that he said to us, 'Today is Christmas for me.' We went into the church one by one, lit our candles, kissed the icons, said our prayers and left."

After the Corsica left Djibouti, Andreas noticed a horrible stench coming from the cargo hold. "After we left Africa, that's when the potatoes began to rot. It was the heat. People were vomiting everywhere because of the stench. Anyway, they tossed those rotten potatoes into the ocean before we reached Colombo."

To make matters worse, sea water had entered some of the cabins on the bottom deck. "I was sleeping on the top bunk in my cabin and when I went to climb down, my feet were suddenly standing in a foot of sea water. Right there on the floor of our cabin. Can you believe it?"

In Colombo, Andreas visited the zoo where he climbed onto an elephant. "Normally you would have to pay to ride the elephants but the man there didn't charge me anything. I had ten pounds on me from Cyprus. By the time I arrived in Melbourne, I only had two pounds left."

From Colombo to Fremantle, Andreas experienced a 'black market' on the ship. "If you wanted fresh drinking water, you had to buy it – one shilling a bottle. This Loukia woman from Paphos who was travelling with us, paid for my water. This way I was able to save my money. After Colombo, many people became very unhappy with the Corsica."

After fifty-four days at sea, the passengers finally reach their destination. "When we arrived at Port Melbourne we are not allowed to dock until the Government people came on board to inspect the ship. We sat in Port Phillip Bay for two days. I remember lots of men in boats coming out to greet us and throwing chocolates up at us. Everybody was on the deck leaning over the rails talking to the men and catching chocolates. The ship was leaning so much that the captain kept calling out, 'please move to the other side.' Some people listened, some didn't. The men in the boats had migrated to Australia before us. I guess they were relieved that we had arrived safely because no one had any idea what had happened to us. Many of the family members and friends who were waiting for us in Melbourne feared the worst."

When the Corsica was finally allowed to berth at Station Pier, Andreas was greeted by his neighbour Christodoulos who took him to his house in South Yarra. "I was lucky that he didn't charge me any rent. The first night when I arrived at his house I was surprised to see so many men sharing rooms. There must have been four or five men per room. Christodoulos put me in a room with an old man; when I say old, he must have been around fifty. Well this man snored all night. I couldn't sleep - so I got up and went outside and just sat there in the dark. 'Where have I come?' I kept saying to myself. 'What will become of me?' Christodoulos told me to be patient but I couldn't. I left after a few weeks. I went to live with Loukia Papastylianou, my friend who was on the Corsica with me. She was living on Glenferrie Road in Malvern with her fiancé."

Andreas was surprised to learn that there was a lot of unemployment in Melbourne when he arrived. "I started to get worried," he admits. "Luckily, I found a job after two weeks. It was at a shoe shop in Swanston Street, however I only lasted a month. There were too many customers and I couldn't keep up. Then I found a job at the AJC Jam Factory in Prahran. My job was to go down to Port Melbourne with a truck to fill hessian bags with coal to bring the coal back to the factory so they could heat the machines to make the jam. This would happen four times a day, I was earning about twenty-two pounds a week at AJC."

After a few months, Andreas left AJC and went to work as a spot-welder for a refrigeration company in Mentone. "I lied about my age," he admits. "I told them I was twenty-two so I could earn a higher wage. I worked there for eighteen months. The unemployment office only paid one or two pounds a week. In 1953, I went to work for the railways in Newport. I also moved out of Loukia's house, and bought my first house in Malvern, near the railway station."

On the 1st of May, 1955, Andreas married Maria Kounelis. She was the eldest of five children and had migrated to Melbourne from the island of Lesvos in Greece in 1953. Like most Greeks in Melbourne during the 1950s, Andreas and Maria were married at the Evangelismos Greek Orthodox Church on Victoria Parade in East Melbourne.

In 1956, their son Nicholas (Nick) was born followed by two daughters; Despina (Desi) in 1962 and Evdokia (Vicky) in 1969.

According to Andreas, many migrant men would finish work and go to visit the Greek clubs in the city. "There were two clubs," he explains. "The Acropoli on Bourke Street, under the Trivoli cinema and the Democritus, which was on the corner of Russell and Lonsdale Streets. The clubs were a great meeting place for all new arrivals. We came here penniless without knowing anything, without knowing the language, but somehow, we were able to adjust to this new country.

My mother didn't want me to stay in Australia. She would always write to me and say, 'come back son. I will sell some property and pay for you to return back home'. I would write back to her and say, 'Australia is my home now.' For us migrants, Australia was a good home."

ACKNOWLEDGEMENTS
I would like to thank Andreas Nicolaou for allowing me to publish his story of migration. Special thanks to his daughter Desi Meimaarakis for her help and support.

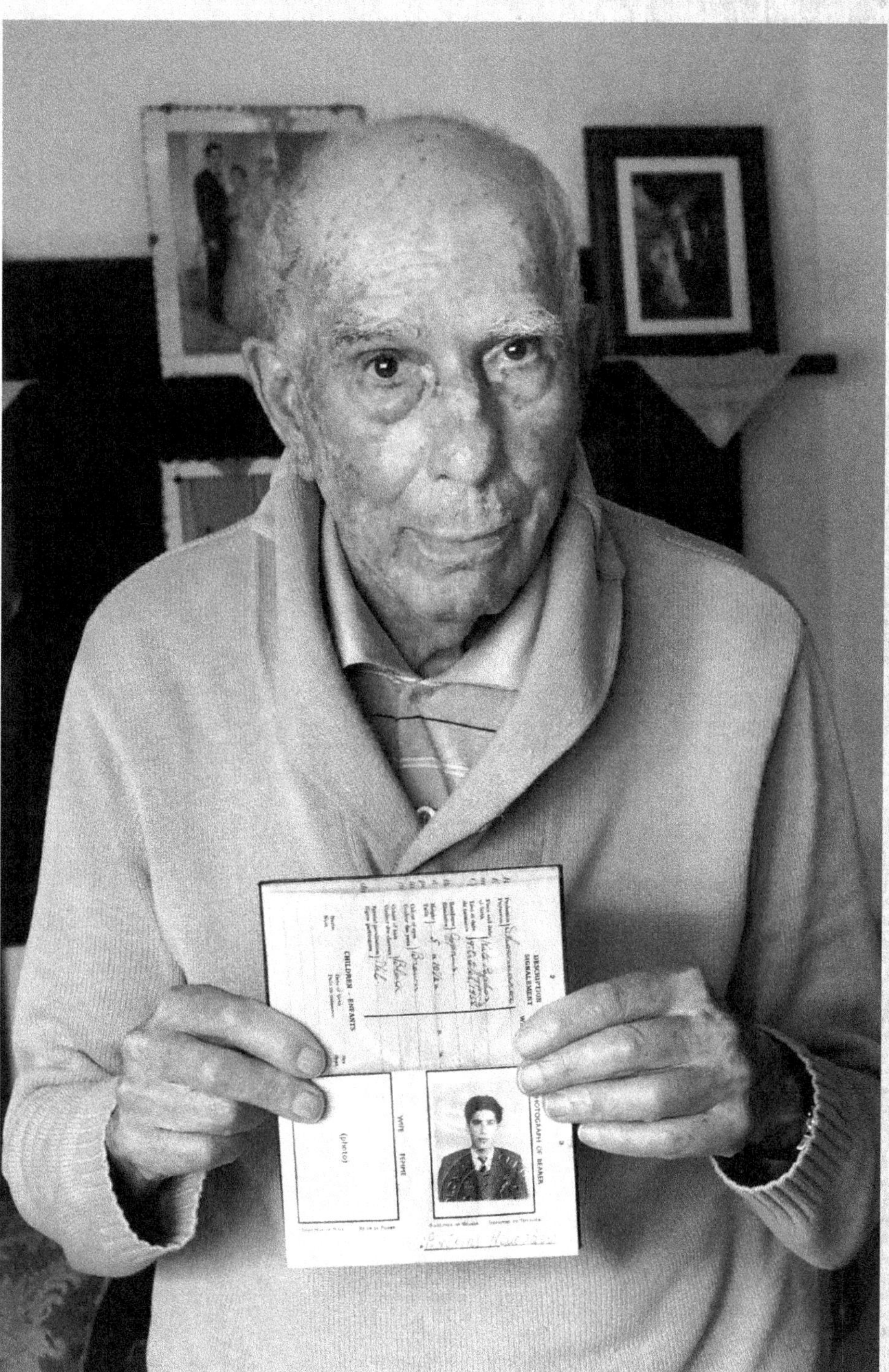

Andreas Nicolaou with his British Passport in July, 2019.

ANDREAS ARTEMI

Andreas Artemi was born on the 27th of November, 1925 in Anogyra, Limassol. He grew up in Anogyra and Ktima, Paphos and was the son of Artemis and Chrystalla. He came from a poor family and after the early death of his father Andreas he was forced to stop attending school at the age of twelve and go to work to support his widowed mother and three siblings, Loukia, Stavros and Eraclis.

His first job consisted of carrying and laying heavy rocks to build a harbour near the castle in Paphos. Andreas soon left this back breaking work to train and work as an electrician with the Paphos Power Station in Ktima.

In June 1951, Andreas married Efstathia Efstathiou. He was twenty-five and she was twenty-one.

Efstathia was born in the village of Arsos, Limassol in 1929. Her parents Efstathios and Myrofora owned the only olive press in the village. Efstathios was also the first person in Arsos to own and drive a truck. Sadly, he was killed in a motor vehicle accident before Efstathia was born. She was still in her mother's womb when her father died. Her brother died six months later as a result of the accident.

After Andreas left Cyprus for Australia, Efstathia moved to Paphos to live with her mother-in-law, Chrystalla. Andreas left Cyprus in the hope that he would find

Efstathia Efstathiou (seated) with her friend Erato. Cyprus, 1946.

their arrival on their forearms. He would regret doing this years later. My father maintained close friendships and contact with many of his fellow passengers from the Corsica," explains Miranda.

Andreas' wife Efstathia arrived in Melbourne in 1954 and after a few years, they purchased a block of land in North Coburg on which Andreas would build their first family home. Because he did not drive, he would ride his bicycle (carrying planks of wood and building materials) from his rented house in Fitzroy to the property which was a distance of around eight miles. The first room he built was the laundry, in which he lived with his wife until the rest of the house was finished.

Later in life, Andreas purchased land in the outer northern suburb of Campbellfield, on which he would build houses to sell.

In June 1961, Andreas and Efstathia were blessed by the birth of their daughter Miranda followed by their son Artemis, in March 1962. The children were both christened at the same time at the Evangelismos Greek Orthodox Church in East Melbourne.

Andreas passed away in 1995 followed by his wife Efstathia in 2014.

ACKNOWLEDGEMENTS

I would like to thank Miranda Manolopoulos for allowing me to publish her father's story of migration.

better employment opportunities to help him support his family.

Andreas and the other passengers were concerned that the Corsica would not be able to complete the journey as they travelled through the rough seas of the Indian Ocean. "My dad told us how they used sacks of potatoes in the cargo hold as extra weight (or ballast) to help balance the ship and keep it steady," his daughter Miranda tells me. "However, when the potatoes began to rot, they were thrown overboard into the sea which caused the ship to list (lean) for the remainder of the journey. Dad also talked about the stench they all endured as a consequence of the potatoes rotting in the hold."

When he first arrived in Melbourne, Andreas rented a room at a house in Fitzroy which he shared with others including Evagoras and Olga Papadakis. He worked on building sites in Melbourne as a carpenter in the early 1950s. "After he arrived in Melbourne my father and a few of the other male passengers from the Corsica got together and agreed to get a tattoo of the ship and the date of

Efstathia Efstathiou (on the right) with Olga Papadakis. Melbourne, circa 1954.

Andreas and Efstathia (on the right) with Efstathia's brother and his wife Maria (on the left) in the back of the North Coburg home.

ABOVE: Father Kourtessis christening Miranda (Myrofora) at Evangelismos church in East Melbourne, 1962, Miranda's brother Artemis was christened on the same day since they are only nine and a half months apart. The Godmother is Olga Papadakis.

BELOW: Group photograph at Miranda and Artemis' christening with the Godparents and guests. Melbourne, 1962.

Panayiota Agathangelou was born in the village of Peyia, Paphos in 1937. In December 1951, she boarded the ship Corsica with her mother Eleni (aged thirty-nine) and her four siblings, bound for Australia. "We were on our way to be reunited with our father Michalis who had migrated to Adelaide two years earlier," she explains. "I was fourteen and the eldest child. My brother Georgios was ten, Maroulla (Maria) was six, Andrianou was four and Chrysi was only two and a half years old."

Panayiota had just finished primary school and was hoping to attend high school when her father wrote and insisted that the family should leave Cyprus and join him in Australia.

"We were struggling to earn a living in Peyia," Panayiota tells me. "A drought that lasted several years had destroyed our crops. It didn't help that some bad people poisoned our carob trees. After they poisoned and killed our two cows, my parents decided to sell everything they owned to come to Australia. Anyway, I wanted to leave Cyprus because my father was already there."

Panayiota states that her father had to work two or three jobs before he was able to save enough money to afford their passage to Australia. "I remember crying a lot when we left Cyprus. Being the eldest child, I guess I felt the sadness more than my younger siblings. It was difficult saying goodbye to everyone. A week before we left, friends and relatives kept coming to our house to say their goodbyes and they were crying like it was a funeral."

Once on board the Corsica, Panayiota realised that she was not the luxury ship she had expected. "It was a terrible ship," she states boldly. "The food was terrible. The meat was terrible. Thank God my mother had thought to pack a big basket full of *paximathia* (Greek rusks). She baked them herself before we left Cyprus. We also had a small barrel full of halloumi cheese. My mother was wise to pack so much food for the trip. We survived on *paximathia* and *halloumi*."

When her mother Eleni became terribly seasick on the ship Panayiota had to care for her as well as look after her younger siblings. "Fortunately, some kind crew members regularly made soup for my mother. My younger sister Maroulla would negotiate the meals with the crew while I looked after my other siblings. Even though she was only six, Maroulla took on that role."

When the Corsica arrived at various ports, Panayiota and her family stayed in their cabin. "We remained in our cabin because my mother was too sick to walk. Besides, it was too difficult for her to leave the ship with so many young children. I remember the only time my mother felt strong enough to leave the cabin and go ashore was when we finally docked at Fremantle in Western Australia. That was almost two months after we left Cyprus."

The Corsica was a dangerous ship for young children to wander around. Especially on the deck. Panayiota clearly remembers the low guard-rail surrounding the deck. "A young child could have easily slipped through the gaps in the guard rail and fallen into the water," she says. "One day, my younger sister Chrysi gave us all a fright when she tried to climb through the rails. She was watching a man from our village dangling our sister Andrianou over the water, as a joke, and she must have got jealous, so she tried to climb through the railing herself. I grabbed her just in time. I also remember that the window in our cabin was broken and would remain open. One day some fish came flying through our window and landed on the floor of our cabin. My siblings and I started screaming. When we finally arrived in Melbourne, I remember everyone made the sign of the cross."

Panayiota's father Michalis had travelled from Adelaide by train to meet the family when they docked at the Port of Melbourne. "My father had spent some time in Melbourne when he first arrived but due to an industrial strike, he moved to Adelaide. Apparently, the houses were cheaper in Adelaide so he ended up buying a house on Westbury Street in Hackney. That's where we all went to live once we arrived."

Unfortunately, two years after Panayiota and her family had arrived in Australia, Michalis Agathangelou was tragically killed in a train accident. He was thirty-seven years old. "My father went to disembark a moving train at a railway station but somehow misjudged his step and fell through the gap between the train and the platform. It was just before Christmas Day in 1954. My poor mother was now a widow and left with seven children (six girls and a boy) to look after. My younger siblings, Lola and Michele, were born in Australia. In fact, my mother was seven months pregnant with Michele when my father died. That was a very difficult time for my family. Imagine the pain of leaving your homeland to arrive in a new country with the promise of a great new life and then you lose your father. We all suffered so much after my father died. It was a very difficult time for all of us, especially my mother. My parents really loved and cared for one another."

A local radio station 5AD reported the tragic death of Michalis Agathangelou on Christmas Eve and before long, many local people from Adelaide turned up at the family home with donations of gifts, toys for the children, food and money. Even Michalis' boss and the workers from the Chrysler Aircraft Division where he worked donated £530. Panayiota became the family translator during this very difficult period.

Shortly after Michalis died, Panayiota and her brother George were forced to leave school and go and work to help support their family. Panayiota found a job at the Arnott's Biscuit factory and George found work with a local butcher. "I only knew a little bit of English at the time," she says. "I was meant to work for two years and then resume my studies but unfortunately, things did not turn out that way for me. I was married at twenty. My husband Vasili lived across the road from our house in Adelaide. He was from Peloponessos. We had three children. So you see, after I left Cyprus I had to grow up very quickly."

Panayiota visited Cyprus in 1990; thirty-eight years after she had left.

ACKNOWLEDGEMENTS

I would like to thank Panayiota Agathangelou for allowing me to publish her story of migration. Special thanks to her sister Maria and daughter Eugenia Fragos for their help and support.

THE CORSICA

PAPHOS

PANAYIOTA & ELENI AGATHANGELOU

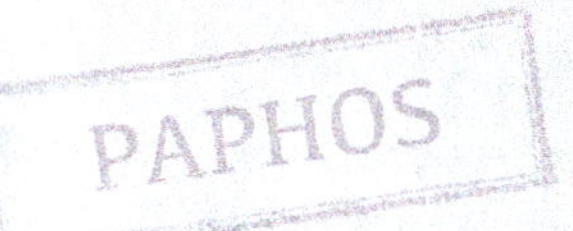

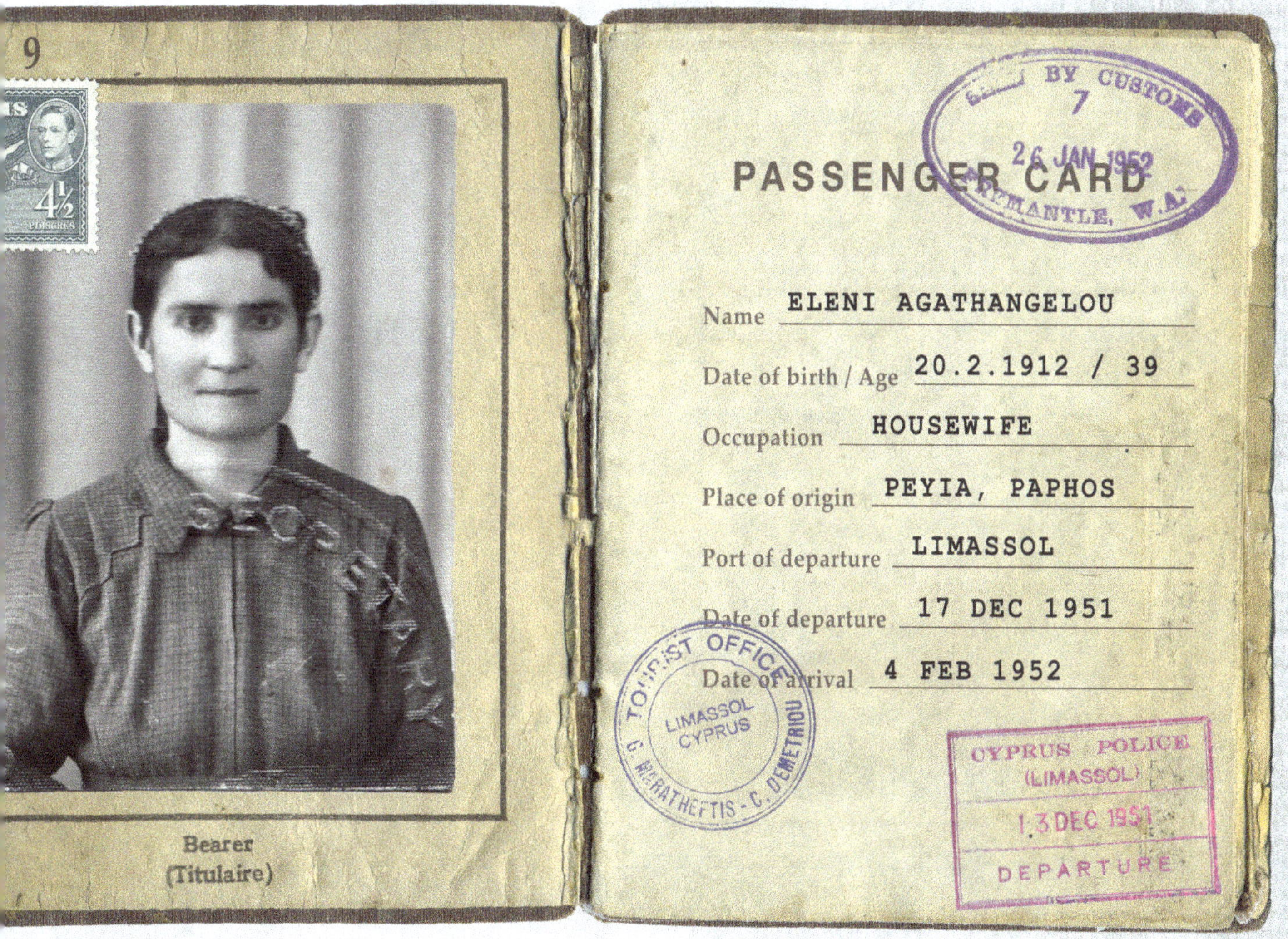
9

Bearer
(Titulaire)

PASSENGER CARD

BY CUSTOMS
7
26 JAN 1952
FREMANTLE, W.A.

Name ELENI AGATHANGELOU

Date of birth / Age 20.2.1912 / 39

Occupation HOUSEWIFE

Place of origin PEYIA, PAPHOS

Port of departure LIMASSOL

Date of departure 17 DEC 1951

Date of arrival 4 FEB 1952

TOURIST OFFICE
LIMASSOL CYPRUS
G. MERATHEFTIS - C. DEMETRIOU

CYPRUS POLICE
(LIMASSOL)
13 DEC 1951
DEPARTURE

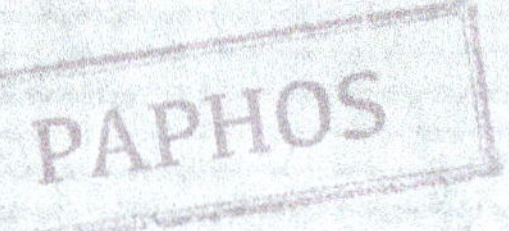

LOUKIA PAPAHARALAMBOUS

CLOCKWISE
- En route to Australia, January 1952. Back row from left to right: Evagoras Papadakis, Avraam Christofi, Unknown and Demetris Parlan. Middle row: Michalis Thesalos, Takis Nicolaides and Andreas Artemis. Front row: Loukia Papastylianou, Olga Papadakis, Andreas Tryphonos, Lella Nearchou and Georgoula Achileos.
- Loukia with her sons, Bambos and Steven. Malvern, early 1960s.
- Andreas and Loukia's wedding photograph. Melbourne, June 1st, 1952.
- Andreas with his sons, Bambos and Steven (with his hunting rifle). Malvern, early 1960s.
- Loukia and Andrea with their son Steven in front of the family car (1959 Morris Major). Malvern, early 1960s.
- Loukia's sons, Steven (left) and Bambos. Malvern, early 1960s.

Name **LOUKIA PAPAHARALAMBOUS**

Date of birth / Age **15.10.1920 / 31**

Occupation **NIL**

Place of origin **VASA, LIMASSOL**

Port of departure **LIMASSOL**

Date of departure **17 DEC 1951**

Date of arrival **4 FEB 1952**

Loukia Haralambous (nee Papaharalambous) was born in Vasa, Limassol on the 15th of October, 1920. Her parents were Papastylianous Papaharalambous and Aphrodite Christodoulou. Papastylianous married Aphrodite when she was fourteen years old and he was twenty-four. They had eight children together; Calliroy, Michael, Haralambos (Humbi), Christodoulos (Ttoouli), Christalla, Gregory (Gregori) and Andreas. Calliroy was born when Aphrodite was only sixteen. She passed away as a teenager. Michael joined the Cypriot Volunteer Regiment during World War Two and was killed in 1941. He is buried in Athens.

When Loukia's father Papastylianous become a priest, he was stationed in different villages and parishes around Cyprus. He later became the permanent priest for the church of Panagia Theoskepasti in Kato Paphos, which allowed him to be together with his family.

Although Loukia completed primary school, she always regretted not attending high school. She enjoyed learning at

were expected to sacrifice their own needs and wants to serve others. Loukia was determined to choose her own fate. In 1951, she decided to leave her village and travel to Australia. Her father did not want her to leave the village. In fact, he even built her a house on the family land to keep her from leaving. When Loukia's cousin Panayiotis (who was living in Melbourne) wrote to her with a request to come and keep his wife company and also to meet his friend Andreas who wanted to get married, she agreed to migrate. She was thirty-one years old and knew no English.

There had been a number of men in Cyprus over the years who had proposed to Loukia but she did not like any of them. Andreas was different. He had sent her many letters throughout 1950 which help her to get to know him by the time she agreed to travel to Australia. In one letter, Andreas wrote that if she came and did not want to marry him, then he would gladly pay for her return trip back to Cyprus. Loukia had seen Andreas once before during World War Two when he drove a British officer to see her father. She remembers spotting him from the window and noticing how good looking he was sitting in the military vehicle in his army uniform. It was only after he got out to stretch his legs (he was wearing shorts) when she was disappointed to see that he had skinny legs. Little did she know then, that she would one day travel to Australia to marry him.

According to her two sons Bambos and Steven their mother had been very sick on the Corsica. Thankfully, there were a few good people who took turns to look after her (such as Olga and Evagoras Papadakis). Someone had brought *'trahana'* (dried wheat and yoghurt) and a small kerosene stove from Cyprus and made Loukia soup in her cabin. Loukia had also mentioned that the tap water on the ship was always rusty and that the food

tasted awful. Thankfully, every time the ship stopped at a port many passengers (those who had some money) would buy fresh fruit and vegetables to supplement their meals on the ship.

Soon after she arrived to Australia, Loukia was introduced to Andreas Haralambous. He was born in Kaimakli, Nicosia on the 25th of November, 1920. Interestingly, he is listed as being two years older on his British passport because he lied to join the Royal Engineers with the British Forces in the 1940s, as well as work for the Nicosia municipality. He had emigrated to Australia in December 1947 on the ship MISR. His father was Haralambos Stylianou, a stone mason and church builder, and his mother was Thekla Hadjiharis.

Loukia stayed with her cousin Panayiotis and his wife Eleftheria in Malvern and helped Eleftheria in the home to look after her son Conn and then later her daughter. She worked in the clothing industry as a seamstress and later as an overlocker. Loukia and Eleftheria looked after each other over the years and became as close as sisters.

Loukia and Andreas were married on the 1st of June, 1952 at the Evangelismos Greek Orthodox Church, on Victoria Parade, East Melbourne.

They moved into a large house off Glenferrie Road in Malvern. Their house became known as a halfway house for many new arrivals from overseas. "From what I was told there was plenty of singing and dancing at the house," says Bambos. My parents experienced happy times with their friends and relatives."

In 1954, their son Bambos was born followed by another son, Steven in 1957.

Loukia and Andreas returned to Cyprus in 1966. They travelled on the Ellinis from Melbourne to Cyprus via Piraeus and returned on the Patris. By all accounts, it was a much better journey than the one experienced by Loukia when she arrived in Melbourne on the Corsica.

ACKNOWLEDGEMENTS

I would like to thank Bambos and Steven Haralambous for allowing me to publish their mother's story of migration and for their kind help and support when required.

Loukia's parents, Papastylianous and Aphrodite Papaharalambous (nee Papastylianou). Late 1930s

school but had to leave at the end of primary school to help look after her younger siblings and to work in the fields and care for their few farm animals. The work was very difficult for such a young child but her father relied on her and her sister to look after the family and help their mother whilst he was away performing his priestly duties.

Loukia could foresee a bleak future for herself in the village. Unmarried women, were expected to look after their parents, siblings and even other relatives. They

Andreas Haralambous' studio photograph which he sent to Loukia in December, 1950.

Loukia (left) with her mother and some of her siblings in Cyprus, 1929.

Loukia (left) with her sister Christalla in Cyprus, 1940.

Loukia with her sons and their cousins in the front garden of their house in Malvern, Melbourne. Early 1960s.

En route to Australia on the Corsica, January 1952.
From left to right: Takis Nicolaides, Andreas (Rikos)
Artemis, Michalis Thesalos, Georgoula Achileos, Lella
Nearchou, Olga Papadakis, Loukia Papastylianou,
Andreas Tryphonos, Evagoras Papadakis, Avraam
Christofi and Demetris Parian.

PAPHOS

ANDREAS TRYPHONOS

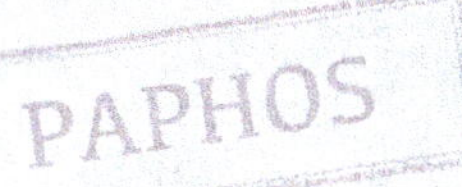

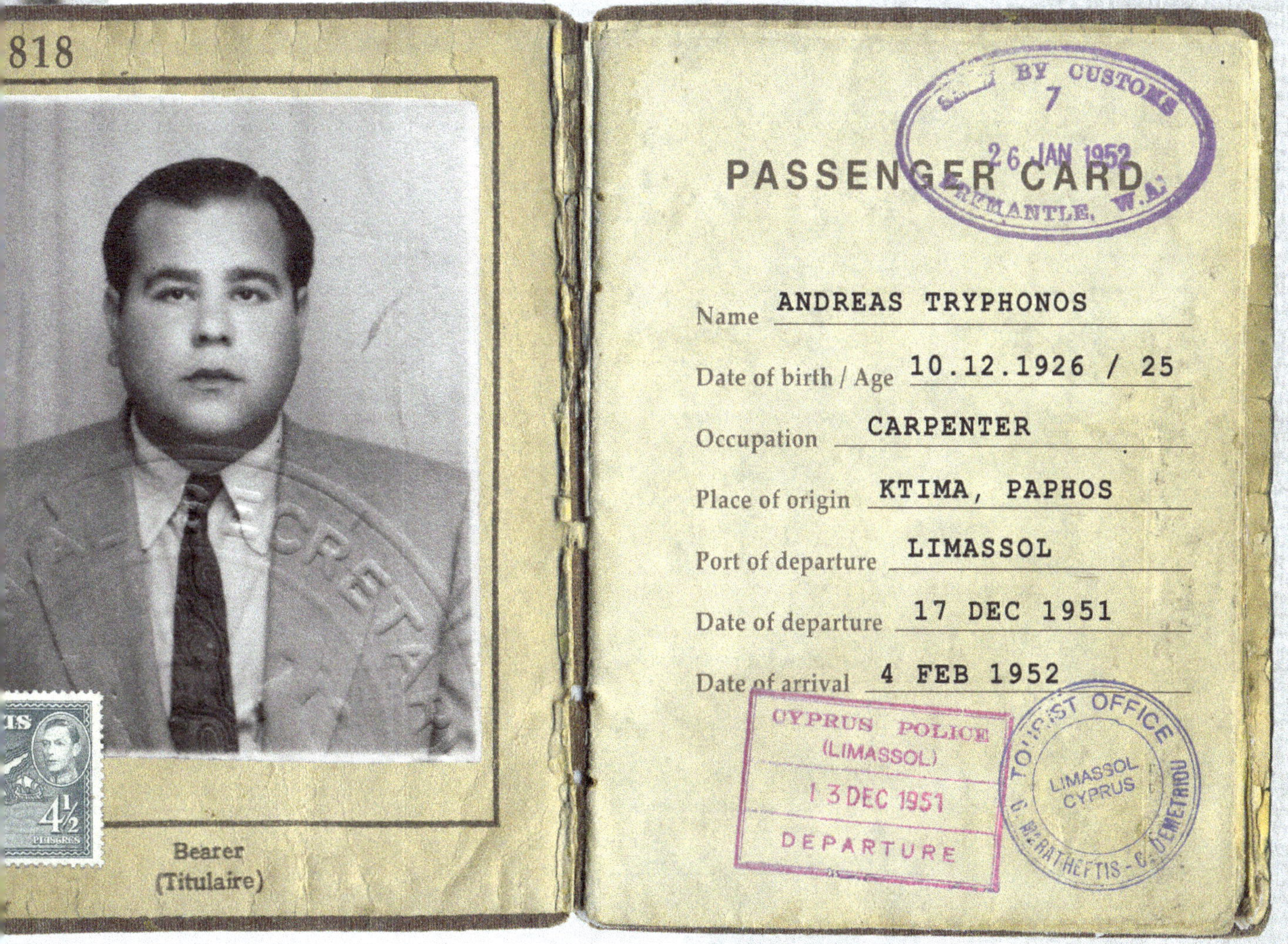
818

Bearer
(Titulaire)

PASSENGER CARD

BY CUSTOMS
7
26 JAN 1952
FREMANTLE, W.A.

Name ANDREAS TRYPHONOS

Date of birth / Age 10.12.1926 / 25

Occupation CARPENTER

Place of origin KTIMA, PAPHOS

Port of departure LIMASSOL

Date of departure 17 DEC 1951

Date of arrival 4 FEB 1952

CYPRUS POLICE
(LIMASSOL)
13 DEC 1951
DEPARTURE

TOURIST OFFICE
LIMASSOL CYPRUS

Andreas Tryphonos was born in Ktima, Paphos on the 10th of December, 1926. His father Tryphon Dimitriou had married Anastasia Stylianou (nee Nicolaou) a widow with three children of her own; Christos, Neophita and Charalambous. Together, they welcomed three more children into their blended family; Nicolas (born in 1924), Olga (born in 1925) and Andreas (born in 1926).

Andreas was apparently a curious and adventurous young boy. When he was ten, he skipped school with his cousin Takis Nikolaou to go and explore the Tomb of the Kings. They were in search of hidden treasure inspired by an urban myth told by his father. The boys' adventure at the tomb was cut short after the police arrived and Andreas' father was summoned to collect them from the police station.

Despite skipping school on many occasions, Andreas managed to complete his education. He eventually found a job at the Electricity Commission in Ktima along with his school friend Socratis (Takis) Nicolaides.

Sometime in the late 1940s, Andreas was introduced to Efpraxia Efstathiou in Ktima. It was an arranged meeting at a picture theatre called Zina which was set up by his *koumbari* (groomsmen). Andreas was in his early twenties while Efpraxia was in her late teens.

Efpraxia was born in the village of Chlorakas in Paphos in 1930. When she was seven, her mother Maria was tragically killed in a farming accident. Maria was pregnant with her fifth child when she went out one day to plough the fields. Suddenly, her donkey was spooked by a noise and jumped backwards causing the handle of the plough to hit Maria hard in the stomach. She died as a result of her injuries leaving behind four young children; Panayioti (born in 1929) Efpraxia (born in 1930), Angela (born in 1934) and Eleni (born in 1936). Her mother's dying words, 'who will look after my children?' would haunt Efpraxia throughout her life.

As the eldest girl child, Efpraxia decided to take on the household duties to look after her family. Thankfully she did receive assistance from her aunties. During the day they all worked together on the family farm which produced various vegetables that were then sold at local markets. This way, her younger siblings could afford to attend school. Unfortunately, her father Efstathios spent most of their income on non-essential items which meant that they were unable to escape poverty.

Andreas' family were not too keen on his choice for a bride. Reacting to their concerns, Andreas decided to leave Cyprus for Australia promising Efpraxia that he would send for her as soon as he had established a foothold there.

In December 1951, he boarded the migrant ship Corsica with several people that he knew from Ktima, including his best friend, Socratis Nicolaides who had worked with him at the Electricity Board. Andreas was aged twenty-five when he left Cyprus.

After a rather exhausting and harrowing two-month voyage, the Corsica finally docked in the Port of Melbourne on the 4th of February, 1952. According to his daughter Mary, her father did not

Sisters, Eleni, Efpraxia (seated) and Angela Efstathiou. Paphos, 1952.

Power Station Employees (Electricity Board) in Ktima, Paphos. December, 1951.
Back row from left to right: Sadik, Christodoulos, Laos, Andreas Artemis, unknown and Loizos. Middle row: Socratis Nicolaides, Andreas Tryphonos and Jamil.
Seated: Petrakis Psaridis, Kostas Kotsalis (Manager), Mayor Christodoulos Galatopoulos, Eftychios Vasseliadis and George Ioannou. Squatting: Andreas Tselepos and Andreas.

talk about the Corsica. "He did tell us that the ship was on its last legs by the time it arrived at the port in Fremantle and it was leaning quite severely."

Andreas was met by his cousin Demitri Demosthenous whom he stayed with for a while at his residence in South Melbourne. Later, he travelled to country Victoria where he worked for the State Electricity Commission on the development of the power station at Yallourn. The work was difficult, manual labour compared to his job in Cyprus as a meter-reader.

Efpraxia waited patiently for an invitation from Andreas so she could come to Australia. During their time apart, they communicated by writing letters, which would often take weeks to arrive. Her friends pleaded with her to forget about Andreas and to marry someone else, however she was strong-willed and confident that Andreas would one day send for her.

Andreas (on the far right) with friends and his brother Nicholas (on the far left). Paphos, circa 1947.

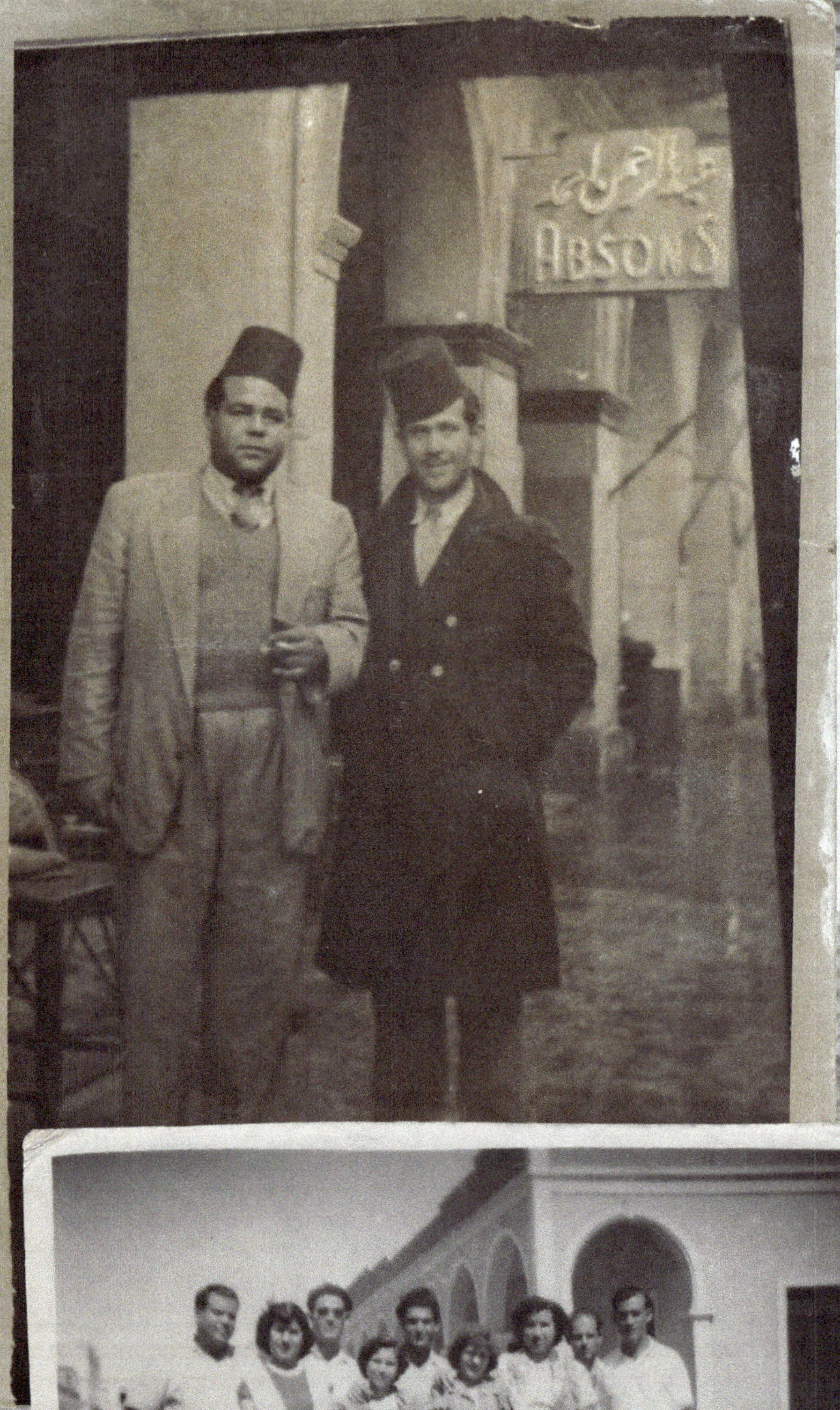

CLOCKWISE

- Andreas Tryphonos (left) and Socratis Nicolaides in Port Said, Egypt. December, 1951.
- Andreas Tryphonos in Djibouti, 30th December, 1951.
- En route to Australia (location unknown), January 1952. Back row from left to right: Evagoras Papadakis, Avraam Christofi, unknown and Demetris Parlan. Middle row: Michalis Thesalos, Takis Nicolaides and Andreas (Rikos) Artemis. Front row: Loukia Papastylianou, Olga Papadakis, Andreas Tryphonos, Lella Nearchou and Georgoula Achileos.
- En route to Australia (location unknown), January, 1952. From left to right: Andreas (Rikos) Artemis, Takis Nicolaides, Andreas Tryphonos, Avraam Christofi and Michalis Thesalos. Front row: Demetris Parlan and Evagoras Papadakis.
- Djibouti, 30th of December, 1951. From left to right: Andreas Tryphonos, Lella Nearchou, Takis Nicolaides, Olga Papadakis, Evagoras Papadakis, Georgoula Achileos, Loukia Papastylianou, unknown and unknown.

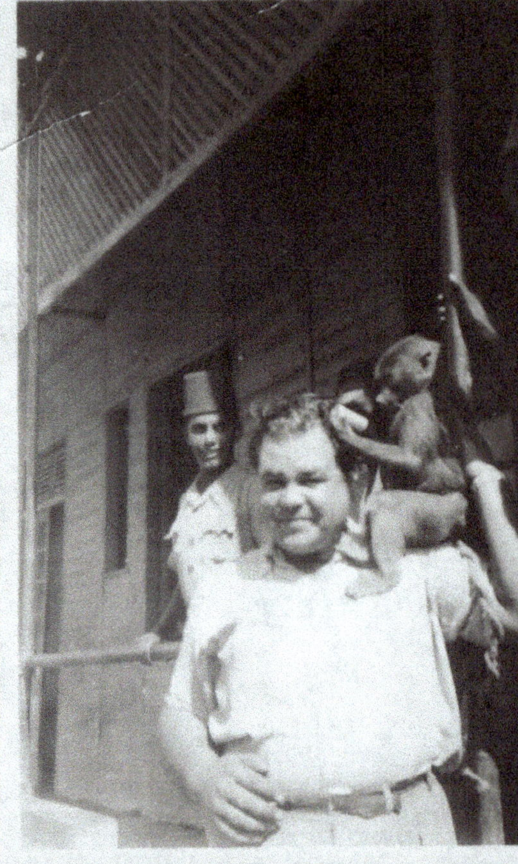

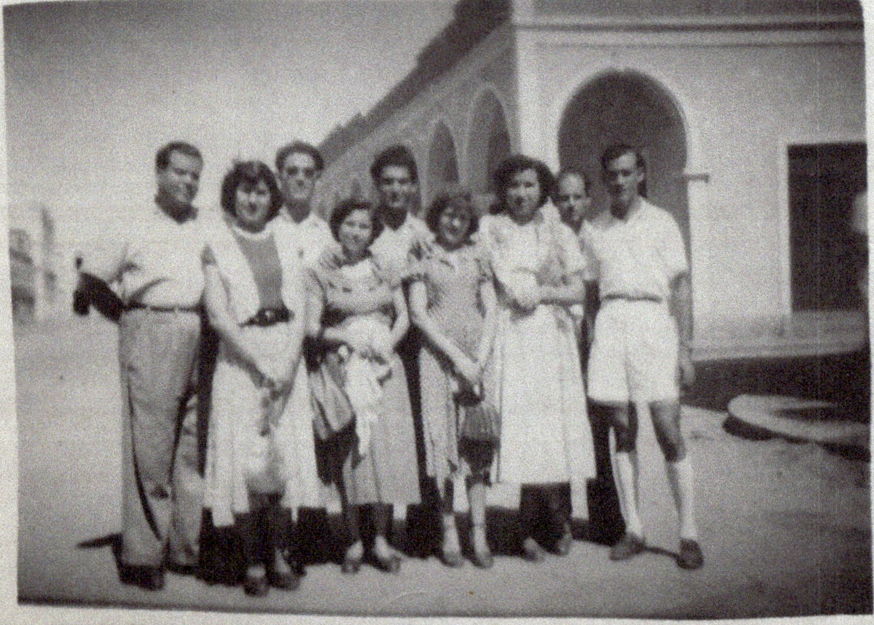

From left to right: Andreas, Efpraxia, Vera and Erotokritos (Eric) at Luna Park in Melbourne, 1956.

Andreas and Efpraxia at Luna Park in Melbourne, 1956.

Back row: Andreas Tryphonos and Takis Nicolaides Front row: Unknown, Michael Neofytou and wwwLella and Neofytos Nearchou at Luna Park in Melbourne, 1956.

Andreas Tryphonos and Socratis Nicolaides at Luna Park in Melbourne, 1956.

From left to right: Michael Neofytou, Unknown, Andreas Tryphonos, Takis Nicolaides (blurred) and unknown friend at the bar in Luna Park in Melbourne, 1956.

Left: Andreas (holding dog) with a friend outside
a pub in South Melbourne. Circa 1952.

In 1953, Andreas left Yallourn and returned to Melbourne where he gained employment at Standard Motor Company in Port Melbourne, assembling British Standard and Triumph motor vehicles.

At one point, Andreas worked briefly at a canning factory called Brookes Lemos on Williamstown Road in Port Melbourne, manufacturing KIA-ORA cordials, jams, chutney, sauces, pickles, honey, canned meats and fruit juices. The factory employed many migrants including Turkish, Greek and Italian nationals. Andreas worked at the conveyor belt packing cans in boxes.

Like so many other migrants, Andreas' ambition was to work hard for a few years and save enough money to bring his beloved Efpraxia to Australia.

Efpraxia never lost hope that Andreas would one day send for her. After three years, tired of waiting, she borrowed money from her sisters Angela and Eleni to pay for her passage to Australia. Angela and Eleni were both seamstresses and decided to make their older sister a wedding dress which Efpraxia gladly packed in her suitcase. She travelled on the migrant ship Anna Salen and arrived at Port Melbourne in March 1955. She recalls people standing on Station Pier shouting up at them. "Go back! There are no jobs here! They've lied to us." Her heart sank, especially since she had been seasick for the entire journey to Australia.

Three months later, on the 21st of May, 1955 Efpraxia and Andreas were married at the Evangelismos Church in East Melbourne. Soon after, they were blessed with four children; Tryphonas, Mary (Maria), Anastasia and Demetrios.

The newly married couple moved in with Andreas' cousin Vera and her husband Erotokritos (Eric) who owned a fish and chip shop in Pearson Street, Brunswick. Efpraxia was appreciative and happy living with her husband's cousin and they all got on very well. They loved visiting the Melbourne Zoo which was close to where they lived.

Efpraxia initially worked at Sniders and Abrahams Tobacconists at Drewery Place in central Melbourne, preparing the tobacco leaves for the making of cigarettes. Later, she suggested to Andreas that they should get their own business. Andreas and Efpraxia helped out in Eric's fish and chip shop learning the finer details of the requirements of owning a business. Eventually, with the experience gained, they bought their own fish and chip shop on High Street in Westgarth. Efpraxia always helped in the fish shop even after each child was born. They owned the shop for twenty years.

ACKNOWLEDGEMENTS

I would like to thank Mary McIlwain for allowing me to publish her father's story of migration. Special thanks to her husband Leigh McIlwain for all his help and kind support.

Left: Andreas in Yallourn. Man on the
horse is unknown. Circa 1952.

PAPHOS

ELEFTHERIOS CHARALAMBIDES

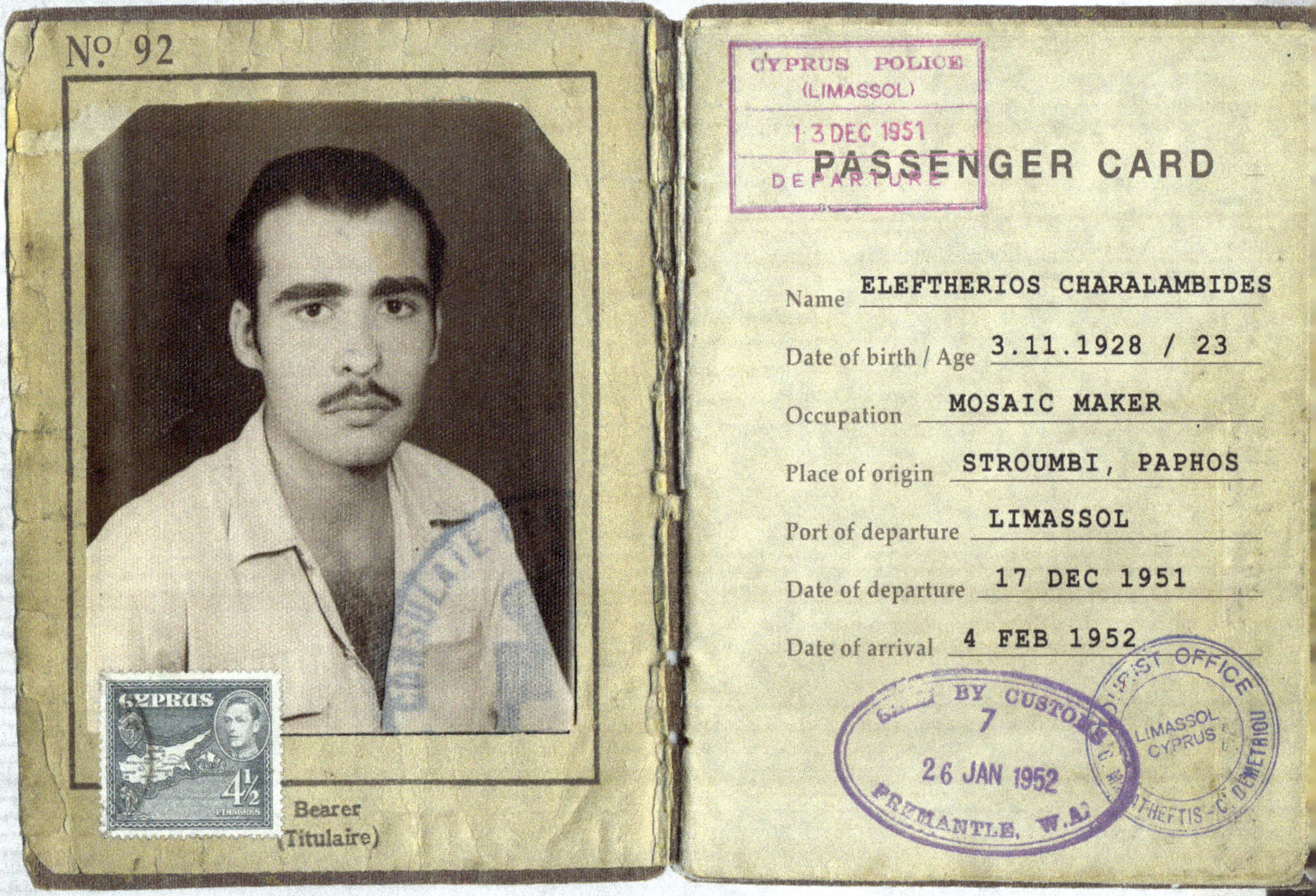
No 92

Bearer
(Titulaire)

CYPRUS POLICE
(LIMASSOL)
13 DEC 1951
DEPARTURE

PASSENGER CARD

Name ELEFTHERIOS CHARALAMBIDES

Date of birth / Age 3.11.1928 / 23

Occupation MOSAIC MAKER

Place of origin STROUMBI, PAPHOS

Port of departure LIMASSOL

Date of departure 17 DEC 1951

Date of arrival 4 FEB 1952

On the pier at Port Said, Egypt. Elefterios (left with cigarette) and Symeon Mesaritis squatting up front. Symeon was aged twenty-five and listed as a carpenter. December, 1951.

experienced great poverty. Eleftherios spent three winters without any shoes. Like most Cypriot youngsters, he would help his father on the farm before and after school. Eleftherios' younger sisters, Androulla was born in Stroumbi and Sotiria in Ktima.

In March 1947, Eleftherios joined the Cypriot Volunteer Regiment (CVR) with the British Armed Forces and served some time at the El Tahag Camp in Egypt. Two years later his mother Eleni suffered a stroke and passed away aged only forty-nine. Army documents indicate that Eleftherios was discharged in 1949, the same year his mother died.

After serving in the CVR, Eleftherios wanted to escape the poverty of Cyprus, so with only twenty pounds in his pocket and an old army trunk containing his most valued possessions, he left for Australia on the Corsica. Unfortunately, he did not discuss the details of his ordeal at sea, only to say that he lived in appalling conditions for almost two months and that the ship was not sea-worthy. It was the trip from hell. On numerous occasions he wished he never got on the ship and wanted to go home.

Upon his arrival in Australia, Eleftherios spent some time at Bonegilla migrant camp before moving to Melbourne where he rented rooms at various locations. During the day, he would work in cafes washing dishes, and then worked night

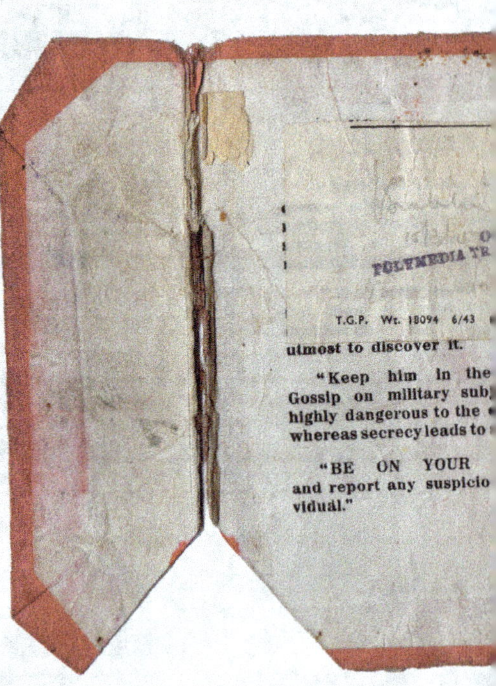

Elefterios' CVR Service book from the years 1947-1949.

Elefterios (left) with Evagoras Papadakis en route to Melbourne on the Corsica, 1952.

Eleftherios Charalambides (also known as Elef Lambides) was born in Alexandria, Egypt on the 3rd of November, 1928, (some official documents show that he was born on 15th of October).

His parents Theophilos Charalambides (formerly Papakyricou) and Eleni Pslate, met in Alexandria where they were married in the Cathedral of Evangelismos around 1920. They were blessed with eight children; Charalambos (born in 1923), Yiannoula (born in 1924), Angela (born in 1927), Eleftherios (born in 1928), Marika (born in 1931), Yiorgos (born in 1934), Androulla (born in 1938) and Sotiria (born in 1941). Theophilos was a decorated soldier who served from 1912 to 1917 in the First World War.

In 1937, when Eleftherios was nine, his family left Egypt to return to Cyprus where they owned some land and a house in Stroumbi, Paphos. With no electricity or running water their new life was a vast difference to their life in Egypt. They sold everything they had and bought land in Kato Pervolia and Ktima and began a new life there as farmers. A wave of nationalism was on the rise in Egypt, causing many Greeks to return to their homelands. Living off the land was difficult for the family and at times, they

shift at Dunlop in Port Melbourne. Although his Uncle Paul owned and operated a cafe in Kilmore, Victoria, Eleftherios did not live with him.

In 1953, Eleftherios met Jean Spotiswoode and soon after, their daughter Karen was born in 1954. In 1960, his younger sister Androulla joined him in Australia.

Eleftherios worked two jobs for many years. With the money her earned, he was able to buy land in Mt Waverley and eventually built his first family home. He worked at the Lockwood factory in Oakleigh for over thirty-five years rising through the ranks from leading hand to class machinist and finally to foreman.

Eleftherios lived his life to the full. He always had a big smile, a hug and kiss when he greeted family and friends. He loved gardening and cooking, and was a one-eyed Collingwood supporter. He loved making traditional Greek food and sweets and in recent times even smoked meats! Despite his ordeal on the Corsica, one of his greatest passions was to travel. He first returned to Cyprus in 1974 and visited many times thereafter. Despite the reason he left Cyprus, Eleftherios had great love and pride for his homeland and his family.

ACKNOWLEDGEMENTS

I would like to thank Karen Charalambidou for allowing me to publish her father's story of migration and for her kind help and support along the way.

Army Book 64 (Part I).

Soldier's Service Book

Soldier's Pay Book, Army Book 64 (Part II), will be issued for active service.)

Entries in this book (other than those connected with the making of a Soldier's Will and insertion of the names of relatives) are to be made under the superintendence of an Officer.

Instructions to Soldier.

1. You are held personally responsible for the safe custody of this book.

2. You will always carry this book on your person.

3. You must produce the book whenever called upon to do so by a competent military authority, viz., Officer, Warrant Officer, N.C.O. or Military Policeman.

4. You must not alter or make any entry in this book (except as regards your next-of-kin on pages 10 and 11 or your Will on pages 15 to 20).

5. Should you lose the book you will report the matter to your immediate military superior

6. On your transfer to the Army Reserve this book will be handed into your Orderly Room for transmission through the O. i/c Records, to place of rejoining on mobilisation.

7. You will be permitted to retain this book after discharge, but should you lose the book after discharge it cannot be replaced.

8. If you are discharged from the Army Reserve, this book will be forwarded to you by the O. i/c Recor[...]

Eleftherios, aged twenty-two in Ktima, Paphos. Circa 1950.

Eleftherios at the Bonegilla Migrant Camp, Victoria. February, 1952.

BLUE ATLANTIC LINE

HEAD OFFICE : BEVIS MARKS LONDON E.C. 3.

This form must be completed and signed by the intending
passenger. No berth can be definitely booked unless this
form is filled up to the satisfaction of the
BLUE ATLANTIC LINE

DECLARATION FORM FOR PASSENGERS TO AUSTRALIA

Ship's name ..... **CORSICA** ..... Class ..... **TOURIST** Berth No. .... Sailing date **12/12/51**

Embarkation port ..... **LIMASSOL** ..... Landing port ..... **SYDNEY**

Surname (in block letters) and full Christian name **CHARALAMBIDES Eleftherios** Sex **male**

Father's name *Theophilo Karakouibides* Mother's name *Alexis Karakouibides*

Relationship to the head of family (in travelling) ....

Marital status A) *Single* Race B) (state explicitly whether Hebrew or not) **Greek European**

Birthplace **Alexandria Egypt.** Birthdate (day, month, and year) **15/10/28**

Nationality C) **Greek** Profession or occupation **Mosaics maket**

Present address **Nicosia Cyprus**

Country of last permanent residence **Cyprus**

Country of final destination (State and Place) **Australia**

Purpose of the voyage **Immigrant** Presumable duration of stay abroad **unknown**

Passport No. **247** issued by **GREEK CON.** at **NICOSIA** on **2/7/51** expiring on **2/7/52**

Visa No. issued by **CYP.GOV.** at **NICOSIA** **29/11/51** expiring on **8/10/53**

Landing Permit No. **C136844** issued by **IMM** at **AUSTRALIA** on **8/10/51** expiring on **"**

Re-entry Permit No. .... issued by .... at .... on .... expiring on ....

A) Single, married, widowed — B) European, Hebrew, Asiatic, African. — C) Italian, British, French, Indian etc.

State as the case may be : 1. engaged under labour contract - 2. to take employment - 3. to join relatives - 4. nomination - 5. for commercial or professional purposes - 6. on family grounds - 7. on study grounds - 8. pleasure, travel, etc.

To THE BLUE ATLANTIC LINE

I hereby certify that I do not come within any of the prohibitions under the IMMIGRATION ACTS OF THE COMMONWELTH OF AUSTRALIA. I undertake to sign - when so requested by an Officer of your Company on board the ship on whclhe I am about to embark - any declaration prescribed by the Australian Authorities. If I should be prohibited from landing in Australia. I will pay the amount of the fare for the return- journey on the ship and in the class and accommodation which may be assigned to me for such jouney. I hereby agree that, if I am called upon to do so by you, I will before embarkation take out a letter of Credit on the Agency at the port to which I am proceeding.

9th December,   51.

.... 19 ....

Signature *Eleftherios Charalambides*

Δ. Π. 29/45/*1749*

ΔΙΟΙΚΗΣΙΣ ΠΑΦΟΥ

Κον *Ευστάθιον Ο. Παναγιωτίδην*

'Αναφερόμενος εἰς τὴν αἴτησιν σας δι' ἄδειαν εἰσόδου εἰς
Αὐστραλίαν, ἐνετάλην νὰ σὲς πληροφορήσω ὅτι ἡ ἄδεια σας
εἰσόδου εἰς τὸ ἐν λόγω μέρος ἐλήφθη παρὰ τῆς Κυπριακῆς Κυβερνήσεως, δύνασθε δὲ τώρα νὰ ὑποβάλετε αἴτησιν διὰ τὴν ἔκδοσιν
διαβατηρίου.

Διοικητής.

[Form M. 28.]

ME...

(For Person...

INST...

In cases where the Medical ...
should state under " REMARKS ...
permanent or temporary nature.

Re...

NAME ..... **ELEFTH...**

ADDRESS ..... **KT...**

1. Have you or any mem...
   serious illness or surg...

2. Have you or has any ...
   institution or attend...

3. Have you or has any ...
   EPILEPSY or been tre...

I hereby certify that th...
in every particular.

Signature of applicant which ...
in the presence of the Med...

NOTE.—This form is ...
(see other side) if travelling t...

Against the headings ...
any departure from norm...

A. Heart .. .. ..

B. Lungs .. .. ..
C. Nervous and mental condit...
   intelligence .. ..

D. Hearing .. .. ..
E. Sight—
   (a) Without glasses ..

   (b) With glasses (if wor...
F. Urine—Is there presence of ...
   or sugar ?.. ..

Age ..

Height ..

Weight..

REMARKS (include partic...

   in answers to above que...

....

....

I CERTIFY that I have ...
set forth above. I further ...
under " Remarks ", each of ...
and not suffering from any ...
upon the public or to preve...

Date.... *Paphos* ...

EXAMINATION.

(Form No. 47A)

(...manent Admission to Australia.)

...MEDICAL EXAMINER.

...le to describe the examinee as being in good health, he
...e of the defect which he finds and whether it is of a

...IFICATE.

...ant to Questions.

...T.H. CHARALAMBIDES...
(...ne in BLOCK capitals.)

...KHOA... CYPRU...

...mily included in this application ever had any
...No

...ur family ever been in a sanatorium or other
...he treatment of tuberculosis? No
...family ever suffered from MENTAL DISEASE OR
...ution for any kind of these diseases? No
...pplied by me to the Medical Examiner is correct

Eleftherios Th. Charalambides

...DICAL EXAMINATION.
...e medical certificate for husband, wife and children
...gle men or women.
...ve, state whether normal or give particulars of

...and, or Single Man	Wife, or Single Woman
normal	
normal	
normal	
normal	
normal L. normal R.	L.
...L. me R.	L.
...is	
...ears old	
...6"	
...mily	

...arture from normal conditions not fully

...ed the above-named and that the results
...ny opinion, subject to any special observ...
...ed is in good health and of sound consti...
...defect which is likely to render him/her a...
...earning his/her own living.

...951
(Signature and Qualifications...)
...ddress... Paphos... Cyp...

ΣΩΤΗΡΗΣ ΤΑΛΑΡΙΔΗΣ

ΙΑΤΡΟΣ

ΕΔΡΑ ΕΝ ΠΑΦΩ

ΤΗΛΕΦΩΝΟΝ 29.

Κτῆμα τῇ 7th MAY 1951

NAME: ELEFTHERIOS THEOFYLAKTOU HARALAMBIDES

ADDRESS: KTIMA PAPHOS
CYPRUS   AGE: 22

X-RAY EXAMINATION OF THE CHEST

Normal appearance of the lungs and the Diaphragme.
No evidence of tuberculosis or any other disease
of the lungs.
The Heart and the Big vesseles of the Heart do not show
any pathological changes.

Dr S Talaridy
Signature................

Certified that the signature appearing above
is that of Dr. BS. Delarides of Paphos CYPRUS.

For Director of Medical and
Health Services
CYPRUS.

11.5.51

No. 1041/1951

GOVERNMENT OF CYPRUS
INTERNATIONAL SANITARY CONVENTION, 1944.
INTERNATIONAL CERTIFICATE OF VACCINATION AGAINST SMALLPOX

THIS IS TO CERTIFY that *Eleftherios Th. Charalam* (Age 22 Sex m.)
whose signature appears below, has this day been vaccinated by me against
Smallpox.
Origin and Batch No. Of Vaccine *Lister* Eng. Sig. of Vaccinator *Komiadaninai*
3542   Official Position *Health Inspector*
(Official Stamp)   Place *Ktima CYPRUS* Date 25/6/51
Signature of person Vaccinated x *Charalambides* CYPRUS.
Home Address Ktima (Paphos) CYPRUS.

IMPORTANT NOTE:- In the case of primary vaccination the person vaccinated
should be warned to report to a medical practitioner between the 8th and
14th day in order that the result of the vaccination may be recorded on
this certificate. In the case of re-vaccination the person should report
within 48 hours for first inspection in order that any immune reaction
which has developed may be recorded.

THIS IS TO CERTIFY THAT the above vaccination was inspected by me on the
date (s) and with the result(s) shown hereunder:-   Result *Reaction*
Date of Inspection   *Accelerated*
28/6/51

Sig. of Doctor *Komiadaninai*
Official Position *Health Inspector* Date 28/6/51
(official stamp)   Place *Ktima CYPRUS*

Use one or other of the following terms in stating the result, viz.
"Reaction of Immunity", "Accelerated Reaction (vaccinoid)", "Typical
primary vaccinia". A certificate of "No Reaction" will not be accepted.
Signature of Person Vaccinated x *Charalambides*
THIS CERTIFICATE IS NOT VALID FOR MORE THAN 3 YEARS FROM DATE OF ISSUE.

118

PAPHOS

HARALAMBOS THEOPHANOUS

Haralambos and Maria Theophanous with their four children. From left, Andrew Koula, Nicki and Theo outside the Greek Orthodox Church in Lygon Street, Carlton, 1958.

Haralambos (Charles) Theophanous was born on the 19th of August, 1910 in Neo Chorio, near Polis Chrysochous. He was the eldest of five children. His brother was George and his sisters were Eleni, Theano and Olga.

After completing primary school, Haralambos was sent to work at a nearby copper mine but was later trained to become a shoemaker. After his

island of Chios who, after escaping from the Nazi occupied island, had been relocated to live in Polis Chrysochous during the remainder of World War Two.

Maria Georgoulis was born on the island of Chios on the 17th of May, 1921. She spent some time in Athens with her aunt before the war, and had an Athenian accent which later captivated Haralambos. After the Germans occupied the island in May 1941, Maria and her sister and brother in law (along with others), stole a boat from the Germans and fled to Turkey as did thousands of other Greeks.

Maria's father could not escape from Chios and he tragically starved to death during the war. After arriving in Turkey, the refugees from Chios were sent to various internment camps around the Mediterranean. Maria and her sister were sent to Cyprus but lived in separate villages on the island. Maria lived in Polis Chrysochous where she met and fell in love with Haralambos. She was twenty-one at the time and he was thirty-two.

In July 1943, Haralambos and Maria welcomed the birth of Koula (Kyriakoulla) followed by two sons, Andrew in 1946 and Theophanis in 1948.

expensive. For some strange reason, Cypriots had to pay over 100 pounds each to travel to Australia. That was like paying around 5,000 dollars in today's money. That's for a one-way trip. Other Europeans only paid around ten pounds under the Australian government's Assisted Passage Scheme. In fact, my father had to sell his field for 100 pounds to help pay for his ship fare. He came to Australia with nothing."

Before leaving Cyprus, Haralambos told his five-year-old son Andrew, 'to look after his mother.' "It was a very emotional farewell," recalls Andrew. "My father and my mother wept a lot on the day he was leaving. In fact, my mother never stopped weeping because of subsequent events."

As far as his father's experience on the Corsica, Andrew explained that his father was very shy and did not talk about the past. "He didn't say much about his life. He only told my mother that the Corsica was a horrible ship and they didn't know if they would survive the journey. After all, it wasn't as if the passengers were getting daily briefings by the captain or the crew. They had no idea what was going to happen to them from day to day. The people who ran that ship should have gone to prison for not providing proper food and water or toilets that work and for allowing such poor hygiene on board the ship. Even after Colombo, things did not improve."

For the families that were left behind, there was no information sent to them about the Corsica and the journey itself. Rumours began to circulate on the island, including in the village of Polis. "We thought that we would be notified when the Corsica arrived in Australia, but after five or six weeks, we had heard nothing. Then a rumour started to spread in the village that the ship had sunk. Everyone was devastated. Our mother was beside herself. No one knew where or when the ship had sunk. Did it sink before it reached Colombo, or at Colombo or after Colombo? I just remember that Colombo was mentioned. The rumour spread like wildfire. The big question at the time was, 'who would look after our family? How would we survive without a father?' My Godfather, who owned the main store in Polis, gave my mother some money to see us through for a while. He even offered to adopt me."

Almost twelve weeks after the Corsica had left Limassol, the Theophanous family

Haralambos' parents, Theophanis and Hariklia Theophanous. Cyprus, circa 1951.

apprenticeship, he opened a small shoe shop in Polis where he made and repaired shoes for both Muslim and Christian customers. At one time, he had a partner who was a Turkish Cypriot cobbler.

In 1942, he met and married Maria Georgoulis, a Greek refugee from the

After the war, Haralambos wanted to leave Cyprus to set up a new life for his growing family in Australia but more importantly, he wanted his children to be educated there. "It was impossible for our whole family to leave Cyprus together," his son Andrew explains. "It was far too

in Polis finally received word that the ship had arrived safely at its destination and that Haralambos was in fact, alive. "We were told that the ship had broken down at Colombo and that was the reason it was so delayed," says Andrew. "It was actually a miracle that the ship made it all the way to Australia. My mother cried every day for two and a half months thinking that our father had drowned at sea. For three months, mum had to rely on charity and the goodwill of others to get by in the village. Later in life, my mother would always go back to this period in her life to remind us how difficult it was for her."

It took three years for Haralambos to earn enough money to partially pay the fares for his wife and sons to emigrate to Australia. "I know that my father was given a loan by the World Council of Churches, which took him thirty-five years to pay back," says Andrew. "Without his shoemaking tools and the means to set up a business, he had to find other work. Thankfully, there was a strong network of Cypriot men who had come to make a better life, and they helped my father find work in the Standard Motors factory at Fishermans Bend in Port Melbourne."

After his father left for Australia, young Andrew began to show a great interest in the Greek Orthodox Church, even learning the divine liturgy by heart. "I used to think of myself as a church person and would pretend to be a priest in the village. I even made my own 'thurible' (censer) with string and bottle tops and would wave it around while conducting my own church service or mock wedding with some of the other village kids. When it was time for us to leave Cyprus, the priest in Polis begged my mother to leave me behind. 'Leave him for the church.

Leave him for the church,' he pleaded with her. 'We will look after him. Your son has a remarkable understanding of religion and will have a bright future with the church here.' Of course, my mother said no and we left Cyprus for Australia."

In August 1954, Maria and her three children emigrated to Australia on the ship Fairsea to be reunited with Haralambos in Melbourne. Koula (Kyriakoulla) was 12, Andrew was eight and Theo was six.

"Our mother was happy to start a new life in Australia. After everything she had to endure on Chios during the war, and then in Cyprus, waiting to be together with her husband, she was glad to reach Australia. Once we arrived and were reunited with our father, we struggled at first to make ends meets. My father worked so hard in factories in those years, including as a welder at the Ford Motor company and later in a firm which made chairs."

Despite their humble beginnings as New Australians, Haralambos and Maria had a very generous approach to hospitality, especially towards other migrants. "I remember my father had a small group of close-knit friends in Melbourne that he knew from his village and they would always meet up at our rented house in Moreland and Albert Park. Friends like Achilleas Demetriou who was also on the Corsica. This is when my mother was in her element. She would cook a feast and put on a huge spread with so many different dishes. Even though we were poor during that period, my parents always had time for their friends and this taught me a great deal about human generosity."

In 1955, Haralambos and Maria welcomed their fourth child, Niki.

Like most migrants, the Theophanous family lived in rented accommodation In the first few years after they arrived to Australia. "One house in Moreland was so

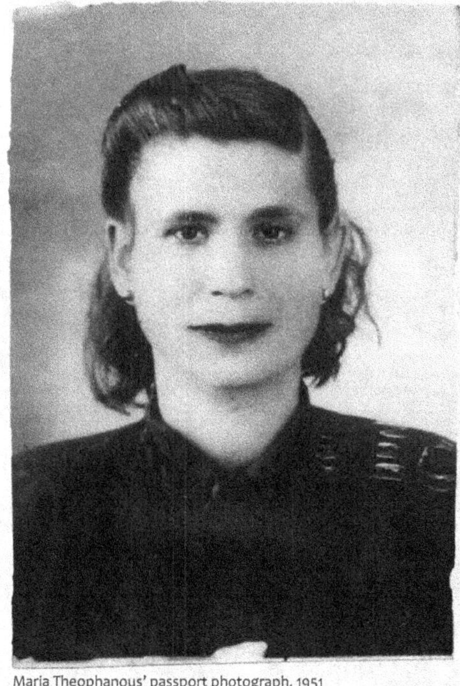
Maria Theophanous' passport photograph. 1951

small that all six of us lived in two rooms," Andrew explains. "This was real poverty. In 1959, we became eligible for a Housing Commission house and thus we were given terms of payment that permitted us to purchase our own small home. The house was on Pascoe Vale Road, in the working-class suburb of Broadmeadows. During these years, my mother also worked at the Australasian Jam Company in South Yarra. It was hard work for years and mum retired after she had an accident at the factory."

Broadmeadows is where Andrew lived for many years until he graduated from Monash University with First Class Honours in Philosophy, before leaving for studies at Oxford University in England. Haralambos left Cyprus because he wanted his children to have excellent opportunities in education. This came true for Andrew and also for Theo, who gained First Class Honours in Politics from La Trobe University. Niki also graduated from university. Unfortunately, she died at the early age of forty-three years.

Haralambos lived to see his sons achieve outstanding results in Australian society. Andrew served twenty-one years in the Australian Parliament as a Member of the House of Representatives. He was Parliamentary Secretary (assistant minister) to Prime Minister Paul Keating. Theo served many years in the Victorian State Parliament, including Minister for Industry and Energy and other portfolios.

Andrew says of his father. "He was a man of huge compassion. He loved all of humanity. His love of education came from his innate wisdom. He supported my love of, and studies in, philosophy. His struggles in life taught me many lessons about the importance of social justice and equality amongst all human beings."

Haralambos passed away on the 5th of September, 1995. His beloved wife Maria died on the 22nd of May, 2002.

ACKNOWLEDGEMENTS

I would like to thank Andrew Theophanous for allowing me to publish his father's story of migration. Special thanks to Kathryn Eriksson and Steve Savva for their help and support along the way.

Phoklon with young Timothy, (son of Kostas Casimatis) outside the Casimatis home in Sandy Bay, Hobart, Tasmania. Circa 1956.

PHOKION
PAVLIDES

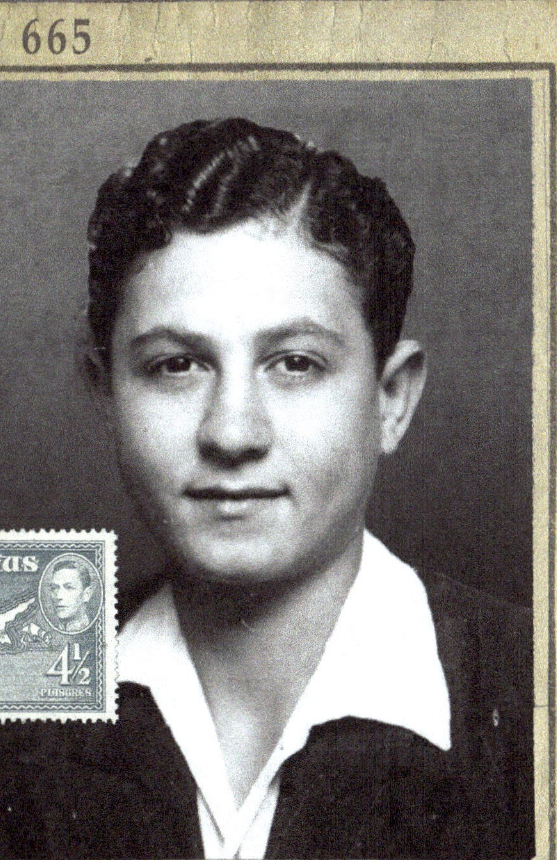

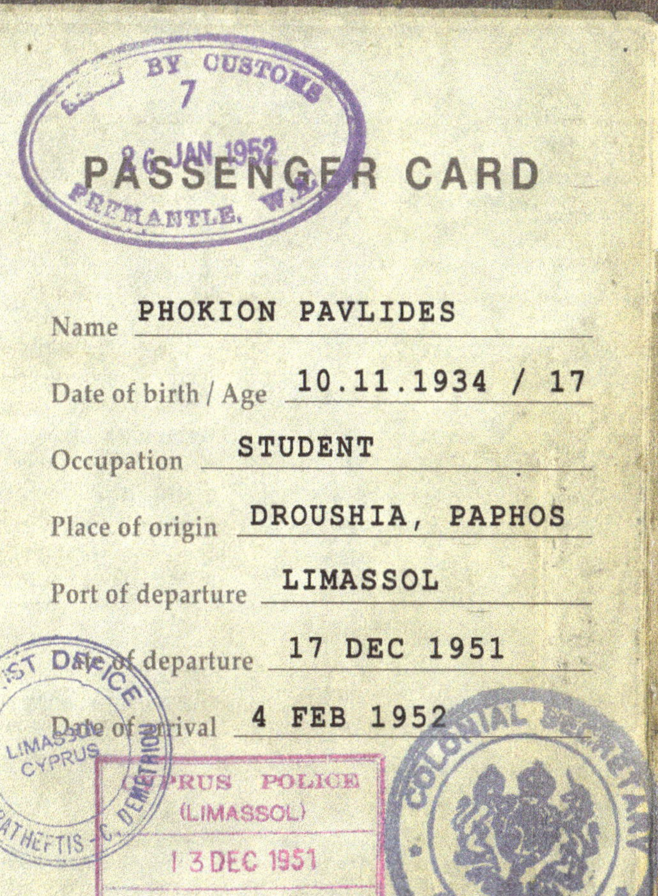

Phokion (right), his brother Haralambos (left) and unknown friend (middle). English School College in Paphos, 1951.

Phokion Pavlides was born in Droushia in 1934. His parents were Giorgios and Despina Pavlides. In the village, Giorgios operated a flour mill that was driven by a diesel motor. Phokion would help his father at the mill during the school vacation.

"Well as you know, after the Second World War people started to become fanatical about *Enosis* (union) with Greece. My teachers were especially keen to promote this idea and they would force us to protest or demonstrate against the British. Schools began to close. My father was the one who said to me. 'You would be better off leaving this island because things will get worse. That's why I left.'"

Phokion wanted more than anything to stay in Cyprus to complete his secondary school education. "Back then, I knew that in order to find work in Cyprus you must know English so I enrolled in an English school in Ktima. My father had spent some time in America so he was able to help me with the language. In this way, I was able to excel in my studies."

When Phokion's father Giorgios travelled to America in the 1930s, he met and worked briefly with a Kytherian family named 'Casimatis' who owned a restaurant in Piraeus. When Kostas Casimatis migrated to Australia and opened a restaurant in Tasmania, Giorgios asked him to sponsor his son Phokion.

Grigorios Kasimatis (Gregory Casimatis) had been approached in the early 1910s by Panayiotis (Peter) Galanis, a fellow Kytherian, to become business partners in a fish shop in Hobart. After only fifteen months, Galanis sold his share to Gregory, who then took on his younger brother Antonios (Anthony) as a partner. Their shop, the Britannia Cafe, was fitted out with upstairs dining rooms and subsequently became Tasmania's first Greek run restaurant.

"On the day I left Cyprus, my father took me to the harbour in Limassol. I remember sitting there with my father and we could see the Corsica anchored out in the distance. There must have been around 2,000 people gathered there. As we were sitting there, my father turned to me and said. 'Phokion, now that you are leaving, I won't be able to look after you anymore. You'll have to look after yourself.' I nodded and replied, 'Yes, I know father,' He then said. 'Son, when you get to Australia you will find flies and bees.' I'm thinking what is my father trying to tell me. I'm about to board the Corsica and he wants to talk about flies and bees. Anyway, he said. 'You know what flies do and you know where flies like to sit.' I nodded. 'And you know what bees do. When you get to Australia, you have to decide whether you will be like a fly, or whether you will be like a bee.' I understood what my father was trying to say and I never forgot his simple words of wisdom."

It was late in the evening by the time Phokion was allowed to board the Corsica. He remembers seeing a cargo of potatoes being loaded onto the ship. "We didn't move for two or three days and many passengers were getting angry. They just kept us there in Limassol while they loaded the potatoes in the cargo hold. I remember the crew were all Italian. We couldn't understand them and they couldn't understand us. I remember one Cypriot man became so angry he grabbed one of the crew members to hit him and this poor man shouted back, 'I'm not the Capitan, I'm not the Capitan.' Tensions

Phokion (left) with Grigorios Kasimatis (Gregory Casimatis) shortly after arriving in Hobart, 1952.

were high. We finally left at night and arrived at Port Said the next day through the Suez Canal. It's the first time I had ever seen black people. All these black people everywhere."

After leaving Port Said, Phokion recalls how they stumbled across a Greek Orthodox church in the port town of Djibouti. "It was a Sunday and a few of us decided to venture through the town. Suddenly we heard the familiar sounds of the Orthodox liturgy. To our surprise there was a small church in front of us. The small congregation there welcomed us with open arms and invited us to join them in the church. After the service they served us food and drink and wished us safe travels.

According to Phokion, it was after Djibouti when the Corsica began to break down. "One of the engines broke down and the ship started to zig-zag like a snake. The potatoes began to rot because of the heat. I saw them throwing sacks of rotten potatoes overboard. Then the fridges in the ship's kitchen broke down. That's when I saw them throwing whole carcasses of beef overboard. I was being sick overboard when I saw them throwing a whole carcass or half a carcass into the water. I remember seeing sharks attracted to the meat in the water."

Phokion also recalls the food on the ship being quite dismal. "They

didn't have anything else to feed us, just *macaronia* (spaghetti). They fed us *macaronia* for breakfast, *macaronia* for lunch and *macaronia* for dinner. Because the refrigeration on the ship broke down, there was also no fresh water. We had to buy bottled water. This became the trip from hell. To make matters worse, somebody stole my money. I had fifty pounds in my suitcase and someone stole this money. I don't know who but someone took it."

Phokion shared a cabin on the Corsica with three other men. "I don't quite remember where they were from. I think two were from Paphos. I remember there were quite a few Yugoslavs and Pontian passengers on the ship. They would gamble and fight amongst themselves. The Captain of the ship would turn off the lights at night so they couldn't gamble. This would make them even more furious and they would shout and throw tables and chairs around. It was a sight to see, all that destruction. I also remember that the toilets weren't working. What a mess. As for seasickness, we all had it pretty bad. Let me tell you, this ship was not a passenger ship. The Corsica was not a passenger ship. It was a cargo ship. It wasn't meant for people. I have very bad memories of this ship. I wouldn't wish this trip on anyone."

Phokion passed the time on the Corsica talking to his fellow passengers. "We just sat around talking to one another. I was the only one who could speak any English. I had an uncle on the ship who was from a neighbouring village close to Droushia. He spent most of the time crying. Apparently he sold everything, all his animals to buy his ticket. 'Don't cry Uncle,' I would say, trying to comfort him. Everything will be okay when we get to Australia. I've heard good things about this country. 'I don't have any money,' he would reply. 'I can't speak any English.' Anyway, I ended up becoming his translator."

After he arrived in Australia, Phokion went to work with Kostas Casimatis and his brothers at the Britannia Cafe in Hobart, Tasmania. "It was a very upper-class restaurant. I stayed with Casimatis for two and a half years. I was paid six and half pounds a week peeling and cutting potatoes and doing all sorts of jobs. There were three brothers all working together. None of them married. They looked after

me, I can't complain. They treated me like family."

Phokion even served in the Australian army for a few months since he was still a British subject. "Let me tell you, I went in as a lamb but came out as a lion because

of the training. I even learned how to drive in the army. I remember being paid fifteen pounds a week."

In 1953, Phokion found work as a cook at the Women's Hospital in Hobart. With the money that he saved (approximately 320 pounds), he eventually bought a grocery store on Murray Street in Hobart. Over time, Phokion was able to bring a few of his siblings from Cyprus to Tasmania. He helped them resettle, get educated and find employment. "In those ten years after arriving to Australia on the Corsica, I was able to earn enough money to pay off my father's debts in Cyprus and to help many of my siblings migrate to Hobart to be with me."

In 1962, Phokion met and married Panayiota Santarmis. He explains how they met. "My sister Artemis worked at the Women's Hospital which was opposite my grocery store. She became friends with a Greek woman named Panayiota and introduced me to her. I was twenty-eight and Panayiota was twenty-three at the time. That's how I met my wife. We got married on the 27th of December, 1964. In fact, I had a double wedding with my brother Athinodoros and his fiancé Katerina. It was huge with orchestras and

a huge feast."

Phokion eventually purchased a farm in Tasmania (known as the Golden Egg Farm) and managed a successful egg business. At one time, his farm was home to 20,000 chickens.

Phokion and Panayiota Pavlides relaxing at Seven Mile Beach in Tasmania, 1969.

"I must say that Australia was very good to me. I can't complain. I've had a good life living here. It's funny, I remember once, these two Aussies started to beat me up outside my shop however, when they discovered that I was Greek, they stopped and hugged me. The Aussies liked the Greeks because we helped them during the war. They didn't like the Italians much."

According to Phokion, his legacy in Hobart is his family. "There aren't many Cypriots over here. Most of them are related to me or connected to my family. When we all get together, I know everyone, young and old - we're all connected. To think, that when I first arrived, I was on my own. I was the only Cypriot in town. There were no churches and no *kafenia* (coffee houses). It's amazing to think how far we have come."

ACKNOWLEDGEMENTS

I would like to thank Phokion Pavlides for allowing me to publish his story of migration. Special thanks to his granddaughter Domonique for her help and support along the way.

PAPHOS

ELENI SAVVA

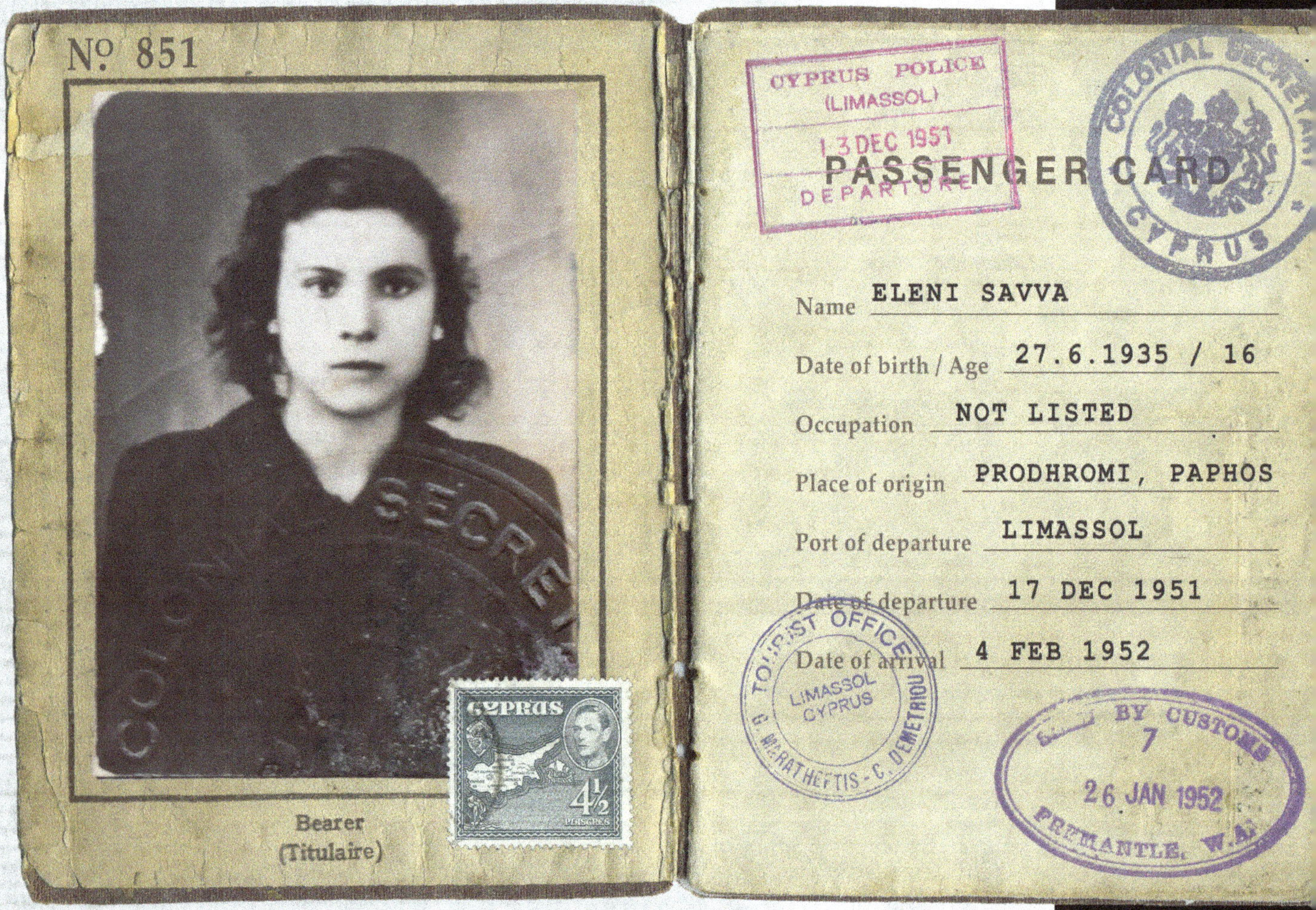
No 851

Bearer
(Titulaire)

CYPRUS 4½ PIASTRES

CYPRUS POLICE
(LIMASSOL)
13 DEC 1951
DEPARTURE

COLONIAL SECRETARY CYPRUS

PASSENGER CARD

Name ELENI SAVVA

Date of birth / Age 27.6.1935 / 16

Occupation NOT LISTED

Place of origin PRODHROMI, PAPHOS

Port of departure LIMASSOL

Date of departure 17 DEC 1951

Date of arrival 4 FEB 1952

TOURIST OFFICE
LIMASSOL CYPRUS
G. MARATHEFTIS - C. DEMETRIOU

BY CUSTOMS
7
26 JAN 1952
FREMANTLE, W.A.

Eleni Savva was born on the 27th of June, 1935 in the mixed village of Prodromi, Paphos. The village lies between the ancient town of Polis Chrysochous and the popular coastal community of Latchi. She was the fifth daughter (and seventh child) of Savva Christoforou and Maria Panayiotou. Eleni's siblings are Christophoros, Antigoni, Xenou, Hariklia, Chrystalla. Agathangelos, Myrianthi and Aristotelis. Eleni's eldest sister Antigoni, died suddenly in 1942, aged only eighteen. Eleni remembers her mother as only ever wearing black clothing since the death of Antigoni.

In March 1937, Eleni's eldest brother Christophoros (aged fifteen) accompanied his Aunt Mirianthi on the ship Patris to go to Australia. Having a large family proved to be a financial strain for Eleni's parents so they thought that Christophoros might have a better future living and working in Australia.

According to Eleni, her father Savva was a strict man but always determined to teach his children the value of a good education. She remembers how he would return home from the *kafenion* (coffee house) in the evenings and make her read to him the things she had learnt at school that day. Eleni did not share a close relationship with her mother Maria. She remarked that there was no open display of affection or love directed towards her. "I have no memory of my mother ever hugging me," she says softly. "She was a quiet, shy and softly spoken woman who didn't show emotion easily. I guess people behaved differently in those days." Eleni would reflect on her mother's lack of affection with a sense of disappointment throughout her life.

After completing fourth grade in primary school Eleni was expected to work in the fields and perform annual rural duties with her parents such as harvesting and threshing of crops.

Of all her siblings, Eleni was particularly close with her sister Chrystalla (also known as Tallou). They spent many hours together during the day and at night slept next to each other in the same bed. "We all slept in the same bed," explains Eleni. "My older siblings would sleep at one end of the bed while the younger ones would sleep at the other end. We didn't have any toys either. I would play with my sisters and the other children in the village with sticks and stones. Sometimes we had dolls that we made ourselves from rags, and spare scraps of material."

With so many children to look after, Eleni's parents could not afford to have them all living at home. Besides, their house was not big enough. Eleni's eldest brothers, Christophoros and Agathangelos were persuaded to leave home as teenagers and continue their education in Nicosia while Eleni and her sisters were expected to stay in the village and work in the fields. As the children grew older, they were married off one by one or sent to live with relatives overseas. For instance, Christophoros accompanied his auntie to Australia, whereas Agathangelos migrated to Toronto, Canada where his Uncle Kiriakos lived. Antigoni, Xenou and Hariklia were all married by *proxenia* (arranged marriage) whilst still in their late teens.

In January 1951, Eleni's sister Xenou emigrated to Australia with her husband Phillipos Socratous and their young son Christophoros. Within a fortnight of their arrival she gave birth to her second child, Maria. By this time, Christophoros had established himself and was married with two children of his own. He wrote to his father asking if any of his other siblings were interested in migrating to Australia. Initially, Chrystalla offered to go but soon changed her mind. "My sister Chrystalla didn't want to go to Australia," says Eleni. "She wanted to stay in the village, so I volunteered to take her place. That's how it happened that I would come to Australia. I was only sixteen at the time."

A few nights before she left Cyprus to travel to Australia, Eleni grabbed a hand-woven table runner and a set of bed sheets and secretly placed them in her suitcase without her mother's knowledge. The heirloom table runner was hand woven by her mother in the traditional manner prior to her marriage in 1919. "I wanted to take something to remind me of her," says Eleni. "In fact, my sister Chrystalla saw me pack these items in my suitcase and she quickly removed them, stating that they were her *prika* (dowry) and therefore belonged to her. But I managed to sneak them back into my suitcase without anyone knowing before I left for Australia."

On the day of her departure, Eleni's mother Maria wished her well on her journey. She did not offer her daughter any words of advice or express any emotional feelings. Eleni bid farewell

Eleni Savva (left) aged fourteen, with her older sister Chrystalla (aged nineteen) at a *panayiri* (festival) in Polis Chrysochous, 1949.

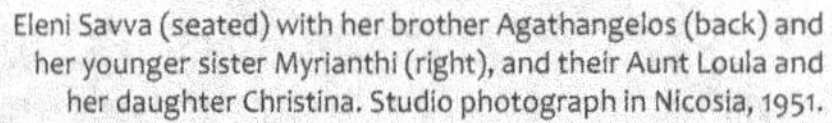

Eleni Savva (seated) with her brother Agathangelos (back) and her younger sister Myrianthi (right), and their Aunt Loula and her daughter Christina. Studio photograph in Nicosia, 1951.

Savvas Christoforou (Eleni's father). The photograph was sent to his daughter, wishing her a Happy New Year for 1954. Studio Photograph in Polis Chrysochous, 1953.

to her family and friends in the village, and walked quietly with her father, and older sister Hariklia down the main road towards the town of Polis Chrysochous. They boarded a bus to Limassol, passing through Ktima along the way. Once they arrived in Limassol, they stayed overnight at the house of Xenou's brother-in-law.

The next morning, Eleni and her father and sister went down to the port in Limassol. "When we arrived at the port, we discovered that there was going to be a long delay before I could board the ship. Unlike my mother, my father became quite emotional when it was time for us to say goodbye. I remember that he wished me well and told me to be careful. He also gave me two pounds for the journey."

Eleni shared a cabin on the Corsica with Chrysi Georgiou from the neighbouring village of Kathikas in Paphos and Katina Lambi from Karpaseia (*Karpasha*), a small Maronite village in the north of Cyprus. Chrysi and Katina were older than Eleni and travelling to meet their fiancées in Australia. "I remember that shortly after we left Limassol, the ship stopped. I'm not sure why, but it did not move for several days. No one told us what was going on, and so we didn't know anything. We waited and waited and then the ship started again and we left Cyprus behind us."

Eleni's cabin was located at the bottom of the ship. "Our cabin was cramped, uncomfortable and there was no privacy," she exclaims. "The humidity and heat were terrible. At least I had my own bed. It was the first time in my life I had my own bed to sleep in. I remember that there were people who were unhappy with where they were sleeping. The rooms were small and everyone was feeling cramped. It was hot inside and many times we had to go outside. We spent a lot of the time outside on the deck."

On board the Corsica, Eleni would meet Cypriots from different parts of Cyprus. This was a new experience for her as she had rarely left her village in Paphos. "Some of the passengers came from the same village. Some were travelling on their own, and others were with their families. I was on my own. Actually, that's not quite true. I did know Andreas Socratous. His

The family of Theodoros and Eleni Apostolou in the courtyard of their double story home in Agios Theodoros. The family were wealthy land owners. Their eldest child, Apostolis is the only one missing. From left to right standing: Demitris, Katelou, Evridiki and Zafiro. Front row seated: Theodoros Apostolou with young Elisaveth and Eleni Apostolou holding Andreas and Kostas. Agios Theodoros, Larnaca, 1953.

brother Phillipos was married to my sister Xenou. Andreas looked after me on the ship. He would always ask me how I was, and he would reassure me that everything would be okay. A few of the other women were also friendly to me. I think that they could sense that I was afraid and not as confident as they were. The ship was crowded. There were people everywhere. There were a lot of men. I would listen to the other passengers complaining and talking about how disappointed they were. Anyway, I was young. I didn't know any better. But I remember everyone was complaining and getting upset."

Like most of the passengers on board the ship, Eleni could not speak any English. "I remember that the people working on the ship were Italian. We couldn't communicate with them and they couldn't communicate with us. It was very difficult. We couldn't explain what we wanted. Most times we tried to find out things by asking other passengers. Someone would know something and that's how we would find out."

With regards to the smell on the ship, Eleni remembers that many passengers became quite sick. "It was a terrible smell. It was everywhere. The girls and I were lucky that we didn't get sick, others did, but we were fine. Everyone was complaining and talking about the smell. We were told that the smell came from rotting food. It was only later that I learnt it was potatoes. The toilets were also very dirty, and always smelt. No one came to clean them. For the women it was very upsetting that we had to live like this."

Eleni remembers that the food on the Corsica was another cause for complaint by the passengers. 'They gave us the same food every day. We were eating macaroni. It was something simple like you would give to a child. How did they expect us to eat the same food every day? The other thing is that they didn't even have water for us to drink sometimes. We heard that it was dirty or that they didn't have enough water for everyone. I remember that some of the men became very angry with everything on the ship. They would even yell at the waiters. There was frustration because they could not understand and nothing could be done. We had to put up with everything until we got to Australia. In the end, we were all waiting for the day when we would reach Australia and get off the ship."

When the Corsica docked in the Port of Colombo, passengers were able to disembark the ship. Eleni recalls how Andreas would accompany her, Chrysi and Katina on their walk around the local streets.

When they finally reached Melbourne, Eleni was met at the pier by her brother Christophoros with his wife Maroulla (Maria), and her sister Xenou with her husband, Phillipos. Eleni had no memory of her brother Christophoros back in Cyprus. He had left when she was still a toddler. Now it was like she was meeting him for the first time. Also reunited on the pier were Maroulla with her sister Kalesteni

Eleni Savva (left) aged sixteen with her two cabin friends, Catina Lambi (aged eighteen) and Chrysi Georgiou (aged twenty-three) on board the Corsica. They are all wearing the same type of necklace, bought in Colombo, Ceylon. January, 1952.

Apostolis and Eleni Theodorou on their wedding day, outside Evangelismos church in East Melbourne. Saturday the 15th of October, 1955.

and Phillipos with his brother Andreas.

Within a few days Eleni found a job at the Jam Factory in South Yarra. "I was living with my brother Christophoros and his family in South Yarra. They were renting a house there. I shared a room with Kalisteni. It was close to the Jam Factory so I could walk to work and home. My job was to select and separate the fruit that was used to make the jam."

After a few weeks Eleni left the Jam factory and went to work in a number of different factories that specialised in the manufacture of women's and children's clothing. She even worked for a short time as a kitchen-hand in a cafe/restaurant on Elizabeth street in central Melbourne.

Eventually, Eleni left Christophoros house and went to live with her older sister, Xenou and her family. Xenou, who was a stubborn person, would always insist that Eleni come and live with her in Hawthorn East.

In early 1955, Eleni, then aged nineteen, was formally introduced to Apostolis Theodorou. He was almost ten years her senior. Apostolis was born on the 12th of December, 1926 in the mixed village of Agios Theodoros in Larnaca. He was the eldest of eight children, and had migrated to Australia in September 1951 on board the Italian ship, the SS Florentia. Like so many other young migrants, Apostolis' intention was to work for several years in Australia and then return to Cyprus.

Eleni and Apostolis met at the Evangelismos Greek Orthodox Church in East Melbourne and later they spent some time at the Alexandra Gardens getting

to know each other. A few weeks later, they met again, this time at Eleni's sister's house where she was living. "I remember entering the lounge room with a tray of small cups with Greek coffee to serve the guests. As I approached Apostolis with his coffee, everyone turned to watch us." Shy, self-conscious and aware that everyone was looking, Apostolis picked up the small cup with trembling hands. Though he was instantly attracted to Eleni, she did not feel the same way towards him. He seemed to be shy and quiet and she didn't consider him to be handsome. Even so, she was prepared to accept her fate without hesitation. At the age of nineteen, she saw marriage as her opportunity to leave behind her dependence on her brother and his family, and an abusive relationship

between her sister and brother in law, to start her own life.

By mid 1955, Apostolis and Eleni were engaged, and were in regular contact with each other. They were married several months later, on Saturday the 15th of October, 1955 at the same Greek Orthodox church where they were first introduced.

After they were married, Eleni and Apostolis rented a room at a house in Coppin Street, Richmond. Two months later, in January 1956, they moved into their first house on the same street in Richmond. It was a solid brick, double fronted, three bedroom Victorian house that was constructed in 1887. It cost them 4,000 Australian pounds.

In 1959, Eleni and Apostolis were blessed with their first child, Theodoros followed by another son Savva (Steven) in 1961.

In 1963 Apostolis, purchased a plain sewing machine and an overlocking machine and Eleni began working from home, servicing various local factories, including a knitwear factory and the Pelaco shirt factory in Richmond. Apostolis, would collect the fabric from the factories and would later return them, once Eleni had completed her work.

In 1969, Eleni began working for the Slade Knitwear company which was also located in Richmond. She would work there until her retirement in 1988.

When asked if she regretted leaving Cyprus, Eleni said. "No, I don't regret leaving. I wanted to leave. Even though I was scared sometimes, I still felt that I wanted to leave my life in the village behind. What was I going to do there? Just work in the fields. I had no future in the village. I was saved from a life in the fields. Saved from a life of threshing and harvesting. Saved from the sickle."

Eleni's marriage to Apostolis lasted for forty years, until his sudden and unexpected death on Wednesday the 4th September, 1996.

ACKNOWLEDGEMENTS

I would like to thank Eleni Savva for allowing me to publish her story of migration. Special thanks to her son Steven Theodorou for his kind help and support.

Eleni Theodorou outside Andreas and Olga Socratous' house in Richmond, 1958.

THE CORSICA

PAPHOS

ELENI & MARIA CHRISTODOULOU

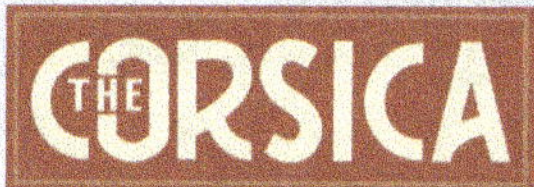

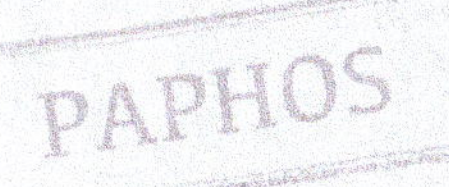

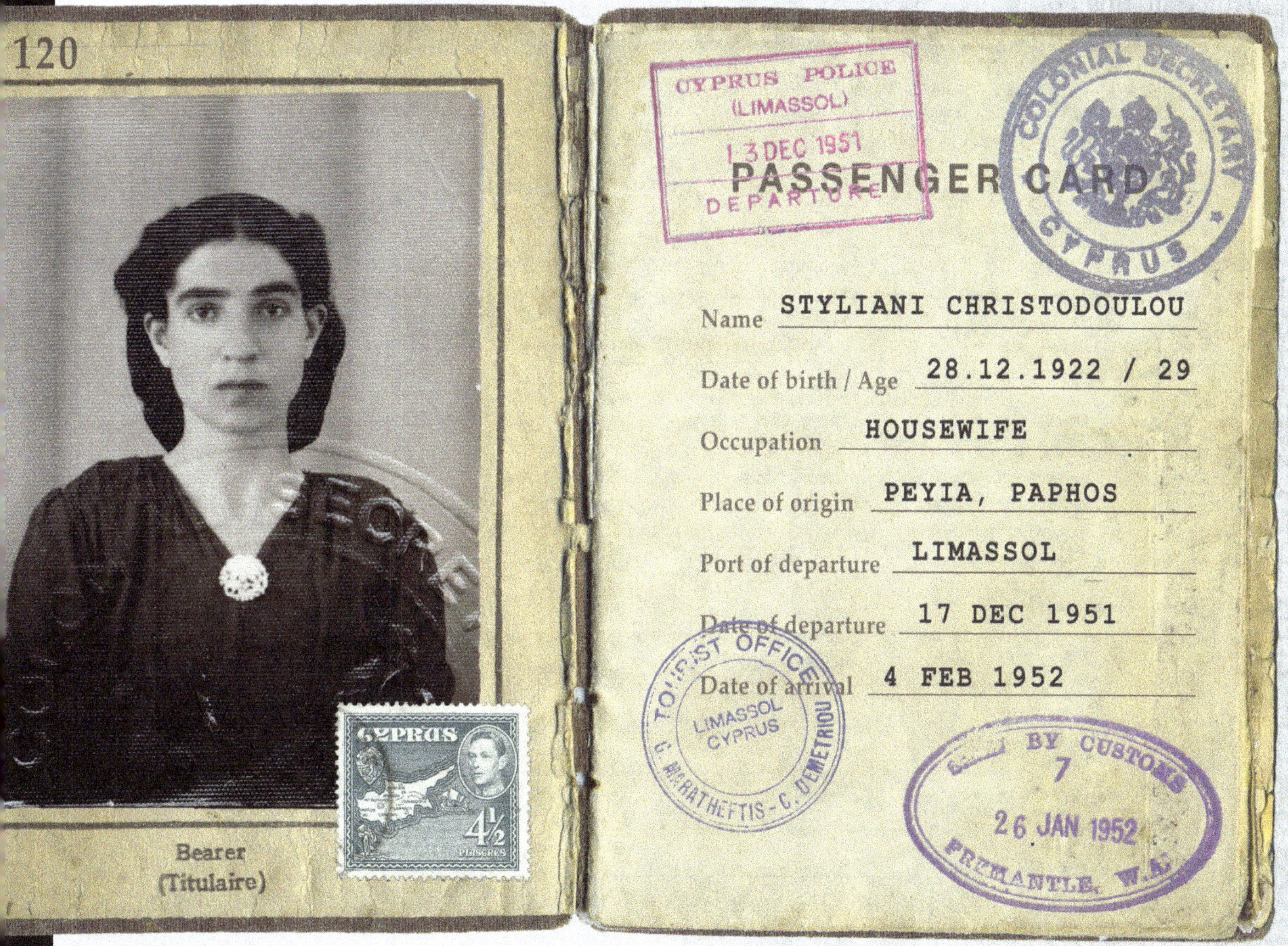

120

Bearer (Titulaire)

CYPRUS POLICE (LIMASSOL) 13 DEC 1951 DEPARTURE

COLONIAL SECRETARY CYPRUS

PASSENGER CARD

Name STYLIANI CHRISTODOULOU

Date of birth / Age 28.12.1922 / 29

Occupation HOUSEWIFE

Place of origin PEYIA, PAPHOS

Port of departure LIMASSOL

Date of departure 17 DEC 1951

Date of arrival 4 FEB 1952

TOURIST OFFICE LIMASSOL CYPRUS G. HARATHEFTIS - C. DEMETRIOU

BY CUSTOMS 7 26 JAN 1952 FREMANTLE, W.A.

Varnava and Stella Christodoulou's engagement photograph. Ktima, Paphos, May 1945.

Stella's parents, Haralambos and Eleni Hadjiharalambos with Stella as a baby. Peyia, 1923.

Eleni and Maria Christodoulou were born in the village of Peyia, Paphos. Their parents were Varnava and Stella (Styliani) Christodoulou. They were only toddlers when they left Cyprus with their mother to be reunited with their father in Australia. Eleni was five years old and her little sister Maria was only three, so it is no surprise that they do not recall the voyage itself. "All we know is what our mum told us," says Eleni. "She often spoke about the trip and how terrible it was. It's only through her stories that we know anything about the Corsica."

"It was dad's wish for us to leave Cyprus," adds Maria. "Mum didn't want to leave. Our dad was always a restless man. He wasn't one to sit still, or to stay in our village to raise his family. He liked adventure and going to Australia was a big adventure for him. Mum on the other hand, didn't want to leave Cyprus or her family. She was content to stay in the village."

Varnava Christodoulou left Cyprus by areoplane in 1949 and landed in Darwin in December that year. Like most migrants at that time, he left seeking a better life for his family. "Mum was pregnant when dad left," Maria tells me. "However, our sister Elpitha died soon after she was born. Mum had lost another child (Chrystalla) a couple of years earlier so you can imagine her heartbreak. I think that was the main reason she didn't want to leave Cyprus."

Stella's biological mother, Chrystalla died two weeks after she was born and she was adopted and raised by Haralambos and Eleni Hadjiharalambos. "Mum's adoptive father Haralambos wanted her to stay in Australia for a few years and then return to Cyprus," says Eleni. "It devastated her that she would never see him again. For most of her life, she never really settled in Australia." Maria nods in agreement. "She left Cyprus with one baby in her arms, holding the other by the hand and carrying a basket with food from the village. She never got over the fact that she left Cyprus and her adoptive parents."

Varnava Christodoulou's mother also passed away when he was quite young. His father chose not to remarry. In 1929, at the age of thirteen, Varnava left his family and village of Peyia to travel to Nicosia where he found work as a house-boy. He worked hard for many years, sending what little money he earned (outside his expenses) back to his sisters in Peyia. He was particularly close to his youngest sister Maria who was apparently the best seamstress in the village. Maria was keen to save all the money that her brother sent her to one day buy a sewing machine. Unfortunately, she was tricked by a gypsy to bury the money under a tree with the promise that it would multiply, but instead the gypsy stole the money and ran away. Maria died quite young, in her twenties; some say due to the heartbreak she suffered from losing all the money her brother had sent her.

During the Second World War, Varnava joined the Cypriot Volunteer Regiment and spent time with the British Armed Forces in a non-combative role in Palestine, Italy and Egypt. He worked as a clerk due to his knowledge of English.

In October 1945, Varnava returned to Cyprus and married Stella Hadjiharalambos who was also from Peyia. In fact, they were third cousins. He was twenty-nine and she was twenty-one.

According to Maria, her mother Stella hated the journey on the Corsica. "Mum told us that she was violently ill for most of the trip," says Maria. "So was Eleni. We stayed locked up in our cabin. Apparently I was a rather excitable child and kept running around. Poor mum was scared that I might climb up to the top deck and fall into the ocean. There were no safety barriers on the ship. Anyone could have easily slipped overboard. Thankfully, there was always a kind man who would find me running around and bring me back to our cabin. I can only imagine the fear that my mother must have felt. It must have been terrifying for her."

Maria and Eleni were too young to remember but their mother Stella had

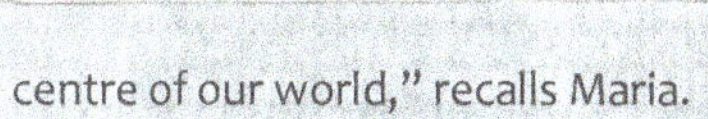

CLOCKWISE:
- Stella Christodoulou and daughters Eleni (standing) and Maria. Stella sent this photograph to Varnava in Australia. Circa 1950.
- Pilgrimage to the Monastery of Apostolos Andreas. Far right is Stella, her mother Eleni and Varnava. April, 1946.
- Family portrait in Melbourne, 1957. Left to right: Maria, Stella, Varnava and Eleni. Front: Nick, Charlie, and George.
- Varnava's passport photograph, 1949.

certainly mentioned the rotten potatoes and onions and of course, the awful stench. Their mother also mentioned the Italian food and the fact that at one point the ship had run out of fresh water. "I don't remember the journey but I do remember the day we arrived in Melbourne," recalls Maria. "I remember my dad had hired a small boat and came out to greet us while the ship was docked in the bay. He was wearing a brown suit and was throwing chocolates up at us. There were other men on the boat. After we docked, our dad took us to a house in Northcote and I remember there were biscuits on a table and balloons pinned to the walls."

Stella struggled to settle into her new homeland. She couldn't speak a word of English and she missed her family and friends in Cyprus terribly. The family soon moved into their own home in Niddrie. "Although our house was small, it had a huge backyard and open paddocks for miles around which we children made use of," says Maria. "At the end of our street there was Essendon Airport. There was no security in those days which meant we would wander around the Arrivals/ Departures lounges and the kind maintenance workers would allow us to board a TAA or ANA airplane to play in and look around."

Stella gave birth to five sons in Australia: George, Charlie, Nick, Andrew, and Peter. Due to their father working at Dunlop Rubber in Abbotsford and thus not being on hand to take Stella for hospital visits, Eleni and Maria would take it in turns to go by tram to The Queen Victoria Hospital on Lonsdale Street to be interpreters for their mother's pre-natal appointments. "Of course we would also visit the Greek shops," laughs Eleni. "Our favourite was owned by a man named Violaris. Mum would buy things like Halva, Greek newspapers, the latest 78RPM records from Greece, olive oil, etc. We would visit Yiannopoulos in Swanston Street, as well as Myer to buy sweets to take home and share together."

By late 1959 the family moved to West Sunshine to a larger house with running hot and cold water. "There were so many Cypriot people there, and of course the Church of Saint Andreas became the

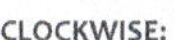

centre of our world," recalls Maria.

As the family embraced their new life in Australia there were sad times too, particularly when Stella received letters from Cyprus informing her that her parents had passed away. "Our poor mother never did get to see her parents again. The last time she saw them was in December 1951 at the Port of Limassol before she boarded the Corsica."

Varnava passed away in October, 2010, and Stella in September, 2014. They left behind a legacy that can never be broken with their seven children, ten grandchildren and seven great-grandchildren.

ACKNOWLEDGEMENTS
I would like to thank Eleni and Maria for allowing me to publish their story of migration. Special thanks to Maria's daughter, Nicole Nightingale for her kind help and support along the way.

CHRYSI GEORGIOU

CYPRUS POLICE
(LIMASSOL)
1 3 DEC 1951
DEPARTURE

PASSENGER CARD

Name   **CHRYSI GEORGIOU**

Date of birth / Age   **8.4.1928 / 23**

Occupation   **DRESSMAKER**

Place of origin   **KATHIKAS, PAPHOS**

Port of departure   **LIMASSOL**

Date of departure   **17 DEC 1951**

Date of arrival   **4 FEB 1952**

TOURIST OFFICE
LIMASSOL
CYPRUS
C. HERATHEFTIS - C. DEMETRIOU

BY CUSTOMS
7
26 JAN 1952
FREMANTLE, W.A.

Chrysi (second from left) with friends in Kathikas. May, 1948.

Chrysi in Kathikas. Circa 1946.

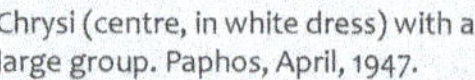
Chrysi (centre, in white dress) with a large group. Paphos, April, 1947.

C hrysi Georgiou (nee Taramidou) was born in the village of Kathikas, Paphos on the 8th of April, 1928. She was one of seven surviving children born to Georgios Taramidis and Athina Christou (six other children had died quite young). Her siblings were Kyriakou, Maria, Alexandria, Dionysios, Georgios and Galatia.

Chrysi's family were deeply religious and well respected in Kathikas. Her uncle was the village priest and played a significant role in fostering and influencing her Christian beliefs. Like most of the inhabitants in the village, Chrysi attended church every Sunday.

By all accounts, Chrysi had a blissful childhood in the village. She had plenty of friends and enjoyed more than anything, to help her mother prepare the family meals. She was close to her father Georgios too, and they would spend many hours together in the fields. His premature death in 1936, when she was only eight years old, had a profound impact on her and she suffered his loss immensely.

In 1940, after completing primary school in Kathikas, Chrysi was sent to Ktima to learn how to sew and become a dressmaker. Although her education was cut short, Chrysi's love for knowledge never waned throughout her life. She was highly intelligent and ambitious. Her brothers Dionysios and Georgios also left Kathikas after completing primary school. They were sent to Nicosia where they worked as cooks, waiters and valets for the British Governor at Government House. In 1950, they both left Cyprus and migrated to Australia.

Apparently, when Chrysi was in her late teens, she fell in love with a young man from Kathikas. Soon after they were engaged however, he contracted Tuberculosis and was sent to London for emergency treatment. After months had passed without a word, Chrysi feared the worst. Grief stricken, she left Cyprus to join her two brothers in Melbourne. In December 1951, she bid her family and friends farewell and boarded the Corsica for Australia. Little did she know at the time that she would never see her mother again. She was twenty-three and a qualified dressmaker when she left Cyprus.

On the ship, Chrysi met and shared a cabin with Eleni Savva and Catina Lambi. Eleni was sixteen and from the village of Prodromi and Catina was eighteen and from Karpaseia, a small Maronite village in the north of Cyprus. The three single women became close friends on the Corsica and they managed to help each other endure the boredom, fear and homesickness that they all shared.

When the Corsica finally berthed at Station Pier in Port Melbourne, Chrysi was greeted by her brothers Dionysios and Georgios. They took her to a small terrace home in East Brunswick where she was obliged to obey and follow their strict rules. Within a short time, she found work at a chocolate factory.

Like so many other Cypriot migrants in the 1950s, Chrysi's knowledge of English was extremely limited. At times, she would receive racist taunts from the locals if she spoke Greek with her co-workers on the tram ride home from work. When she went shopping for food, she could only point to the items she wanted. Once a butcher hit the back of her hand with his knife when he thought she was attempting to touch the meat on display.

Chrysi's hand was hurt quite badly. From that day forward, she always kept her hands close to her sides or pressed firmly against her chest whenever ordering food from a delicatessen or butcher.

Chrysi's cousins Theo and Costa Papasavvas had also migrated to Melbourne from Kathikas. Costa was married to Nitsa Tsindos however Theo was still single. Like many Cypriot bachelors in Melbourne during the 1950s, Theo spent many Saturday nights at one of the Greek cafes on Russell Street or Exhibition Street in central Melbourne. Sometime in late 1952, Costa Papasavvas arranged for his friend Antonis (Tony) Demetriou, who worked with Theo in Melbourne, to meet his cousin Chrysi.

In April 1953, Chrysi and Antonis were married at the Evangelismos Greek Orthodox Church in East Melbourne.

Antonis Demetriou was born in the village of Kili, Paphos on the 21st of August, 1929. As a young boy he was sent to work at the docks in Famagusta with his uncle who owned a successful stevedore workshop, repairing small ships and fishing vessels. By the time he was twenty, Antonis worked in plumbing and maintenance in Famagusta. He eventually left his uncle's business to set up his own together with his brother Aryiri and his Uncle Peter.

Chrysi Georgiou (middle) on board the Corsica with her two cabin friends, Eleni Savva (right) and Catina Lambi (left). January, 1952.

After Chrysi and Antonis were married, they moved into their first house on City Road in South Melbourne. They also started working together at a restaurant in St Kilda called Costa's Cafe with Chrysi's brother Dionysios (Denis) and his wife Rita, Chris and Helen Thalas and Theo Papasavva. The restaurant was located on the infamous Fitzroy Street and was open seven days a week from early morning to late at night. It was a successful business and served Mediterranean food which was new to Melbourne at that time.

In late 1955, Chrsyi gave birth to her son James. She found it difficult to juggle life as a new mother and work at the restaurant so business was sold and everyone went their separate ways.

Chrysi and Antonis eventually moved to Pascoe Vale South in 1956 where they bought a fish and chip shop which they named Tony's Fish and Chips. In April 1957, they welcomed the arrival of their second son George followed by Phivos in June 1958 and Andrew in April 1961. After Andrew was born the family moved to a residence behind the fish and chip shop on Bell Street in Pascoe Vale South.

Chrysi now spent most of her time, caring for her four sons and working in the fish and chip shop. Thankfully, her Australian neighbours were very friendly and took turns to help her out with the children. The Demetriou house in Pascoe Vale South soon became a refuge for many of their relatives who had migrated from Cyprus. Even the lounge room was converted into a bedroom to accommodate all their guests.

Chrysi was to experience her happiest moments in Melbourne during the late 1950s and 1960s. Her house was always full of friends and relatives with many parties occurring on the weekends with plenty of laughter and family fun. Her banquets and delicious home-cooked food became central to the family festivities. Chrysi and her brothers were all great cooks, having learned their culinary skills in Cyprus; Chrysi with her mother in Kathikas and Dionysios and Georgios at the British Governor's House in Nicosia. The Demetriou family also went on many picnics with relatives and friends to places such as Elwood beach, Caribbean Gardens, Bacchus Marsh and Donnybrook. When her boys went to university and began to pursue other interests, Chrysi began

Chrysi and Antonis (Tony) Demetriou at a Cypriot function in Melbourne. Circa 1956.

organising weekly card nights at her house with her friends.

In 1961, Chrysi and Antonis moved to Hawthorn and bought a second shop on Burwood Road. At the height of the credit squeeze in 1962 they sold their house and business in Hawthorn and moved back to Pascoe Vale South where they all lived in a small two-bedroom dwelling at the rear of their fish and chip shop. The boys slept in two sets of bunk beds and attended North Coburg primary school and later, Newlands High in North Coburg.

This was a very busy time for Chrysi. She would see her children off to school each morning and then work in the shop until 3pm. After school, she would be available to help the children with their homework. Even though she had difficulty with reading and understanding the words, her maths was always strong. By helping her sons with their homework, Chrysi was also able to learn English and improve her own education. Her thirst for learning and knowledge made her determined to see her sons become highly educated and go to university. Her wishes would eventually come true. James became a successful lawyer, George an accountant with his own business, Phivos a VCE teacher and coach and Andrew a successful business man owning a dental company and then becoming a successful and respected CEO of the Australian Football League.

Chrysi felt extremely proud that all of her children and grandchildren were highly educated. Her sons' interest in sport, in particular football and cricket, also brought Chrysi much enjoyment, although in the early days she would often chastise them for spending too much time playing sport with other local children in the back lanes of their neighbourhood or at the car park of the local Woolworths supermarket. Sport helped Chrysi's sons to break down many cultural barriers. They all played football and cricket at the Pascoe Vale football club and eventually James and Andrew played senior football for the Essendon and North Melbourne clubs.

In 1971, Antonis sold his fish and chip shop business and began selling real estate while Chrsyi went to work at Spicers in East Brunswick. She also attended adult education classes to improve her English, produced two outstanding and moving stories of her life and as a migrant mother and wife.

Sadly, Chrysi passed away in February 2006. She is remembered as a decent, honest and modest woman who loved and cared for her sons and was a great support to them and her husband. She was much loved by her church group and the Red Cross community in her neighbourhood. She is survived by her four sons, ten grandchildren and ten great grand children

Every year in Kathikas, little swallows would return to their nests on the western side of the stone church in the heart of the village. For many years, Chrysi and other elders who had migrated abroad, would return to the village each summer to be reunited. They became known as the *helithonia* (the swallows) of Kathikas. These days, the elders still come together to remember with sorrow, Chrysi Georgiou - the great daughter of Kathikas – for her soul will always be there.

ACKNOWLEDGEMENTS
I would like to thank the Demetriou brothers for allowing me to publish their mother's story of migration. Special thanks to James Demetriou for his kind help and support along the way.

A group of male passengers on board the Corsica en route to Australia. Most of the passengers wore their best clothes during the voyage. December, 1951.

Iacovos Christodoulou is standing at the front on the right and Louis Kyriacou is second from the left.

PAPHOS

IACOVOS CHRISTODOULOU

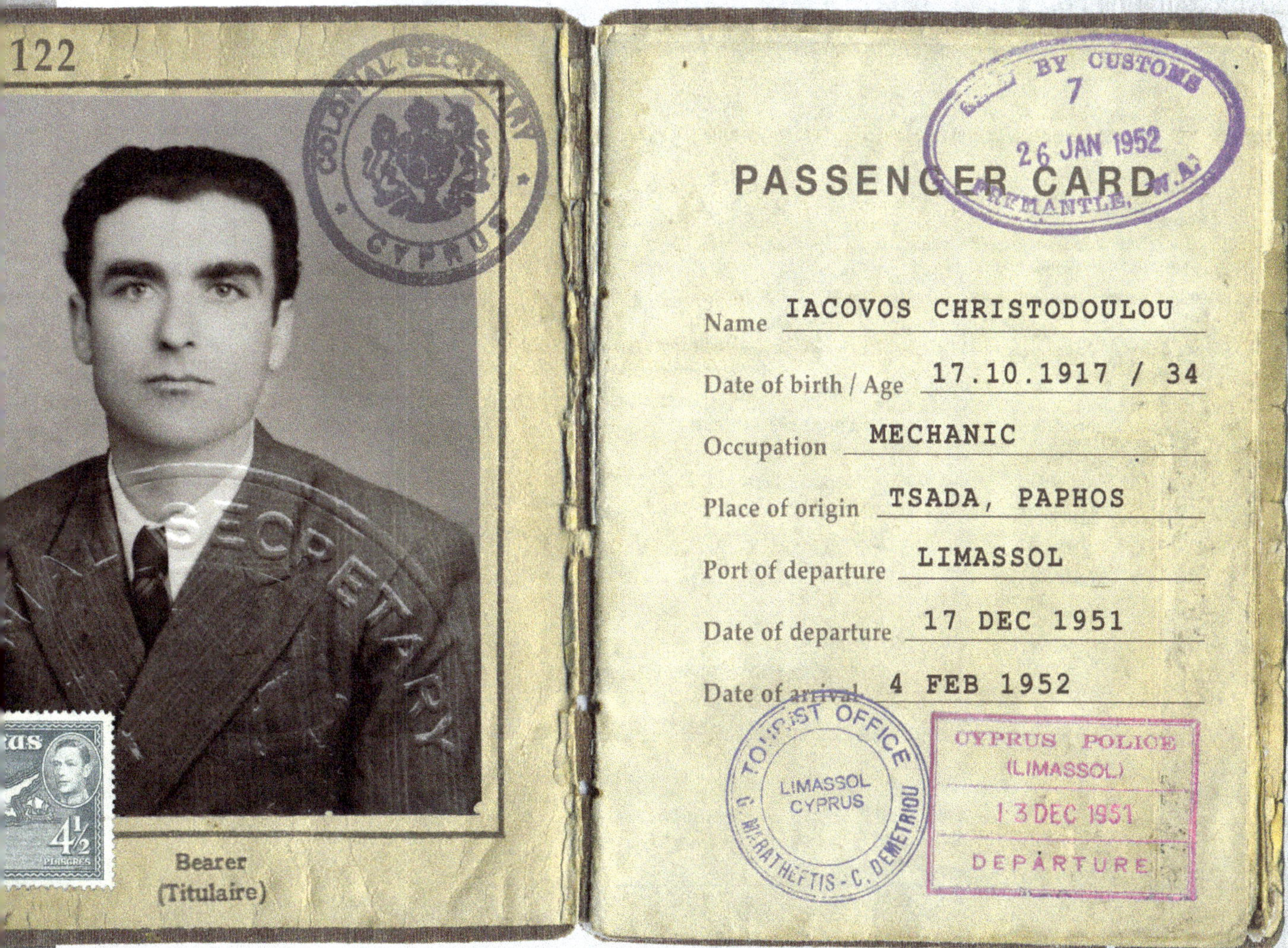

Kyriakoula (centre) with two friends. Komi Kebir, Famagusta. Circa 1949.

Iacovos Christodoulou was born in Tsada, Paphos on the 17th of October, 1917. He was the eldest of four children born to Christos and Kleoniki Makarounas. His siblings were Socrates, Vasiliki, and Georgios.

Iacovos attended primary school until the fifth grade. He was then sent to train as an apprentice for a few years and to learn how to become a skilled engine mechanic for flour mills. In his teenager years he would travel around Cyprus on his motorcycle with his bag of tools installing, repairing and running the diesel engines for a number of village flour mills. In fact, that is how he met his wife Kyriakoula Piera. He visited her father in the village of Komi Kebir in Famagusta until a marriage was organised with his daughter. Kyriakoula was eleven years younger than Iacovos.

Iacovos and Kyriakoula were married in 1949. Their son Louis was born the following year.

When his first cousin (Loukas Neofytou) migrated to Australia in February 1951, Iacovos was inspired to do the same. He decided to travel alone (without his wife and son) to see if Australia was as good as his cousin had told him. If Australia did indeed live up to all stories and assumptions made, then he would arrange for his wife and son to join him there. Kyriakoula's brother Pieris Piera agreed to travel with him.

"At the age of thirty-two, my father was one of the older passengers on the Corsica," his daughter Nicki tells me. "He took on more of a father figure role, looking after the mostly single and young Cypriot passengers, especially when they disembarked to explore the ports along the way. In Djibouti for instance, he was forced to intervene after some of the locals tried to rob them. He shouted at the would-be thieves in Greek and chased them away. By far, the worst thing that my father experienced on the Corsica, was the smell of rotting onions and potatoes. It

En route to Australia. Unknown location. Iacovos is second from the left. January, 1952.

was disgusting. No one could eat because they were so sick and overcome by the smell. He also mentioned that the fresh water on the ship had run out, so when they reached Colombo they would try to buy water there. He felt ripped off and became quite annoyed at the terrible situation they all faced on that ship. He just kept thinking, when will this trip end? When will we reach Australia? It just went on and on and on."

Once he arrived, Iacovos soon realised that Australia may not suit his wife after all, especially considering the lifestyle she was accustom to in Cyprus. Apart from a clash of cultures, there was also the language barrier to overcome. He wrote to Kyriakoula stating that perhaps it was best for her to remain in Cyprus and he would return to her after working for a few more months.

Kyriakoula however, wanted to be with her husband and to be reunited as a family. Being only twenty years old, she felt vulnerable without him. In 1953, she packed

Three passengers on the Corsica. December, 1951.

Iacovos (with hat) and Kyriakoula (holding beer bottle) entertaining their friends at their Charles Street home in Fitzroy. Circa 1955.

her bags and together with her young son Louis, left Cyprus to join Iacovos in Australia.

"Initially my parents struggled to find accommodation in Melbourne," says Nicki. "No one wanted to rent a room to a migrant couple with a child. When they eventually found a place, the landlord was so strict that he told my mum to make sure my brother Louis remained seated or on the bed at all times. He was not allowed to walk around the house. It was really awful."

Kyriakoula's brother Pieris helped her and Iacovos with the deposit to buy their first house at Charles Street in Fitzroy. "The house had four bedrooms," explains Nicki. "My parents and brother would stay in one bedroom while they rented the other three bedrooms to other migrants. It became like a boarding house in the end. On Saturday nights, my father would invite all his friends to our house for a party, especially any new arrivals. They would catch up with all the news from Cyprus, and then eat, sing and dance. My mum would do all the washing and cooking and my father would entertain his friends. It was common for my parents to extend their hospitality to their Cypriot friends and family or any new comers from Cyprus. Their hospitality was always reciprocated, so there were always somewhere to go every weekend."

"But not all migrants looked out for each other in the 1950s," adds Nicki. "My parents often spoke of some unfortunate experiences. For instance, one time my mum was struggling to communicate with a shop keeper at a milk bar in Fitzroy. There was a local Greek man in the shop who could speak English but he refused to translate for my mum unless she paid him first."

In 1957, Iacovos and Kyriakoula welcomed the birth of their daughter Cleonicki (Nicki) followed by another son, Chris in 1962. In September 1965, the family moved to their Malvern East home and then to their new house in Bentleigh East in 1972.

Iacovos worked at General Motors Holden for twenty years mainly as an engine tester on the assembly line at Fishermans Bend. In 1978, he was forced to retire early due to illness. He was very proud to have received a gold watch from the company in recognition of his services.

Kyriakoula worked at the Jam Factory for a while before being trained on the overlocker machine for a number of clothing factories in Fitzroy. "The whole rag-trade industry in Melbourne was established on the backs of migrant women like my mother," says Nicki.

Like most Cypriot men who had migrated to Australia during the 1950s, Iacovos enjoyed visiting the Greek club on Russell Street to meet his fellow compatriots. He would visit on Sundays and mix with the early migrants and new arrivals from Cyprus, relishing any news from the homeland.

He also enjoyed getting up before the dawn to go hunting with other Cypriot migrants including his brothers-in-law Pieris and Petrakis.

"My parents were very proud of their achievements in Australia," Nicki exclaims. "They embarked on an unknown journey with a hope of a better life for themselves and their children. They were very happy and grateful for the friendships they had formed and maintained over the years. Perhaps this is a story that resonates with all migrants who are searching for a better future."

Iacovos passed away in November 2001 at the age of eighty-four.

ACKNOWLEDGEMENTS

I would like to thank Cleonicki (Nicki) Rowse for allowing me to publish her father's story of migration and for her kind help and support along the way.

Iacovos at the GMH plant. Fishermans Bend, Melbourne. Circa 1958.

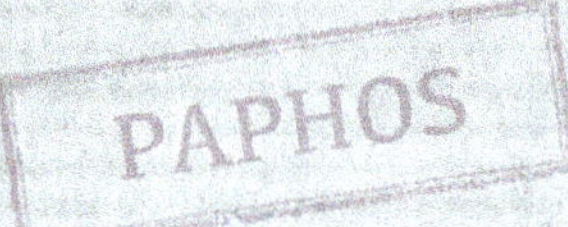

ANDREAS SAVVA

Andreas Savva was born in the village of Choli, Paphos on the 30th of September, 1924. His father Savvas (known as Saouris) was forty-five years old when Andreas was born and his mother Christina was thirty-eight. Andreas was the first of their children to survive beyond childhood. His older siblings had died in infancy or at an early age, most likely from Thalassemia. Andreas' younger siblings were Eleni (born in 1929) and Pavlou (born in 1934).

The village of Choli was small, remote and poor and at the time, had a population of around twenty-four families.

After completing third grade, Andreas was taken out of school so he could help his parents earn a living. He worked long hours each day ploughing the fields that belonged to other villagers, or breaking rocks to help build new roads. It was back-breaking work for a child aged ten and Andreas would suffer chronic back pain for the rest of his life.

Andreas married Elpiniki Nicolaou on the 10th of October, 1947. For their *prika* (dowry), her parents gave them four fields, three mud brick houses, a mill to grind the grains, one cow, one donkey and one goat. The day after their wedding, when the sheets were inspected and Elpiniki's goodness was revealed, they received another mud brick house. Andreas wasn't concerned about receiving any dowry. He often stated that he would have married Elpiniki as she was.

In February 1949, Andreas and Elpiniki welcomed the birth of their son Steve followed by their daughter Niki a year later in February 1950. Soon after Niki was born they were sitting at a *kafenion* in the neighbouring village of Goudi listening to some of the local men discussing a newspaper article about how Australia was looking for migrants. Elpiniki turned to her husband and said, 'Andreas, you should apply'. Several of her relatives had immigrated to other countries seeking a better life and she was anxious to follow their example. Besides, she knew her husband was earning a reputation for expressing strong anti-British views and she feared that one day, he might end up in jail or worse, get himself killed. 'Would you go to Australia?' Andreas asked his wife. 'Yes, yes,' came her swift reply. They both realised it was far better (and safer) to confront the challenges of a foreign country, with its alien culture and

Andreas and Elpiniki Savva with their children Niki and Steve. Taken in a Paphos photographic studio a few days before Andreas boarded the Corsica bound for Australia. December, 1951.

Andreas Savva's parents Savvas and Christina and their granddaughter Christina. Paphos, 1958.

language than to remain in Cyprus and suffer the consequences of a harsh economic and uncertain future.

Andreas went to see a lawyer in the town of Ktima named Nikos Koundoros, who helped him fill out his applications for a visa and a passport. Months went by without word and he began to lose hope. He feared that his left-wing political alliances were responsible for the delay. He began to tour the churches lighting candles and praying, including the monastery of Apostolos Andreas. Eventually he went back to breaking rocks for building roads. People began to say that the lawyer had robbed him and it served him right for thinking that he and Elpiniki could break free of their destiny. Then, one night, the Virgin Mary appeared to him in a dream requesting that he go to her church and light a candle in her honour. He obliged and within a week, his visa arrived. Andreas believed it was a miracle.

In December 1951, Andreas bid his wife and two children goodbye and together with his good friend Charalambos Theophanous, they boarded the dilapidated ship Corsica in Limassol bound for Australia. Andreas was twenty-seven years old. On the day that he left, it was said that the howls of his father could be heard in the next village and he was seen beating his head against a tree trunk in grief. Perhaps Saouris knew that he would never see his son again.

When Andreas arrived at Station Pier in February 1952, he looked down from the ship, but could not see anyone he recognised. Suddenly, he heard someone calling out his name. *'Andreas, ella kato'* (Andreas, come down). It was Panayioti Krassaris, his second cousin. Panayioti took Andreas to a grand old mansion in Essendon that belonged to Savvas Krassaris, who had migrated to Melbourne in 1924. Savvas and Saouris were first cousins and he agreed to sponsor Andrea's migration to Australia. It was quite common for the early migrants like Panayioti and Savvas Krassaris to visit Station Pier frequently in the hope that they might see friends or relatives arriving from their homeland. Panayioti was aware the Corsica was due to dock sometime in late January and early February so he would go to the pier frequently in the hope of meeting his cousin and any other countrymen.

Within a short while, Andreas found a job at the General Motors Holden (GMH) plant at Fishermens Bend where he was required to open up large crates full of car parts. Eager to fit in, he made every effort to socialise with the other workers at the plant. He played cricket with the Aussies, and became a hero one day when he stuck out his hand and caught the ball. His action had won the match, and he was rewarded with beers.

Like some other migrants, Andreas was seduced by the allure of the racetrack and he soon began to gamble away his salary. Unfortunately, he never knew when to stop. One day when he was at the Moonee Valley racecourse, he managed to win an astonishing 800 pounds by the second-last race. In those days, that was equivalent to a year's salary. In one almighty expression of faith however, Andreas bet all of his winnings on the last race and lost it all. Unable to afford the bus fare home, he was forced to walk the four miles from Moonee Ponds to Carlton. One can only imagine just how depressed and dejected he must have felt.

Two years had passed since Andreas had left Cyprus and Elpiniki's father was losing patience and becoming anxious and suspicious. He warned his daughter not to expect Andreas to return to Cyprus or to send for her and that she should divorce him. He pledged to find her another husband. But Andreas had not forgotten his wife and children. In fact, he would often cry at family gatherings and functions in Melbourne because he missed his family so much. In an act of kindness, his cousin Panayioti lent him the money to pay for their tickets and bring them to Australia.

In the summer of 1954, Elpiniki gathered her two children and luggage and prepared to leave Cyprus to be reunited with her husband in Australia. As she closed the door to her tiny house in Choli she began to feel apprehensive. Clutching a child in each hand, she farewelled her brother Georgios, who had taken her to the port in Limassol, and boarded the vessel which was to take her to Beirut to link up with the ship Cyrenia for the voyage to Melbourne. She had only left her village a handful of times in her life and here she was leaving her country, her family, and everything familiar behind. What was she thinking? She relaxed slightly in Beirut after staying in a hotel and eating the best bean casserole she had ever tasted.

The Cyrenia arrived in Melbourne on a beautiful, sunny winter morning in July 1954. When Elpiniki could not see Andreas on the dock, she returned to her cabin devastated and crying. Perhaps her father's warnings were correct after all. She decided she was going to stay on the ship and return to Cyprus. Her son Steven however remained on deck looking out for his father. Moments later, he rushed excitedly back to the cabin, alerting his distraught mother that he had seen his father waiting below. Andreas was wearing the same coat he had worn when he had left the village and young Steven had recognised it and his father. The family reunion was bittersweet. Nicki was wary of her father. He was a stranger to her, and she would hide whenever he approached her.

Andreas and Elpiniki welcomed the birth of two more daughters; Christina in July 1955 and Maria in March 1957. Sadly, Maria died before she turned two and Christina was diagnosed with Thalassemia Major, a life-threatening form of anaemia.

The language barrier was a constant source of frustration for Andreas and Elpiniki, especially when trying to communicate with doctors. Even at home Andreas would fly into a rage if he suspected that Nicki was using English to poke fun at him. Once when she said, 'leave me alone, willya,' he yelled back, 'who is this willya?' He thought it was a disparaging remark. Elpiniki also struggled without English. If she needed eggs, she would take eggshells down to the corner milk bar to show the shop keeper.

Before Maria died, Elpiniki joined Andreas at GMH. Although he was uncomfortable about his wife working, Andreas knew he had no choice, especially with four children to look after - two of them with a serious illness. Australia did not have a public health-care system in those days. Elpiniki was twenty-nine when she started work, and she felt like her life was over. She had left Cyprus because she did not want to work on the farms and here she was on the assembly line at the GMH plant drilling holes into bits of metal. 'I am too old for this,' she would often tell people.

In time, Andreas and his family settled into their new life in Australia. Andreas turned his backyard into a market garden, filling it with fruit trees and vegetables while Elpiniki ensured that the interior of their house displayed elements of their Cypriot culture, especially the lounge room and kitchen. She would regularly bless the house by burning incense and dried olive leaves in a small urn. On Saturday afternoons, the children would go to local cinema to watch American movies. In fact, the Saturday matinees became a critical part of their English tuition. They also played games with the other local children in the street. Steven was eventually enrolled in primary school and his sister Nicki went to kindergarten in Carlton.

ACKNOWLEDGEMENTS

I would like to thank Steve Savva for allowing me to publish his father's story of migration and for his kind support along the way. Special thanks to his sister Niki for letting me paraphrase sections from her book 'So Greek'.

CHRISTODOULOS APEITOS

PASSENGER CARD

Name **CHRISTODOULOS APEITOS**

Date of birth / Age **24.1.1924 / 27**

Occupation **DRIVER**

Place of origin **AGROS, LIMASSOL**

Port of departure **LIMASSOL**

Date of departure **17 DEC 1951**

Date of arrival **4 FEB 1952**

C hristos (Christodoulos) Apeitos was born on the 24th of January, 1924 in the village of Agros, Limassol. He was the youngest of seven children born to Yiannis Georgiou Apeitos and Angeliki Nicolaou. "My mother was only fifteen when she married my father back in 1899. He was twenty years older than her. She had actually given birth to twelve children but sadly five of them died as infants because of illness and disease. That was quite common in those days."

In the 1930's Christos' father Yiannis worked at the Amiantos asbestos mine. The English-owned company employed over 5000 people at one time, attracting workers from many mountainous villages around Troodos. "People were never idle in those days," Christos tells me. "Everybody worked, from six years old to eighty". During his childhood, Christos accompanied his parents in the fields watering and looking after their crops.

When Christos turned twelve, he was sent to live with his older brother Nicholas in Nicosia with a view of attending night-school. He soon found work as an assistant at a *pantopoleio* (grocery store) in the main marketplace. "I remember there was a *jami* (mosque) close to the

Best friends, Christos Polycarpou (left) and Christos Apeitos. Melbourne, 1954.

shop where I worked and every day the *Hodja* (Holy man) would come to our shop to buy various things."

Christos taught himself how to ride a bicycle and he soon became the store's main delivery boy. "My job was to deliver food products to customers all over Nicosia. I didn't get paid but I was provided with free accommodation and all my meals. I worked at this grocery store for five years. On my last day, my boss gave me an envelope with eight pounds in it. Can you believe it? After five years of service I was only paid eight pounds."

In 1942, Christos and his friends Marinos and Giorgios agreed to join the Cypriot Volunteer Regiment for the British Armed Forces. His friends however, went ahead and enlisted without him. Feeling abandoned, Christos returned to Nicosia where he found work as a waiter in a tavern on Ermou Street.

In late October 1950, Christos was introduced to Antigone Symeou by his good friend Christos Polycarpou, who was Antigone's cousin. Antigone soon discovered that the two friends were getting ready to leave Cyprus. "It was a very quick meeting," said Christos. "We talked for a little while and then I told her I was leaving for Australia in two months. 'Take me with you', she said all of a

sudden. I was surprised to hear her say that. I'm not sure why she said it but I can tell you, it left a lasting impression on me. I told her that once I was settled in Australia I will write to her."

In December 1951, Christos Apeitos and his friend Christos Polycarpou left Cyprus for Australia. "Polycarpou left on a different ship called the Ravello and I left on the Corsica," says Christos. "I can't remember why we didn't leave on the same ship. Well, as it turned out the Ravello arrived one month earlier than the Corsica. That shows you how old and slow the Corsica was. As I recall, it was an old renovated and converted battleship. There were about a thousand Cypriots on board, and a few hundred men and women from various Greek islands. There were four of us from Agros. I remember we arrived at Limassol harbour on the 12th of December expecting to board the ship but there was a delay and there was no ship to board. It was the holy feast day of Agios Spyridon. Everyone had to find a place to stay in Limassol overnight. Those who had relatives went to stay with them. Others rented rooms at various hotels. Those from Agros, stayed with the Christostomos family. The next day the harbour staff ferried the passengers out to sea using small boats so we could board the Corsica. There was no pier in those days. Once we were on board the ship, we remained there until the 17th of December I think. About five days. I'm not sure why there was such a delay. If they told us, I can't remember. We were told by the shipping agent in Limassol that the ship

Christos and Antigone's official wedding photograph. Melbourne, May 1955.

had swimming pools, theatres, everything, but there was nothing like that. Yes, there was a pool on the ship, but it was empty – there was no water in it. Some people say that because the travel agent had so many Cypriots anxious to leave Cyprus, he was forced to find any old ship that could transport them to Australia. That's how he came to book the Corsica."

Before he left Cyprus, Christos bought a bag of lemons. "I was told that if I sucked on the lemons I wouldn't feel seasick. I tried this and it worked. I didn't feel seasick. I remember sitting on the deck next to one of the captains and we had a pleasant conversation. We sat together talking for quite a few hours. Although the majority of the crew were Italian, the captains were all Greek so we could talk to them. I remember that when we stopped at Port Said in Egypt, two boys sneaked onto the ship. Stowaways. I think they were Greek. Anyway, the Corsica was one of the last ships to pass through Port Said at that time because of the Suez Crisis and Coup that took place in Egypt in 1952."

Christos believes that the potatoes that were stored in the hull, began to rot after the Corsica reached Africa. "That's when we started to smell the potatoes. It was after we arrived at Massawa. I remember the ship had to stop at each port for repairs and fuel. Apparently, it was damaged during the Second World War and it was never repaired. We were lucky we didn't sink. We all slept down below in a narrow space. We had bunk beds. I remember in the opposite bunk was Halloumos and Vroullias. We were all from Agros. I remember when we were disembarking at the port in Colombo, there was a mother with her young daughter who lost her footing and they both fell in the water, waist high. Some of the crew jumped in the water and helped them back onto the gangway. It was lucky that no one drowned that day."

Christos did not forget Antigone. Their fateful meeting on a dark street in Nicosia kept playing over and over in his mind. In 1954, he finally sent her a proposal for marriage. Antigone immediately sought her father's approval. At first, her father Symeon, was not very happy at the prospect of sending his daughter to the other side of the world to get married. He did, however, know that the Apeitos family from Agros were well respected and this was enough for him to give his consent. Antigone wrote to Christos in Melbourne stating that she would indeed marry him. He was working for the Country Roads Board at the time and once he received her reply he decided to move back to Melbourne to look for a house to buy. "I had to find a house," he tells me. "I couldn't let her come and meet me in the bush." At the time Christos was working at Eildon to build the dam that would become the Eildon Weir.

On the 6th of January, 1955, Antigone arrived in Melbourne on the SS Neptunia. She was twenty-three years old. Christos was there to greet her and took her to his newly acquired home in the south-eastern suburb of Oakleigh. They were married on the 1st of May, 1955 at Evangelismos Church in East Melbourne. The wedding reception was held at their house in Oakleigh with over two hundred guests in attendance.

Christos and Antigone were blessed with three children; Yiannis (John) born in 1956, Polixeni (Pauline) born in 1957 and Giorgios (George) born in 1960.

Christos had left his job at the Country Roads Board and went to work at Elmaco in Carnegie which manufactured plastic electrical parts. The factory was owned by two Jewish brothers. Before their first child was born, Antigone would join him there. "I couldn't believe it," she exclaims. "I was earning ten pounds and four shillings a week. Back in Cyprus when I was caring for my sick uncle, I was paid six pounds a month and that was considered a lot of money in those days." Antigone was also shocked to discover that in Australia she was only required to work forty hours a week and her weekends were free to do as she pleased.

When asked if he had any regrets about leaving Cyprus to settle in Australia, Christos smiles and says. "None at all. I've had a good life here. Especially after Antigone agreed to come here to marry me. No, no - Australia has been good to me and my family."

ACKNOWLEDGEMENTS
I would like to thank Christos Apeitos for allowing me to publish his story of migration. Special thanks to his sons, George and John for their kind help and support and to Antigone for her wonderful Cypriot hospitality and her delicious home-made treats.

Christos Apeitos standing on the left with his work colleagues outside a factory in Leveson Street, North Melbourne which manufactured stainless steel tanks for storing milk.

LIMASSOL

NICOS
JONIS

PASSENGER CARD

Name **NICOLAS JONIS**

Date of birth / Age **20.9.1934 / 17**

Occupation **STUDENT**

Place of origin **AGROS, LIMASSOL**

Port of departure **LIMASSOL**

Date of departure **17 DEC 1951**

Date of arrival **4 FEB 1952**

Nicos' parents, Savvas and Christina in Agros. Year unknown.

left Limassol bound for Australia. I remember Limassol was full of people, and it was raining quite a lot. My father knew someone who owned a hotel so we stayed there for one night. The next day on the 13th, the Corsica finally arrived and was anchored about a mile out of port. My father and I hugged and said goodbye. It was very emotional. How could I know that it would be another twenty years before I would see my parents again? Thank God they were still alive. I know many migrants who were not so lucky – their parents had died by the time they returned to Cyprus. Like I said, we were allowed to board the ship on the 13th of December but we just sat there, in the ocean, outside Limassol for four days. I remember I could see the mountains of Troodos in the distance, all covered in snow. Thank God, I had company with me. There was Christos Apeitos and two others men from my village."

Nicos does not recall much about the journey itself only that he ate oysters in Colombo for the first time. "I didn't like them, but after I came to Australia I loved them."

Once Nicos stepped off the Corsica onto Station Pier at Port Melbourne, his uncle Christos Violaris was there to greet him.

Nicos Jonis was born on the 20th September, 1934 in the village of Agros. His parents were Savvas Jonis and Christina Violaris and his siblings were Maria and Haralambos. Nicos' father owned one of the six coffee houses in the village. He was also a butcher and blacksmith.

When he was seventeen, Nicos was sent to Australia to live with his mother's brother Christos Violaris. "My Uncle Christos had been living in Australia since 1924 and initially he wanted my sister Maria to come to Australia for a better life. My parents didn't want my sister to leave Cyprus so they sent me instead. But I have no regrets."

Nicos remembers the day he left the village with immense clarity. "It was Wednesday the 12th of December which was the holy feast day of Ayios Spyridon. We attended church in the morning and then set out for the Port of Limassol. When we arrived, the Corsica wasn't there. The ship hadn't arrived yet. Another ship named the Ravello had just

Nicos Jonis at Colombo Zoo. January, 1952.

ABOVE:
A group of migrants posing with the priest of the Greek Orthodox Church (Saints Constantine and Helen) in Djibouti. Nicos Jonis is standing second from the left. On his left is Andreas Malais and the woman squatting on the far right is Chrysi Georgiou. Sunday the 30th of December, 1951.

INSET:
Somewhere in Djibouti. Christos Apeitos is on the far left next to Nicos Jonis. Sunday the 30th of December, 1951.

LEFT:
From left to right: Frixos Violaris, Amalia Violaris, Christos Violaris, Eleni Violaris and Nicos Jonis. Sitting at the front Christos' house in West Brunswick, Melbourne, 1954.

LEFT:
Outside Evangelismos Church in East Melbourne, 1955. From left to right: Nicos Christofi, Nicos Chartas, Christos Apeitos, Theo Violaris, Nicos Jonis and Andreas Malais.

BELOW:
Standing from left to right: Chrysoulla Maros, Amalia Violaris, Christos Violaris, Voni Panos, and Maria Violaris. Front Frixos Violaris and Nicos Jonis. Halpin Street, West Brunswick, Melbourne, 1954.

Christos Violaris was born in 1904 in the village of Agros. He was the youngest of four siblings including Nicos' mother. He had migrated to Melbourne in 1924, when he was twenty. "Everyone knew my uncle," says Nicos. "He was very well respected in Melbourne. After I arrived I went to live with him at his West Brunswick house. I even worked at his *pakaliko* (grocery store and delicatessen) which was located on Lonsdale Street, opposite Saint Francis Church. I remember he paid me around three pounds a week. My uncle had the first Greek *pakaliko* in Melbourne. All the Cypriot and Greek migrants would shop there during the 1950s. It was the only place you could buy traditional Greek food and ingredients. I really had a good time in Melbourne during the 1950s. I was young and had plenty of company. One of the highlights of my life was going to the opening and closing ceremony of the Olympic Games in 1956."

A year after he arrived, Nicos was conscripted for national service with the Australian Army and was stationed at the Puckapunyal Army Camp near Seymour.

Nicos worked with his uncle at his grocery store for eight years. He then found work as a waiter at Hotel Cecil and later at the Capers restaurant on Collins Street. "I made more money in tips than in wages in those days. I then ventured into my own business. First I had a cafe and hamburger shop in Sunshine called Dagwoods Den and then I opened a cafe

in East Melbourne, next to the Greek Orthodox Church called Lansdowne Coffee Lounge, right there on Lansdowne Street. I was there for twenty-five years."

Nicos married Arete Tsouna on the 22nd of August, 1964 and together they have two children; Sam born in 1965 and Christina in 1969.

"I only have one regret in coming to Australia," Nicos tells me with a sigh. "I regret that it took me twenty years to go to Cyprus to see my mother."

ACKNOWLEDGEMENTS

I would like to thank Nicos Jonis for allowing me to publish his story of migration and for his kind support.

Studio photograph of Nicos and wife Arete after their engagement in 1963.

Nicos and Arete with their children Sam and Christina. Venus Studio on Russell Street in Melbourne, 1973.

OLGA ANGELLIS

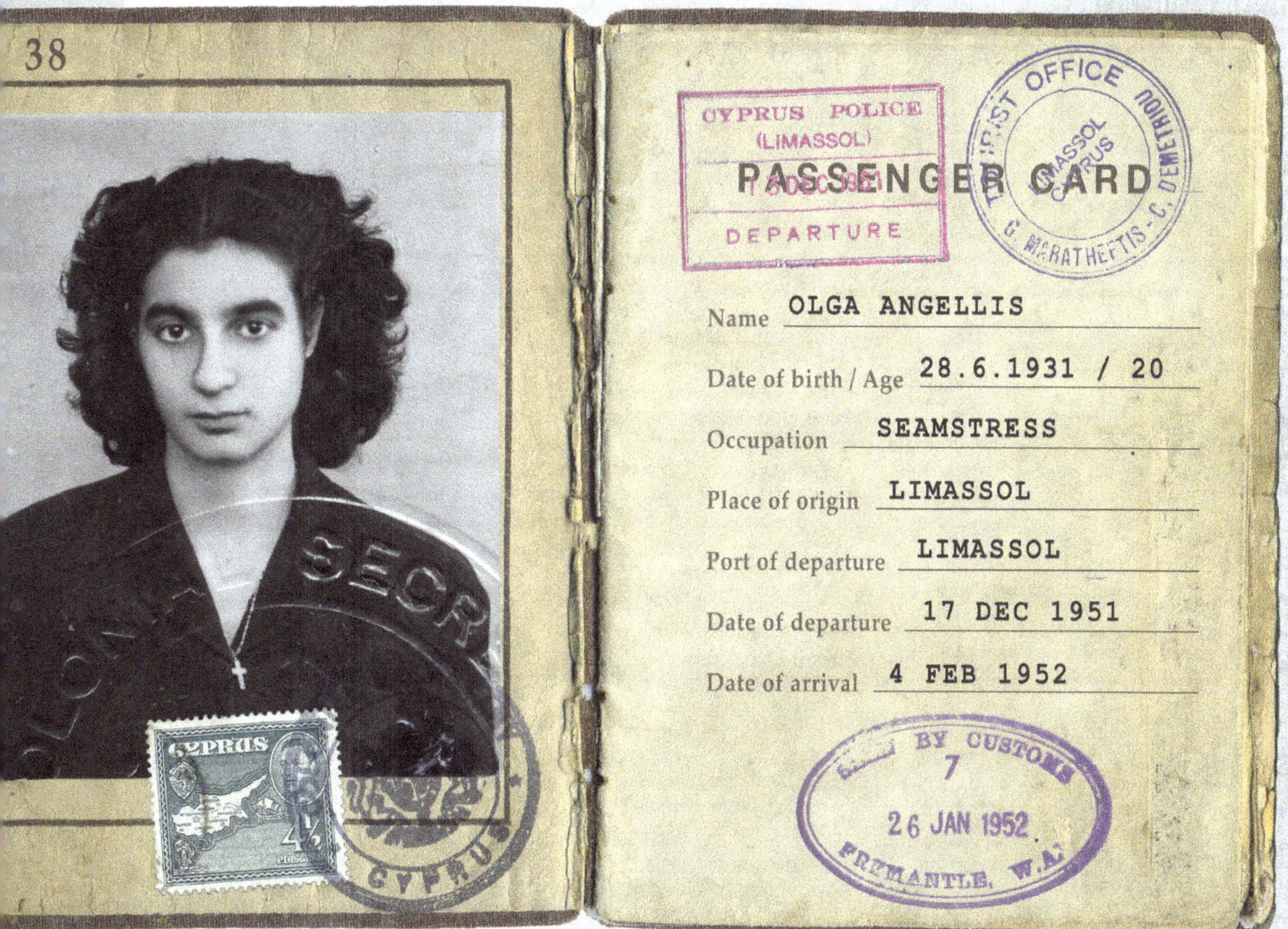

Olga was born in Limassol town on the 28th of June, 1931. She was twenty years old when she travelled with her mother Anna on the Corsica. Her father Constantinos Angellis had migrated to Australia in 1948. He worked as a baker in Limassol. After sustaining a serious injury to his leg pulling a heavy bread cart, he made the decision to leave Cyprus and travel to Australia to establish a new life before sending for his family to join him three years later. "After I finished high school, I had a chance to go and study in Athens," Olga tells me. "I had won a scholarship, you see. My mother however, wrote to my father to ask for his permission. He became very upset and told my mother that unless we both came to Australia he would not send us any more money or see us again. So you see, my parents managed to convince me to leave Cyprus with a promise that I could go and study at a university in Melbourne."

Olga's life in Cyprus had been a happy one. She enjoyed her school years and was an intelligent and successful student. She was surrounded by her family and friends and the security this provided. She was infatuated with one of the local boys and also recalls watching the handsome British soldiers who were stationed in Cyprus during the war. It was therefore, with sadness and regret that she left this life behind to come to Australia.

Olga and her mother stayed in a cabin on the Corsica. "We were down below near the potatoes and onions," she says. "The ship was full of potatoes and onions on their way to Australia. There were other people in our cabin, I can't remember how many but they were very nice. I remember a lot of people were complaining about the stench on the ship." Olga also recalls the dining room where the food was served. It was like a cafeteria. They served strange food, not the Greek food to which the passengers were accustomed. She remembers people playing games on board the ship such as cards and billiards. The atmosphere was buoyant and people were hopeful and looking forward to their new lives in Australia.

One day as Olga was sitting on the deck of the ship with her mother getting some fresh air, she noticed a man sitting nearby looking at her. "My mother noticed that he was looking at me, that he was admiring me and decided to talk to him.

Studio photograph of Olga in Limassol. Circa 1949.

We discovered that his name was Costas Anastassiades and he was from Morphou. He was on his way to Australia to study. When we arrived at Port Said my mother asked me to go ashore with Costas. I wanted to stay on the ship but my mother insisted that I should get to know him. When another couple agreed to come with us, I consented and we all left the ship and went ashore to a restaurant. I remember Costas ordered brains and he paid for everyone's meals."

"I knew from the start that he liked me. He wouldn't leave our side. He always wanted to be around me and my mother. There were other men from his village on the ship but he preferred to stay with us to be close to me. When we first boarded the Corsica, my mother wouldn't let me out of her sight. She wanted me to always stay with her. She was very protective of me. I think because I was her only child. But after she met Costas, she allowed me to go out with him a few times on the ship. However, I also remember my mother warning me to be a good girl as she did not want me to get into any trouble."

When they arrived in Melbourne, Olga's father Constantinos was there to greet them and take them back to his house in Richmond. "I couldn't believe it. My mother persuaded Costas to stay with us in our house in Richmond. He didn't have anywhere to stay. I was upset with my mother for a while. She had told my father that Costas was interested in me.

Costas would sometimes knock on my bedroom door and whisper, 'Olga, how are you today. Come out and get some fresh air.' He was a gentleman. He never tried to do anything. He was caring and ambitious and I liked that about him. I had plans to go to university to study domestic science but Costas wanted to marry me. I finally agreed to his proposal and we were married on the 11th of September in 1952. Our daughter Elpida was born in 1956 and our son Christopher was born seven years later in 1963."

Olga's husband eventually became a station master in Melbourne. Later he and Olga owned a couple of fruit shops. They managed one each, Olga in Hartwell, and Costas in Ringwood. They made a good, hard-working team and were successful in this venture. Costas went on to become a taxi driver and Olga worked at Sportscraft, a clothing factory in Hawthorn. She became passionate about workers' rights and fair pay. She eventually became the shop steward and worked tirelessly to improve the working conditions of employees. One of her strongest memories is meeting the Prime Minister, Paul Keating and expressing her views to him about what she perceived were the problems with the textile industry's treatment of workers.

Overall, Olga's life in Australia had its ups and downs. She has lived a full life, surrounded by her two children, six grandchildren and at the time of writing, one great grandchild.

She never returned to Cyprus.

ACKNOWLEDGEMENTS

I would like to thank Olga Angellis for allowing me to publish her story of migration. Special thanks to her daughter Elpa Theodorakis for her help and support.

Costas Anastassiades' passport photo, 1951.

CLOCKWISE
• Olga and Anna Angellis on the Corsica en route to Australia, January, 1952.
• Olga Angellis and Costas Anastassiades on the right with three other passengers (names unknown) on the upper deck of the ship, January, 1952.
• Olga (right) and a friend on the Corsica. January, 1952.

LOIZOS
PANAOURIS

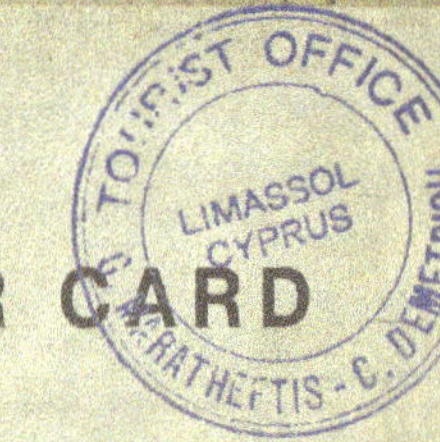

PASSENGER CARD

Name   **LOIZOS PANAOURIS**

Date of birth / Age   **21.7.1933 / 18**

Occupation   **FARMER**

Place of origin   **GERMASOGEIA**

Port of departure   **LIMASSOL**

Date of departure   **17 DEC 1951**

Date of arrival   **4 FEB 1952**

CLOCKWISE FROM TOP
- Loizos Panaouris in Yermassoyia.
- Loizos at a local dance hall in Melbourne, 1953.
- Loizos in Yermassoyia, 1949.
- Elli Panaouris with her daughter Stella. Prahran, 1957.
- From left to right: Frixos Pavlou (Elli's brother), Loizos Panaouris and a friend. Limassol, 1948.
- Loizos Panaouris in Melbourne, 1951.

Just engaged, Elli Pavlou and Loizos Panaouris in Yermassoyia, 1954.

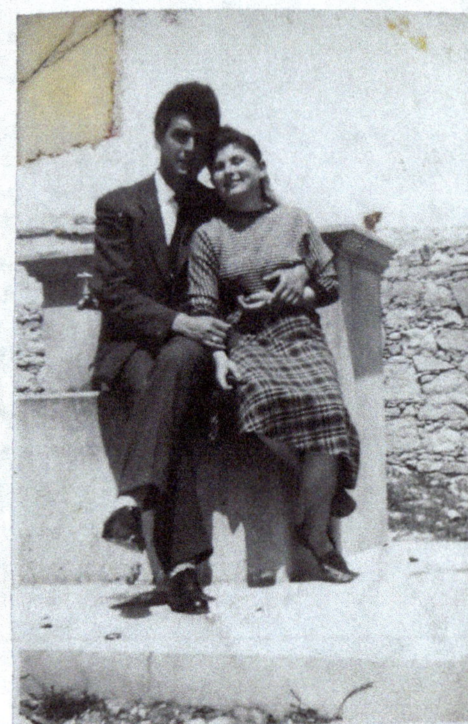

Loizos (Louis) Lambros Panaouris was born on the 21st of July, 1933 in the village of Germasoyia, Limassol. Louis was born to Lambros and Stella and was the youngest of seven children. His brothers were Panayioti, Antoni, and Vassili and his sisters were Panayiota, Parthenopi and Elisabeth. Louis' father bred various types of livestock on the land that he owned and he also grew crops and harvested an orchard of olive trees.

Louis finished high school in Limassol and was fluent in English but he was not able to find satisfying work so he was easily persuaded to travel to Australia with three of his friends from his village. He was only eighteen when he left Cyprus in December, 1951.

According to his wife Elli, Louis had always stated that the Corsica was a terrible ship. "Most of the passengers were seasick, as the ship was continually moving from side to side. It wasn't moving in a straight line. Conditions on the ship were not good. Louis told me stories about the terrible food that they were given to eat and he mentioned the onions and the potatoes and how they spoilt due to the heat and that made the whole ship smell horrible."

Elli Pavlou and Louis Panaouris grew up in the same village. "We went to the same school and he was friends with my brother Frixos," she says. "I knew Louis from afar – as they say. Louis was almost three years older than me. After Louis and his three friends left Cyprus, I remember many mothers in our village feared that the Corsica had sunk, especially when they didn't hear news from their sons for over two months. Louis told me that the ship made many stops for repairs and to get fresh water. He also told me that he kept to himself on the ship and really only spoke to his three friends. This was probably because he was so young and still quite shy."

According to Elli, Louis became homesick soon after arriving in Australia. "He didn't like the accommodation or the food and he soon decided that he wanted to return home. He worked very hard so that he could raise enough money to return to Cyprus. He even worked in Mildura picking grapes during the summer in 1953." Louis only stayed in Australia for two and a half years before returning to Cyprus in 1954.

Shortly after Louis returned to Cyprus he saw Elli at a carnival in Limassol. After a few months, he proposed and Elli agreed to marry him. Louis struggled to find work in Cyprus however, in particular, a job where he could use his English speaking and writing skills and he again became restless. He told Elli that he wanted to live in Australia.

"When I agreed to marry him, I thought that we would live in Cyprus," explains Elli. "I reluctantly agreed to go

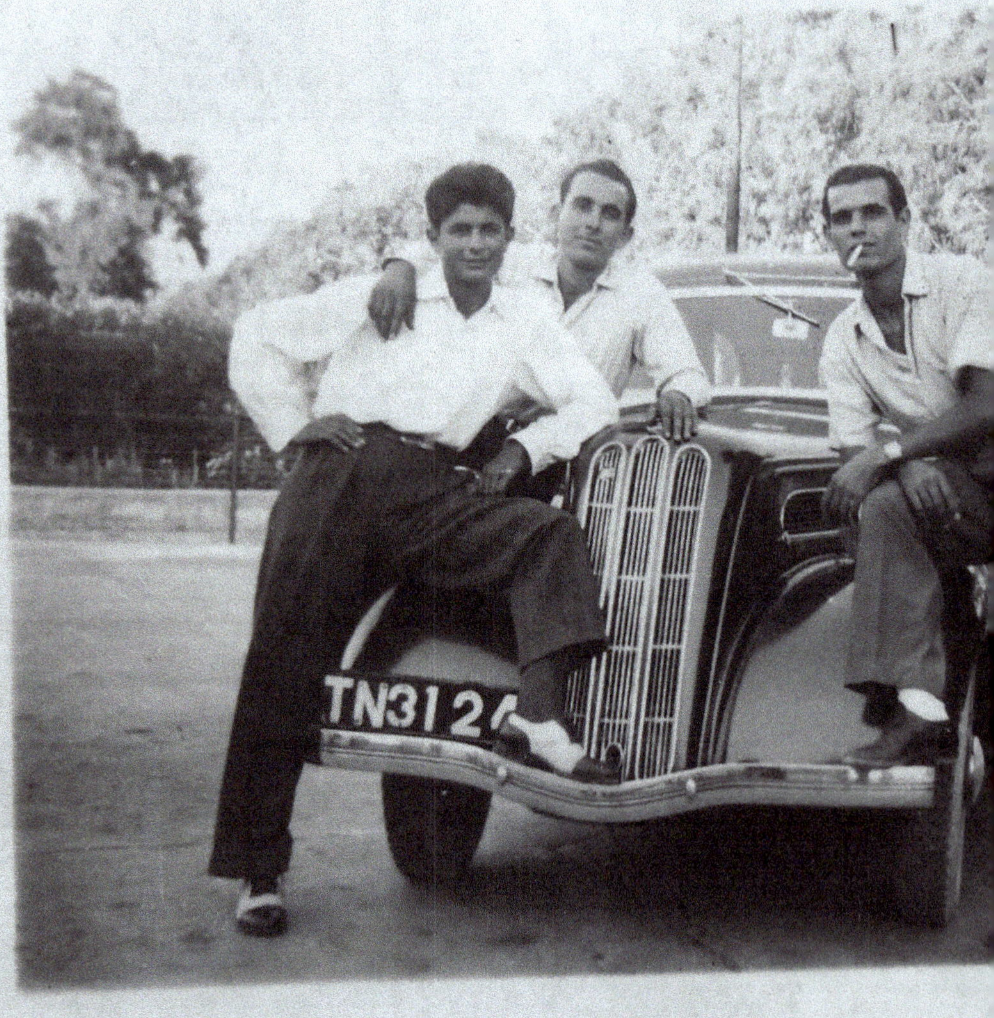

Loizos (far right) with three friends including Frixos Pavlou (left) in Limassol, 1949.

Loizos at the window of his rented room in Carlton where he lived with other Cypriot migrants, 1952.

to Australia with him but my family, especially my mother, were very sad and upset."

Louis left before Elli to go to Australia in order to find work and to organise their accommodation. In March 1955, six months after they were engaged, Elli arrived to Melbourne on the passenger ship Anna Salen.

Louis and Elli were married at the St Eustathios Greek Orthodox church in South Melbourne on the 15th of May, 1955. They have two children, Stella born in 1957 and Pavlos born in 1958.

ACKNOWLEDGEMENTS

I would like to thank Stella Haralambos and Paul Panaouris for allowing me to publish their father's story of migration and for their kind support.

Nikos Charalambous and Loizos Panaouris (right) at Brighton Beach, Melbourne, 1953.

ANDREAS CHARALAMBOU

Name   ANDREAS CHARALAMBOU

Date of birth / Age   15.8.1932 / 19

Occupation   FARMER

Place of origin   KATO PLATRES

Port of departure   LIMASSOL

Date of departure   17 DEC 1951

Date of arrival   4 FEB 1952

Andreas Charalambou (middle) with his cousins Georgios Papanicolaou (left) and Georgios Costantinou (right). Nicosia, Cyprus. Circa 1948.

Andreas Charalambou was born in the small village of Kato Platres on the 15th of August, 1932. He was the eldest of six children and the only son of Haralambos Michael Psomas and Eleni Michael. His sisters were Koralia, Augusta, Maroulla, Panayiota and Popi (Penelopi).

"When I was growing up, there were eight luxury hotels in Platres," Andreas remarks proudly. "I even worked at the Forest Park Hotel as a waiter for about a month. In fact, one day I met and served King Farouk from Egypt who was a regular guest at the hotel. He loved to gamble and I would watch him playing cards for money. During the summer months, tourists would camp under the trees in Platres and sleep in tents."

Andreas left primary school at age eleven to become an apprentice electrician. "My father wanted me to attend high school but I didn't like school that much. I would get bored easily and sneak out of class. I preferred to help my father with his herd of goats. He had around 500 goats. We owned land near the village of Agios Nikolaos and that's where we would graze the goats so they wouldn't destroy the forest."

At thirteen, Andreas became apprenticed to an electrician in Platres. Afterwards, he moved to Nicosia to study with another master electrician. "Once I completed my apprenticeship, I began working with an electrical engineer named Efklides Papadopoulos. The company was called Jupiter Electrical Co. and the manager was J. Michaelidis. My job was to install lights in homes in and around Nicosia. At that time, electricity was very new to the island. Most people still used kerosene lamps. There were some weeks when I would earn between ten to fifteen pounds. That was a lot of money back then. Most workers were lucky to earn a few shillings a week."

The idea to travel to Australia did not occur to Andreas until he was sent to repair the wiring at the Rialto cinema in Limassol. "I was at the Rialto with my work friends when we met this man who began telling us that he was leaving Cyprus to go and work in Australia. After this man left, my friends and I decided just for fun, to see if we could also apply to go to Australia. We went down to the office of Louis Loizou, the main travel agent in Limassol. Louis sent us to a photographer named Kyriacos who had a shop down at Molos. We didn't think our applications would be accepted. We really only did this as a joke. There were six of us who applied that day but I was the only one whose application was approved by the Australian Government. My friends were very disappointed. At first, I decided not to go to Australia since my friends weren't going but when my cousin Kyros Efstathiou told me he was leaving, I decided to go with him. My father was not happy. He did not want me to leave. 'Why would you leave Cyprus?' He said to me. 'You've got a good job. You're earning good money.' Anyway, we talked for a while, I told him a few little lies and I managed to convince him that I would go for a few years and then return. He signed my passport application, because I was still underage and needed his permission. My passport cost around ten pounds and my father gave me 100 pounds to add to my 100, so I could buy a first-class ticket from the Louis Travel Agency. I paid 200 pounds in total for that ticket. I could have paid a lot less but I didn't want to stay on the lower levels of the ship cramped with the other passengers, like cattle. It was very expensive to leave Cyprus in those days. Many people had to borrow money or sell their land to buy a ticket. Can you imagine if immigration was free, I think everyone would have left Cyprus and the island would be empty."

Andreas' parents and five sisters accompanied him to the Port of Limassol on the day of his departure. "Looking back now, I wasn't that sad to leave Cyprus or my family. I remember feeling excited because I saw this trip as an adventure."

As far as Andreas was concerned, the Corsica was doomed from the start. "They put us on the ship in Limassol and we stayed anchored there for a week. We didn't move and they wouldn't let us leave the ship. We were stuck there. It was probably just as well, because if we were able to leave the ship we would have killed that travel agent. Anyway, it was only later when we found out the cause of our delay. They were loading potatoes and onions to take to Colombo. Because they were loading them at night, we couldn't see anything. The ship finally departed Limassol on the 17th of December, 1951. I remember it was 8am in the morning."

On the ship, Andreas shared a cabin with his cousin Kyros and two other men from the village of Aradippou. "I can't remember their names but I know that these two other men ended up in Adelaide."

Two days after leaving Limassol, the Corsica reached Port Said. "I discovered that the local people in Port Said could speak many different languages. I think they learnt these languages by meeting people from the different nationalities at the port. We were in the Suez for one day, but we stayed on the ship."

After the Corsica left Port Said, it made its way down the Suez Canal to the Port of Suez to refuel and get fresh water.

Andreas Charalambou (right) with his cousin Kyros Efstathiou on board the Corsica. December, 1951.

"We would stand on the deck and look at the view and we could see all these little camels on the land. The canal was very narrow with steep walls on either side. I remember a bridge at the end that would lift and open up to let the ships through."

After a few days at sea, Andreas began to feel less excited and more anxious. "They were feeding us large white beans and spaghetti every day. That's all we ate. I was also shocked to see the showers on the ship. They were disgusting. Some of the passengers saw the drain hole for the

Andreas Charalambou (left) with his cousin Kyros Efstathiou on a rickshaw in Colombo. January, 1952.

shower and thought it was a toilet, they didn't know the difference. They would do their business over the hole just like in the village. It was terrible. No one came to clean up the mess in the showers."

In Massawa, Andreas was surprised by the behaviour of the locals. "The locals living here were very friendly to us. I think this is because the Italians who govern the country had made them tame. As soon as we set foot on land, they rushed up to us and begged us to go out with their sisters or daughters. I was shocked at the way they treated their women. I couldn't believe that the mothers would take you to their daughters, who were aged somewhere between twelve and eighteen years old. I've never seen anything like this before in my life. The poverty must have been very bad in this country for people to behave like this."

Andreas admits he spent some time with a young local girl in Massawa. "She came up to me and took my hand confidently. We walked back to her house hand-in-hand. When I asked her how old she was, she told me she was fifteen. She lived in a tall, three-storey house. I was very scared because I was on my own, I was wondering whether I should stay with her or not. In the end I decided to follow her up the steps and into her house. When we got inside, there was a big black man standing there. I immediately became frightened. The girl said, 'this is my father.' At this stage I was so scared I almost wet my pants. Her mother and brother were also in the room. I was trembling. They asked me to sit at a table and we all ate together. Afterwards, her father warned me not to ruin his daughter because she was still young. 'You can kiss her but that's all,' he said. Anyway, as it happened I ended up staying the night at this girl's house. I slept in her room. We communicated in broken English. In the morning, her parents fed me breakfast and I spent the day together in Massawa with this girl. The next day, she even came to the port to bid me farewell. In fact, she came onto the ship with me. Who knows - perhaps she was hoping to come to Australia with me. The other passengers became very curious about this girl. I told them she was my cousin. Anyway, in the end I gave her two pounds and sent her on her way."

Andreas' cousin Kyros didn't get to explore Massawa because he was too sick to move. In fact, according to Andreas, Kyros spent most of the trip confined to his bed in their cabin.

In Massawa, Andreas bought a few live chickens and baby goats from a local trader who slaughtered and cleaned them so he could cook them on the ship. "I bought two *okes* (around five kilos) for fourteen shillings. One of the men from Aradippou who was staying in our cabin, had a burner and some pots and he cooked these chickens with rice for us to eat. Later he cooked the baby goat meat with potatoes and onion and made us a *tavas* (baked rice and meat)."

According to Andreas, the Corsica left Massawa on the 28th of December and after two days and nights at sea, they reached the Port of Djibouti. "I remember we stopped here to refuel. The blacks in Djibouti were quite different to the ones we saw and met in Massawa. There were many thieves here. They tried to rob us but we outsmarted them instead. Djibouti was governed by the French but it was quite a dirty place, much dirtier than Massawa. The locals were very tall and skinny and looked unclean. The only place that was any good as far as I could tell was the port itself and the Shell refinery."

In his diary Andreas writes, that they went to church in Djibouti (Agios Konstantinos and Eleni) where they worshipped and stayed for liturgy. He says that the Bishop from the church came on board the ship to bless the passengers with *ayiasmos* (holy water).

After Djibouti, the Corsica took ten days to reach Colombo. "For those ten days we did not see any land at all. Colombo was one of the nicest places I had seen so far. There was a zoo there which had every animal you can think of. There was also a lovely museum and many beautiful old buildings. The Port of Colombo was very nice. There were probably around 100 ships in the port the day we arrived. It was very busy. We spent three days in the town and many passengers went exploring and shopping. I left Cyprus with fifteen pounds in my pocket, so I bought a lovely table ornament, an ash tray that was decorated with lions and crocodiles and I even bought a watch. Colombo was very green. The trees were really unusual and different to what I had ever seen before."

With regards to the rotten potatoes and onions, Andreas explains that the local authorities in Colombo insisted that the Corsica must be towed out to sea so they could dispose of the smelly sludge from the cargo hold into the ocean. "I remember they used pumps to pump the sludge into the sea. They left us on the land for five days while they cleaned the ship so the smell could go away. We stayed in a hotel during this time. The hotel must have been paid for by the ship's captain or crew. There's no way we could have paid for it. I can't remember much about the hotel to be honest, we only went there to sleep. I remember we went to this one Greek restaurant in the town to eat. When the owner found out that we were Greek, he got very excited and treated us to a free meal. We met some good people on this trip. I didn't expect to find people in these places who looked after us like they did."

"And let me tell you another thing," Andreas says rather excitedly. "The Greeks can be found all over the world. Everywhere we stopped with the Corsica we found Greeks living there. It was quite amazing."

Andreas recalls that on New Year's Day there was a fight on deck between the Italian and Greek crew members. "I think they were fighting because they each wanted the New Year celebrations to follow their own traditions. The fight became very violent. They grabbed all the deck chairs and threw them at each other. Most of the chairs ended up in the Indian Ocean. Even a few Cypriot passengers joined in the fight. When we got up the next morning to go up to the deck, we couldn't find any chairs to sit on."

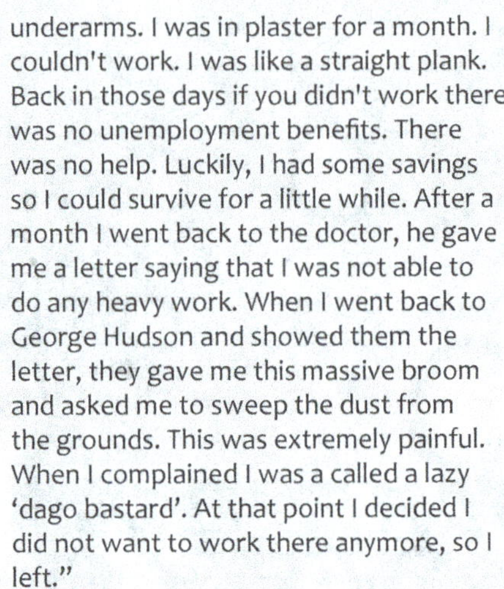
Andreas (left) in Wagga Wagga with a work colleague from Romano's Hotel, 1957. Andreas was fixing his own car.

"We departed Colombo on the 13th of January, 1952," recalls Andreas. "We were told that the water on the ship was running low and to reduce the amount of washing or showers we were doing. Maybe down below they ran out of water but on the second level where I was staying, we had water. The next stop for us was Fremantle. I don't remember much of Fremantle. I can't remember if we were allowed to leave the boat or the port. I do remember that from what I could see, there was not much there."

After arriving in Melbourne, the ship was not allowed to travel any further. Andreas and other passengers bound for Sydney were taken to the train station. "I remember the train from Melbourne to Sydney. Somewhere along the way, our train stopped. We had to get off the train because there was a bush fire near the tracks up ahead. We walked about two miles to the next train station where we got onto a bus to take us all the way to Sydney. It took us two whole days. Our suitcases stayed on the first train and came later after we had already arrived in Sydney. I arrived at Central train station where my cousin Yiannis Moustakas was there to meet me. He didn't recognise me because I was all black and dirty from smoke on the train."

In Sydney, Andreas went to live in Kings Cross. He lived in a terrace house with a few other Cypriot migrants. "As soon as we arrived in Sydney we had to look for work. We didn't have any money, so we needed a job. My first job in Sydney was at the George Hudson Timber yard. This was a hard job. I was working on the cranes. It felt like I was being lifted into the sky, standing on huge timber logs. I worked there for around six months. I had an accident one day, where the crane that was holding the timber log I was standing on, was detached from the claw that was holding it on one side, so I slid off too and I fell to the ground from quite a height. After I fell, I was taken to the hospital. My watch that I had bought in Colombo was shattered, totally destroyed. At the hospital I was left sitting there for a long time in pain. Finally, a nurse came and gave me two tablets and sent me home in a taxi. When I got home, I couldn't move. I was groaning in pain. An older Cypriot man who was living next door heard me crying out in pain and came to check up on me. This man looked after all the young Cypriot men. He would help us with paperwork and anything else we needed. Anyway, the next day he took me to see a doctor. The doctor took some x-rays which showed that I had broken three bones in my back." Andreas laughs as recalls the day. "They put me in plaster from the pelvis all the way up to my underarms. I was in plaster for a month. I couldn't work. I was like a straight plank. Back in those days if you didn't work there was no unemployment benefits. There was no help. Luckily, I had some savings so I could survive for a little while. After a month I went back to the doctor, he gave me a letter saying that I was not able to do any heavy work. When I went back to George Hudson and showed them the letter, they gave me this massive broom and asked me to sweep the dust from the grounds. This was extremely painful. When I complained I was a called a lazy 'dago bastard'. At that point I decided I did not want to work there anymore, so I left."

Andreas left Sydney and moved to Newcastle to look for work. After searching for a week he moved to Wollongong to try his luck there. "When I arrived in Wollongong, there was a strike at the Steel Works and they wouldn't employ anyone new. Everything was closed. The only work I could find was at Harry Peter's Fish Shop, where I began peeling potatoes and washing anything that was thrown at me. I had to do whatever to earn a living. While I was working there a man who owned a cafe in Port Kembla called Lobster Cafe offered me a job and I worked there for a year. From Port Kembla I then decided to go to Cooma where I worked at a cafe called The Majestic Cafe as a cook. In those days we only cooked steak, sausages, chips and mashed potato. The reason we ended up in Cooma was because we actually wanted to go and work in the Eucalyptus oil farming. I went with three other Cypriots. To get work in the Eucalyptus business you

Andreas with his Raleigh Car in Wagga Wagga. Circa 1957.

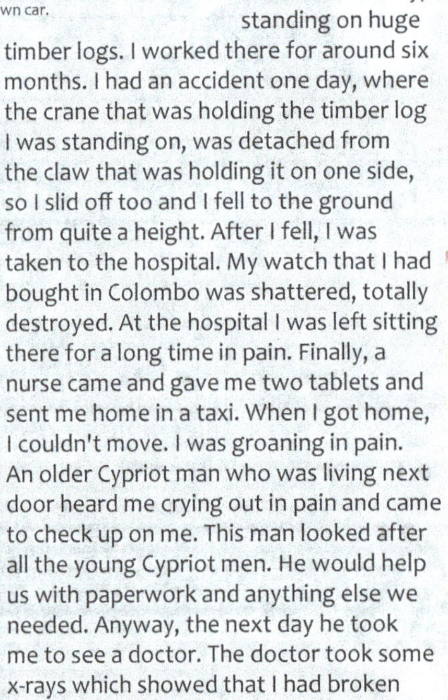

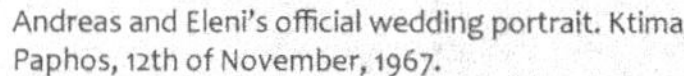

Andreas and Eleni's official wedding portrait. Ktima, Paphos, 12th of November, 1967.

had to have an agent. It took a year to find an agent. At that time, we were taken up to the Snowy Mountains, somewhere near Adaminaby I think. We bought a tent and lived in the forest for two years. We had to pick the leaves from the Eucalyptus trees by chopping down the tree. We would fill these massive drums with leaves. Using heat and steam, the oil is collected in another drum. It would take about two weeks to fill a drum. We made some good money doing this."

Andreas moved to Tumut, also in the Snowy Mountains, where he worked for two years on the Snowy Mountains Hydro Electric Scheme. "I worked in the kitchens for a little while and then they needed a driver to drive the big trucks in the tunnels to the junction shaft to empty the loads. In 1956 when Prince Phillip toured Australia, he came to visit the site. I remember we were all waiting for him to arrive. I was standing only a few feet away from him."

"I moved to Wagga Wagga after Tumut, because I found a job there, working at Romano's Hotel. This was a fancy hotel at the time, and I think it still exists to this day. In Wagga Wagga I bought a house, which I renovated by myself. After a while I sold the house and moved to Barellan where I bought a cafe, called the Barellan Cafe. I paid 1,000 pounds for it back then. I remember the day after I got access to the cafe I was there to clean it up and I got a knock at the door. It was the Health Inspectors.

They told me they were there to close the cafe down. I asked them, why didn't you come last week to close it down - then I would have paid nothing for this place. Anyway, I managed to fix up the cafe, so I had everything anyone could ask for. Living in that county town was great. It was a close-knit community, and everyone was friendly. I remember one Sunday, I left the front door open, I went there to clean up and set up for the next day, and when I got there the shop was full of people. They had come from Church and went into the shop to cook their breakfast. There was a woman at the grill cooking bacon and eggs for everyone, so I sat down, and she cooked for me too."

"Barellan is also where I watched Evonne Goolagong as a very young girl hitting her ball against the wall behind my cafe. I remember her father; he was a nice man. She came from a large family. One day a man from Sydney came and saw her, and the whole community gave money to support Evonne moving to Sydney to be coached. "

"Living in Australia in those days was hard. It wasn't as easy as I thought it would be, we had to work extremely hard. People were not very nice to us. We were called 'dagos', and abused for speaking Greek in public places. Actually, I remember being thrown off a bus one day with my friends because we spoke Greek. I was too embarrassed to go back to Cyprus too soon, in case people thought I was unsuccessful in Australia."

In 1967, when Andreas turned 35, he did return to Cyprus bringing his beloved Toyota Crown vehicle with him. He left Australia on the Ellinis, arriving in Limassol on the 27th of March, 1967.

Soon after he arrived, Andreas met Eleni Savvas Zaloumi, a twenty-six year old nurse from Paphos, and the second daughter of Savvas Petrou Zaloumi and Solomoni Christodolou. "Eleni saw me with my fancy Toyota Crown car and thought who is this handsome man," laughs Andreas. "She stood on her balcony and shouted down to me 'If you don't marry me I am going to jump off and kill myself' So what could I do, I had to marry her so she didn't kill herself." In truth, Andreas met Eleni through his youngest sister Popi who was a friend of Eleni at work in the General Hospital in Nicosia. One day, Andreas went to visit his sister at the hospital's cafeteria, soon after having returned from his adventures in Australia and met Eleni. A few months later they decided to get married.

Andreas and Eleni were married on the 12th of November, 1967, at the church of Agios Kendeas in Ktima, Paphos.

After their wedding they moved to the village of Kato Platres, where they lived for a year. During this time Eleni stopped working as a nurse and helped Andreas on his fruit orchards where they grew apples, peaches, pears, grapes and plums. Most of their land was located in the village of Agios Nikolaos in the Troodos Mountains. A year later, feeling sorry for his brother-in-law (who had no money and no job), Andreas offered him the land to work, which he gratefully accepted. Andreas and Eleni then moved to Limassol where they bought and opened a cafe, which Andreas named the Boomerang Cafe. They both worked there together for a short while, until Eleni fell pregnant and was ordered by her doctor to stay in bed for the duration of her pregnancy to avoid the risk of losing the baby. Eleni moved back to Paphos to live with her parents while Andreas stayed and worked the cafe. After a year, Andreas gave up the cafe because his brother-in-law could not continue working the farms and Andreas did not want to let these be destroyed, so they moved back to Kato Platres. There, they raised their three children, Maria, Sonia (Solomoni) and Michael.

After the Turkish army invaded Cyprus in 1974, the Prime Minister of Australia, Gough Whitlam, declared that any Cypriot with a British Passport could not enter Australia after the 31st of December, 1974. Andreas and Eleni had British passports that were about to expire so they decided to leave Cyprus with their children before the stated deadline to stay in Australia until the war was over. As it happened, they have remained in Sydney ever since where they live happily with their three children and four grandchildren, Bridgette, Stephanie, Ellie and Christina.

ACKNOWLEDGEMENTS

I would like to thank Andreas Charalambou for allowing me to publish his story of migration. Special thanks to his daughter Maria for her kind support over the last few years.

CHRYSANTHOS THEODOSIOU

Chrysanthos Theodosiou on the Corsica. January, 1952.

PASSPORT

This Passport con
32 pages.

Ce passeport con
32 pages.

Given at Nicosia, the 28th
of September, 1951.

By Command of

His Excellency the Acting Governor,

C. J. THOMAS,

Acting Colonial Secretary.

NAME OF BEARER
NOM DU TITULAI

ACCOMPANIED BY
(Maiden nar

ACCOMPAGNÉ DE
(Née)

NATIONAL STATUS

British s

FAR LEFT
- Chrysanthos Theodosiou with his niece Sophia (left) and a friend on the Corsica. January, 1952.

LEFT
- From left to right: Tsikkinis Kyprianou, Chrysanthos, Melanie Nathanael, unknown and Panayiota Efstratiou. Front: Sophia Theodosiou (kneeling) Athinoulla Efstratiou, unknown, unknown and Christakis Nathanael. On board the Corsica. January, 1952.

Sophia Theodosiou on board the Corsica. January, 1952.

Chrysanthos Theodossiou was born in the village of Kellaki, Limassol on the 10th of December, 1920. He was the second-youngest of nine children born to Theodosis Hadjiyianni Koumi and Sophia Theodosiou Hadjioannou. At the age of twelve, he was taken out of school by his father to help with general farm duties on the land, such as growing and harvesting fruit and vegetables and also selling the seasonal produce at the markets in Limassol. The journey from the village to Limassol was approximately seventeen miles and mostly conducted by donkey or mule or by village bus. Chrysanthos' father owned a lot of land in Kellaki and the surrounding areas near Limassol.

Chrysanthos married Xanthippi Christofi Araklidiou on the 13th of November, 1949. Their daughter Chrystalla (Stella) was born in 1951. Xanthippi's father had built the couple a small house in the village. Before migrating to Australia, the couple operated a small *bakaliko* (grocery store) in the village, although they struggled financially as most customers were obliged to use *verisie* to take goods on credit.

In 1951, Chrysanthos agreed to escort his niece Sophia to Australia to marry Phillipos Demetriou (also from Kellaki). Phillipos had migrated to Australia in January 1948 (on the ship Partizanka) when he was twenty-one. After working for a few years, he set up his new home in Sydney and sent word back to Cyprus that he was ready to marry Sophia. Apparently, the couple had developed strong feelings for one another 'from afar' when they were young.

Sophia and her two siblings (Maria and Michalis) were orphaned from a young age after their mother passed away quite young. Their father Ioannis, (Chrysanthos' older brother) later remarried and decided to move away from Kellaki with his new wife. Sophia and her two siblings were more or less adopted and raised by Chrysanthos' parents. During this time, Chrysanthos became very close to his niece Sophia and took on the role of carer. It was therefore not surprising, that when the opportunity arose, he volunteered to escort his twenty-year-old niece to Australia to marry Philippos. In fact, he had to borrow 200 pounds from one of his brothers to pay for their ship fares and travel cost.

In December 1951, Chrysanthos bid farewell to his wife Xanthippi and eight month old daughter Stella and boarded the Corsica, together with his niece Sophia. Not much is known about their living arrangements onboard the ship, although it is likely that Sophia shared a cabin with other young women while Chrysanthos stayed in the male quarters down in steerage. Once they arrived in Australia, Chrysanthos and Sophia stayed with Philippos' brother and his wife in accommodation in the eastern suburbs of Sydney. Shortly after, he moved into separate lodgings and began night school to learn English whilst also working to support himself, earn some money to send to his wife and to save for their future.

Like so many other migrants, Chrysanthos soon found work at various factories in Sydney before moving to Murwillumbah where he worked for a while at a banana plantation. When his wife Xanthippi and three-year old daughter Stella arrived in Australia in early 1954, they joined him in Murwillumbah where they lived for a year or so. In 1955, their son Kosta (Con) was born and soon after the family moved to the inner-Sydney suburb of Darlinghurst, where Chrysanthos had rented a small flat on the first floor of a house.

A few years later, Chrysanthos bought a house with his *koumbaro* (best man) in West Ryde before moving his family to a house in Concord West behind a fish and chip shop that he and Xanthippi operated for six years. Soon after they bought their own home in Concord, which the family owned until Xanthippi passed away in 2016. Chrysanthos and Xanthippi worked hard to set up their new life in Australia. Their second son Andrew was born in 1957 followed by another daughter, Despina (Debbie) in 1965. According to his eldest daughter Stella, Chrysanthos did not discuss his voyage on the Corsica in depth, other than to mention the 'stench' and how utterly awful it was and that it took so long (almost two months) to arrive in Australia in the most unbearable of conditions. Stella believes that perhaps the experience was so terrible for her father that he may have chosen to block it from his mind. Chrysanthos Theodossiou sadly passed away, aged almost seventy-five in November 1995.

ACKNOWLEDGEMENTS

I would like to thank Stella Stylianou for allowing me to publish her father's story of migration.

CLOCKWISE
- Vintage postcard - Nicodimou family album, 1950s.
- Eleni Haji Kleanthous - passport photo, 1956.
- Loukas Nicodimou with young Costas (Angelis Dimitris' nephew). Botanical Gardens, Melbourne. Circa 1953.
- Loukas at the Army barracks, in Puckapunyal, Victoria. Circa 1954.

LOUKAS NICODIMOU

PASSENGER CARD

Name **LOUKAS NICODIMOU**

Date of birth / Age **17.10.1934 / 17**

Occupation **TAILOR**

Place of origin **AGIOS THERAPON**

Port of departure **LIMASSOL**

Date of departure **17 DEC 1951**

Date of arrival **4 FEB 1952**

Loucas and Eleni on their wedding day at Evangelismos Church in East Melbourne, together with George Nicou and best man Anthimos Savva. September 13th, 1959.

oukas Nicodimou (Nicodemou) was born on the 17th of October, 1934 in the village of Ayios Therapon, Limassol. He was the youngest of three children born to Persefoni Theodis (nee Georgiou) and Nicodemou Theodis. Sadly, his mother died when he was around seven years of age leaving Loukas to be cared for mainly by his uncles, aunts and cousins in the village, while his widowed father struggled to earn a living.

Although Loukas finished primary school and was considered a bright child, he had no prospects of attending high school. At the age of fifteen he moved to Limassol where he was apprenticed to a tailor. His two older sisters, Maroulla (born in 1931) and Despina (born in 1928), both worked as housekeepers from a young age in Limassol.

At age seventeen, Loukas decided to travel to Australia where he had several cousins and childhood friends.

On the 13th of December, 1951, he boarded the Corsica. While Loukas did not share too many stories about the Corsica, he did mention the constant smell of rotten green potatoes, which made many people sick for days and even weeks. This was something that he never forgot.

It is believed that Loukas was the only person on the Corsica from Ayios Therapon, however he did befriend others, including a man from Agros who was known to Loukas' future brother-in-law, Angelo Savides. There were other passengers who did not speak Greek making communicating with each other difficult. Despite this, all the passengers tried to help each other.

Loukas recalls eating pasta day and night and having a glass of wine. It seemed that all of the waiters and cooks were Italian.

After arriving in Melbourne, Loukas chose to stay in Richmond with Angelis Dimitris his first cousin's husband who had migrated to Melbourne in 1949. Like so many other migrants, he soon found employment on the production line at the General Motors plant in Dandenong.

In 1953 he was conscripted into the Australian Army and completed his three months training at Puckapunyal, in Central Victoria. He would return there every fortnight for the following three years for further training.

In 1956 when Angelis' wife, Angeliki and four of their five daughters arrived from Cyprus, Loukas continued to live with the family in a single fronted weatherboard house in Richmond for another two years. After this the family moved to Ballan and Loukas moved to South Melbourne. Angeliki's mother,

Aremioni and Loukas' mother, Persofoni were sisters so the bond between Loukas and the Dimitris family were particularly strong. This bond continued for many years as quite a few Sundays were spent at the Dimitris' family home once the family moved back to Richmond in the early 1960s.

For approximately one year from late 1958, Loukas moved to Bacchus Marsh to work in the fish and chip shop of his childhood friend, Anthimos Savva who had arrived in Australia in the late 1940s.

As was customary at the time, Loukas met Eleni Haji Kleanthous in March 1959 through an arranged family meeting. Occasionally, Eleni would travel with Loukas to Bacchus Marsh to visit Anthimos and his parents as Eleni had arrived in Australia on the same ship as Anthimos' mother and father in 1956.

Eleni and Loukas were married on the 13th of September, 1959 at the Evangelismos Greek Orthodox Church in East Melbourne. Loukas' friend Anthimos Savva was the best man.

Eleni Haji Kleanthous was born on the 28th of December, 1934 in the village of Sanida, which is approximately nineteen miles north-east of Limassol. Eleni was the youngest of thirteen children born to Kleanthous Thomas and Myrianthi Christofi. Her siblings were Philippos (born in 1911), Erasmia (born in 1913), Evanthia (born in 1915), Michalis (born in 1917), Christofi (born in 1919), Olympia (born in 1923), Petros (born in 1925), Maroulla (born in 1927), Paraskevi (born in 1929), and Patroklos (born in 1933).

"My mother Myrianthi was only twelve when she married my father, and became a mother at thirteen years of age," says Eleni.

With regards to schooling, Eleni's experience is no different to thousands of other young Cypriot children growing up in rural Cyprus during the 1930s and 40s. "I

boarded the ship, they wanted to put me down below (in steerage) but I argued with the crew. There was no way I was going to stay down the bottom of the ship, especially after I knew my mother had paid for a first-class ticket. I was crying and shouting at the crew until they finally moved me upstairs into a cabin."

At first, Eleni did not like living in Australia. She regretted leaving Cyprus and spent most days in Melbourne crying to herself. "I was so sad and homesick. I don't know why I left my village. My poor mother offered my brother a thousand

In 1961 the Nicodimou family moved back to Melbourne and settled in Glenroy where they bought and operated a milk bar next to the Hutchinson's Flour Mills for twelve years. "We were lucky in those days," says Eleni. "I had good neighbours. They were Don and Una Scully and they looked after my children while Loukas and I worked at the milk bar. We wouldn't have been able to run our business if it wasn't for the kind support we received from our Australian neighbours."

In 1973, Loukas and Eleni purchased a cafe in the London Stores Emporium on the corner of Elizabeth and Bourke Streets. After some years they went on to establish several other cafes including Macey's in Little Collins Street and a cafe near the corner of Bell Street and Sydney Road in Coburg.

In 1980, while working in their Coburg cafe Loukas suffered a severe stroke which affected his speech and mobility. He was forty-six years of age. He spent the next six months recovering at the Royal Talbot Rehabilitation Centre in Kew, Melbourne. Thankfully, he managed to regain his speech and most of his mobility.

As a result of Loukas' time in the Australian Army, he became a member of the Glenroy RSL. He always attended the dawn service on ANZAC day until his health began to deteriorate. After he retired, he began volunteering at the RSL's many fundraising events. He enjoyed nothing more than supporting his community, family and the church.

In 2011, Loukas was awarded the Australian Defence Medal in recognition of his service in the armed forces. According to his daughter Soulla, he was the first Cypriot to have this award bestowed upon him. He was a keen lawn and indoor bowls player and won many trophies in National, Victorian and RSL competitions.

Loukas passed away on the 15th of July in 2019.

Eleni Nicodimou with son Nicos (aged two and a half) and daughter Soulla (nine months) in the back of their milk bar in Glenroy, February, 1963. The milk bar was part of Hutchinson's flour mill, a major employer in Glenroy during the 60s and 70s.

was allowed to complete primary school," she exclaims. "But after that, my parents wanted me to stay at home and work on the farm to look after the cows and goats. I did this throughout my teenage years. It was my brother who finally said, 'leave the village life and go to Australia. You can't spend your life working on the farm like this.' So, my parents arranged for me to travel to Australia. I was twenty-one years old." Eleni's sister Paraskevou and her brother Petros were already living in Australia.

Eleni arrived in Australia in 1956. "I remember it was a long and horrible journey," she tells me. "When I first

pounds to send me back to Cyprus."

After they married, Eleni and Loukas packed up their belongings and moved to Tasmania where her brother Petros lived. They bought and operated a small cafe in the township of Burnie. "My brother Petros was living in Tasmania," Eleni explains. "He invited us to join him and his family there. At that time, there was only one Greek family living in Burnie. I had to learn how to speak English on-the-job because all our customers were Australian." In 1960, Loukas and Eleni welcomed the birth of their son Nicos. Their daughter Soulla was born in 1962 and a third child, Christopher was born in 1970.

ACKNOWLEDGEMENTS
I would like to thank Eleni Nicodimou and her daughter Soulla for allowing me to publish Louka's story of migration and for their kind support along the way.

MELANIE NATHANAEL

Name   **MELANIE NATHANAEL**

Date of birth / Age   1912 / 39

Occupation   HOUSEWIFE

Place of origin   GERMASOGEIA, LIMASSOL

Port of departure   LIMASSOL

Date of departure   17 DEC 1951

Date of arrival   4 FEB 1952

Colombo Zoo, Ceylon. January, 1952.
From left to right back row: Tsikkinis Kyprianou (Melanie's brother-in-law), unknown, Agathangelos (Vangeli) Pavlou, unknown.
Middle row: Panayiota Efstratiou, Melanie Nathanael, unknown, unknown.
Front row: Athinoulla (Panayiota's daughter), Christaki (Doug) and Eleni Nathanael, unknown and Chrisostomos (Christopher) Nathanael.

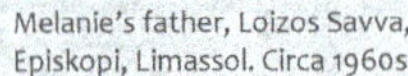

Melanie's father, Loizos Savva, Episkopi, Limassol. Circa 1960s.

Melanie Nathanael (nee Loizou) was born in the village of Episkopi in 1912 but she grew up in Potamos tis Germasogeia. As a young girl, Melanie was sent to Limassol to learn how to become a seamstress. That was where she met and fell in love with mechanic, Nathanael Chrisostomou who was six years her junior (he was born in April, 1918). They were married in 1942 and had three children Chrisostomos (Christopher), Christaki (Doug) and Eleni (Helen).

In 1950, Melanie's husband Nathanael migrated to Australia following in his brother's footsteps and seeking the promise of a better life. Nathanael's intention was to go to Melbourne, find work and set up accommodation before he could arrange for his wife and children to join him. His youngest son Christaki was two years old when he left. Whilst in Melbourne, Nathanael changed his name to George Nathanael.

True to his word, George arranged for Melanie and his children to come and join him in Australia in 1951. Christopher, who was nine years old, recalls the day they left. "I remember getting there and was no pier at Limassol and we had to be ferried out to the Corsica. I know we stayed in a cabin but I can't remember much about the trip itself – only bits and pieces. I do remember going through the Suez Canal and seeing camels on the land – a caravan of camels which was fascinating. There was sand on both sides and we were travelling in between. It was quite a sight. When the fresh water ran out, I remember this Cypriot man who worked in the kitchen, began selling bottles of water to the passengers. The tanks on the ship must have been old and

Back row from left to right: Philippos Nathanael (George's brother), Melanie Nathanael, Christaki Nathanael, Chrystalla Chrisostomou (George's mother), George Nathanael, Kyriacou (George's sister), unknown woman, unknown man. Front row from left to right: Elias (George's cousin), Eleni Loizou Savva (Melanie's mother), unknown baby, Chrisostomos Nathanael, unknown older woman, unknown boy, Elisavet (George's sister), Eleni Nathanael, Leila (George's sister), and Katerina (she was married to George's brother Simeon). This photograph was taken Germasogeia in 1950 and may possibly be a farewell gathering for George Nathanael before he departed for Australia.

Passport photo; Melanie Nathanael (age thirty-nine), with her three children, Chrisostomos (aged nine), Christakis (aged four) and Eleni (aged seven). Limassol, 1951.

rusty and so the water was undrinkable except for the tank in the kitchen. That was the only one that had drinkable water and so this man was very enterprising to say the least."

Eleni who was only six when she travelled on the Corsica also recalls a few moments. "I don't remember much about the trip or the ship itself," she tells me. "Just bits and pieces. I remember the barge in Limassol that took us out to board the Corsica. I remember seeing rust everywhere. The ship must have been very old. Of course, I remember that awful smell of rotting potatoes. It was a terrible smell. It was really bad. Food-wise, I don't remember much but I can tell you that my younger brother Doug became friends with the ship's baker and he would bring us fresh bread. Thankfully, Mum also brought food from Cyprus. It was strange, I remember there was this black man on the ship. He must have been a stowaway. I remember he was tied with ropes to a post on the deck."

In Colombo, Christopher remembers seeing the open sewers and the drains in the street. "I remember the stench," he says. "The place stunk."

When the Corsica reached Fremantle, the family went ashore to inspect the port town. "I remember we walked into a fruit shop," says Christopher. "It was a spotlessly clean shop with all this beautiful fruit neatly laid out. We had never seen anything like it before. Oh, it was fantastic and we were all in awe." "That's right," adds Eleni. "I remember mum bought us bananas for the first time."

When the Corsica finally reached Port Melbourne, George Nathanael was there to greet his family. "It was so exciting for us children when we finally docked at Station Pier," exclaims Christopher. "Our father was there on the pier with two of his brothers. I remember hanging off the ship's rails and waving down at them. Oh, it was very exciting. He took us to his house at Drummond Street in North Carlton where we had a bit of a celebration."

"Everyone stayed at this house with us," adds Eleni. "Our Uncle Tsikkinis who was also on the Corsica with us, lived with us for over a year. When his wife and five children arrived in 1953, they all stayed with us. It was crowded but we had fun. We got a TV in 1956 and I remember our neighbours would come over to watch the shows with us. I also remember you needed three-pence to operate the gas meter. Times were so different in those days. We used to play cricket on the street, using the light pole as the stumps. We even gathered wood from the Carlton cemetery to light bonfires on Guy Fawkes Day. On Sundays we would walk to the Evangelismos church in East Melbourne."

George Nathanael was working at General Motors Holden (GMH) at Fishermans Bend at the time when his wife and children arrived on the Corsica. Before GMH, he worked on the Snowy Mountains Hydro-Electric Scheme for a while. Melanie found work at a dry-cleaners shop owned by a Greek man in Carlton before moving to a shop in Flinders Lane where she sewed dresses.

Christopher speaks fondly about his first few years in Australia. "Right from the word go, we were adopted by the local community in North Carlton, and by the local Australian children. We were their friends. Our neighbourhood was 100 percent Australian and they embraced us. As kids, we went to Lee Street State School, around the corner from Drummond Street. I learned how to play cricket before I learned how to speak English. We were involved in everything, with the whole community. We were all friends. There was no 'dago', or any nasty words said to us. We were all part of the gang – all part of the community there and it was one of the loveliest, growing up periods of my life. We were invited to birthday parties, and other events. I played every sport under the sun. I played Aussie Rules and Cricket and Tennis. We made skates, we made bonfires. It was amazing. There were no fights, no arguments, we were just part of the community - all the time."

In 1960, the Nathanael family moved from North Carlton to Sunshine. "My father George was keen to grow a vegetable garden so we moved to a house with a big backyard," says Christopher. "I had just started High School at Princes Hill," adds Eleni. "I had to travel by train from Sunshine to go to school."

ACKNOWLEDGEMENTS

I would like to thank the Nathanael family for letting me publish their story of migration. Special thanks to Christopher and Helen for their help and support.

Tsikkinis and Nitsa Kyprianou's official wedding portrait. Cyprus, 1946.

LIMASSOL

TSIKKINIS KYPRIANOU

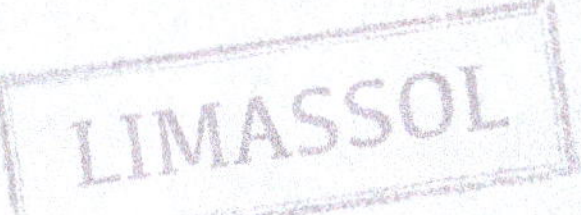

819
Bearer
(Titulaire)
CYPRUS POLICE
(LIMASSOL)
13 DEC 1951
DEPARTURE
PASSENGER CARD
Name TSIKKINIS KYPRIANOU
Date of birth / Age 2.2.1924 / 27
Occupation BARBER
Place of origin GERMASOGEIA, LIMASSOL
Port of departure LIMASSOL
Date of departure 17 DEC 1951
Date of arrival 4 FEB 1952
BY CUSTOMS
7
26 JAN 1952
FREMANTLE, W.A.
TOURIST OFFICE
LIMASSOL
CYPRUS

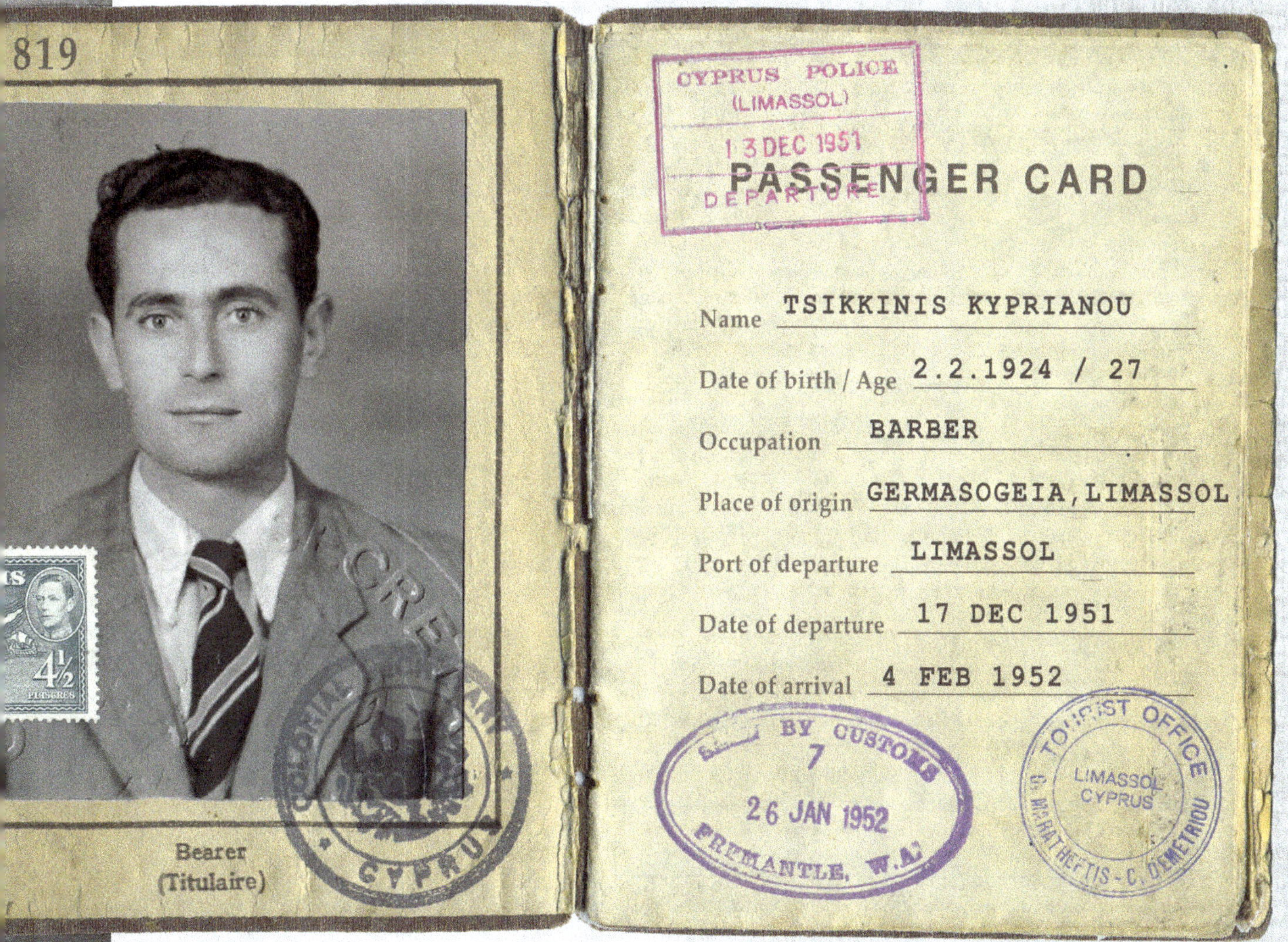

Nitsa Tsikkinis with her five children; from left to right: Panayiotis, Vasilakis (Vas), Louie, Stavroulla and Kypriani (Kim). Limassol, 1953.

Tsikkinis Kyprianou was born on the 2nd of February, 1924 in the village of Germasogeia, Limassol. His parents were Kyprianos Tsikkinis and Panayiota Kyprianou. Tsikkinis was their only child until his brother Kostas was born in 1940.

Like most children at the time, Tsikkinis helped his parents to earn a living by working on the land. His mother Panayiota earned a bit of extra money selling fabric at the local markets and going door-to-door. She never went to school but she had a sharp mind and good negotiating skills.

After the outbreak of the Second World War, Tsikkinis joined the Cypriot Volunteer Regiment as part of the British Forces. Although he was under age he signed up in December 1940 after telling the recruitment officer that he was eighteen, when in fact he was only sixteen and a half. "Dad didn't really talk about his time in the army," his daughter Kim tells me. "He did mention that he went to Palestine and Egypt where he was trained to be a barber and thereafter he was instructed to give the other soldiers haircuts. It was in the army when he met a man named Pambos Louizos from Epikospi and they became best friends."

After the war, Tsikkinis left the army and opened up his own barber shop in Germasogeia. He would charge one shilling for a haircut and a shave. Most of his customers paid him in produce, such as eggs and chickens, as money was scarce in those days. One day his friend Pambos introduced him to his sister Nitsa. Although she was older than him, Tsikkinis

was determined to marry her.

Tsikkinis and Nitsa were married in 1946 and soon after, they built a house in Germasogeia and started a family. They were blessed with three sons and a daughter in a matter of four years, (Panayiotis, Vasilakis, Louie and Stavroulla).

Now a father, Tsikkinis struggled financially to make ends meet. At his barber shop, his customers would ask for credit and promise to pay later but most never did as they genuinely had no money. His decision to migrate to Australia was largely based on the poor economic circumstances and the political instability that the island was facing after the Second World War. "One of the reasons my dad decided to migrate to Australia," explains Kim, "was because as a British subject he could go there with a British passport. He had also heard stories from other people that there was plenty of work in Australia and that the workers were earning large sums of money. He must have thought that Australia was a land of 'milk and honey' or the lucky country."

As it happened, Nitsa's sister Melanie was leaving Cyprus in December 1951 with her three children to be reunited with her husband and their father George Nathanael. George had migrated to Melbourne two years earlier. Tsikkinis jumped at the opportunity to travel with his sister-in-law on the Corsica leaving his wife and four children behind. In fact, Nitsa was pregnant and expecting their fifth child, Kypriani (Kim) when he left.

According to his son Vas (Vasilakis), his father did not say much about his

trip to Australia. "Dad didn't tell us a lot about the Corsica only that he would cut some of the passengers' hair for money to buy fresh water. The fresh water on the ship had run out."

Back in the village, Nitsa was becoming increasingly anxious about the Corsica, especially since she had not heard from Tsikkinis for two months. "No one had heard any news about the ship or whether it had reached Australia," remarks Kim. "Rumours started to circulate in the village that the ship had sunk and that everyone had drowned. Some people would even say to my mum. 'You see Nitsa, now you will never see your husband again.' They were quite cruel."

When Tsikkinis arrived at Port Melbourne, his brother-in-law George Nathanael was there to greet him and of course, to be reunited with his wife Melanie and children. George arranged

Nitsa with her children and mother-in-law. Limassol, 1953.

for Tsikkinis to stay at his house in North Carlton and even found him a job the at the General Motors Holden (GMH) plant at Fishermans Bend where he worked.

Tsikkinis began saving his wages for a deposit to buy his own house and to bring his family over from Cyprus. In his spare time he earned extra money by cutting hair for other migrant men and people that he knew. "I think that dad would have preferred to have worked as a barber in Melbourne," says Kim, "but because he couldn't speak any English he was unable to do the course and to get his barber's certificate. He therefore stayed at GMH for his entire working life in Australia."

Two years after he left Cyprus, Tsikkinis was finally able to arrange for his family to join him in Melbourne. His wife Nitsa gathered her five children and boarded the ship Fairstar for the journey. As it turned out, the ship was so overcrowded (due over booking), that when they reached Cairo, all the women with young children were allowed to continue their journey to Australia by plane. Unbeknown to Tsikkinis, Nitsa and her five young children were instructed to disembark the ship, without any of their luggage, and taken to the airport to board a KLM plane. "It took us ten days and ten nights to get to Australia," Kim recalls. "In those days aeroplanes didn't fly at night. We landed at Sydney airport in May 1954 and we were taken to Central Station to get on a train to Melbourne. When we arrived at Spencer Street Station, there was no one there to greet us. Dad was under the assumption that we were still coming by ship."

Kim was born six months after her father left Cyprus on the Corsica. By the time she met him in Melbourne in 1954, she was almost two.

According to Kim, her father Tsikkinis was very easy going and rarely raised his voice. He loved to play cards with his friends, joke around with his children, and always made time to take his family on outings every Sunday. He loved to socialise with friends and everyone was warmly welcomed in his home. He especially loved how the local Aussies were so relaxed and easy going."

ACKNOWLEDGEMENTS

I would like to thank Vas Tsikkinis and Kim Stavrou for letting me publish their father's story of migration and for their kind help and support along the way.

Tsikkinis Kyprianou in his army uniform after joining the Cypriot Volunteer Regiment. Cyprus, 1940.

LEFT: Tsikkinis (left) with two other Cypriot Volunteers. Jaffa, Palestine, 1943.

STAVROULA ANTONIOU

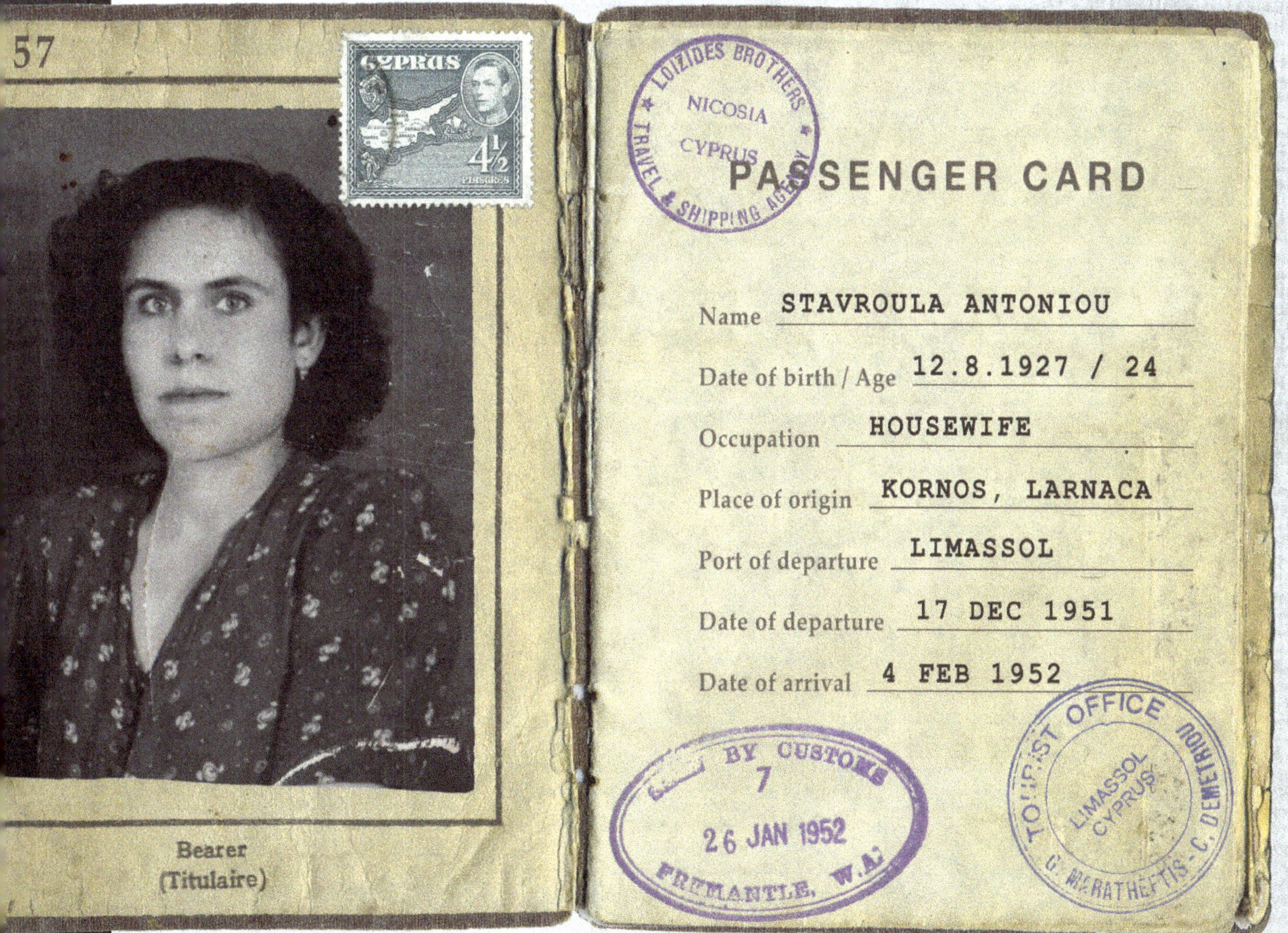

PASSENGER CARD

Name **STAVROULA ANTONIOU**

Date of birth / Age **12.8.1927 / 24**

Occupation **HOUSEWIFE**

Place of origin **KORNOS, LARNACA**

Port of departure **LIMASSOL**

Date of departure **17 DEC 1951**

Date of arrival **4 FEB 1952**

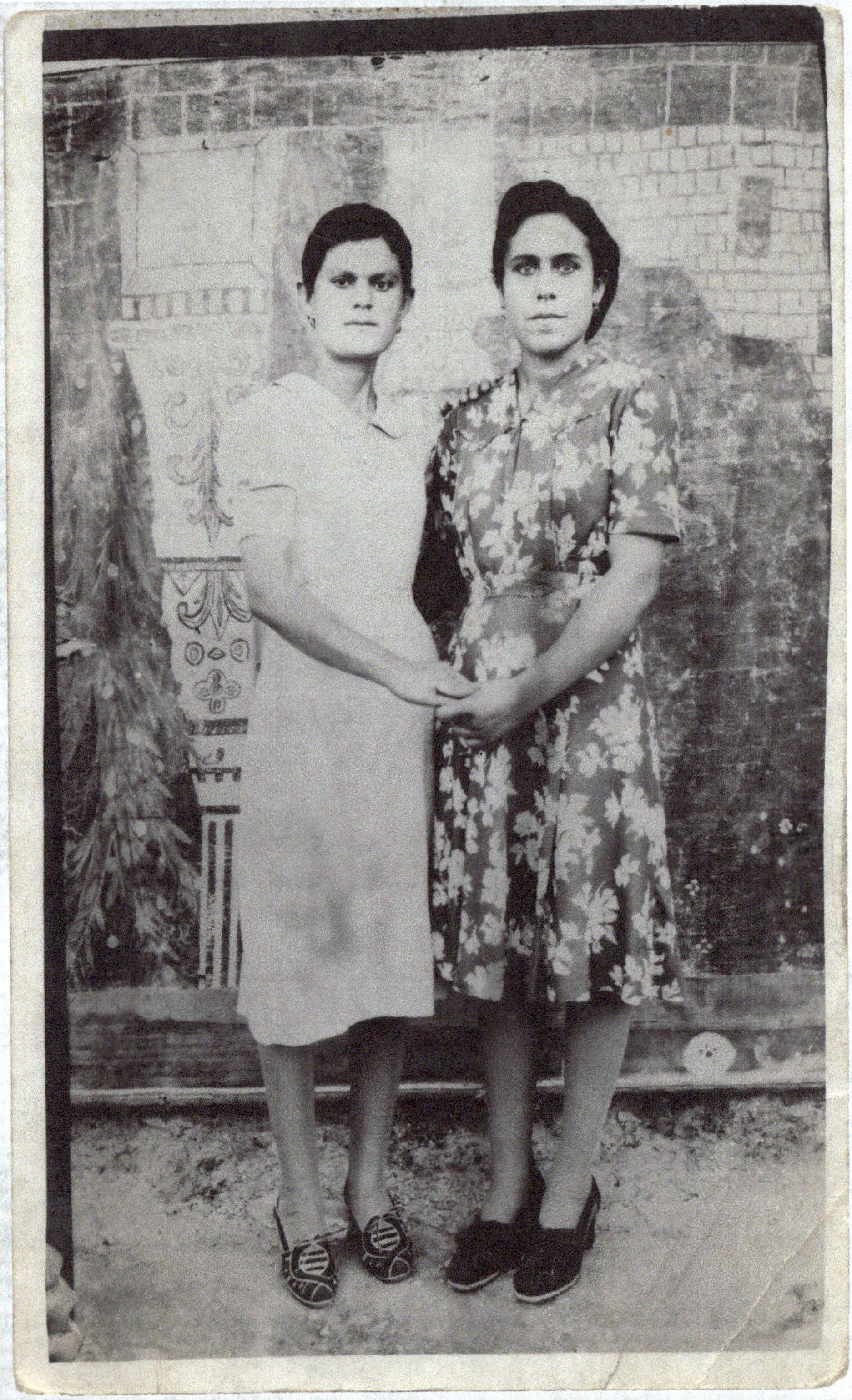

Stavroula Georgiou with a friend in Kornos. Circa 1944.

Stavroula Antoniou (nee Georgiou Hangoudis) was born on the 12th of August, 1927 in Kornos, Larnaca. Her parents were Erato and Georgios Hangoudis and her siblings were Christofi, Evagoras, Kostas, Christaki, Maria and Andreas.

At the end of 1951, Stavroula left Cyprus with four young children to travel on the Corsica to Australia to be reunited with her husband Nicos. "My husband had left for Australia a year earlier on the ship Cyrenia," she explains. "I was married at eighteen and a mother by nineteen. Can you imagine what it was like for me? I was travelling with my twin babies, Erato and Androulla who were ten months old and my five year old son Georgios and daughter Eleni, who was three years old. I was only twenty-four. I remember that I paid 120 pounds to travel on that ship. We stopped at Port Said for a few days and then on our way to Colombo the potatoes started to really stink. I don't know why they had potatoes on our ship. We heard they were destined for Singapore. Anyway, they slowly poured the rotten potatoes overboard but unfortunately the smell remained on the ship."

As you might imagine, travelling on a migrant ship in the 1950s was especially challenging for any mother with just one child, let alone for someone like Stavroula who had four children under the age of five. "For me, it was especially difficult," she says. "A woman with four small children. I had the two babies together in a basket and the other two, I always kept them close to me. I was afraid to let them leave the cabin – they were so little and so young. Thankfully, there was a Greek-Egyptian woman who sometimes looked after my two babies. She would say, you go up and eat with your older children and I will stay here in the cabin and look after your babies. If it wasn't for her, I would have remained a prisoner in that cabin for two months. I couldn't even go upstairs and stand on the deck of the ship. I was too scared that my children would fall into the ocean. I was like a prisoner on that ship. Trapped in my cabin. Any mother who travelled with children became a prisoner."

According to Stavroula, most of the women on the Corsica were either married

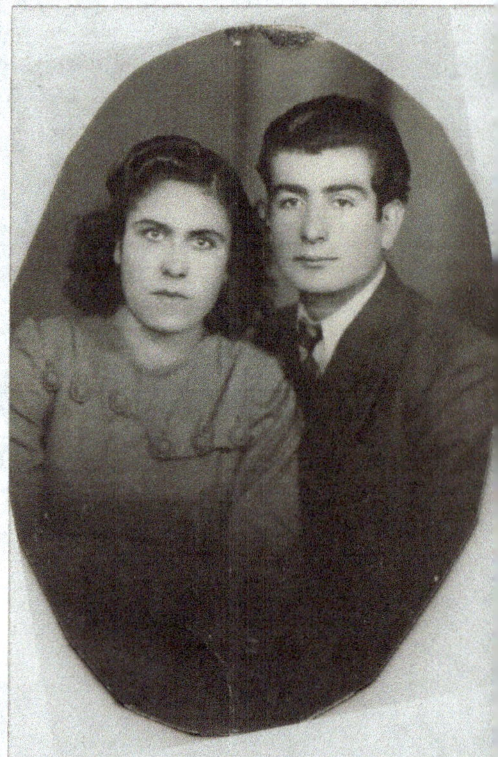

Stavroula and Nicos Antoniou. Circa 1946.

Left: Stavroula's mother Erato with her grandchildren. On her right is Doula, and in front from left to right is Eleni, Erato, Androulla and Georgios. Kornos, Larnaca. Circa 1951.

Above: The Antoniou family at Luna Park in Melbourne, 1953. Front row from left to right: Androulla, Erato, Georgios and Eleni.

or engaged and on their way to meet their husbands and fiancées. "There were very few single women on the ship," she recalls. "Of course, the majority of the passengers were men, and mostly single young men. I also had a large basket full of food with me from Cyprus. I brought plenty of food from Kornos with me. I didn't like the food on the ship. All they fed us was macaroni. Always macaroni mixed with everything, tomatoes, everything. It was awful. My children wouldn't eat. I would say to them, you have to eat – there isn't anything else."

"Why did your husband Nicos decide to leave Cyprus?" I ask Stavroula. She smiles at me and sighs before she replies. "My husband had a good job in Cyprus. He had served in the British Army during the Second World War and after the war he found work with the English. Unfortunately, one day he got caught trying to steal some petrol for a friend and lost his job. He struggled after that to make ends meet. He found odd jobs here and there but it was never enough."

With regards to the problems that were evident with the Corsica, Stavroula shakes her head and remarks. "I remember from the start, there was something wrong with that ship. It wasn't going straight. It seemed to be zigzagging across the ocean and leaning over to one side. It was moving up and down and side to side – like a snake. When the weather was bad, the bottles for my babies were tossed around the cabin. Then we ran out of water. People were drinking from the hose on the deck. I tell you, it was a miracle that we made it all the way to Australia. The children did not recognise their father when we arrived. They barely knew him. Only my eldest child Georgios remembered something about him."

Stavroula's husband was at the pier at Port Melbourne when the Corsica finally docked on the 4th February, 1952. "Nicos was there to greet us when we arrived," she says. "He took us to a small house on Market Street in South Melbourne. I remember there was no gas, no hot water. I had to burn wood in our backyard to heat up the water to wash our clothes. It was not a good start to our life in Australia. We suffered a lot. I never dreamed that my life would turn out like this. I never thought that one day I would have to travel on a ship with four children, alone. To travel so far and to leave my homeland to start a new life in Australia. The first ten years were especially difficult. We bought our first house in Albert Park and then we sold that and bought a fish and chip shop in Moray Street, South Melbourne. We lived in the back of the shop. In 1970 we moved to Northcote where I still live today.

My husband became a taxi driver so I worked at the shop on my own. Can you imagine trying to raise four children while you work all day in a fish and chip shop. I did that for ten years. Once we sold the fish and chip shop I found a job at the Commonwealth Army Barracks in Coburg as a machinist. I was making the army uniforms there."

ACKNOWLEDGEMENTS

I would like to thank Stavroula Antoniou for letting me publish her story of migration. Special thanks to her children, Androulla, Erato, Elly and George for all their help and support along the way.

Nicos Antoniou at the front of his Milk Bar in South Melbourne with a young customer. Circa 1960.

THE CORSICA

LARNACA

TAKIS IOANNOU

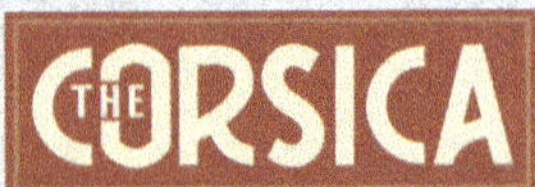

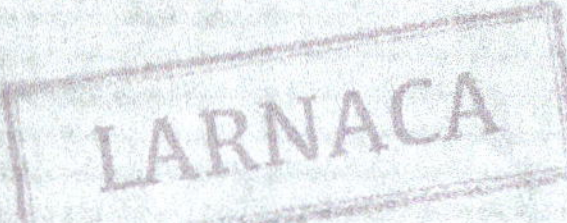

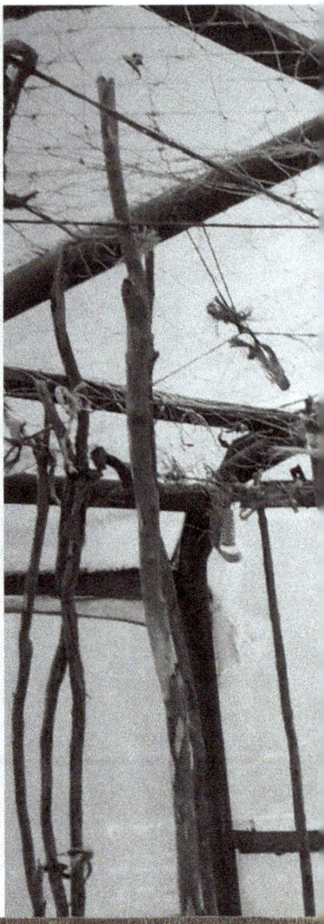

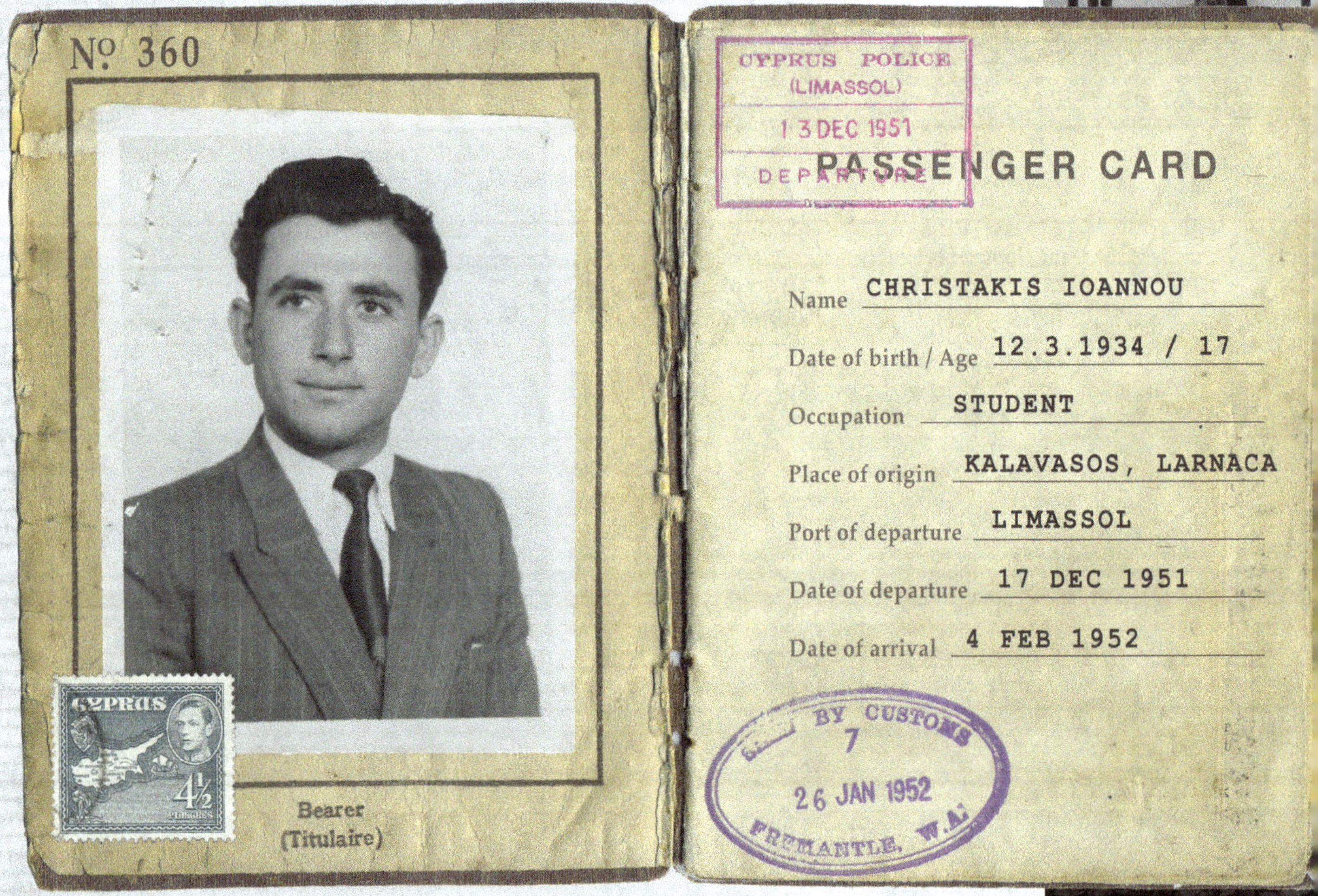

Nº 360

Bearer
(Titulaire)

CYPRUS POLICE
(LIMASSOL)
13 DEC 1951
DEPARTURE

PASSENGER CARD

Name CHRISTAKIS IOANNOU

Date of birth / Age 12.3.1934 / 17

Occupation STUDENT

Place of origin KALAVASOS, LARNACA

Port of departure LIMASSOL

Date of departure 17 DEC 1951

Date of arrival 4 FEB 1952

BY CUSTOMS
7
26 JAN 1952
FREMANTLE, W.A.

The anticipated departure day of the Corsica at the Port of Limassol. December 13th, 1951.

Takis Ioannou was born on the 12th of March, 1934 in the village of Kalavasos, Larnaca. He was the eldest child of Ioannis and Argyroula Papamatheou followed by his two younger sisters, Athoulla and Athinoulla.

When Takis completed primary school, he was required to help his parents with a variety of agricultural tasks such as ploughing, sowing, threshing and harvesting. He was even given the responsibly of operating their flour mill. "I was a man at twelve," he says proudly. "Our mules were six-foot-tall and I was this little boy working amongst them."

When he turned seventeen Takis took a leap of faith and boarded the Corsica to travel to Australia with the single-minded intention of paying off his father's debts which amounted to a thousand pounds.

"It was raining a lot in Limassol that week when I arrived to board the ship. I remember they were trying to load these sacks of potatoes and onions in the rain. When the ship took off, I looked back towards the harbour and I could see my

According to Takis, the Corsica was terribly understaffed. "I remember that the Captain would pay passengers to help in the ship's kitchen or to help the crew load or unload goods at the ports. I met my good friend George Demetrios (Tsimboukas) in the kitchen on that ship."

When the Corsica docked at Port Said, Takis was immediately harassed by the Arab beggars who had gathered at the port to pester the passengers for money. "These beggars would stretch out their hands towards me and shout *pakshish, pakshish,* (money, money). They looked desperate. Port Said must have been a very poor town. I ignored the beggars and spent my money on ice cream and soft drinks instead."

When they arrived at Colombo, Takis visited the zoo with his friends. "The zoo in Colombo was nice but their market was terrible. It stunk and there was mud everywhere. I was with six young boys and two young girls from my village. I was the youngest. It was in Colombo when they had to get rid of the rotten potatoes and onions. That's when the smell really hit us. Every time the wind changed direction, the smell would hit us and we would all have to move quickly to get away from it."

parents standing on the wharf. That's when I saw my mother crying. It was the first time I saw her cry. Anyway, the smell on the ship was awful. The potatoes and onions had turned to mush because they got soaked in the rain back in Limassol. Many passengers became sick."

Travelling with Takis were six men and two girls from his village. There was also a man named Ioannis Constantinou who would one day become Takis' father-in-law. Takis knew Ioannis from his childhood. "When I was a boy I would catch a ride on top of his bus as he transported carobs from Kalavasos to a factory in Zygi. Even though he was on the Corsica with us, I didn't know that one day I will marry his daughter."

Once the ship left Colombo, Takis recalls more problems with the Corsica. "I had heard that the pump that pumped water into the engine wasn't working. It was a coal-fire engine and it nearly blew up. This fellow that boarded the ship at Massawa, he knew something about engines and he told the crew that there was something wrong with the pump, that it wasn't pumping water into the boilers or something like that."

Takis arrived to Australia with only two pounds in his pocket and feeling quite anxious about securing work and somewhere to live. "I left Cyprus with twelve pounds and by the time we arrived I only had two pounds. Can you believe it? I was seventeen years old with two pounds to my name. Anyway, within a week, I was able to find a job at this glass factory in Spotswood. I was on the production line and I had to clink together freshly made beer bottles to check that they didn't crack or break. I was only wearing a leather apron and gloves for protection. I worked at the glass factory for a few weeks and them my friend George Antoniou got me a job at the Rosella factory in Richmond. My job there was to take cans of fruit and sauce by trolley to the steam cookers. For me, the best part of the job at this factory was working with so many women. There were around 2,000 women there and only ten men."

Takis was also able to secure accommodation as soon as he arrived. "I was renting a small room with some other Cypriot migrants in a small house on Drummond Street in Carlton, but then I moved into my Uncle Alekos' house in Windsor, where I shared a room with my cousins. This house had four bedrooms and each bedroom was rented to a different family."

In 1959, Takis met Loulla Costantinou at his uncle's house during a late-night supper celebrating the Greek Orthodox Easter. "My uncle had invited Loulla's family to join us for supper after church. They had travelled to Melbourne for Easter from the country town of Traralgon."

Loulla was only eight when her father Ioannis left for Australia on the Corsica in 1951. She remained in her village of Pentakomo with her mother Ermioni and her older brother Costa until they were finally reunited in 1956. Loulla admits that when she first saw Takis at his uncle's house it was love at first sight. "I just loved the way he looked," she says.

 Takis Ioannou (right) with Themistoclis Haralambous (middle) and unknown passenger in a local taxi in Djibouti. December 30th, 1951. Inset: Takis resting after cutting timber on a vineyard in Mildura, 1953.

Takis' Uncle Aleco, Aunt Stavroulla (his mother's sister) and his cousins Athina, Panayiota and Gayle. Windsor, Melbourne. Circa 1952.

Once engaged, Takis moved to Traralgon to be closer to Loulla. He found work at the Australian Paper Mill (APM) where his father-in-law worked. Traralgon had many Cypriot residents. They moved there because of the promise of steady employment with companies such as the State Electricity Commission and the paper mill.

Takis finally paid off his father's debt and bought his first house in Traralgon.

On the 19th of September, 1959, Takis and Loulla were married in the Church of England in Traralgon. A few months later on the 17th of January, 1960 they were married again, this time in the Greek Orthodox Church of Evangelismos in East Melbourne. Nine months later, their first child John was born.

Between 1962 and 1964, Takis worked at the Hazelwood Power Station.

In 1963, Loulla gave birth to a daughter whom she named Emy (after her mother Ermioni). A year later, Takis built a new house for his growing family. He also went back to APM in Traralgon where he worked for twenty-seven years until he retired in 1991.

Between 1967 and 1971, Takis took on a second job delivering milk by horse and cart in the evenings. His milk rounds began at 5pm and would finish three hours later. If his horse was sick, his wife Loulla would be required to drive a milk truck while he delivered the milk on foot. Apparently, the horse would listen to instructions from Takis but had also memorised the route and knew where to go. For Takis, the horse was easier than using a truck to deliver milk.

In 1969, Takis and Loulla welcomed their third child, a daughter they named Roulla after Takis' mother Argyroula.

ACKNOWLEDGEMENTS

I would like to thank Takis Ioannou for letting me publish his story of migration. Special thanks to his daughter Roulla Charilaou for all her support.

Takis and Loulla on their wedding day outside Evangelismos Greek Orthodox Church in East Melbourne. January 17th, 1960.

PASSPORT

By His Excellency Sir Andrew Ba...

M.P. Nº 515162.

PASSPORT

By His Excellency Sir Andrew Barkworth Wright, Knight Commander of the Most Distinguished Order of Saint Michael and Saint George, Commander of the Most Excellent Order of the British Empire ...

This Passport contains
32 pages.
Ce passeport contient
32 pages.

1

35

**PASSPORT.
PASSEPORT.**

CYPRUS.

38080

of PASSPORT }
du PASSEPORT } 38080

E OF BEARER }
DU TITULAIRE } *Vasilios An...*

MPANIED BY HIS WIFE
(Maiden name) }
MPAGNÉ DE SA FEMME
(Née) }

{ and by .... children
{ et de .... enfants

NAL STATUS
...ritish subject; Citizen of the Un...
...Kingdom and Colonies.

BRITISH PASSPORT

CYPRUS

38080

Vasilios ANDREOU

the ...

By command of

His Excellency the Governor

VASILIOS ANDREOU

PASSENGER CARD

Name **VASILIOS ANDREOU**

Date of birth / Age **1.1.1932 / 19**

Occupation **LABOURER**

Place of origin **ARADIPPOU, LARNACA**

Port of departure **LIMASSOL**

Date of departure **17 DEC 1951**

Date of arrival **4 FEB 1952**

asilios Andreou was born in the village of Aradippou on the 1st of January, 1932. His parents, Andreas Theodoulou and Varvara Kakoulis had six children and Vasilios was the second eldest. His siblings were Maria, Anika, Michalis, Stellios and Kiriakou.

Vasilios was eleven years old when he worked at the mines digging marble. His family were very poor and struggled to make ends meet. After the Second World War many people in Cyprus struggled to find work so they migrated to other countries to help support their families.

"I was one of forty-eight people to leave Aradippou to travel to Australia," he remarks. "Most of us were young, single and carefree. There were only a few older men amongst us, perhaps in their sixties. I was the first of my family to leave Cyprus at the time, and I was the only one from my immediate family to come and settle in Australia. Others migrated later, but they went to England. I had a lot of company on the Corsica. My close friends were Pandelis Kazis, George Petrou and Antonis Marinos. They stayed in Melbourne but my other close friends ended up going to Adelaide with me."

According to Vasilios, the reason there were so many Cypriots travelling on the Corsica at one time was mostly due to difficulties or perhaps deliberate delays by the travel agency trying to find a ship that would go to Australia. "We had been waiting for three months for a ship to arrive to leave Cyprus," he says. "There were no ships for three months. We all had our tickets and were ready to leave but we had to wait for a ship. It wasn't until this travel agency in Limassol was able to book the Corsica and we all ended up leaving at the same time on the same ship. I remember my ticket was £220. I also remember the Corsica was an Italian ship and all the crew were Italian which made it impossible to communicate with them. Those who knew a bit of English could exchange a few words with them."

"We waited for eight days in Limassol on board the ship until it final took off. At least I had the company of my friends from Aradippou. We thought the ship was great. We were all very excited. How would we know. We've never seen a ship like this before. We all slept on bunk beds that were positioned along the walls of the ship. When I say bunk beds, I mean

Studio portrait of Vasilios Andreou. Circa 1953.

they were more like the hammocks you see on battle ships. For the first week or so everything was fine. Before the ship left Limassol, we sat together in the dining rooms and ate our food and drank our wine and it was actually very good. The dining room was full of people enjoying themselves and eating and drinking and having a good time. But let me tell you, once the ship took off and after the potatoes began to rot the dining room was empty after that. Everyone had escaped to the upper levels and outside on the deck to get fresh air."

Vasilios' recalls that the first leg of the journey between Limassol and Port Said was quite pleasant and easy going. "Once we left Port Said everything was bad after that," he remarks. "It wasn't just the rotten potatoes. It was everything. The toilets were filthy. No one was cleaning them. Everything was filthy and stinking. The water was filthy, you couldn't drink it. They were giving us sea water to drink. Whenever the ship docked somewhere people would rush ashore to buy fresh water and return with bottles of water. What could they do. I tell you it was a black tragedy for us. This terrible life that we all had to endure, I wouldn't wish it on anyone. It was worse than a prison. Even prisoners did not suffer the way we suffered on that ship. It wasn't just the passengers who suffered but also the crew. I felt sorry for the crew of the ship."

"After a while, people began to sleep upstairs in the dining rooms, away from the filth and stench down below. They slept on the floors, on the chairs, on the tables – anywhere – as long they were away from the stench. You have to understand, people were tired and desperate to get some sleep. Let me tell you another thing. When they lifted up the *tsoupallia* (sacks) of potatoes you could see they had turned to sludge, and the potato juice had leaked everywhere. Even after they managed to remove all the sacks of potatoes from the cargo hold, the sludge and rotten juice remained. The smell never went away."

"I felt sorry for the young women on the ship. Especially the young children. This wasn't a suitable place for them. I remember one poor woman who had four children. The poor woman. My friends and I took turns to hold her children and give her some peace. I think she had twin babies."

Unable to cope with the conditions on board the ship, Vasilios was able to convince a crew member to let him sleep in a cabin at night. "I tell you, that rotten smell took over the ship. *Paw paw paw*, (oh dear) that smell, no one could sleep down below anymore. I got angry with one Italian crew member who was looking down at us and laughing. I began to argue with him after I found out he had a lovely cabin to himself. I noticed there were two beds in the cabin. The one bed was for him and the other bed was spare so I convinced him to let me use the spare bed. First, he said that I could use the bed only during the day time but I said to him sternly, no, no, no I want the bed at night too. He finally agreed and I spent about a month in his cabin, away from the lower decks and away from the stench of the rotten potatoes."

Vasilios describes the Corsica as the 'ship from hell'. The journey through the Red Sea and the Indian Ocean was particularly stressful and traumatic. "I've got to say, travelling on that ship has been the worst experience of my life. I've never suffered as much as I did during that trip on the Corsica. It was horrible. What was worse is that no one knew what was going on or what to do. No one was telling us anything. A worst experience you would never have in your life. It was that bad. No one had any idea about the route we were taking. When we ended up in Djibouti we asked each other, 'what the hell are we doing in Djibouti?' No one knew anything. The only good thing about Djibouti was when we stumbled upon a Greek Orthodox church. It was a Sunday and they did a special liturgy for us. I'll never forget it. (Vasilios becomes emotional). The bishop said to us. 'Try and be patient. Things will turn out okay.' I will never forget his words."

On the 1st of January, 1952, Vasilios celebrated his twentieth birthday on board the Corsica.

"How did you pass the time on the ship?" I ask him. "What could we do," he replies. "We played cards, we played *tavli* (backgammon), we used to do *Karaghiozis* (puppet theatre). There was one guy who would set up a *Karaghiozis* theatre and he would entertain us. He would set up in a corner and we would sit around and laugh at his jokes. If we had some money we would buy drinks. There was also this Cypriot who was from Larnaca and he would play his violin. We used to sing and dance. That's how we passed the time."

After reaching Melbourne on the 4th of February, most of the passengers from Aradippou, boarded a train to Adelaide. "The Corsica was broken by the time we docked at Melbourne. It couldn't move any more. I stayed in Melbourne for about four months, sharing rooms with other migrants, before I went to Newcastle. During that time, the ship remained stationary. It wouldn't start again. The engines were broken."

Australia was a huge culture shock to the young Cypriots migrants. They were impressed with the Australian wide-open spaces, buildings, parkland and markets. "I didn't know how to use the traffic lights," he laughs. "One day a police officer sees me and grabs me by the ear to show me how to use the traffic lights. 'Red means stop and green means walk,' he shouted at me. He also warned me not to jaywalk. That was my first Australian lesson."

Communication was another great challenge for Vasilios and the other new arrivals. Most couldn't speak or understand English. He eventually secured a job in a glass factory making beer bottles. He worked there for four months before moving to Newcastle to meet up with his first cousin Antonis Nikolas who went by the nickname '*O Englezos,*' (the Englishman). Vasilios stayed with Antonis and helped in his fish and chip shop.

In 1953, Vasilios eventually moved to Adelaide where he teamed up with his best friend from Aradippou, Kiriakos Skouroumounis to open a fish and chip shop. Putting their skills to work they created a very successful business together.

In 1954, Vasilios met sixteen year old Eleni John. He met Eleni at her father's house when he went to buy bags of potatoes for his fish and chip shop. Eleni's father, Charalambos Yiannis was known in Adelaide as Charlie John. As the story goes, when Charalambos arrived in Australia in 1928 the immigration officer took one look at his name on his passport and shook his head and said. 'How do I bloody pronounce this one?' Another officer looked at it and said, 'just put him down as Charlie John'. The name stuck and he was thereafter known as Charlie John.

Charalambos was a commission agent at the East End Market in Adelaide. He would bring Vasilios's potato orders home and store them until Vasilios came to collect. For Vasilios, it was a good excuse to see Eleni and finally ask for her hand in marriage from her father.

Eleni's mother Bandelou Hadgikostandi was also from Aradippou and knew Vasilios's family well.

Vasilios and Eleni were immediately attracted to one another. In fact, Vasilios became a regular customer buying more potatoes from Charalambos than he needed.

Vasilios (Bill) and Eleni (Helen) were married on the 8th of December, 1957 in the Greek Orthodox Cathedral of Archangels Michael and Gabriel on Franklin Street in Adelaide. They were soon blessed with four children; Pandelitsa (Patricia), Varvara (Barbara), Paraskevi (Betty) and Andreas (Andrew); eight grandchildren and eleven great-grandchildren.

Although leaving Cyprus to migrate to Australia was extremely difficult for Vasilios, he persevered and managed to overcome all the hardships to live a happy and comfortable life in Adelaide. He has no regrets. Like so many Cypriots from his generation, he enjoys retelling stories of the past and spending time with his family and grandchildren.

At ninety years of age, Vasilios still drives to church with Eleni most Sundays. Every Christmas Eve, he lights up his beloved *fourno* (wood-fired oven) and prepares a traditional Cypriot feast for his family to enjoy.

He has no regrets.

ACKNOWLEDGEMENTS
I would like to thank Vasilios Andreou for allowing me to publish his story of migration. Special thanks to his daughter Pantelitsa (Patricia) for her help and also Andrea Johns for her ongoing support over the last few years.

KYRIACOS CONSTANTI

CLOCKWISE
- The christening of Costas Zannettides. Kyriacos and Myrofora Constanti are standing on the right. The old woman is Myrofora Kyriacou. Sydney, 1960.
- Myrofora and Kyriacos with their sons, Con (in the sailor suit) and George Sydney, 1959.
- Kyriacos with his friends on Redfern Street, Redfern,1952. From left to right: Socrates Kyriacou, Unknown, Antonis Kayias, Charlie Theodorou, George Antoniou, George Livatiotis, Kyriacos Constanti (second on the right) and Panayis Vasili. The man squatting was known as Italos.

Kyriacos was born on the 14th of February, 1931 in the village of Troulloi, Larnaca. His father was Kostas Constanti and his mother was Chrisi Vakkos. "My father's father died before he was born," says Kyriacos. "He went to intervene in a fight between two men - I think they were relatives - and he was accidentally stabbed in the leg. In those days, there were no doctors or hospitals and his leg became gangrenous and he died soon after."

Kyriacos was trained as a carpenter from a young age. "I was ten years old when my father took me out of school after completing the third grade. From there I started my apprenticeship. I worked in the village of Athienou (near Troulloi) for a while then I managed to find work in Scala at a Turkish Cypriot-owned factory. I used to live with my *Mastoras* (Master) and slept in the same room as his children. I was taught how to build windows and doors for houses. I also worked at a soap factory in Scala where I was required to build wooden boxes for the soap to be exported. I remember earning two and half pounds for six days work at the soap factory."

After the Second World War, there was very little work for tradesmen like Kyriacos. "My father wanted me to get married but I told him I wanted to go to Australia instead, to look for work. I had a brother who had emigrated to South Africa but he didn't like it there. My other brother went to England but he kept complaining about asthma from the coal pollution. That's why I chose Australia. My father loaned me 120 pounds for the ship fare. Before I left Cyprus, he gave me some good advice. 'Be careful not to marry a foreign girl, not even if she is from Greece. If she does not want to live in Australia anymore, where will your children go? Their mother will want to return to her village in their country and you will return to Cyprus, but think about your children. Where will your children go? I thought that was good advice."

In 1951, Kyriacos discovered that there were no ships available that year to bring migrants from Cyprus to Australia. That was until the agents in Limassol booked the Corsica. "There was another ship called the Ravello that came from Italy. Yes, I remember now. The Ravello left Limassol on the same day as the Corsica but it reached Melbourne on the 9th of January, 1952. That's almost a month before we arrived. That's how slow and old the Corsica was."

Once the passengers were allowed to board the Corsica in Limassol there was a delay. "I shared a cabin with five other men. We would go to bed and wake up the next morning and we were shocked to find that we were still in the waters outside Limassol. We knew the delay was because they were loading the potatoes and onions onto the ship. When we asked the crew members why the ship wasn't moving they told us that the sea was rough and prevented them from loading the potatoes. The captain, who was Greek told us, 'in forty years I haven't encountered a rough sea like this'. Remember, it was winter - December - and there were plenty of storms at that time."

According to Kyriacos, when the Corsica arrived at Port Said, Egypt, another 290 passengers boarded the ship. "They were from different backgrounds. Two of the men and myself would go on to marry women in Australia who were sisters. Three sisters. As we continued our journey to Australia many of the passengers became seasick including a few of the men in our cabin. I worked in the kitchen with the ovens making bread under the main cook who was Italian. He often warned me to make sure that I locked the door before leaving the kitchen, as food seemed to be disappearing. I would without his knowledge fill a bag with food to bring back to the cabin so that my friends could eat (without ever being caught). The bag that I put the food in was a bag that my mother had given me before I left Cyprus which was filled with *paxamadia* (rusks). I shared these with the other passengers."

For Kyriacos, the trip to Australia on the Corsica was relatively good. "Because I found work making the bread in the ship's ovens, I had a better journey than most of the passengers as I could eat what I wanted. I didn't get paid. Many of the passengers I heard got sick of the spaghetti with sauce they were served every day. I used to tell the cooks in the kitchen not to put sauce on my spaghetti. Once the potatoes started to rot, the ship began to stink. Furthermore, the rotten juices from these potatoes somehow entered the water tanks on the ship making the water dirty and undrinkable. I resorted to stealing fresh water bottles from the ship's kitchen to give to the passengers who couldn't afford to buy their own. Like I said, the water that came out of the ship's taps was undrinkable"

In Massawa, Kyriacos met a Greek man who owned a pharmacy store. "He gave us free medicines. There were plenty of Greeks in Massawa."

When they reached Djibouti, an Italian policeman at the port warned Kyriacos and his friends to be careful walking around the town because the locals were wild. "We left the ship in groups of ten. One Cypriot man who was with us had his wallet stolen. This man jumped down from a wall and grabbed his wallet and ran off. That wall must have been ten foot high. We all gave chase, caught him and took him to the nearest police station. The police sergeant said, 'don't worry I will take care of this man for what he did'. I was thinking to myself, he will surely cop a beating. After that incident we all went to church. There was a Greek church in Djibouti. The Bishop was there that day. I had a chat with him. 'Are you heading for Korea?' He asked. No, Australia I replied. 'In that case I will come to your ship to do a blessing for the passengers with holy water.' And he did. Afterwards, he stayed for coffee before we took off."

According to Kyriacos, when the Corsica docked in Colombo, the authorities were able to transfer all the sacks of potatoes that weren't rotten onto the port and dump the rest into the Indian Ocean. "We travelled mainly by tram in Colombo, except once, we took a taxi to go to the Zoological Gardens. The Indian driver quoted us one pound for a round trip. When we returned to the taxi after spending two hours at the zoo he demanded that we pay him another pound claiming that the original fee was only for an hour of his time. We began to argue with this man when a policeman approached the car. We told him our side of the story. The policeman took the one pound from my hand and offered it to the taxi driver telling him to take us back to the ship. The driver took the money and took us back, and that's how we got out of that mess."

When the Corsica stopped at Perth, the passengers were greeted by Greeks at the port. 'Stay here' they would shout at us. 'There is plenty of work here'. I told them that I didn't know anyone in Perth and that I was heading to Sydney where I had relatives."

Kyriacos and Myrofora Constanti's wedding portrait with wedding party. Esma Photo Studio, Oxford Street, Sydney. February 6th, 1955.

Kyriacos met his cousin at Port Melbourne on the 4th of February, 1952, on the day the passengers were finally allowed to disembark from the Corsica. "My grandmother's brother lived in Melbourne but he had gone hunting on the day I arrived, so I didn't get to see him. I had to leave Melbourne the next day to go to Sydney to meet up with my relatives there. I was told that in the same week, the Corsica left Australia with a cargo of wheat destined for Kenya. I'm not sure if that's true."

Kyriacos travelled from Melbourne to Sydney by train, however, he encountered yet another delay along the way. "Just before we got to Albury, our train had to stop because there was a broken down train up ahead and we couldn't proceed any further. Many of us were hungry so we climbed out of the train and onto some trees to collect fruit to eat. A guard told us off and we had to come down. Anyway, a few buses arrived and took all of us to a restaurant for food and then dropped us off at a station that was located after Albury and past the broken-down train."

Kyriacos was greeted at Central Station in Sydney by a few relatives and friends who were also from the village of Troulloi. They took him to Redfern where they lived. One of his first tasks was to write a letter to his parents to inform them that he had arrived safely to Australia.

"My uncle told me to place my letter in the letter box on the street so it could be sent to Cyprus. Not knowing, I placed my letter in a telephone box. Luckily, my cousin saw me and showed me what a proper 'letter box' looked like. How would I know? In Cyprus, our letters are dropped off at the *kafenion* (coffee house) in the village"

Kyriacos soon found work in Sydney. "I went to work at the Crown Crystal Glass Works factory in Alexandria. I worked at the ovens there for fifteen years. I looked after four ovens. I eventually was able to repay my father the 120 pounds he had loaned me for the ship fare."

Remembering his father's warning to not marry a foreign girl, Kyriacos was in conversation with his cousin's wife Despinou Vasili, when she asked him if he was ready to get married. Kyriacos replied, "if you know anyone as good as you, then I am more than happy to get married." Despinou wrote a letter to her cousin in Cyprus (Myrofora Georgiou Stassi) and Kyriacos wrote to his father (Kosta) who then went to meet the young lady and her family in Aradippou. They then agreed that she would be sent to Australia to meet Kyriacos and if she approved, go on to marry him. Myrofora was twenty years old and Kyriacos was twenty-three.

Myrofora arrived in Australia in January 1955 on a ship Castel Felice. "We met up and had a conversation. I said to her, if you like me we should get married. I was a very decent man. That's how my mother raised me. Luckily, she agreed and we were married three months later in the Church of Ayia Sophia and we had four children together; three sons and a daughter (Con, George, Chrisi and Chris). We were married for fifty-nine beautiful years before her passing in 2014."

Soon after he was married, Kyriacos bought his first house in Sydney. "I paid 800 pounds for this house. It was a large house in Darlington with seven bedrooms which we rented out to families and migrants. At one stage, we had eighteen tenants who were each renting a bed for twenty-five shillings a week."

Kyriacos eventually invested in a mixed business and later a service station where he worked very hard to help raise his family and educate them.

ACKNOWLEDGEMENTS

I would like to thank Kyriacos Constanti for allowing me to publish his story of migration. Special thanks to his children Con, George, Chrisi and Chris and his daughter-in-law, Eva Costanti for their help and support along the way.

From left to right: Charalambos Athanasiou, Mamas and a cousin (name unknown). Agios Theodoros, Larnaca. Circa 1942.

CHARALAMBOS ATHANASIOU

PASSENGER CARD

Name	CHARALAMBOS ATHANASIOU
Date of birth / Age	1.2.1916 / 35
Occupation	MASON
Place of origin	AGIOS THEODOROS, LARNACA
Port of departure	LIMASSOL
Date of departure	17 DEC 1951
Date of arrival	4 FEB 1952

Family portrait sent to Charalambos in Melbourne. From left to right: Ntinos, his mother Christina, Areti, Maroulla and Soula. Larnaca, Circa 1957.

Constantinos (Ntinos) Charalambous was only six years old when his father Charalambos Athanasiou left Cyprus in December 1951 to migrate to Australia.

"I remember I went to the Port of Limassol to farewell my father," he tells me. "I was with my Aunt Angeliki, my dad's sister. I was standing on a big box and I could see the Corsica ship in the distance, leaning to one side. I think there were two ships out there. I remember it was a stormy day and there were a lot of waves. I could see people on the pier getting onto barges to go out to the Corsica."

According to Ntinos, his father didn't say much about the Corsica only that it was a very terrible ship. Of course, he did mention the rotten potatoes. "My father told me that if he ever went back to Cyprus, he would find the person who organised this ship and punch him up. It would be many years before my father managed to return to Cyprus. You see, he didn't want to travel by ship again. When he left, I was six years old. My sister Areti was four, Maria was two and Soula was only a few days old."

Ntinos did not see his father again until he was eighteen years old. "He was gone for twelve years," he says. "I never knew him. I never heard his voice and it was so difficult for me to call him papa. I did however developed a lot of love and respect for him when I got to know him. He was a very hard working man. I realised how much he also went through without a wife and children for so many years. The truth is that he never abandoned us. He was sending money to my mum every month."

Charalambos Athanasiou was born in the village of Agios Theodoros on the 1st of February, 1916. His father was Athanasios Georgallis and his mother was Areti. Charalambos was the second eldest of five children. His siblings were Ioulia, Katerina, Angeliki and Odysseas. Sadly, Katerina died aged seventeen from Typhoid. Angeliki also contracted Typhoid but managed to be saved because her mother Areti was able to find someone in her village to exchange a gold coin into pounds so she could pay a doctor in Larnaca to save her life. Tragically, Odysseas died from Pneumonia, aged nineteen when he was living in Egypt.

Charalambos' father was a builder and was known to have built many houses in the village. By all accounts, he was quite a gifted builder who was able to calculate the dimensions and circumference of arches and doorways despite not having attended school. The family also owned and managed the main olive press in the village. At the end of Autumn, during harvest time, the inhabitants would bring their olives to the mill operated by Charalambos and his father so they could press them and produce their oil. According to Ntinos, even the olive seeds were sold for the production of gelatine. "In those days nothing went to waste. My parents were very industrious. Even after my father left, my mother would make her own *zivania* (alcohol) to sell. My parent's were not poor. They were making good money at the time. That's why I don't believe my father had to borrow any money for his ship fare. It's unbelievable for that time, but I think his parents had enough money to pay for his fare."

"When my dad left, I remember my *pappou* (grandfather) would cry every day," recalls Ntinos softly. "He would sit on the bridge above our house and cry. Don't forget, he lost a daughter, then another son and now another child was leaving him. When my *pappou* would sit at the table to eat, he would often burst into tears and not touch his food."

I ask Ntinos to explain why his father left Cyprus. "His dream was to open up a business producing olive oil but he didn't have any money. So he thought to go to Australia and work hard, make enough money and then return to the village and set up his business. He had two friends in Melbourne, Dimitri Hadjinicola and Christos Constantinou so he decided to join them there. Dimitri actually sponsored him. A lot of people left from my village after the Second World War. In fact, because my father was gone for so long (twelve years) I became known as *'O Ntinos tis Christinas'* (Christina's son Ntinos). They didn't say Charalambos. People forgot about my father."

His wife was Christina Papapeiri (her father was the local priest in the village of Agios Theodoros). They grew up in Agios Theodoros. "My mum's parent's had arranged for her to marry someone else in the village and when my dad found out, he went and made a fuss so she could marry him. That's how it happened. They waited until they had built a house for her before they got married."

Charalambos and Christina were married in Agios Theodoros on the 16th of July, 1944.

In April 1945, Charalambos and Christina welcomed the birth of their first child, Constantinos (Ntinos). In December 1946, their daughter Areti was born followed by Maroulla (Maria) in February 1948 and Soula (Athanasoula) in December 1951. "My mother gave birth to my youngest sister a few days before my father left Cyprus. On the day he went to Limassol to board the ship, my mother stayed in bed because she had just had a baby."

According to Ntinos, his father spoke about the rotten potatoes and the fact that the food on the ship was bad. He was lucky to have some halloumi cheese with him that his mother had given him for the trip. "I don't know if anyone else from the village left with my dad. I didn't ask him that question and he never told me.

All I know is that he told us he planned to return to Cyprus after five years. I remember he said five years. But when the troubles began in 1955 and 56, he decided to stay in Australia to see if the situation would get better. I know he didn't want us to come to Australia. He always wanted to come back to Cyprus and to live his life in the village. It was hard for him too."

According to Ntinos, his father worked extremely hard in Melbourne in order to support his family. He was upset at his situation and desperate to find a solution. "He didn't realise how tough it was going to be in Melbourne," says Ntinos. I know that he worked very hard and would send money to my mother every month. It was about twenty-five pounds a month. When I was in high school, I was living with my dad's sister Angeliki in Larnaca. He would send her money to look after me. For that I can't fault him. He always sent money."

After Charalambos arrived to Australia, he was employed by a large construction company as a plasterer to work on buildings in the city of Melbourne. "He also worked for himself on weekends doing private jobs for people," explains Ntinos. At the time, he was living with his friend Dimitri in Prahran together with a number of other migrant men. He then moved to Albion Street in Brunswick to stay with another friend named Christos and his family. I know that my father suffered emotionally because he was living away from us for all those years. As a way of comforting himself, he deliberately chose to stay with friends who had young children. That's how he coped with the separation from his family. It was a very tough time for him."

After his father left, Ntinos embraced the duty and responsibility of looking after his mother and sisters. "When I was very young, I remember people would try to take advantage of my mother in the village, financially I mean.

As I grew older I was able to protect her and make sure that they didn't try to trick her or steal her property. Ntinos managed to complete his primary and secondary education with top marks.

When Ntinos turned sixteen, he decided to write a letter to his father expressing his desire to come and study in Australia. "I told him that I was very keen to go to university in America or the United Kingdom. If however, he arranged for me to come to Melbourne to study then he could also reunite the family. I told him to act quickly. Apparently, he was so moved by my letter that he agreed and immediately arranged for my mother and sisters to come in 1962 and then I arrived a year later once I had completed my high school education. They arrived on the ship Patris in November 1962 and I arrived in July 1963, also on the Patris. Three days after I finished high school I left Cyprus. I remember my father greeted me at Station Pier. He was taller than me. He was somewhat disappointed that I didn't speak proper Greek but instead, I spoke pure Cypriot from the village."

Once Ntinos was reunited with his family, they lived in a house that his father had purchased in Prahran. "It was a three bedroom house on Princes Street but we only stayed there for a few years because the Housing Commission forced us to sell the house in 1969. My father then bought another house in Malvern."

Ntinos speaks fondly of his mother Christina. "I admire her so much for what she did for us. She sacrificed so much and always gave us good advice. Can you imagine what she went through? She was left alone in the village with four young children and had to deal with everything. She was quite an amazing person to put up with what she did. I'm not blaming my father because after I got to know him and I found out what he went through on his own in Melbourne, it wasn't easy for him. Let me tell you. My dad's departure gave me the opportunity to make my own decisions and face life in my own way. His departure created such a strength and confidence in me that I doubt I would have been the same person had he stayed. He was very strict and I believe he would have restricted my plans for the future. I became a stronger person in his absence and because of his absence."

Charalambos Athanasiou died in 2008. He was aged ninety-two.

ACKNOWLEDGEMENTS

I would like to thank Ntinos Charalambous for allowing me to publish his father's story of migration and for his kind help and support.

Charalambos sent this postcard of Melbourne to his family in Cyprus in December 1953, ten months after he arrived. The postcard reads: "To my dear and unforgettable children and my dear wife. I wish you happiness for the New Year 1953. I didn't imagine my children that I would leave you to come to this dark foreign land to live. I kiss you, your father Charalambos."

LARNACA

IBRAHIM RIFAT

CLOCKWISE:
Back row, left to right: Zeka Hashim, Huseyin Rifat, Sefki Murat. Front row: Ibrahim Rifat, Suzan Huseyin, Fatma Mustafa, Tahir Salih (squatting) and unknown child. Fatma was betrothed to marry Tahir Salih. Melbourne, 1955.

Suzan Huseyin, Glaszner Studios, Larnaca, 1954.

Left to right: Huseyin Rifat, Fuat Hashim, Zeka Hashim, Tahir Salih, unknown. unknown man squatting. North Melbourne, 1951.

Ibrahim Rifat, aged 29. Melbourne, 10th January, 1953.

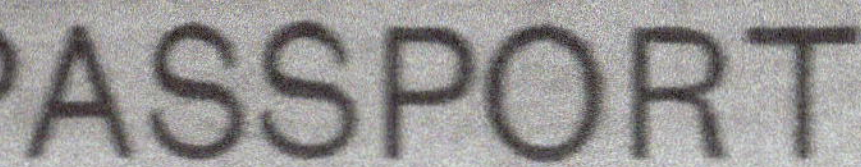

PASSPORT

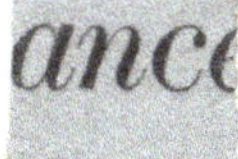

Rickshaw drivers in Colombo, Ceylon. Ibrahim is seated second from the left. The other men are unknown. January 8th, 1952.

Ibrahim Rifat was born in the village of Menoyia, Larnaca on the 3rd of March, 1923. He was the fifth-born child of Rifat Hassan and Amber Receb, who had nine children in total (six boys and three girls). Ibrahim's older brothers were; Niyazi, Hassan, Nazim, Behcet and his younger brother was Huseyin. His sisters were; Serif, Harise and Muhube.

The village of Menoyia consisted of both Greek and Turkish inhabitants. Although they lived, worked and socialised together, they valued and respected each other's cultural heritage.

From an early age, Ibrahim worked before and after school. He would help his parents to sow and harvest crops and to care for their farm animals. Like most children in Cyprus at the time, he was expected to work hard to ease the financial burden on his family and to improve the welfare of the village. His primary education was therefore cut short and he completed only four years of schooling.

Around the mid-1940s, Ibrahim's family experienced a series of financial and personal tragedies. First, his father, Rifat Hassan, lost an inheritance dispute in court, which forced them to sell their family home in order to pay the legal fees. Then Rifat's appendix ruptured and he passed away in 1948. Ibrahim now had the responsibility of looking after his widowed mother and his three unmarried sisters. He had to work even harder and accepted any job that was available such as harvesting, shearing, fruit picking and even road construction. As was the custom, he also provided for his sisters' dowries so they could marry. In time, he was able to secure his mother's comfort and independence by buying her a small house in Menoyia.

Despite the many challenges he faced, Ibrahim felt no resentment or indignation towards his family. In 1951, however, he decided to migrate to Australia. He felt that his life in the village was becoming tedious and restrictive. He longed to start in new life in Australia where he had heard that work and labour were always in demand. His youngest brother Huseyin had migrated there a few years earlier as did some other men from his village. They had positive things to say about the so-called 'lucky country,' in their letters which convinced Ibrahim to follow their lead.

When Ibrahim arrived at the Port of Limassol on a cold and wet December morning in 1951, he was full of hope and dreaming of a better future. He hugged and kissed his family good-bye; not knowing that he would never to see his mother again nor return to his homeland. As he boarded the Corsica, he felt the weight of poverty, hardship and family obligation slip away and he prepared himself for a new adventure abroad. This was a decision that he would never regret.

According to his daughter Ozal, Ibrahim never really talked about his journey to Australia. "My father didn't say much about his experience on the Corsica although he did mention that the ship seemed to be going backwards and not forwards. That's how slow it was. He also mentioned that there were a lot of potatoes in the cargo hold that had gone bad. They had to throw them all out in the ocean when they reached Colombo."

After a long and exhausting seven-week journey, a nervous and apprehensive Ibrahim finally set foot onto Station Pier at the Port of Melbourne. His good friend Tahir Salih was there to greet him. He had migrated to Australia six months earlier with the migrant ship Protea. Ibrahim was surprised to learn that Tahir had organised his accommodation in Melbourne, and had paid the first month's rent in advance. Tahir even secured him a job at General Motors. Two days after arriving in Melbourne, Ibrahim commenced working the afternoon shift on the production line at Fishermans Bend. In those days there was no need for an interview, resume, aptitude test, medical examination or police check. All you needed was a verbal recommendation and the job was yours.

"My father would never forget Tahir's kindness and assistance to help him settle in Melbourne," his daughter Ozal tells me. "He was amazed when he received a pay packet at the end of his first week at General Motors. He couldn't believe it. Back in Cyprus, he would work for others and then have to chase them for weeks or sometimes months, begging them to pay him. Now he was getting paid straight away, at the end of each week without fail. He started to save his money and eventually bought himself a house in Abbotsford."

Like so many Cypriot migrants, Ibrahim could hardly speak or understand a word of English. This was particularly challenging and a source of great frustration for him. His frustration would be tested one extremely, foggy night after finishing work. He decided to catch a taxi home rather than endure public transport. He showed the taxi driver his address which was written on a piece of paper. When the driver parked in front of his house, Ibrahim became disoriented and refused to leave the taxi. He didn't recognise the house. All the houses were Victorian Terrace homes, so they all looked alike. Perhaps it was the dense fog that clouded his senses. He was certain that if he paid the driver and left his taxi, he will be stranded in the middle of nowhere. Sensing his apprehension, the driver guided Ibrahim to the front door. Pointing to the door, the Driver commanded, "Push! Push!". Ibrahim was horrified. He thought to himself, "what in the world have I done to this man for him to call me a *Pusht*?" Luckily one of the boarders

in the house, heard the commotion and opened the door before any altercation occurred.

Although his command of English was very limited, Ibrahim knew Greek reasonably well. He had learnt the language on the streets of his village as a young boy by interacting with his neighbours and the other Greek inhabitants. His knowledge of both Turkish and Greek made it easier for him to communicate with his co-workers at General Motors.

During his bachelor days in Australia, Ibrahim mainly socialized with other Cypriot bachelors. On weekends, Ibrahim would meet his Turkish friends by the banks of the Yarra River, where they would sit, drink and exchange stories or share their weekly adventures with one another. Sometimes he would frequent a popular Greek club on Lonsdale Street,

Three sets of brothers from Menoyia, Cyprus. Standing from left to right: Huseyin Rifat, Tahir Salih, Ali Salih and Fuat Hashim. Seated: Ibrahim Rifat and Zeka Hashim. Melbourne, April, 1952.

where he could socialise with other Cypriot migrants and eat a familiar Cypriot meal.

In 1953, a year after he arrived, Ibrahim decided it was time to get married. He wrote to his mother in Cyprus and asked her to find him a suitable bride. His mother Amber approached Huseyin Chavoush and Vasviye Huseyin in the neighbouring village

of Klavdhia (Klavdia), to discuss a marriage between their daughter Suzan and her son. They agreed. Soon after, Suzan and Ibrahim started to send each other letters and photographs, in an attempt to get to know one another. "My mother was hesitant about coming to Australia," recalls Ozal, "so my father wrote and advised her that the Olympic Games were coming to Melbourne. He promised her that if she came to Melbourne, he would take her to the Olympics. As it turned out, when the Olympics games commenced, my mum was heavily pregnant, so she stayed at home and my father went to the Olympics on his own."

Suzan Huseyin Chavoush was born in Klavdia in 1938. The inhabitants of her village were all Turkish Cypriot. When Suzan was quite young, her family moved away from the village, to live and work on a farm (*chiftlik*) in Arpera. The surrounding

farms were owned or operated by Greek Cypriots. Suzan naturally learnt to speak Greek, through interaction with her neighbours and farm workers.

Ozal recalls her mother telling her, "When the family was living and working on the *chiftlik*, her mother would take the sheep out to pasture with her older sister. The neighbouring farmers also took their

From left to right: Tahir Salih, unknown, Fuat Hashim, unknown, Huseyin Rifat, Zeka Hashim and Ibrahim Rifat. Botanical Gardens, Melbourne, 1954.

herd of sheep out to the surrounding pastures. Not once, did any man approach my mother or her sister or say a nasty word to them." Here was my mother and aunt in the middle of nowhere surrounded by sheep and the men kept their distance and left them alone. This is an example of the respect that all communities and families had for one another.

When Suzan became a teenager, she went to work alongside a dressmaker, as an apprentice in Larnaca. Suzan learnt to sew and become a seamstress. It was during this time that she became betrothed to Ibrahim.

After two years of written correspondence with her future husband, Suzan was granted permission by the Australian government to migrate to Australia. Part of her application to enter Australia, included a clause, stating that a bond of 100 pounds be provided (by Ibrahim) that may be used by Suzan to pay for her return passage to Cyprus if she decided not to marry him. This was a form of travel insurance. The bond would only be returned to the applicant, after the 'proxy bride' had married and resided in Australia for over a year.

In May 1955, Suzan Huseyin bid farewell to her family and friends and boarded the ship Skaugum bound for Australia. She was only seventeen years old. Apparently, some of the families in Klavdia were not happy that she was leaving to marry a man in Australia. "There were fathers with sons who were not pleased to see my mother leave," says Ozal. "At the coffee shop, some of the village men would approach my grandfather and say, aren't the young men in our village good enough to marry? Why does your daughter have to travel so far to get a husband? My mother was so young at the time, so she did what her parents had decided for her."

Suzan was travelling to Australia with her friend Fatma Mustafa. Fatma was engaged to Ibrahim's friend Tahir Salih. They reached Port Melbourne on the 2nd of June, 1955. Ibrahim and Tahir and a number of their male friends were waiting for them at the pier. After the initial greetings and introductions, they went to Ibrahim's newly acquired house in Abbotsford. "I remember my mother telling me that she was very shy and nervous. My father had invited his friends to the house because they wanted to

hear from my mother Suzan, all the news from home. My mother told me it was the first time she had sat down at a dinner table with unrelated men, all chatting and laughing. In Cyprus, she had only dined with male family members. Suzan felt very uncomfortable with the boisterous chatter, so she excused herself after serving the food and went and sat in another room to eat alone."

Two weeks later, Suzan married Ibrahim at the Registry Office in Melbourne. Her friend Fatma also married Tahir on the same day.

Suzan slowly settled into her new environment. Her Polish neighbour, Stella was very kind to her and helped her when Ibrahim went off to work. Abbotsford in the 1950s was a suburb with many immigrants from Europe.

In late 1955, Suzan's sister Baykan arrived as a proxy bride. She married a Cypriot man name Shefki Mourat from Paphos. Shefki had also migrated to Australia aboard the Corsica. Baykan's arrival gave Suzan a sense of family.

In 1956, Ibrahim and Suzan were blessed with a son named Ozgun. In 1960, their daughter Ozal was born followed by another son Huseyin in 1962. In 1964, Ibrahim sold his house in Abbotsford and moved his family to Glenroy.

Ozal has fond memories of her childhood. She remembers as children growing up that they socialized with their cousins, other Turkish Cypriot families, went on picnics and attended the Turkish Cypriot club in Richmond. Mixing with other Cypriots provided her parents comfort and a connection to their homeland, but at the same time they celebrated Australian life. The family would enjoy going on outings to the Moomba March, Royal Melbourne Show, to fairs, to the Cinema, the beach during summer and country drives.

For her parents, life in Australia was enormously different to their life in Cyprus. Their Abbotsford home had electricity and

running water. There were trains, trams and taxis to travel on. They shopped at the Victoria Market, which had an abundance of meat, fruit and vegetables.

Ibrahim worked hard in Australia, which enabled him to buy a home and raise his family. Australia gave Ibrahim and Suzan security and provided an education to their children. If you were willing to work hard, one could achieve a comfortable lifestyle in comparison to Cyprus at that time.

Although they embraced the Australian way of life, Ibrahim and Suzan passed on their Cypriot culture to their Children. Suzan always cooked Cypriot foods at home and they encouraged their children to learn the Turkish language. Cypriot culture is based upon family unity. Ozgun, Ozal and Huseyin treasured the love and devotion bestowed upon them by their parents. They valued honesty, loyalty and hard work. Their disciplined and loving upbringing enabled them to become caring and principled individuals.

Ibrahim Rifat passed away in May, 2007 at the age of eighty-four. His wife Suzan passed away in September, 2019 at the age eighty-one. Ibrahim and Suzan felt fortunate and were thankful to raise their family in Australia, but their Cypriot culture always ran through their veins.

ACKNOWLEDGEMENTS

I would like to thank Ozal Halil for allowing me to publish her father's story of migration and for her kind help and support along the way.

COMMONWEALTH OF AUSTRALIA

APPLICATION FOR PERMIT TO ENTER AUSTRALIA.

(Immigration Act...)

CLOCKWISE
- Suzan's father Huseyin Chavoush and her brothers, Hasan (left) and Tevfik (right). Glaszner Studios, Larnaca, 1955. This photo was sent to Suzan after she had migrated to Australia.
- Suzan Huseyin, aged fifteen. Glaszner Studios, Larnaca. November, 1953. She sent this photo to Ibrahim, shortly after she had agreed to become his bride. When Ibrahim received this photo, he wrote back and requested a full-length photograph. Suzan would later tell her daughter Ozal, 'Perhaps your father wanted to be sure that I wasn't sitting in a wheel chair.' She designed and made the dress she is wearing.
- Ibrahim's mother Amber Receb (seated) and sisters Harise and Serif. His Aunt Emine Mahmut is on the right. Cyprus. 1949.
- Suzan's family. Her mother Vasviye Chavoush (left), sisters Baykan (seated) and Jale and brother Erol. Glaszner Studios in Larnaca. September, 1954.

(7) My last place of permanent residence was *Mennaya, Larnaca. Cyprus*

(8) My present occupation is... *Farmer*

Studio portrait of Kyriacou
Stavrou as a bride in Sydney,
February 8th, 1953.

KYRIACOU STAVROU

Name **KYRIACOU STAVROU**

Date of birth / Age **30.5.1933 / 18**

Occupation **SEAMSTRESS**

Place of origin **PYRGA, LARNACA**

Port of departure **LIMASSOL**

Date of departure **17 DEC 1951**

Date of arrival **4 FEB 1952**

Kyriacou and Christos' engagement photograph. Sydney, 1952.

Kyriacou Stavrou was born on the 30th of May, 1933 in the village of Pyrga, Larnaca. Her parents were Stavros and Maria Stavrou and she was one of seven children whose names were; Shenkou, Maria, Odysseas (Minoshi) Andreas, Kosta, and Loukia.

Kyriacou only attended school until the fourth grade before she was forced to abandon her education to help her brothers Andreas and Kosta on the family farm and in the fields performing various agricultural tasks.

Her father Stavros always believed that there were better opportunities for Cypriots overseas. As a young child Kyriacou remembers her father travelling to America to work, to gather the funds to support his growing family. He worked on the wharfs and did whatever labouring work he could find. He enjoyed his time in America but returned to Cyprus to settle outstanding family issues. Wanting only the best for his children he often encouraged his children to seek better opportunities overseas. In 1951, Kyriacou's older brother Odysseus decided to emigrate to Australia. Reluctantly, her father agreed that Kyriacou should go with him. Odysseus had heard that Australia could provide many opportunities to migrants with regards to employment and making good money. Kyriacou, who had trained as a seamstress, was also keen to earn money to support her struggling family back in Cyprus.

In December 1951, Kyriacou together with her older brother Odysseus boarded the Corsica bound for Australia. For most of the journey, the shy eighteen year old kept to herself and was under the constant supervision of her brother. Like so many other passengers she suffered from sea sickness and nausea, either from the constant swaying and rocking of the ship or from the stench of rotting onions and potatoes coming from the cargo hold. She spent a good deal of time up on the deck consuming lemons to settle her stomach and trying to avoid the stench coming from below. At each port, she would reluctantly disembark onto dry land but made a point to remain within the port area as she did not have the confidence to explore further afield.

Kyriacou's first glimpse of Australia was Fremantle where she disembarked to explore the port township. She was immediately astounded by the hustle and bustle of town compared to the other ports she had visited. She was also impressed by the cleanliness and organisation of the streets, shops and houses. The local residents seemed polite and appeared to take care of their appearance. Her positive first impression of Australia would remain with Kyriacou throughout her life.

After disembarking at Station Pier nine days later, Kyriacou was given tickets to travel by train to Sydney. She initially lived in the suburb of Surry Hills with other Cypriot migrants in a shared terraced house. She found steady work in the city centre cleaning at various cafes and restaurants that were owned or managed by Greeks and Cypriots who did not expect or care that she spoke very little English.

During her first few months in Sydney, Kyriacou discovered that many Cypriot migrants would gather and meet at events that were organised and run by the Greek Orthodox Church of the Holy Trinity located on Bourke St, Surry Hills. These social and community events included weddings and dances. In fact, it was at one of these weddings where Kyriacou was introduced to Christos Serghiou (later known as Christos Sergis), a young Cypriot migrant from Morphou. They were married in 1953 and lived in a house in Wentworthville that Christos had bought in 1952. This is where they also raised their family of three; Harry born in 1953, Stephen born in 1958 and Eva born in 1963.

Over the years Christos and Kyriacou worked together at the Bonds Spinning Mills at Pendle Hill. Despite having children Kyriacou worked at the cotton mills for forty-two years before retiring at the age of sixty-five. She remembered her years at Bonds very fondly as her employer provided her with many work opportunities and was understanding of her needs when raising her family. It was at Bonds where she also mastered the English language.

In July 2012, Christos Sergis sadly passed away. Kyriacou remained in the family home surrounded and supported by her children and their families, including eight grandchildren and eight great-grandchildren until she died on the 8th of May, 2021.

ACKNOWLEDGEMENTS
I would like to thank Eva Constanti for allowing me to publish her mother's story of migration and for her kind help and support along the way.

Kyriaki and Christos Sergis on their wedding day, February 8th, 1953. They were married at the church of Ayia Sofia in Surry Hills, Sydney.

THE CORSICA

LARNACA

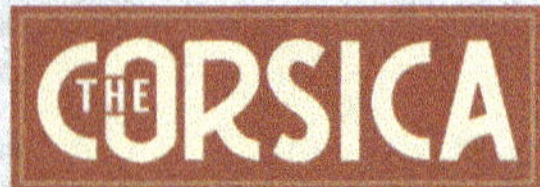

GEORGIOS ANTONIOU

No 52

Bearer
(Titulaire)

CYPRUS 4½ PIASTRES

CYPRUS POLICE
(LIMASSOL)
13 DEC 1951
DEPARTURE

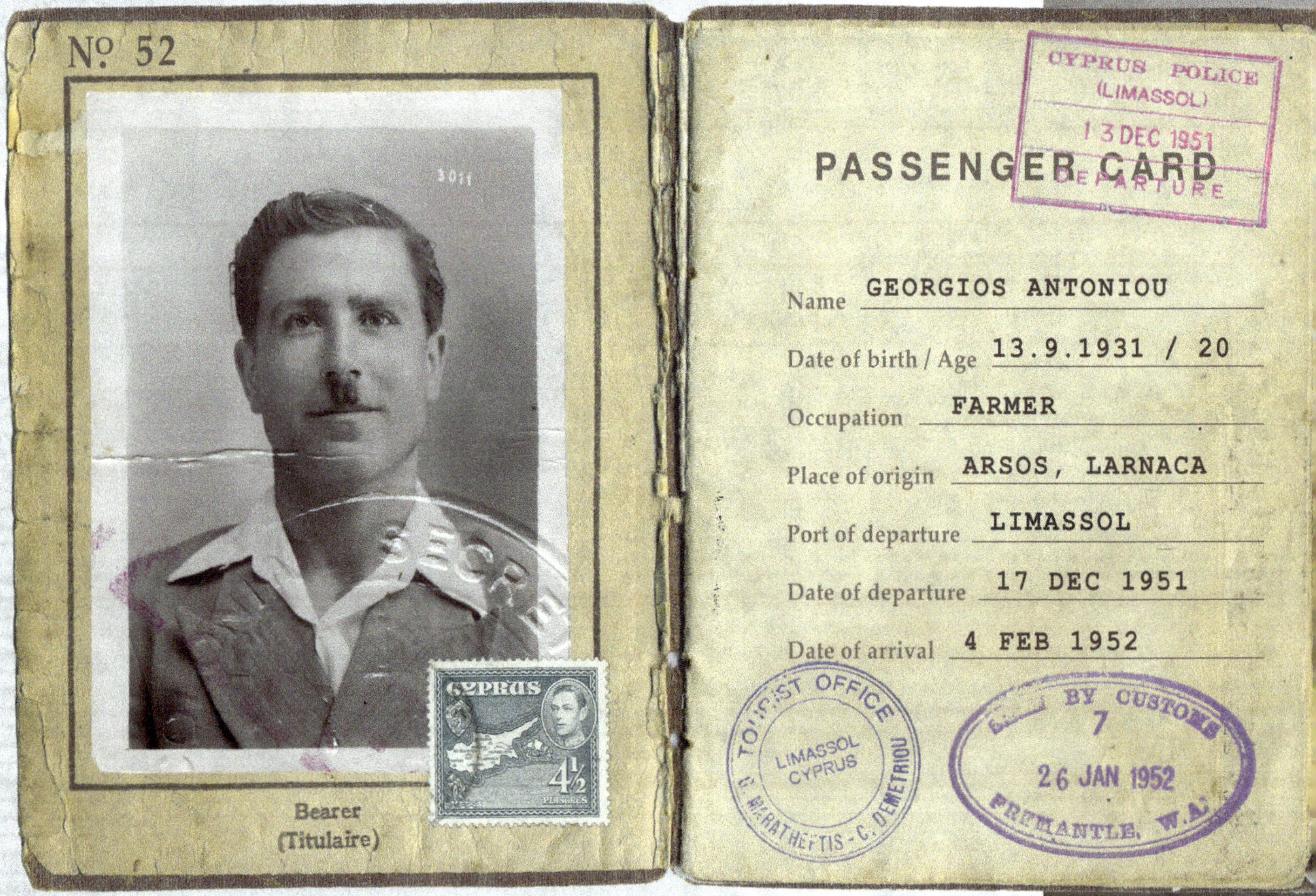

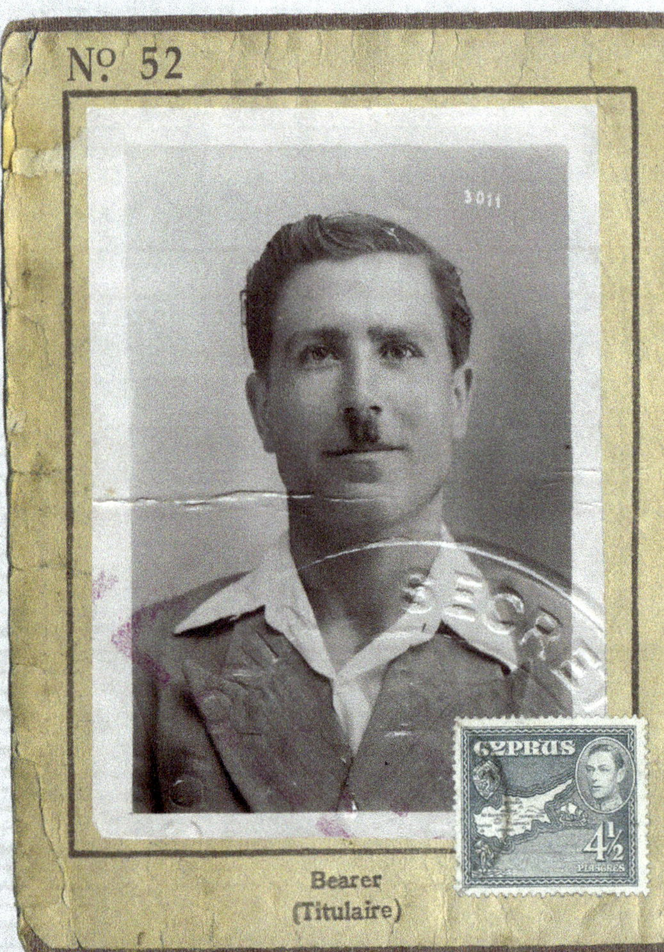

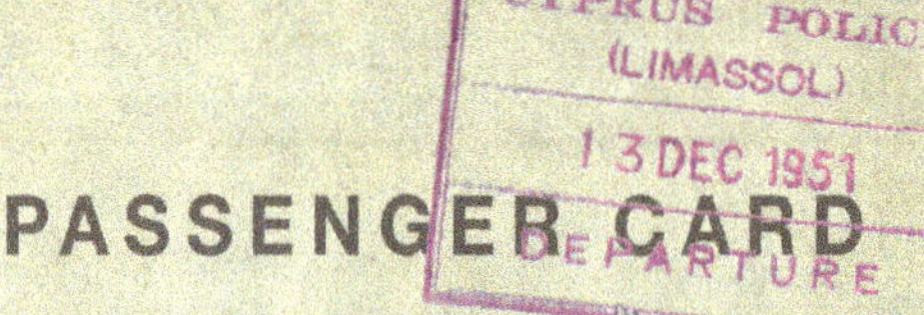

PASSENGER CARD

Name GEORGIOS ANTONIOU

Date of birth / Age 13.9.1931 / 20

Occupation FARMER

Place of origin ARSOS, LARNACA

Port of departure LIMASSOL

Date of departure 17 DEC 1951

Date of arrival 4 FEB 1952

TOURIST OFFICE
LIMASSOL
CYPRUS
C. MARATHEFTIS - C. DEMETRIOU

BY CUSTOMS
7
26 JAN 1952
FREMANTLE, W.A.

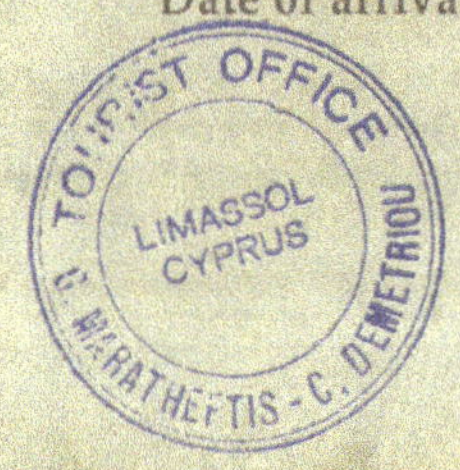

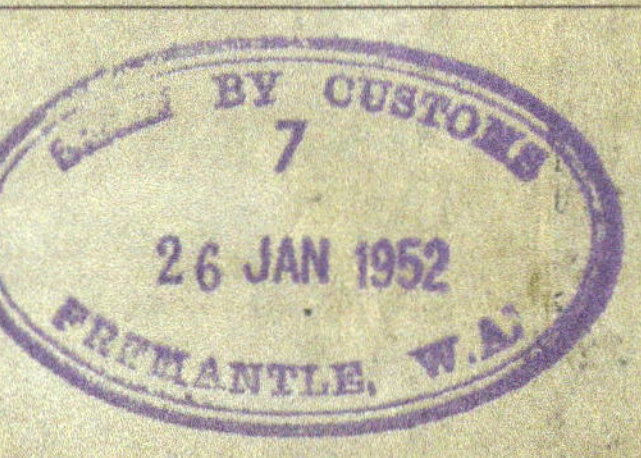

Georgios Antoniou. Paddington, Sydney, 1952.

Georgios Antoniou (centre) with friends. Redfern Street, Redfern, Sydney. Circa 1954.

Georgios Antoniou was born in the small mixed village of Arsos, Larnaca, on the 13th of September, 1931. He was the second of ten children born to Antonis Georgalli and Myrofora Louca; the first being Panayis, then Georgios, Katerina, Anastasia, Kyriakos, Lucas, Andreas, Vasilis, Niki and Dimos.

Arsos was a lush village with approximately 600 inhabitants from both the Greek and Turkish Cypriot community. They lived together freely and in harmony. The social activities that united the community in Arsos included, church on Sundays, the occasional wedding or baptism and if you were male, going to the *kafenion* (coffee house). "Our father was very bright at school," says his son Peter. "He reached maximum elementary level at aged eleven. There was no secondary school in the village and despite the school principal pleading with our grandfather to allow him to continue with his education, this was not an option for our father. Georgios' father owned a prized orchard and he regularly received government donations and support, encouraging him to boost production. Georgios was destined to work in the family field and orchard, along with his older brother."

With little opportunity working on the land and a yearning for adventure, the highly spirited twenty year old embraced the post-war immigration exodus from Cyprus and set off to find work in Australia. He hoped for a better life and economic security. By all accounts, Georgios was a handsome young man and popular with the girls, both Greek and Turkish Cypriot. "When I explored why our father decided to leave Cyprus, our uncle Kyriakos explained that a village of 600 inhabitants was too small for Georgios!"

Georgios boarded the Corsica in late December 1951, for the start of a journey that would change the course of his life. According to his daughter Bobby, her father did not really talk about the Corsica or his migrant journey to Australia. "He rarely spoke about the trip. This may be because it was so treacherous, and he spent so much time in his crowded cabin feeling sick. I do, however, recall him talking about the rotting potatoes and the all-pervading stench that came from the hull."

After a perilous seven-week voyage, Georgios finally arrived at Station Pier in Port Melbourne. Without any financial means or language skills he made his way to Sydney by train, forging a strong and long-lasting friendship with fellow passenger, Kyriacos Constanti. "I don't think my father's sponsor turned up to meet him when he arrived in Sydney" remarks Peter. "Somehow, he contacted the brother of his village schoolteacher who helped him with the immigration and customs officials at the station. "The day he arrived, Georgios was directed to a boarding house on Pitt Street in Redfern, where he shared rooms with other migrant men.

His shipboard friend Kyriakos had heard about work at a local factory. They headed straight to the Australian Consolidated Industries (ACI) glass factory in Waterloo where they were instantly hired and put to work on the production line. Unskilled migrants at that time were often given the dirtiest and most dangerous jobs. Georgios worked day and night shifts, saving as much money as he could, to send back to his family in Cyprus, to make their life a little easier.

He soon moved to the house of a Cypriot acquaintance, Loizos Loizou on Redfern Street, Redfern. "My father worked Monday to Friday at ACI and then on Saturday mornings he would meet the other local Cypriot men at the pub on the corner of Redfern and Pitt Streets," Tony explains. "Back then, I believe the pub opened at 10am and closed at 6pm." "At lunchtime, all the friends and relatives, mostly single young men, would meet for coffee and snacks at the home of Panayis and Zinovia Vasili (Pitt Street Redfern), and the house where Kyriakos was boarding. It was here that my father met Arthur Papageorge, a man who would become a close friend, *koumbaro* (best man) and Godfather to my sister Miranda. Arthur and his wife Eleni were well known and respected in the Cypriot community. They would wait at the wharves when ships arrived to help Cypriots that needed immediate assistance."

On Saturday afternoons the men would head to Andreas Aristithis' *kafenion* on Castlereagh Street, Sydney where other Cypriots would gather. "Andreas, just like Arthur Papageorge, migrated from Cyprus in the 1920s and was responsible for helping hundreds of Cypriot migrants settle in Australia," says Tony. "On Sunday mornings, all the local Cypriot migrants would go to Saint Sofia Greek Orthodox Cathedral in Darlinghurst. They would return to Redfern, where each household took it in turns to host Sunday lunch. After lunch they would walk to Hyde Park or the Botanical Gardens for ice-cream."

Georgios was content in Sydney, and he settled into his adopted home and new lifestyle quite happily. He knew however, that future success hinged on him learning English. Due to financial and time constraints, attending English classes was not an option. Instead, he bought himself a small Greek to English dictionary and taught himself to read, write and speak English within the span of only a few years.

In 1956, Georgios was introduced to eighteen year old Stavroulla Georgiou who had migrated from the Cypriot village of Aradippou. She was the younger sister of Kyriacos Constanti's wife, Myrofora. Stavroulla joined her sister Myrofora in Sydney in search of work and marriage.

Georgios and Stavroulla's engagement. City Road, Chippendale, Sydney. May, 1957.

Georgios and Stavroulla Antoniou's wedding day at St Sophia Church, Darlinghurst, Sydney. July 21st, 1957.

vibration from Stavroulla's sewing machine quickly drove the tenants out, making room for the regular onboarding of family and friends as they migrated from Cyprus. It is here in Redfern where they raised their four children; Miranda (Myrofora) born in 1958, Tony (Antonis) born in 1961, Peter (Pantelis) born in 1966 and Bobby (Kaliopi) born in 1967.

"Dad was a very popular man and made friends easily", says Bobby. "But I remember one morning he arrived home following a night shift at the glass factory, with blood on his face and hands. I was about five or six and it was the first time I had heard the word 'wog', as he explained to my mother that he had been bashed while walking home and that his wallet had been taken. This did not deter him and he continued to embrace his life in multi-cultural Sydney with even more determination."

Unlike many of his peers, Georgios was quite domesticated, happily turning his hand to cooking, preparing school lunches, cleaning and shopping. He was also a keen singer, but too shy to take on the role of church canter, he reserved his singing for home and family gatherings. He had quite the collection of Greek vinyl records, with an eclectic range from popular Greek, classic Tango to Rebetika.

"Our father didn't return to Cyprus until 1978," says Peter. "His mother Myrofora was dying at the time. When he returned to Sydney, I asked him what it was like going back home. He looked at me and said, 'this is my home son', and I've never forgotten that."

"Despite that, he was still very Cypriot," adds Tony. "From all the stories he told over the years about Cyprus and his life over there, we all felt very Cypriot. He was immensely proud of his heritage and ensured we all learned to read and write Greek and to understand our Cypriot customs."

According to his children, Georgios' faith was a stabilising pillar of his life. He participated in community and religious-based events through his beloved Annunciation of Our Lady Greek Orthodox Church in Redfern from its inception in 1968 and served on the church committee for twenty-five years. "Our mother would be up early on Sunday mornings cooking way too much food," Peter says. "Although our father was quite reserved and unassuming, he would always drag

somebody home from church for lunch – be it someone he'd just met, the priest, bishop or even the archbishop! Our home was known as Central Station – our front door was rarely closed."

Since arriving in Sydney, Georgios worked in several jobs, finally returning to the first workplace that gave him hope and opportunity, only to be tragically killed in a preventable industrial accident in 1992.

While it was adventure and opportunity that first brought Georgios to Australia, it was his new friends, family and community that kept him there. He was eventually joined in Sydney by his sister Anastasia and his brothers Lucas and Vasilis. "The anticipation and hope for a better life never faded for our father. His ambitions live on in his children, grandchildren and great-grandchildren," his daughter Miranda concludes.

ACKNOWLEDGEMENTS

I would like to thank Miranda, Tony, Peter, and Bobby for allowing me to publish their father's story of migration and for all their help and support.

She arrived in Australia on the 6th of March 1956 on board the ship Cyrenia. After some initial hesitation, as Georgios was enjoying single life, he and Stavroulla were married on the 21st of July, 1957 at Saint Sophia Greek Orthodox Cathedral. As fate would have it, another Corsica fellow passenger, Demetrios Georgiou married Myrofora's and Stavroulla's sister, Fotoulla. "It's quite amazing that the three men who travelled together on the Corsica married three sisters and became *kouniathi* (brothers-in-laws)," says Tony.

As a qualified seamstress, Stavroulla was employed as a piece worker in factories around Surry Hills. She later worked from home where she could also undertake her domestic duties. At times, Stavroulla would spend up to twelve hours a day at her sewing machine piecing together garments for the mass-production industry, all the while trying to meet unreasonable quotas, for fear of not getting paid.

In 1961, Georgios and Stavroulla had saved enough money to buy their first home on Pitt Street in Redfern. By law, existing tenants could not be evicted by new owners so Georgios and Stavroulla would arrange regular parties and a flow of visitors at their new home. The noise from these gatherings and the constant

Georgios Antoniou at the ACI Glass Factory in Waterloo, Sydney. Circa 1953.

ANDREAS
GEORGALLOU

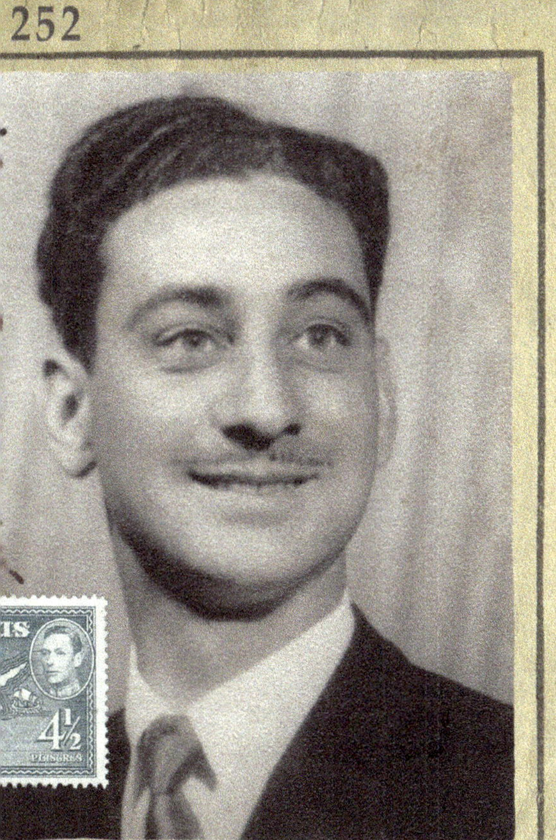

PASSENGER CARD

Name **ANDREAS GEORGALLOU**

Date of birth / Age **17.12.1927 / 24**

Occupation **CLERK**

Place of origin **SCALA, LARNACA**

Port of departure **LIMASSOL**

Date of departure **17 DEC 1951**

Date of arrival **4 FEB 1952**

OPPOSITE CLOCKWISE:
- Ioanna Georgallou, Nicosia, 1952.
- Andreas in Nicosia with unknown child.
- Studio photograph of Andreas Georgallou and his wife Ioanna taken the year they were married in Cyprus, 1945.

Ioanna Georgallou with her daughter Mary in Nicosia. May, 1952.

Andreas Georgallou was born in Scala, Larnaca on the 17th of December, 1927. He was the only child of Antigone Dimitriou Constantinou (from Larnaka tis Lapithou). The name of his biological father is unknown. As the story goes, when his mother Antigone was sixteen, she was sent to work as a child servant and was taken advantage of by one of the men in the house and became pregnant. She gave birth to Andreas when she was only seventeen. Fortunately, she met a kind-hearted tailor from Famagusta named Andreas Kyriacou Georgallou who accepted her and her young son without hesitation. At some point Andreas adopted the same name as his step-father.

When Andreas was around five years old his family moved from Scala to Famagusta for a short time, before settling in Nicosia where Andreas attended the Terra Santa College. Apparently in 1942, when he turned fifteen, he lied about his age to enlist with the Cypriot Volunteer Regiment but was found out and sent home to his parents.

Towards the end of World War Two, Andreas married his neighbour's daughter, Ioanna Pieri. Ioanna was born on the 27th of December, 1916 in the village of Karavas. Her parents were Pieris Charalambou and Eirini Stavri and she was the second of three children, with older sister, Maria (Maritsa) and younger brother George. As a youngster she would work in the fields and the orchards, tending the olive trees and vegetable plots or chasing cicadas in the carob trees rather than attend school. "My mum was a remarkable woman," her daughter Mary states proudly. "She was fiercely independent, intelligent and the personification of love. She was attractive, smart, witty, wise and kind, and above all a wonderful mother, but she was also very strict and the one to meter out the punishment when needed."

Without any formal education, Ioanna became a theatre nurse and worked alongside surgeons at the Nicosia General Hospital and with the Red Cross during the Second World War. When her family moved to Nicosia they happened to live next door to Andrea's family. "My mum had been engaged to a man for five years prior to marrying my dad. For some reason the promise of marriage was broken by her fiancé. My four grandparents, who lived next to each other in Nicosia, arranged the union between my parents, even though my mum was ten years older than my dad, to preserve her reputation. Family honour meant everything in those days and I imagine many a reputation was ruined after a prospective groom did a runner. My parents were married on the 19th of August, 1945 in Nicosia and I was born five years later."

In 1947 Andreas went to work at the Ottoman Bank in Nicosia as a messenger until he decided to migrate to Australia in 1951. He celebrated his twenty-fourth birthday on the day the Corsica departed Limassol. "Apparently my dad had to borrow the money for his ship fare, around 120 pounds, from a shopkeeper near his home," explains Mary. "I can only assume that he didn't earn enough money to pay his own fare. Like most Cypriots, he migrated to escape the hardships that existed in Cyprus at that time."

On the Corsica, Andreas was travelling together with a twenty-year-old clerk named Petros Zachariah Petrides and a twenty-three year old telephone repairman named Andreas Yiangoulli. "Only my dad was married," says Mary. "Petros and the other Andreas were single. Andreas later married Irini Zoe in Melbourne and I was a bridesmaid at their wedding. Petros came to Australia to work and contribute to his sister's wedding dowry and also sent her a gift of a wedding gown."

Mary recalls her father telling her that it was a very difficult journey and that the cargo hold was loaded with potatoes and onions that were rotting and the stench was nauseating. Andreas was originally destined to disembark in Sydney, but due to the horrific conditions on board the ship, he stayed in Melbourne. "In the early days he worked long hours in a variety of factory jobs and even sent money back home to his parents when he could," Mary explains. "He worked for General Motors Holden, Phillips Electrical, Peter Stuyvesant, General Electrics and ten years at the Government Aircraft Factory at Fishermans Bend as a fitter and turner."

Mary and her mother Ioanna travelled to Australia on the ship Largs Bay arriving at Station Pier on the 5th of October, 1953, where Andreas was waiting to greet them. "Not surprising, I didn't recognise my dad," Mary states. "So I cried when he held me in his arms."

The ship 'Largs Bay' that Ioanna and her daughter Mary travelled on. They boarded the ship at Port Said and arrived in Melbourne on 5th of October, 1953.

Andreas and Ioanna worked hard and quickly saved a deposit for their first home in Abbotsford. "When our neighbours in Abbotsford moved to Reservoir, dad bought their house too," says Mary. "Dad knocked down the wall separating the two houses turning them into one bigger home. Our home became a half-way house for many new arrivals. Usually, single young ladies searching for a better life in a new country. Most were accomplished seamstresses so I was never short of a new tailor-made outfit. Many betrothals took place at our house and there was always a party or celebration for an engagement, a birthday or name day. They were usually grand affairs with the women gathering in the kitchen cooking an array of mouth-watering delicacies and sharing stories and jokes with much laughter."

According to Mary, her father Andreas loved music and had taught himself to play the accordion in Cyprus. He also loved to sing. "Dad loved to learn new things and tried his hand at a variety of hobbies including making his own liqueurs, perfumes and even silversmithing. He made some lovely silver and gemstone rings, pendants and brooches that he

Ioanna with a patient at the Central Hospital in Nicosia where she worked.

proudly presented to mum. After mum passed away, dad rediscovered his faith and joined the chanters at Saint Nektarios Greek Orthodox Church in Fawkner, Melbourne and later chanted Divine Liturgy in his rich baritone voice at the Greek Orthodox Parish on the Sunshine Coast. He had a wicked sense of humour, a beaming smile and a loud and hearty laugh that was quite infectious. He did everything with great gusto and loved a party and a good game of *tavli* (backgammon)."

ACKNOWLEDGEMENTS

I would like to thank Mary Andreas for allowing me to publish her father's story of migration and for her help and support.

Andreas (left) with some friends at the mock bar in Luna Park, Melbourne. December 25th, 1952.

THE CORSICA

FAMAGUSTA

KATINA PAVLOU

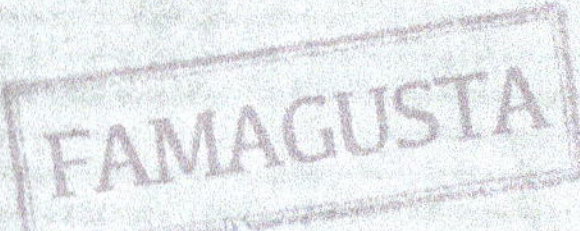

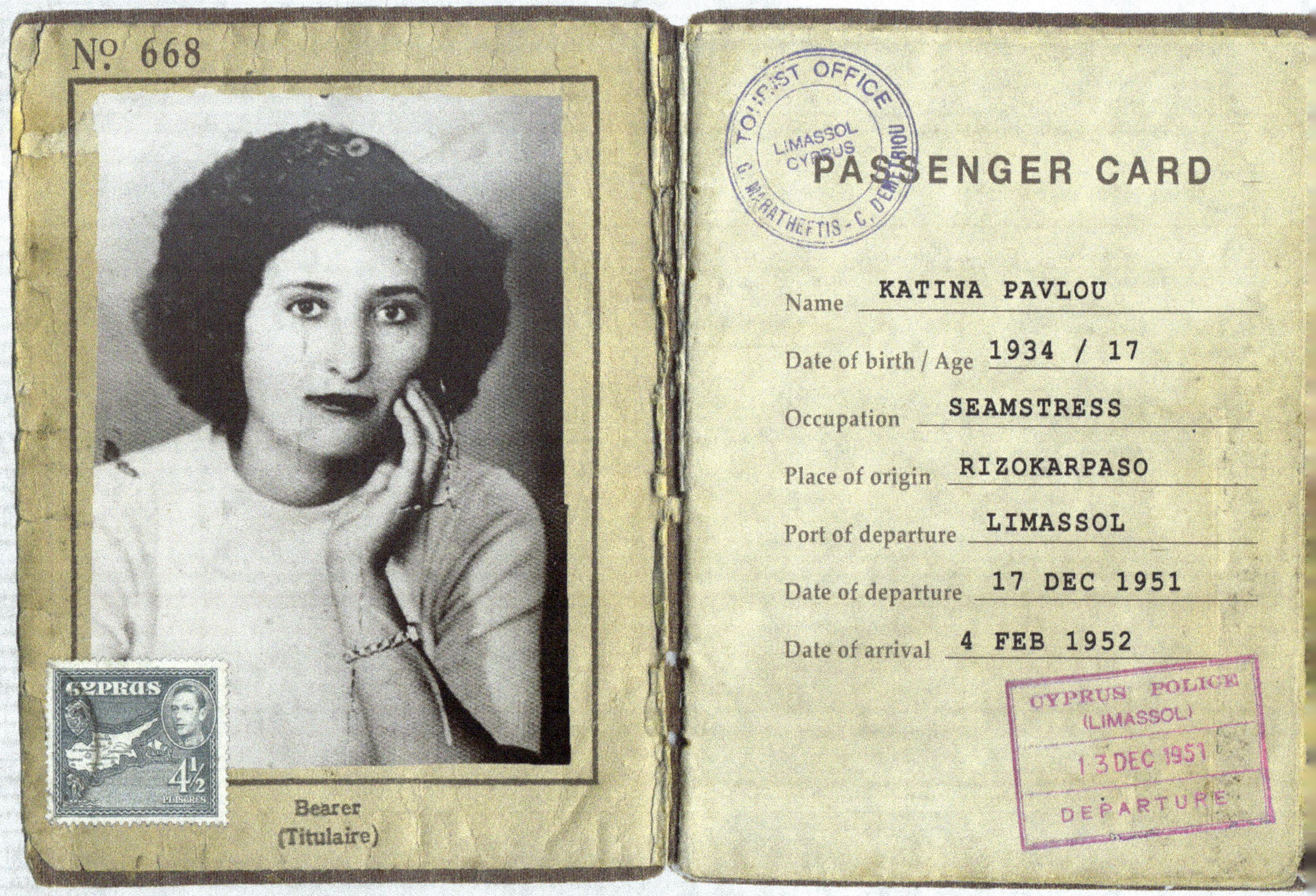

Nº 668

Bearer
(Titulaire)

CYPRUS 4½ PIASTRES

TOURIST OFFICE
LIMASSOL CYPRUS
G. MARATHEFTIS - C. DEMETRIOU

PASSENGER CARD

Name KATINA PAVLOU

Date of birth / Age 1934 / 17

Occupation SEAMSTRESS

Place of origin RIZOKARPASO

Port of departure LIMASSOL

Date of departure 17 DEC 1951

Date of arrival 4 FEB 1952

CYPRUS POLICE
(LIMASSOL)
13 DEC 1951
DEPARTURE

Katina (Katerina) Pavlou was born in the town of Rizokarpaso in 1934. She was the second-eldest of five daughters (Eleni, Andriana, Adelaide and Maroulla) born to Elefterios and Angeliki Pavlou-Chronias.

"My father was not a wealthy man," Katina tells me. "He was a farmer who grew tobacco and sold the leaves to the English. During the summer school break, my sisters and I would sit together on the ground to thread the leaves onto string and hang them to dry. When my father heard stories at his local *kafenion* (coffee house) about how both men and women in Australia were allowed to work and the custom of *prika* (dowry) did not really apply, he decided to send me there."

Katina had always planned to stay in Rizokarpaso and become a teacher. "I didn't want to leave Cyprus but I also didn't want to argue with my father, so for his sake I agreed to leave. I travelled with other girls from Rizokarpaso but we all went our separate ways after we arrived in Australia. I went to Sydney, a few girls went to Adelaide and a few stayed in Melbourne. I remember there was a delay in Limassol with the Corsica so we had to stay in a hotel for about a week. I'm not sure why there was a delay. The company that managed the ship paid for our hotel rooms. My family stayed with me in the hotel until the day I left."

As fate would have it, Katina met Andreas Georgiou on the ship. "He was working as a waiter on the Corsica and therefore travelled for free instead of getting paid. He was from the village of Prastio and had worked at the Famagusta Palace Hotel in Cyprus as a waiter. He would bring food to our cabin and that's when we first saw each other. I realised he must have been attracted to me when he started to bring me different food, better food than the other girls. Even the other girls noticed and started to tease me about his attraction. We didn't spend any time together on the ship. We only saw each other whenever he would bring the meals to our cabin. He asked me once on the ship about my intended destination and I told him I was travelling to Sydney. He told me that he was also traveling to Sydney but after we arrived in Australia we parted ways."

Andreas, like so many Cypriot migrants at the time, left Cyprus for economic reasons. His intention was to work for a few years and then to return home

Katina and Andreas's passport photos. Cyprus, 1951.

with enough money saved to live a more comfortable life. At least that's what he told his mother, who wept bitterly when he announced his intentions to travel abroad. He was twenty-one at the time.

When the Corsica reached Colombo, the passengers were told to go ashore while the crew dumped all the rotten potatoes and onions and cleaned the ship. "The authorities in Colombo wouldn't allow the ship to continue its journey until it was cleaned."

Katina does not remember how the fresh water supply on the ship had run out. "All I remember is the turbulent waters of the Indian Ocean and how I became violently ill after eating a banana. I wouldn't eat another banana for many years after that."

Once we arrived in Port Melbourne, everyone had to disembark from the Corsica and those passengers heading to Sydney had to travel there by train. "I believe the ship was either not allowed to go any further by the Australian authorities or perhaps the ship engines were in such a poor state that it couldn't travel any further. That is why we had to go to Sydney by train. I didn't see Andreas on the train, but when we arrived at Central station I saw him from afar and he saw me. We waved at each other and then went our separate ways. It was a while after that when a mutual friend in Redfern brought us both together. I think Andreas was making enquiries, trying to find me. When he asked me to marry him I was living with an elderly Cypriot couple in Redfern who didn't have any children and I mentioned Andreas to them. They were the ones who helped us to get married.

Meanwhile, back in Cyprus our parents met. His parents went from Prastio to Rizokarpaso to meet my parents."

In August 1952 Katina and Andreas were married. "It was our fate," explains Katina. "We met on the Corsica and we were married in Sydney, six months after we arrived. He didn't know anyone in Australia and neither did I. Over time, my sisters Eleni, Andriana and Adelaide all came to Australia and settled in Sydney. In 1962, my youngest sister Maroulla and my parents arrived and my family was finally reunited. Our father had sold our family home in Rizokarpaso and all our property."

Katerina and Andreas were blessed with three children; Angela (born in 1953), George (born in 1955), and Valentina (born in 1965).

In terms of employment, Katina worked at the Federal Match Company in Alexandria, making matchsticks, before finding work at the Smith Family, sorting clothes. She then joined the printing factory WA Pepperday in Marrickville. Andreas worked at Spurways during the 1960s which was a metal works company in Alexandria, that manufactured nuts and bolts. He also worked at Gilbarco, also in Alexandria making petrol bowsers and for a short time at Tip Top before settling at Hunt Holden in Lakemba as a car detailer. His final job was with Small's which later became Lifesavers.

ACKNOWLEDGEMENTS

I would like to thank Katina Pavlou for allowing me to publish her story of migration. Special thanks to her daughter Valentina Jones for her help and support.

LOIZOS
KYRIACOU

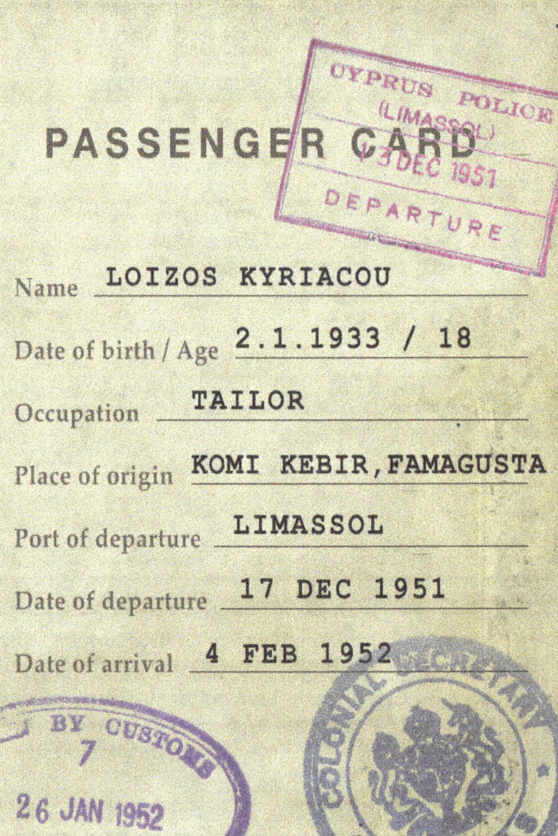

L ouis Kyriacou was born on the 2nd of January, 1933 in the village of Komi Kebir, near Famagusta. He was the second youngest of five children born to Kyriacos and Eleni Pavlouri. His siblings were Fotini (born in 1925), Andreas (born in 1928), Vasiliki (born in 1930) and Myrofora (born in 1935).

From a young age, Louis did his best to support his family and to please his father. "My father was a strict man with a very bad temper. He would ask me to water the vegetables and if I didn't do a good job then *taka* (bang), he would hit me. If he wasn't happy with my work, then *taka, taka, taka*. He would hit me. I eventually gave up. I wasn't going to put up with a beating, so I stopped watering the vegetables."

As for his education, Louis admits that he couldn't get along with his teachers and abandoned his studies in the fifth grade. "There was this one teacher named Triphonas," he tells me. "He was crazy. He tried to get me to sing at these PEK-run events. PEK was for the right-wing fascists and AKEL was for the communists. I refused to sing, so he made me stand in the corner of the school as punishment and he told the other children not to talk to me. I went to school to study - not to sit in the corner. I wasn't going to let this crazy teacher tell me what to do so I decide to leave the school. We Cypriots are crazy. From the moment we are born everything becomes political."

Like so many young Cypriot boys in the 1940s, Louis was swept away by the frenzied support of communism. "I used to read everything that was written by Stalin," he says. "Of course, it was all propaganda. I know that now. But at that time, many young boys, especially those who lived in poverty like me, really supported the views expressed by Karl Marx. His views really appealed to us."

After leaving school, Louis completed an apprenticeship with a local tailor in the village named Savvas Demosthenous, although he had dreams of becoming a carpenter. As fate would have it, his future belonged abroad. In 1951, Louis made plans to travel to Australia. "All of my older siblings had gone to England. My sister Fotini was the first to leave. We had relatives in London so she went to seek work there as a qualified seamstress. My brother Andreas followed her and eventually, so did Vasiliki. My sister Fotini

did not want me to travel to England. I think having one domineering brother over there was more than she could bear. I had read in the newspaper that there were plenty of jobs in Australia so I decided to immigrate to Melbourne instead. I was eighteen years old."

Despite his strict demeanour, Louis' father agreed to borrow the money to pay for his ship fare to Australia. "My family were quite poor. We had no disposable income to speak of. My father went to the *tokoliphtes* (money lenders) to borrow the money. I think the fare for the Corsica was around 130 pounds. That was a lot of money back then. I didn't even have half a *grossi* (penny) to my name. I remember how I would hide in the corner of the *kafenion* (coffee house) because I was so embarrassed that I couldn't even afford to buy a coffee."

There were five other young men, who left Komi Kebir with Louis to travel to Australia.

According to Louis, the Corsica was overcrowded with around 1,200 passengers, all of whom were Cypriot men aged between eighteen and twenty-three. He recalls that the journey took sixty-five days (nine weeks) before they reached Port Melbourne. "There were only young Cypriot men on the Corsica," he tells me confidently. "I don't remember seeing other nationalities or any women for that matter. We thought it was strange that after we paid the travel agent, he didn't give us any tickets. No one had tickets as far as I could tell. We paid our money but there were no tickets to prove that we paid. The travel agents took advantage of all of us. We were robbed. They charged us far more than what the journey was worth. Bloody bastards – those travel agents were."

Louis left Cyprus with a small suitcase and ten pounds in his pocket. "I remember being very excited at the time. After a

delay of four days in Limassol, the ship finally departed. I believe the delay was caused because they were loading the potatoes onto the ship which were stored down below. Most nights, my friends and I slept on the deck of the ship because of that stench from below. You couldn't sleep near the potatoes. It was that bad. Those potatoes began to rot because the Corsica took so bloody long to reach Ceylon. They were dumped in the ocean near the Port of Colombo."

According to Louis, the Corsica was forced to stop at Djibouti to refuel. "It was funny. Every time the Corsica stopped at a port, all the passengers would rush to one side to have a look at the town. This caused the ship to lean over. The captain would shout at us to go to the other side but no one ever listened. At Fremantle we disembarked because we wanted to buy fruit. No one could speak English so we had to point at the fruit so the shop keepers could understand us."

When asked about the food and service on the ship, Louis laughs loudly and says. "What service? There was no service. My friends and I became so agitated and angry at the lack of proper service that we started to throw the cutlery, plates, chairs and even the beds overboard. We really wrecked the place. I remember that the plates were made of metal, like the ones the soldiers used during the war. Our destruction occurred mostly at night, when the crew couldn't see us. I remember we became angry when they wouldn't give us enough food to eat. Some of us would sneak onto the lifeboats to eat the tins of food that were stored there. That's what we ate. Other times we would go into the kitchen and fry potatoes to eat. We had brought oil with us from Cyprus and the kitchen staff allowed us to fry the potatoes in their kitchen. Anyone who brought food with them from

Louis (left) with friend in Regional Victoria, 1952.

Louis in Coote Street, South Melbourne where he was boarding with the Solomou family. Circa 1954.

their village ate it all on the ship. For breakfast, I remember eating boiled eggs with bread and olives."

When the Corsica finally docked at Station Pier in Port Melbourne, Louis was greeted by a friend named Pantelis Solomou. "Pantelis had arrived a year earlier and managed to buy his own house in South Melbourne. All us new migrants split up at the port and went in different directions. At times, we would all meet up again at the Democritos Club, or the Orpheas Club or the Limassol Club or the Cyprus Cafe on Russell Street. In those days, we would rent rooms at various houses around the city. I paid around ten shillings a week to rent a room which I shared with six other migrants."

Unlike most new arrivals, Louis sought the company of the locals in order to learn how to speak English. "I would visit the pubs and drink VB with the Aussies. In those days, the pubs closed at 6pm so we had to rush and drink our beers before the bar closed. This was called the six o'clock swill. I met a lot of Aussies in the pubs back then. This is how I managed to learn the language."

When he wasn't in the pub drinking beer with his Aussie mates, Louis was busy chasing the Aussie girls. "You can imagine, coming from a place like Cyprus, where it's not allowed to even talk to girls, in Australia it was very different. I was going out nearly every night trying to meet girls."

During the first few years after his arrival, Louis spent a lot of time in regional Victoria, doing itinerant manual labour. He became a 'jack-of-all-trades' with the Victorian Country Roads Board. When he returned to Melbourne he began shift-work at IXL, a prominent canned fruit and jam manufacturer in South Yarra.

In 1955, Louis returned to Cyprus to marry Eleni Georgiou from the village of Pano Lefkara. As it happened, his friend Pantelis Solomou was her first cousin (their fathers were brothers) and he had

shown Louis a photo of Eleni insisting that he should marry her. "Eleni agreed to marry me," says Louis, "as long as I went back to Cyprus to marry her there. There was no way she was coming to Melbourne by ship to meet me, even if her cousin told her family that I was a good guy and could be trusted. She wanted me to marry her in Cyprus."

Before returning to Cyprus to meet Eleni, Louis wrote to his father Kyriacos warning him not to ask Eleni's father for any *prika* (dowry). "I told him I want nothing – only Eleni. I told him that I will achieve my own wealth one day and buy my own property."

Louis and Eleni were married in Pano Lefkara in 1955.

In August 1956, Louis and a very pregnant Eleni boarded the Egyptian migrant ship Gumhuryat MISR to travel to Australia. For Louis, married life in Australia was a much better and safer prospect than staying in Cyprus. In the mid-1950s, political tensions and civil disobedience on the island had escalated. The future for the island's inhabitants, both Muslim and Christian now seemed unstable. Eleni's parents were not happy when Louis announced his intentions to return to Australia with their daughter, especially now that she was pregnant. As fate would have it, a few weeks into their journey on the ship Gumhuryat, Eleni gave birth to her first child, a daughter named Kyriaki. "The Gumhuryat was worse than the Corsica," remarks Louis. "At one point, I tried to get the passengers to revolt against the travel agency who booked this ship, but most people were too scared and did not want to cause any trouble."

After arriving in Melbourne in September 1956, Louis and Eleni rented a room in various houses that were owned by established Cypriots until they could afford to purchase their first house two years later (located on Gladstone Grove, South Melbourne).

In 1959, Louis and Eleni welcomed the birth of their son George. When their daughter turned five, she was enrolled at

the Dorcas Street Primary School but the teacher couldn't pronounce Kyriaki and called her Julie instead. The name stuck.

During the 1960s, Louis started working for the furniture manufacturer Gainsborough as a cabinet maker, learning his trade on the job. He later became a union activist and eventually a shop-steward for the Federated Furnishing Trades Society. "The union was weak as piss in those days," he remarks boldly. "We were the lowest paid workers in the country. I helped to change all that. I remember some of the Aussie workers were not happy with me as a unionist and would shout, 'go back to your country you bloody wog,' but that didn't bother me. I knew what I had to do. Even though I received many threats, even death threats, nothing scared me off. I wasn't scared of anyone."

Throughout his working life in Australia, Louis fought hard to improve the working lives of the union members he represented. Some of his achievements included, equal pay for women, increases to the minimum wage for glass workers, better and safer working conditions and the introduction of a thirty-five hour working week.

ACKNOWLEDGEMENTS

I would like to thank Louis Kyriacou for letting me publish his story of migration. Special thanks to her daughter Julie Pagonis for her help and support over the last few years.

Louis outside his house on Coote Street, South Melbourne. Circa 1954.

From left to right: Elpida Loizou, Savvas Antoniou, Agathi Loizou (Elpida's sister-in-law) and Agathi's son, Nicos (age four).
Colombo, Ceylon. January 9th, 1952.

ELPIDA LOIZOU

The Loizou family in Cyprus before anyone migrated to Australia. Back row, left to right: Adamandia, Anastasios, Eleftheria, Loizos and Elpida. Front row: Elli, Georgios, Parthenopi (Elpida's mother), Nicholas (Elpida's father), Mahi and Andreas. Famagusta, Cyprus. Circa 1948.

Elpida Paraskevas (nee Loizou), was born in Varosi, Famagusta on the 14th of November, 1931. Her father Nicholas Loizou was a very proud man, who felt very strongly about his Greek Cypriot heritage. The three great loves of his life were; Cyprus, the Hellenic Republic and his five daughters whom he named Mahi (Battle), Eleftheria (Freedom), Elpida (Hope), Adamandia (Diamond) and Elli (Ellada). Apart from her four sisters, Elpida also had five brothers. Their names were; Loizos, Anastasios, Georgios, Andreas and Phrixos. Unfortunately, Phrixos died when he was very young. He was Elli's twin.

As a young girl, Elpida was very close to her siblings. She would often pack her overnight bag and go stay with a married sibling, mainly to get away from her endless household chores and duties. She was not too keen on cooking and cleaning, preferring to jump on the back of her brother's motor bike and go for joyrides. She was often scolded by her mother Parthenopi, but that did not deter her. Regarded by many as a bit of a 'tomboy', she did however go on to become a qualified seamstress.

In 1948, Elpida's brother Loizou decided to migrate to Melbourne, Australia. Two years later, he was joined by his wife and children and his brother Georgios. In early 1951, Elpida's father Nicholas also migrated to Australia. Later that year, Georgios arranged for his wife Agathi, and young son Nikos, to join him in Australia, Elpida agreed to accompany them. They all boarded the Corsica in Limassol along with Mihali Kaili, who was married to Elpida's sister Mahi. By 1963, most of Elpida's family had migrated to Australia. Only her sisters Eleftheria and Adamandia remained in Cyprus.

"I remember that when we arrived at the Port of Limassol to board the ship, there was some sort of delay and we had to stay overnight in Limassol," recalls Elpida. "There were a lot of family friends also travelling on the ship. We met up at the port and I was excited at the prospect of us all being together."

One of those friends, was a young girl named Olga Angellis, who was travelling with her mother Anna. On board the ship, Olga met and fell in love with her future husband Costas Anastassiades. Another friend of the family was a lady named Anastasia Plisi, who was travelling with her young son Andreas. Even though these ladies each had their own cabins, they spent most of the time with Elpida and Agathi. "We eventually, all shared the

Mihali Kaili in Colombo, Ceylon. January, 1952.

same cabin," says Elpida. "I remember us all bunking in together, sleeping head to toe and I would cuddle my young nephew. We ate together, we laughed together, we sang together and we cried together. They were tough times, but we managed. We had to manage, we had nowhere else to go, so we made the best of it. We shared whatever we had, just to get by."

Shortly after departing Cyprus, Elpida recalls that food became scarce on the Corsica, and that the sea became quite rough. "I remember how the ship was leaning and the ship's Captain would shout through loud speakers for passengers to move to the other-side so that the ship wouldn't lean so much. A lot of the passengers' luggage fell overboard because it was leaning so much. Those poor souls were left with only the clothes on their back and what little they had in their cabins."

According to Elpida, the passengers on the Corsica were not properly fed so they began eating the food that they had packed from Cyprus to bring to Australia. "I was a young rascal and I would climb down to the cargo hold of the ship, to steal potatoes and onions and bring them back to my cabin. The women would peel the potatoes and onions and then take them to the kitchen, where they would fry them so that we could eat something. No one liked the food they were serving on the ship. They gave us nothing but macaroni. We couldn't eat that rubbish."

Apart from befriending other Cypriot passengers on board the Corsica, Elpida met a young Cypriot man named Savvas Antoniou, who found work as a waiter on the ship and would bring her food to eat - whatever he could find. "Savvas was really good to me, and we became good friends. He really looked after us and would give us good advice."

Regarding the fresh water on the ship, Elpida recalls that it was undrinkable. "You couldn't drink the water," she exclaimed with a heavy sigh. "I used to give my brother-in-law, Mihali some money, so he could buy us bottled water, but it was so expensive. When our money ran out, we had to resort to boiling the water from the taps before we could drink it."

According to Elpida, there were mice scuttling around on the ship, more so after the potatoes and onions began to rot. "It was terrible. Passengers complained about the stench and many were violently sick.

Most stayed in their cabins. The sea was very rough and many passengers became seasick. We showered only once a week, and the toilets were also disgusting".

Elpida recalls also having good times on board the Corsica. "I had a great time with the people I met. We used to sit and sing together. It was a tough journey, but it was also quite good."

A highlight of Elpida's journey to Australia, was arriving at Fremantle on the 26th of January, 1952 and exploring the port town. "As the ship was delayed for a couple of days, we were allowed to get off the ship and wander around the port. Agathi was a little reluctant to buy food, as she did not have a lot of money. Whatever she had, she was saving for when she reached Melbourne. I had some money, from Cyprus, so I was glad to help out. We sat down at a cafe and ordered what was on offer. I think it was fish and chips. When the owner of the cafe heard that we had migrated from Cyprus, and I mentioned that we were from Varosi (Famagusta) he rushed to tell his wife. When she came out to greet us, there were hugs, tears and kisses all round. It turned out that the cafe owner's wife was my childhood friend. She had migrated earlier with her husband and set up shop in Fremantle. Of course, it goes without saying, that the food we ate that day was on the house. Cypriots are very hospitable in that way. They will feed their own people at no cost."

When Elpida arrived in Melbourne, she was greeted by her father and brother Georgios who took her to their rented accommodation in Fitzroy. A few months later, she was introduced to a man named Andreas Paraskevas.

According to Elpida, Andreas was a dashing young man who looked a lot like Clark Cable. He was born in Limassol and had migrated to Australia in 1949. They were married on the 21st of August, 1952, and lived in a room they rented in Kensington. Elpida's friend from the Corsica, Olga Anastassiades, became her bridesmaid and was later honoured in christening their daughter, Nikki.

Elpida filled her days by venturing out and going on short walks around the neighbourhood. When she became lost, she would ask a local how to find her way home. Most of the people in the area were Greeks, and knew each other, one way or the other.

Elpida and Andreas eventually bought a small single-fronted house in Richmond, where they raised their four children; Paris (born in 1953), Nikki (born in 1955), Sozos (born in 1956), and Mary (born in 1958). By 1960, they left Richmond, and bought a house in North Sunshine.

Elpida and Olga often reminisce about the old days and how once upon a time they were beautiful and carefree young girls.

At age ninety, Elpida is blessed with seven grandchildren and thirteen great-grandchildren.

Elpida with her father Nicholas taken shortly after she arrived in Melbourne in early 1952.

ACKNOWLEDGEMENTS

II would like to thank Elpida Loizou for allowing me to publish her story of migration. Special thanks to her daughter Nikki Theochari and to Mary Calombaris for their kind help and support.

FAMAGUSTA

SAVVAS ANTONIOU

CYPRUS POLICE
(LIMASSOL)
DEPARTURE

PASSENGER CARD

COLONIAL SECRETARY · CYPRUS

Name **SAVVAS ANTONIOU**

Date of birth / Age **26.11.1928 / 23**

Occupation **CARPENTER**

Place of origin **VAROSI, FAMAGUSTA**

Port of departure **LIMASSOL**

Date of departure **17 DEC 1951**

Date of arrival **4 FEB 1952**

avvas Antoniou was born on the 26th of November, 1928. He was born in the village of Akanthou but grew up in Agios Theodorou. His siblings were Andreas (born in 1925), Froso (born in 1926) and Takis (born in 1931). "My father Ioannis was an orphan from when he was nine years old," he tells me. "Even though he was about fifteen, he joined the Cyprus Volunteer Corp. during the First World War and served with the British army in Greece, Egypt and other places. After the war, when he was about eighteen, he became a policeman. He was earning three pounds a month, which included the money to feed his horse."

As a young boy, Savvas completed an apprenticeship in tailoring. "The apprenticeship lasted two years with no pay. After that, I earned a shilling a week. I worked six days a week for one shilling. If I went to the *kafenion* (coffee house), I could buy a coffee for one *groshi* (penny).

Before migrating to Australia, Savvas was working in Varosi, as a guard for the office of a British army major known as Major Whitehead. "During the Second World War, I went to volunteer for the British Armed Forces but I was too young. After the war, I saw a film that was promoting Australia as a possible destination for young hard-working men. I went to this travel agent in Varosi named Evagoras and paid 150 pounds. I paid for a cabin on the ship which I shared with three other men. One was Turkish Cypriot, another was from Scala and I can't remember the third man."

The following text has been translated from the journal that Savvas wrote during the voyage. "The Corsica arrived at Limassol on the 12th of December, 1951.

Men and boys outside the police station in Lefkoniko. Savvas' father, Ioannis is seated in front of the broom repairing a bicycle with a friend. Savvas' older brother Andreas (aged fifteen), is seated in the foreground and his younger brother Takis (aged around eight) is standing next to the doorway. Savvas Antoniou (aged twelve) is standing on the far right.

The shirtless men and the man seated near the truck are English soldiers. Circa 1942.

I was one of the first passengers to be allowed to board the ship on account that my brother Andreas was a *chaoushi* (police sergeant) and he had some influence. There were twelve people in my family who were policemen. The ship was the Corsica. All the workers were Greek except for the accountant who could speak Italian, Greek and English. He told us they were looking for men to work on the ship so I signed up as a waiter to work in the big dining room upstairs. There was also a smaller dining room downstairs. One day we were serving rabbit. For a joke I told the passengers in the dining room, 'today we have lovely food, it is hedgehog.' Some laughed, some ate the food, others didn't eat. People often complained about the food I was serving. What did they expect? Certain passengers were feeling unwell and could not go to the dining room to eat. There were around eight of them confined in their cabins. On the ship, if you wanted to eat, you must come to the dining hall. That's how it was. I used to sneak food out of the kitchen and deliver it to the cabins of these sick people. In this way, I met a girl who was from Varosi who was travelling with her sister-in-law. Her name was Elpida Paraskevas. Her brother Louizos was in Melbourne.

Our first stop was Port Said. When we got to Djibouti we went to a Greek Orthodox church. It was the first time the church was full of people. The priest was very happy. We went to the museum in Djibouti.

On Tuesday 15th of January, 1952 at 5am we passed the international dateline. There was a celebration on the ship and the crew threw water on us."

I started work on the Corsica straight away. I was washing dishes, peeling potatoes and serving food. I was promised one pound a day. I wrote down in my little journal that they owed me fifty-four pounds in total as I had been working every day of the trip. The accountant however, only paid me forty-five pounds. I had to argue with him to pay me what they owed. They tried to rob me but you see I wrote everything down in my journal, so I knew what they owed me. If I remember correctly, there were around fifty people working in the ship's kitchen. I knew everyone and they all knew me. On the first day of the trip, from Cyprus to Egypt, nearly all the passengers got dizzy. I was lucky. I never got seasick."

Once he arrived in Melbourne Savvas struggled to find work. After three months, he found a job at the Standard Motor Company in Port Melbourne. He was renting a room at a house on High Street, Prahran until he was able to save enough money to purchase his first house in Richmond. Sometime in 1954, he went to work for a Jewish man at his fruit shop in Richmond until he became a signal man for the railways. "I was one of the first migrants to buy an automobile in Melbourne," he says proudly. "It was a Holden of course."

Savvas met a woman on the Corsica named Anastasia Plisi who, in time, would arrange for him to marry her niece, Niki Ioannou. "Anastasia was sick on the ship and I would take food to her cabin. She must have taken a liking to me. After we arrived in Melbourne many of the migrants who were on the Corsica would meet up at the Democritus Club on Russell Street, including Anastasia and her husband. She remembered me from the ship and begged me to marry her niece Niki who was back in Cyprus. At first, I said no, but she kept insisting until I finally agreed. In 1953 my parents and my sister went to Karavas to meet Niki and to arrange our marriage with her parents. Niki was nineteen years old. Listen in those days, whether you wanted someone or not, you did whatever your parents wanted. You married who they wanted you to marry. That was the way it was."

"My parents did not want me to work in the fields," Niki tells me. "They wanted me to stay at home. My father was a builder and found regular work in Karavas, Lapithos and Kyrenia. My mother would

Savvas Antoniou in Lefkoniko village, holding a turkey. Circa 1937.

Savvas' Uncle Loizos Michaeliou in Trikomo, with his donkey and cart. The writing on the back of this photograph reads, 'I am sending you this photograph so you can see how I travel around.' Circa 1940.

On the deck of the Corsica.
In the centre is Savvas Antoniou, standing far right
is Augustis Nicholas (from Arsos), seated with
white shirt is Varnavas Varnava and on his left is
Varnavas Loizou. January, 1952.

Niki Ioannou aged nineteen in Nicosia, 1953.

give us spending money from time to time. If we were going to Nicosia or Kyrenia, she would say, 'go to the *toulabi* (cupboard) and get some money. No, we didn't go to work and my mother worked in the fields for other people."

In March, 1955 Niki bid goodbye to her family and friends and boarded the ship Anna Salen to come to Australia and meet the man that her parents had arranged for her to marry.

Savvas and Niki were married on the 26th of June, 1955 at the Evangelismos Greek Orthodox Church in East Melbourne. "Once married, we enjoyed life," says Savvas. "I remember taking Niki to Luna Park for the first time and forcing her on the Scenic Railway. She screamed with terror all the way up, all the way down and all the way around. From her fear we never went again. We also went to the Astor Theatre in Prahran to watch movies even though we didn't understand them - it was still wonderful to be out. We would also stroll through Chapel Street at night. One occasion we purposely went to look through the Maples store shop window as there were TVs so we could watch the moon landing in 1969 with many other people. As more Cypriots migrated to Australia, socialising and meeting at each other's houses became a regular event. We would eat meals together, drink coffee and the women would share recipes from their own village. We would also meet up in the country for picnics. The Australians were so friendly, probably because of the delicious aroma of the BBQs. We would ask them to join us for a meal and a beer. Of course they never refused."

In 1959, Savvas and Niki welcomed the arrival of their first child, a son named Antonis (Tony). Seven years later in 1966, a second son, Andreas (Andrew) was born and finally a daughter Mary in 1968.

ACKNOWLEDGEMENTS

I would like to thank Savvas Antoniou for allowing me publish his story of migration. Special thanks to his daughter Mary Kechichian for her help and support.

A page from Savva's notebook in which he documented key moments from his journey on the Corsica, including dates, times and stop-overs.

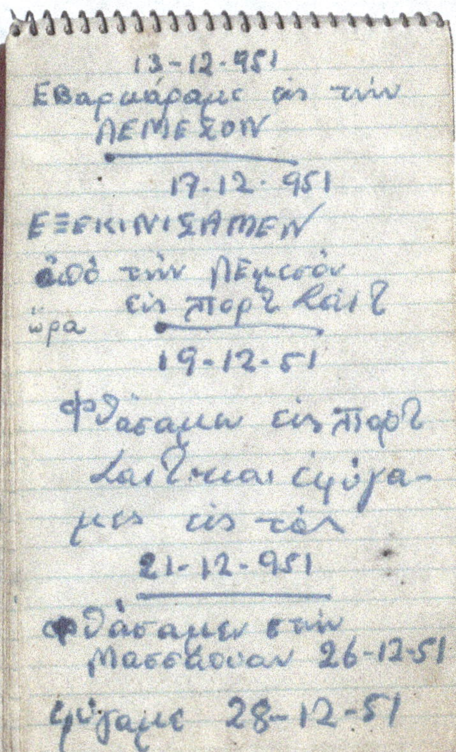

Niki Antoniou dancing on her wedding day with her maid of honour, Gika Kalis, bridesmaid Eleni and flower girl. Melbourne, 1955.

Savvas Antoniou clowning around with friends on the Corsica while Elpida Loizou (seated) looks on. January, 1952.

COSTA LEONIDAS

PASSENGER CARD

Name **COSTA LEONIDAS**

Date of birth / Age **24.4.1930 / 21**

Occupation **CARPENTER**

Place of origin **AGIOS MEMNON, FAMAGUSTA**

Port of departure **LIMASSOL**

Date of departure **17 DEC 1951**

Date of arrival **4 FEB 1952**

C osta Leonidas was born in the village of Agios Memnon on the 24th of April, 1930. His parents were Leonidas Georgiou and Maria Angeli. He was the eldest of seven children. His siblings in order of birth were; Tasoulla, Georgios, Andreas, Christina, Evangelia and Pandelitsa. Costa's youngest sister Pandelitsa, was born in January 1952 whilst he was travelling on the Corsica en route to Australia. They would meet for the first time, twenty years later, when Costa returned to Cyprus to visit his family.

Once he completed primary school, Costa went to Famagusta to work for a furniture maker named Poliori. "I went there to learn the trade," Costa explains. "I was working with six other men making quality furniture using wood obtained from walnut trees. I initially wanted to go to high school and university when I was younger but my father couldn't afford to pay the school fees. There was also the cost of boarding, books and uniform. As the eldest child, I felt a sense of duty to find work and support my family. After the Second World War however, there was not enough work for me. So, that's when I applied to travel to Australia."

Costa stayed in a hotel in Limassol until the Corsica was ready for boarding. "I said goodbye to my parents and they went back to the village. I remember having to borrow 100 pounds from a money lender, a lawyer, who also charged me a lot of interest. He added a percentage to the loan so I owed him 120 pounds. After I arrived in Australia, he started sending these letters, begging for me to repay him. I kept sending him money whenever I could and by the end of it, I must have paid him double what I owed."

On board the Corsica, Costa slept in the lower level of the ship with many other male passengers in army-style bunk beds. Before too long he even managed to find work on the ship. "As soon as the ship took off for Egypt, the captain of the ship asked for qualified tradesmen to work on the ship. I put my hand up and was taken to an area that was absolutely filthy and filled with broken bits of furniture. The stench was very powerful, I couldn't stay down there for long. I complained to the foreman that I cannot work in such terrible conditions. The smells affected me. Anyway, there was a Greek man named Themis who was part of the crew on the Corsica. He was only a few years older

Costa (on the left) with a fellow Corsica passenger, Andreas Falconas, honing their music skills in Melbourne, 1952.

than me and he worked in the kitchen. When he heard me complain about the conditions down below, he came up to me and said. 'Do you own a blue suit and a bow tie?' 'Yes, I do' I replied. He then asked me to get dressed in my suit and report to the Italian boss in the kitchen to ask about getting a job as a waiter. I had absolutely no experience as a waiter, but when the Italian boss saw me in my blue suit, he was convinced that I had worked as a waiter in Cyprus and he offered me the job on the spot. I ended up getting paid around twenty to thirty pounds for my service on the Corsica. I worked every day on the ship, except for the days when the ship was at port. You see, the Corsica made many stops along the way and that's when many passengers would go and eat at the restaurants or cafes near the port."

Being a waiter, Costa claimed that he ate better than the other passengers on the ship. "Once our shift ended, I would sit in the kitchen with the cooks and waiters to eat. We had more food to choose from than what we served to the passengers. There were times when I used to fry potatoes, you know chips, as extra food to pass on to the passengers, especially if I knew that they didn't like the food that was being served in the dining hall. All the cooks as far as I could tell were Italian.

There were two dining halls. A larger one for the lower classes and a smaller one for the upper class passengers. I teamed up with Themis. The waiters always worked together in pairs. There was a difference in the way the food was served depending on which class you were. For example, in the larger hall, Themis and I would carry a large pot of food and empty it into the plates that were already on the tables. In the smaller hall, the food was served on the plates directly from the kitchen. The food was also different according to the class. I remember the Italian head cook was very strict. We had to serve the food on time and as efficiently as possible. One day I became so seasick that I abandoned my duty and ran to the side of the ship to throw up. My boss was not happy because I was late serving the food that day."

According to Costa, most of the potatoes began to rot soon after they left

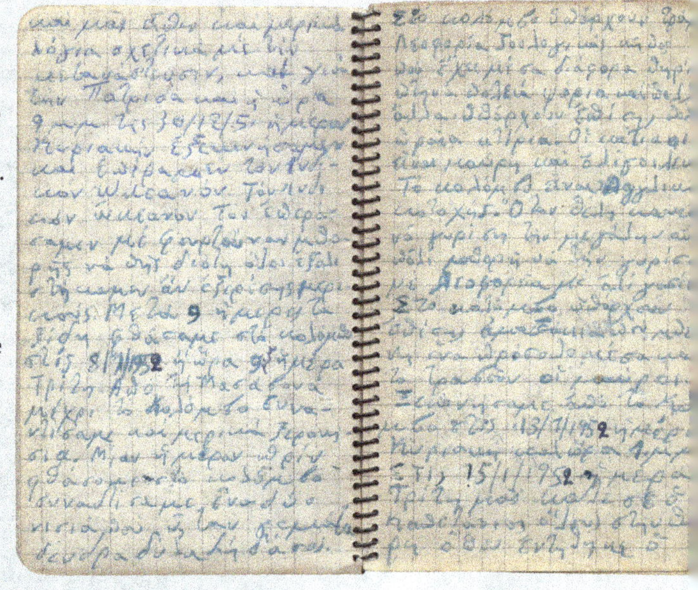

Costa's journal from the Corsica.

Port Said in Egypt. "We were somewhat grateful that there were enough good potatoes left over to cook or fry. Thank God there were potatoes on that ship that we could feed to the passengers who couldn't eat the other food we were serving."

Costa left Cyprus with six pounds in his pocket. "Thank God I found that job on the ship which earned me some extra money. I was so busy, that I didn't have time to think about anything else. This job helped me to forget about my problems and not think too much about my family."

Costa grew to like his Italian boss in the ship's kitchen. "He was strict but he was also very kind and wanted to make sure everyone had plenty of food to eat, especially the children. He would send me quickly, quickly to take food to the cabins to feed the children. That was one good thing about this Italian boss, he really cared about the children on the ship. The bread on the Corsica was good. They had bakers in the kitchen who made fresh bread daily."

Costa worked during the breakfast, lunch and dinner service. There was no supper service. When the dinner service was over, he would often stay behind and help with the cleaning up in the kitchen.

When Costa stepped off the ship in Africa he was surprised to see local women walking around topless, with just a cloth covering their torso and legs. "That was the first big surprise for us migrants," says Costa. "The other big surprise happened when we arrived in Melbourne. We had never seen such wide roads with so many fancy cars. We thought, there must be plenty of rich people living here!"

In early January, 1952 the Corsica crossed the equator en route from Colombo to Fremantle. Costa has fond memories of that day which he has documented in his journal. "The captain invited all the passengers out onto the deck dressed as Poseidon, God of the sea. After the captain's speech, the sirens went off and the captain instructed the crew to spray us with champagne. We all cheered and applauded. Then we were all treated to ice cream. This was a very special day and a rare celebration on the Corsica. Apparently, all sailors celebrate crossing the Equator."

When the Corsica finally docked at Station Pier, Costa was greeted by a man named Adamos Koumi. He was from the village of Paralimni. "It was 6pm by the time we were allowed to disembark. The first thing I wanted was a drink of water. So many of us passengers were thirsty. I was with two Cypriots, one from Paralimini and the other from Famagusta. Their names were Eraclis Nisiphorou and Stavros Symeon. Little did I know that one day I would marry Stavros' sister Theodora (Lola) and Eraclis will end up marrying her younger sister. Adamos took us to his house in Fitzroy and then later I stayed with Michalis and Georgios in Footscray. They were also from Paralimni. I soon found work as a carpenter at a factory called Baltic Simplex which was in Spotswood. The company manufactured agricultural and dairy farm machinery. My English was very poor at the time. I could only say simple words like, yes, no and hello."

Costa eventually gained employment at AGM, where he became head carpenter and foreman until his retirement. "I worked there for thirty-seven years," he says proudly. "But I wasn't promoted until the last six or seven years. Many of us migrants worked very hard to get ahead. I used to always hear the local Aussies complaining and saying, 'bloody new Australians. You've been here for five minutes and you already have a house. How do you do it?' I can't tell you how many times I've heard them say that. I used to reply. When I knock-off work, I go straight home - but you go to the pub and drink, drink, drink."

"When we first arrived in Melbourne, you had to be careful when you went out because the local Aussies were not very friendly and they were wary of us. It was only years later when they finally accepted us and they became friends with us. We did all the worst jobs back then, the filthy jobs. Also, if you had an accent, it was difficult to get a job. I was lucky."

Soon after Costa arrived in Melbourne, he visited the Cyprus Club on Lonsdale Street. "This was a common first stop for many new arrivals from Cyprus because we would be treated to a familiar meal, make friends, meet acquaintances and find accommodation and employment. When I first went to the Cyprus Club I was standing around like a fool. I didn't know anyone and I was the only person from my village who arrived on the Corsica. This club was open for twenty-four hours. The Cypriots who were already here in Melbourne, those who arrived before us, were very kind and supportive to us new arrivals. They really helped many of us to get settled."

Costa eventually settled into a new life in Melbourne. In March 1956, the woman that he would eventually marry, arrived with her family on the ship SS Cyrenia. Her name was Theodora (Lola) Petzierides. "Our families knew each other back in Cyprus," he tells me. "When I was working in Varosi, her brother Stavros was also working there as a car mechanic. He left Cyprus on the Corsica just like me. In fact, my family picked up Stavros and his family to drive to the Port of Limassol on the day I was leaving. I remember that his sister was in the car. I didn't know at the time that one day she will become my wife."

Costa and Theodora were married in 1958 and eventually moved to the western suburb of Sunshine where Theodora 's family lived. Their only daughter Mary was born there.

After retiring from the workforce, Costa and Theodora moved to Oakleigh to be close to their daughter Mary and their grandchildren.

ACKNOWLEDGEMENTS

I would like to thank Costa Leonidas for allowing me to publish his story of migration. Special thanks to his daughter Mary Liveriadis for her help and support.

Costa and Theodora prior to getting married. Melbourne, 1957.

35369

STAVROS SYMEON

S tavros (Steve Symeon) Petzierides was born on the 21st of January, 1932 in the village of Agios Sergios (Seryios), in the district of Famagusta. His father was Symeon Symeou and his mother was Maritsa Christodoulou from Varosi.

"My father owned and operated a mixed business and coffee shop in our village," he tells me. "After completing three years at secondary school, I left to learn the automotive mechanics trade at a well known firm in Famagusta known as Prastitis. I was there two years until I turned seventeen. After a work dispute, the brothers at Prastitis wouldn't let me work there anymore. Work became scarce for me after that. Luckily I had two cousins; one was in England and the other

opportunities for me there."

Stavros brought a notebook with him onto the Corsica in which he documented his journey to Australia. His first entry describes the day he left Cyprus.

"I remember it was the Feast Day of Agios Spyridon on the 12th of December when we got the bus from Varosha to go to Limassol, early in the morning. With me on the bus was Kochoffi, Kyriacos and Costas Leonidas. When we arrived, the ship was there but we had to wait four days until they loaded all these sacks of potatoes for Colombo. After all that, on the 17th of December at 11:30pm we took off for Port Said."

"In those first few days in Limassol, the seas were very rough and the crew couldn't load the potatoes," explains

weight, I would have to fill the ship with water to get you to Australia."

Stavros didn't know what they were loading on the ship. "We could see them loading something but we didn't know it was potatoes"

His parents waited on the wharf until it got dark and then they went back to Varosi.

According to Stavros, when the Corsica arrived in Limassol, it was gleaming and as white as milk. "You could tell it was freshly painted. I couldn't see any rust. This was a cover up by the travel agent. Before the ship arrived people were angry. For six months he promised passengers who paid their fare that 'the ship was coming, the ship was coming,' but it was all bullshit. What he wanted to do was get enough

Stavros (with hand on hip) with his work colleagues (names unknown), Famagusta. Circa 1949.

one was in Australia. They both sent me invitations to immigrate. I chose Australia because I thought it was a new country and everything would be different. I didn't look at the map. I chose Australia because I thought there would be more

Stavros. "Many passengers started shouting because of the delay and all of a sudden we could hear the captain's voice through the speakers saying, 'boys, calm down. I cannot travel unless I put weight in the ship. If I cannot load the cargo for

passengers to fill the ship so he could hire the Corsica and make a big profit. We heard that passengers had stormed the offices of the agent in Limassol and smashed all the windows. They wanted to kill him. Some people had been waiting for nine months for the ship to arrive. Most of them had taken big loans to pay for their ship fare and were paying back interest without setting foot on the ship. There was another ship called the Ravello which arrived in Cyprus at the same time as the Corsica. We saw it. The passengers on the Ravello got to Australia one month before we did."

Stavros was told that the Corsica was in a shipyard somewhere waiting to be demolished before Louis commissioned it and had it painted white to cover all the rust. "I read somewhere that before Louis got this ship, it was used to carry animals. A cargo ship for animals. They had to refurbish and turn it into a passenger ship. When we first went on board we realised it was a big ship, long and very deep. It was very deep. I remember when there were large waves, the ship would shake and a lot of times, the propellers were coming above the water. Maybe the ship didn't have enough weight."

Like so many other passengers, Stavros paid around 125 pounds for his ship fare. He had borrowed the money from his Uncle Georgios. "I was placed down below at one end of the ship. I shared a cabin with three other men. When I say cabin, it was a tiny room with no door and there was a bunk bed on each side of the room. That's it, nothing else. These cabins were scattered all around at the bottom of the ship. The toilets were separate and shared by everyone. One day it was very hot. This was soon after we came out of the Suez Canal. We couldn't bear it. I had some tools in my suitcase (screwdriver, shifter and a pair of pliers). I opened the porthole window and a nice cool breeze came in. All the windows were screwed shut. From there we went to Massawa. I remember after Massawa, they served us this terrible steak on the ship. It was black and as tough as leather. Nobody ate it. They never gave us steak after that. For breakfast we ate feta cheese, olives from Vólos and freshly baked bread. Whatever olives were left over we would take with us downstairs to eat later. I had a *briki* (coffee pot) with me and I would make Greek coffee for me and my friends to drink. You see, the crew let me use the stoves in the kitchen to make the coffee."

Stavros befriended a crew member named Sotiris. "He was from Greece and aged about fifty. One day I asked Sotiris, why is the ship going so slow. He said to me in Greek, 'if you knew what was happening down below, you would get off this ship at once.' He told me that the ship has twelve burners and the ship's mechanics were constantly trying to fix them. They were oil burners but they kept burning themselves out. Out of the twelve burners only six were working. Sotiris also told me that one of the ships propellers was doing thirty revolutions and the other one was doing twenty. Generally, a migrant ship propeller in the 1950s should be expected to do around 100 revolutions per minute. That's why the ship was moving like a snake. One day I asked Sotiris if I could go down below to have a look. He said 'yes'. Boy you wouldn't believe what I saw. Everything was filthy, covered in grease and dirt. The Italian mechanics down there were completely covered in dirt. One of the mechanics said to me, 'everything is bad down here. Everything is bad.' I just had a quick look and I got out of there before I got dirty. Sotiris said to me, 'we are lucky that we have a good Captain. He knows the route and he knows the sea. He will take us to Australia. That's why he is going slow and staying near the coast.' Anyway, that's what Sotiris said."

When the Corsica docked in Djibouti, Stavros and his friends went ashore to explore the town. "It was a Sunday morning. At around 11am we are walking down the main street and we come across a church. A Greek Orthodox Church. Everyone went in to light a candle. It was only a small church, maybe around nine metres by nine metres in size. Before we got to the church we went into a European-style shop, like a grocery store and we were surprised to see a Greek man running it. Anyway, we went into the church but the service had just finished. There was an Archbishop there, and he said, 'don't worry we will do a *paráklisis* for you all (a special service for the welfare of the living). I remember, the singers were all Greek school children with a teacher. He gave us the *paráklisis*, said a few good words, wished us all the best and we left."

When the ship docked at the pier of Colombo, Stavros and around ten other young men, decided to jump into the water. "It wasn't that far down or deep. You could see the bottom of the ocean. After we jumped, and we swam towards the pier. Suddenly we heard the captain's voice come over the ship's speakers. 'Boys, get out of the water. The sharks are coming.' Sure enough, when I looked towards the end of the ship, I could see that there were sharks in the water. Anyway, we got out of the water and sat on the edge of the pier. We could see plenty of fish swimming in the water below us. Anyway, this young boy who was about my age, his name was Pikshashi from Varosha, he said to me, 'when we go into town, we should buy some hooks.' He had the idea of catching fish from the pier. The Corsica had to get some repairs so we knew we were going to be in Colombo for a few days. Let me tell you, walking from the pier into town towards the markets, you had to hold your nose. It stunk. I had twenty pounds on me from Cyprus. So what did we do? We bought coconuts so we could drink the water and eat them on the ship. Me and two other boys who were with me bought twelve coconuts between us. We then wanted to catch a taxi to take us back to the ship but the driver wanted a lot of money for a short trip so we decided to walk instead. Anyway, me and Pikshashi bought the hooks and we went fishing at the pier in Colombo. We must have caught around thirty fish. I'm not sure what they were but we brought them on board the Corsica and gave them to our Greek friend Sotiris to fry them up. We waited on the first day – no fish. Then a second day passed, then a third. By the fourth day we approached Sotiris to find out what happened to our fish. 'You wouldn't believe it boys but the fridge broke down and everything became rotten so we had to throw your fish out.'"

Stavros recalls that at many of the ports, desperate poor people would approach the passengers from the Corsica trying to sell their goods. "They all came to the ship and would try to get anything out of you. I remember when we were docked at Port Said just about ready to leave, all the Arabs would be down below trying to sell their goods. Passengers were buying watches, souvenirs, and stuff like that. You would lower a basket on a rope so they could place the item into the basket and if you liked it you would lower the money down to them. Just before the ship took off, some of the passengers would take the item without paying. That's when the Arabs would really get angry and start screaming up at us. In Massawa,

The Corsica berthed at Station Pier in Port Melbourne, February 4th, 1952.

we were approached by all these young girls, African girls who were probably only twelve or fourteen years old. Being young ourselves, they all rushed towards us. *'Jigi-ji, jigi-ji'*, they would say to us. I had a pen in my pocket. One of these girls said to me, 'I'll take your pen for *jigi-ji.*' An older Cypriot man (Christoforos Kotsiofis) who was standing next to me grabbed my shirt and said, 'you're not going anywhere son. These girls are full of disease.' Anyway, a lot of the passengers went with these girls and they got sick. I would have gone too if Kotsiofis didn't stop me. We were warned by the ship's crew not to walk on our own."

As far as Stavros was concerned, there were some young people on the ship, Cypriot girls and boys who did misbehave.

"We even met three young girls who were travelling with an Aunt and we became quite friendly with them. One of the girls was on her way to Melbourne to meet her fiancé. We spent a bit of time getting to know these three girls. By the time, they repaired the Corsica in Colombo its cargo of potatoes and onions had completely rotted and had to be thrown into the ocean. After Massawa we could smell the potatoes going bad. When we walked around the ship there was definitely a bad smell in the air. They were good until Massawa. Between Massawa and Colombo that's when they started to serve us lots of fried potatoes. Boy they tasted good. They must have realised the potatoes were going off and decided to feed us as many potatoes as they could.

We were lucky also, that the ship had plenty of feta and olives, and spaghetti. That's all we ate."

Stavros had an opportunity to work on the Corsica, not as a mechanic, but as a waiter like a few other male passengers, such as Costas Leonidas and Savvas Antonio. "I didn't become a waiter because you had to work every day. They told us that if you miss one day of work, you will lose two days' pay. I was worried that if I got sick I would work for nothing. In fact, I did get quite seasick between Cyprus and Egypt."

As far as the ship's lean, Stavros remembers how many of the passengers would go and sit or stand on the side of the ship that was getting the sun. This would increase the lean of the ship.

The Greek captain was always shouting in his microphone for the passengers to spread out. When we arrived in Port Melbourne the ship had tipped over so much that you could touch the hands of the people standing on the pier. The captain was always shouting for us to move to the other side."

With regards to the fresh water on the Corsica, Stavros remembers it started to run out in the final weeks of the trip. "When the fresh tap water started to run out, you could pay around two shillings for a bottle of water. I think they increased the price near the end of the trip when the supply of fresh water on the ship was very low."

Stavros spent most of his time on the ship playing cards with his friends (not for money) or playing a Cypriot game called *Ziziros*. "There was a passenger named Nestoras Efstathiou who would play his violin and entertain us."

When they arrived at Fremantle, Stavros was surprised to see flowers in the middle of the street. "They were roses and their perfume reminded me of Cyprus. I loved it. I remember thinking, if Melbourne is like this, I'll be very happy. When we arrived in Melbourne, they kept us on the boat for two days until Immigration could check the ship to make sure that everything was okay. We learned later that the president of the Greek Community of Melbourne and Victoria, Floros Dimitriades had intervened to speed things up. There were people waiting on the pier every day, waiting for us to disembark. The trip took fifty-four days, twice as long as what most passengers expected. Because of this, some families back in Cyprus thought that their sons or daughters were dead. When they didn't hear any news from them after twenty-two days they of course feared the worse. I was told that a lot of mothers in Cyprus were crying their eyes out and even arranged for a church service for their dead child."

When Stavros and the other passengers were finally allowed to disembark onto Station Pier, he was met by his cousin Kosta Hadjipourki who drove him to his house in Footscray

where Stavros stayed for a while. As he unpacked his suitcase that first night, he was surprised to find a small notebook hidden there. "My mother Maritsa placed a small notebook in my suitcase before I left Cyprus in which she had written some important advice for me.

'Stavro…. these words that I have written, read them and they will remind you of me. Be careful always with the company you keep. Don't boast that you are wealthy. Money is always the enemy of man. Friends, should be few but good. Don't tell anyone your secrets. Your cousin Kosti writes that he will always be with you however, we don't know if you will stay over there. Be nice and quiet in the house and love the people who live there. Love from your family, may your time abroad pass quickly. God is great.' My mother also wrote down a few recipes in case I had to feed myself."

During his second week in Melbourne, Stavros visited the unemployment office in Footscray where he secured a job at a local Ford dealership. "My cousin's brother-in-law took me there," says Stavros. "At that time, I was getting five shillings a week from the Australian Government. When I went to the Ford dealership in Footscray I met the owner, Alec Foster. I told him I had worked on Fords in Cyprus and he gave me the job. I used to speak a little bit of English at the time, London English they called it. I worked there for ten years. Most of the workers were Aussies but we got along pretty good. Only once, this man called me a 'dago'. I said to him, 'what's that' and he said 'you're one of these ten pound migrants'. I said, 'excuse me, but I paid 125 English pounds to come here which is around 200 Aussie pounds.' After that, he shut up."

To improve his skills, Stavros also attended trade school.

In 1956, Stavros helped his parents and siblings to emigrate to Australia.

The following year, he met his wife Constandia Kyriakou (Connie) and they were married on the 22nd of November, 1958. Constandia was born in Larnaca on the 26th of January, 1936. She was the daughter of Kyriako and Maria Costantantinou and the third born of nine siblings. In 1957, at the age of twenty-one, she made a difficult decision to leave her much-loved family to migrate to Australia. On her arrival, Constandia lived with her Auntie Fotini and Uncle Panayioti and her

four cousins. That same year, Constandia met Stavros after a chance encounter where he accidentally spilt a glass of beer on her beautiful new yellow dress."

After they were married, Stavros and Constandia moved into their new home in Coronation Street, North Sunshine and were blessed with five children (Simon, Mary, Ken, Dora and Andria).

Stavros continued his line of work as a motor mechanic and eventually owned his own garage and service station. "I was the first Cypriot to manage a service station in Sunshine. The building wasn't even finished when I signed up with Mobil. A fellow named Ted Crisp gave me a loan of 2,000 dollars to buy the place. When the man from Mobil came to inspect the books he said to me, 'congratulations, in our books you are supposed to sell two and a half thousand gallons of petrol a month and you have sold seven thousand gallons.' Stavros then moved to another workshop and service centre on Couch Street in Sunshine, until he retired.

Sadly, Stavros lost his battle to illness and passed away in 2021, ironically on the day of his wedding anniversary. His brave voyage from Cyprus to Australia in 1951 set the course for a rich and fulfilling path. His memory and legacy lives on through his five children, twelve grandchildren and eight great-grandchildren.

ACKNOWLEDGEMENTS

I would like to thank Stavros Symeon for allowing me to publish his story of migration. Special thanks to his niece, Mary Liveriadis for her help and support.

Stavros with his father Symeon cooking a BBQ at Rippleside Park in North Geelong, Victoria, 1959.

MICHALIS MAVROGENIS

ichalis (Michael) Mavrogenis was born in the village of Rizokarpaso on the 6th of September, 1933. His father was Georgios Mavrogenis and his mother was Katerina Spyridonou. He had two brothers and two sisters.

Michalis wanted to leave Cyprus to join his two brothers who had already migrated to Australia. "There were two travel agents in Limassol," he explains. "Mantovani and Louis. I remember standing in a long queue of people who had come to collect their passports. In those days, all the passports were held my village. When it was his turn, he said to the man behind the desk, 'why are you charging ten shillings?' The clerk behind the desk replied, 'so you can take your passport.' This man shouted back. 'I'm not giving you any money. You give me my passport now or I will call the police and I then take my business elsewhere.' He then turned to face us and shouted, 'these men are thieves. Don't give them any money.' He then stood guard as we took our passports without paying."

According to Michalis, the travel agents in Limassol were selling first, captain asked everyone to gather in this big open space and he said to us. 'Listen, there is plenty of room upstairs. If anyone wants to stay in first class, you must pay an additional twenty pounds. For second class, it will cost ten pounds.' So, in other words, it didn't matter that my father paid the travel agent for second class, I was placed down below into third class. Once you were on the ship, there was no way of knowing who paid for what. I remember seeing perhaps thirty people, who had the money, pay to go up to first class. Most of us however, were ushered down below."

Michalis (seated far right) on the Corsica with other Cypriot migrants, en route to Australia. January, 1951.

by the travel agent. Anyway, they were asking each person to pay ten shillings before they handed over their passports. I happen to be standing behind a man from second and third class tickets for the Corsica. "My father purchased a second class ticket for me, however once we boarded the ship, everything changed. The Michalis stayed in the lower deck of the ship and remembers the sleeping quarters. "There was a long narrow corridor, perhaps about five foot wide.

On either side of the corridor were bunk beds. Each bunk had two beds made of mesh. Like army-style beds. The men and the women were in separate quarters. It was very crowded and hot down below. Most of the passengers were young men. There were twenty-seven men from my village alone. I tell you, lucky we were all young, fit and healthy. If we were older, we wouldn't have survived the journey – that's how bad it was. Once the potatoes and onions began to rot, many of us would grab a blanket and go and sleep up on the deck. The smell was so bad no one could stay down below."

Michalis did not know why there was a cargo of potatoes and onions on the Corsica. "I remember watching the ship's crew in Limassol loading the sacks but no one seemed to know where they were going or who they were for. We had to wait four or five days for them to finish loading the potatoes and onions before we could take off."

With regards to the food that was served on the Corsica, Michalis' experience was similar to that of other passengers I had interviewed. "They served us *macaronia* (spaghetti) every day. Eat it or don't eat it, it's up to you. That's what you got. When they served meat, it was as tough as the leather soles on your shoes. Even if you had good teeth, it was unchewable. You couldn't eat it. This young man from my village had a portable kerosene stove and we would use it to fry potatoes on the deck. Another boy from Yialousa worked in the kitchen as a *manjipas* (baker) and he would bring us fresh bread to eat. After we ate, a man named Nestoras would play his violin and we would all sing and dance. This is how we entertained ourselves. There was nothing else to do."

When the Corsica arrived to the Port of Colombo, many young men were paid by the ship's accountant to help throw the sacks of rotten potatoes and onions into the ocean. Michalis was offered the job but declined. He remembers fondly his time spent in Colombo, visiting the markets and the zoo. "We paid the locals two shillings to show us around the town on their rickshaws. I remember at the market, we paid five shillings for a large bunch of bananas which we bought back to the ship."

According to Michalis the water tanks on board the Corsica became contaminated because of the rotten potatoes and onions, so he was forced to buy bottles of fresh water. "I had around ten pounds on me from Cyprus. Most of my money was spent on bottled water. It was two shillings a bottle. You couldn't drink the water from the taps on the ship, it was red in colour and looked disgusting. Some passengers who couldn't afford to buy drinking water had to drink rain water. There was a young boy from my village, Andreas (Andy) Angoura was his name and he was about sixteen, traveling with his parents (Despina and Stylianos) and sister (Stella). They were all staying in first class. When the fresh water ran out on the ship, Andreas climbed onto the life boats where he knew there would be containers of fresh water stored. There were eight life boats so he found eight containers. He came and told us about the containers on the lifeboats and from that day forward we didn't have to buy any water. We just rationed the water from the lifeboats amongst us."

Michalis had heard a rumour that the water tanks on the ship were sabotaged by the crew, in protest of their working conditions.

"When we arrived at Port Melbourne, the Corsica was anchored about a mile out from the pier waiting to be quarantined. My brother Zacharias would hire a small boat and come out to greet me. 'What do you need?' He would call up to me. 'Do you have any water?' I would reply. 'Bring me water.' There were plenty of men who would hire these boats and come to see their loved ones who were stuck on the ship. After the Corsica was tugged into port, it remained there for several days. It was in very bad condition. I don't think it made another trip after that. I remember that our arrival on the Corsica made it to the front page of the local newspaper."

Like most new arrivals from Cyprus, Michalis would visit the two main Greek clubs in the city to mix with his fellow countrymen. "We'd go down to Russell Street to the Democritus Club which was run by Kyriakos Konstantinos or the Cyprus Club which was run by Christos Morphitis. Kyriakos was from the village of Liopetri, Famagusta and he arrived in 1949. There were billiard tables at his club. Most migrants would meet at these clubs to socialise, talk politics and help each other to find work and accommodation. The Democritus club was officially known as the Greek Democritus Workers League Club. For us migrants, Australia was not what we expected. You couldn't even find bread or oil at that time. We had to use dripping to cook. Some suburbs didn't have hot water, or gas or even electricity. Sunshine was all paddocks back then. I remember we would gather wild artichokes. We would walk along the railway sleepers and collect artichokes. I remember when I first visited Sunshine with my friends we met a man who was trying to sell us blocks of land for 100 pounds each. You just had to pay one pound a week to the real estate agent and you could own a block of land in those days. Most of us had plans to return back to Cyprus. We came here to work and go back in a few years. No one thought that Australia would become our permanent home. Melbourne was not what we expected. You had suburbs that had bad reputations and were filthy too. Suburbs like Port Melbourne and Fitzroy. We had never seen Aborigines before. The Exhibition Gardens were full of them. They scared us. When we would leave the clubs on Russell street we would always make sure we were in a group of say five or six men. You would never want to walk alone. We didn't want them to beat us up. Another popular place we would go to visit was Yiannoupolos, on Swanston Street near the corner of Lonsdale Street. We would go there to buy records, newspapers, books, and dictionaries to learn English."

Michalis eventually saved enough money to buy a fish and chip shop in the suburb of Highett. "I bought the shop in 1956 and I sold it in 1962. I then found a job with BHP where I stayed for thirty years."

After his wife Maroulla (Maria) died in 1998, Michalis married Eleni who was once his neighbour back in Cyprus.

ACKNOWLEDGEMENTS

I would like to thank Michalis Mavrogenis for allowing me to publish his story of migration and for his kind help and support along the way.

Georghia Kefala and her cousin Andreas Kyriakou on board
the Corsica. January, 1952.

GEORGHIA KEFALA

Georghia (Georgina) Kefala was born in the village of Agios Ilias, Famagusta on the 4th of September, 1927. Her parents were Antonis Kefala and Katerina Nicholas.

Georghia was the eldest of four children. Her younger siblings were Michael, Nicholas and Anthoulla.

Georghia left Cyprus to find work as a seamstress in Australia, as her brother Michael was already living there.

Her daughter Sandra (Sotiria) gives a brief account of what her mother had told her about the Corsica. "My mother always mentioned the stench of the potatoes and the sticky sludge. She told me that as she walked around the ship with her friends, their heels would stick to the sludge on the floor. My mum always mentioned the stench and the sludge throughout her life. Apparently, the crew weren't cleaning the floors and quite a few women had their shoes ruined on that ship."

Georghia travelled with her cousin Andreas Kyriakou who was four years younger. Andreas had told her that the crew were all Italian and couldn't speak any English therefore, there was little to no communication between the passengers and the crew. "Apparently, the food was always spaghetti," says Sandra, "and the water on the ship was salty. When my mother had a shower, the soap wouldn't lather, perhaps because of the salt in the water. Passengers were told they could only shower once a week

Georghia Kefala with her cousin Andreas Kyriakou (left), on board the Corsica (the other passengers are unknown). January, 1952.

which was very unhygienic, especially for the women."

"The journey was extremely long across very rough seas and many passengers were sick," adds Sandra. "My mother developed a real phobia of the ocean after her trip on the Corsica. She was definitely traumatised by the Corsica. She never travelled on a ship or a ferry again or went anywhere near the sea after that trip. 'I don't want to see the sea, I never want to see the sea again,' she would say to us. My mum often referred to that ship as a stinking prison. She was sick for most of the trip."

Georghia travelled to Sydney by train with her cousin Andreas where she was met by her brother Michael at Central Station. Michael was already living in Surry Hills. She stayed with him initially and he introduced her to his friend Alexandros Therapou. They married in 1952. Alexandros was born on the 1st of April, 1924 in the village of Kythrea, Nicosia and came to Australia in 1949.

When Georghia was pregnant with her first child Sandra in 1955, she arranged for her family in Cyprus to immigrate to Sydney before the birth. "My mum's family were all reunited by the time I was born. We were all living in Surry Hills at the time. My grandparents had intended to stay in Sydney, buy a new house and start a new life. Unfortunately, my grandfather Antonis died from a stroke in 1959. My grandmother ended up living with us and helping my parents raise the family. My mother was able to work and became a very good seamstress in Sydney."

ACKNOWLEDGEMENTS

I would like to thank Georghia Kefala for allowing me to publish her story of migration. Special thanks to her daughter, Sandra Pericles for all her help and support.

CHRISTOS
GEORGALLIS

C hristos Georgallis was born on the 22nd of January, 1933 in the village of Koma tou Yallou in the district of Famagusta. He was the fourth of eight children born to Georgallis Toffi and Maria Nicolaou. "My father worked as a forest ranger," Christos tells me. "But he struggled to earn an income to support our large family. We were so poor that on some days, were didn't have any food to eat."

Like most post war immigrants, Christos left Cyprus for economic reasons. "There was no work for me in Cyprus," he says. "I was a mason and I would find work for one month and then be unemployed for three months or sometimes up to six months. That's why I left."

After his older brother Andreas emigrated to Australia (around 1949), Christos decided to join him there, in the hope that he could secure steady work. "I went to a travel agent in Varosi, named *Xomatas* and I remember paying 120 English pounds for my ship fare. When it was time to leave, I bid my family farewell and I caught a bus from my village and travelled on my own to the Port of Limassol. I remember arriving early – before the other passengers. It was raining and I was feeling quite sad. I saw these men at the port loading sacks of potatoes and onions onto the Corsica in the rain."

"After I boarded the ship, I discovered that the Corsica once belonged to the Kaiser. That's what the crew told me. It was a strong and big vessel but it was as slow as a camel. It didn't go more than ten miles an hour. Thankfully, I didn't get seasick but others around me, were throwing up. I was used to the water, because my village was near the sea."

Travelling with Christos was his neighbour Mihallis (Mouzoura) Perikla (listed as Michael Pericleous) and first cousin Nicos (Toffi) Georgaki (listed as Nicos Neoklis).

When the Corsica arrived at Port Said, Christos went ashore and bought himself a pair of shoes for around two pounds. "Before I left Cyprus, my poor father had sold a piece of land for two hundred pounds. He bought me some new clothes for the trip and gave me 100 pounds to take with me for emergencies. It was the first time in my life I had worn new clothes."

In terms of entertainment on the ship, there was a Cypriot named Vassos Katsiamis from the village of Xeros. He would eventually become Christos' brother-in-law in the late 1950s after meeting and marrying his sister Ellie. Katsiamis would eventually form a band in Melbourne and perform at many Greek Cypriot weddings together with a Cypriot violinist named Matheous and a Greek migrant named Thomas playing guitar.

When the ship arrived at the Port of Massawa, Christos noticed plenty of fish in the water. "There was so much fish swimming around, big fish too. I remember thinking to myself, if only my village had this much fish, our people would have had a better life."

With regards to the rotten potatoes and onions, Christos can't quite remember when the stench first became apparent. He does remember seeing the sacks dissolve into sludge when the crew threw them overboard. "The sacks of potatoes turned into this black stinking water. When the wind would blow, the passengers would run to the other side of the ship to escape the smell. The ship would lean onto its side because there were so many people gathered there. The captain of the Corsica offered to pay us passengers ten pounds a day to help empty the rotten potatoes into the sea. That was a lot of money in those days, but no one took up the offer. No one wanted that job. Those potatoes turned into black sludge and the onions as well. I'm sure they got wet in the rain back in Limassol and then they just melted in the cargo hold which was quite hot."

I asked Christos how he managed to endure the stench on the ship, especially in the sleeping quarters of the lower deck. "There was no stench where I was sleeping. The stench was coming from somewhere else. I'm not sure where, but there was no stench where I was. The way I remember it, you could climb down these steps from both sides of the ship – from the front and from the back - to the central part where I sleeping."

Christos spent most of the time on the upper decks and verandahs of the ship. He recalls that after they left Colombo, the food and the fresh water on the ship began to run out. "There was hardly anything left to eat. If it wasn't for my first cousin Nicos, we would have starved. You see, Nicos got a job in the ship's kitchen and he would secretly bring us fried chips

to eat. We would sit on the deck and eat chips. That's how I remember it."

As for the lack of drinking water, Christos remembers how in the dining hall, the waiter would only place one small bottle of water on the table for all to share. Weeks earlier, passengers were each given their own bottle. "Myself and my friends were fine," he states. "We didn't suffer. As I said, my cousin Nicos worked in the kitchen and he would give us plenty of food and water."

Interestingly, apart from the lack of food on board the Corsica, Christos admits that he had a fairly good trip. The rolling of the ship and the seasickness, never bothered him. When asked about Colombo, Christos remembers that there was a lovely post office there and that the coconuts were very cheap. "I bought some coconuts for about six pence – something like that. It's the first time I had tasted coconuts in my life. A local man showed us how to drill two holes with a knife to drink the coconut water."

When Christos first set eyes on the coast of Western Australia, he remembers thinking, "will this be the land of my dreams or will this turn out to be a nightmare."

Seven days after leaving Fremantle,

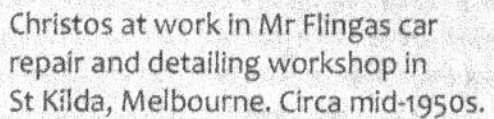

Christos at work in Mr Flingas car repair and detailing workshop in St Kilda, Melbourne. Circa mid-1950s.

the Corsica arrived to the Port of Melbourne. There was a two-day delay while the Australian quarantine officers scrambled on board to inspect the vessel before allowing the Captain to berth at Station Pier on the 4th of February, 1952. "I remember that my brother Andreas and some other men had hired a small boat and they sailed out to greet us on the Corsica which was anchored about half a mile from the pier. I recognised Andreas and we would call out to each other."

When the passengers were finally allowed to disembark, Christos carried his suitcase through the Immigration check-in and met his brother Andreas at the end of Station Pier. "My brother drove there with a friend and he took me to his accommodation on the Esplanade in St Kilda where he was renting a room with his wife. In fact, the man who owned the house, a Greek named Giorgios, made me stay in a shed on the property because there was no more room in the house. I remember the shed was made with sheets of corrugated iron and contained crates full of sardines that Mr Giorgios would sell. The shed was not very nice, but it was cheap. I was paying around one and half pounds a week. My brother's wife Anastasia, cooked all my meals, so I managed to get by.

Initially, Christos struggled to find work in Melbourne. Wherever he went, there were long queues of unemployed men. A chance meeting with a Jewish business owner named Mr Flingas would change his luck and fortune. "This man owned a car repair shop and detailing business opposite Luna Park in St Kilda. After learning that I was a skilled bricklayer, he let me work on the construction of an upper storey to his shop. When that job had finished Mr Flingas sent me to an automotive school in Richmond so I can learn a new trade. I would go two nights a week. In those days, my English was very limited. I used to fall asleep during the theoretical lessons but I really concentrated in the practical classes. That's how I managed to learn a new trade. After six months, I knew everything. I knew how to weld, how to do colour-matching, how to spray, the lot. Mr Flingas paid all the school fees. He was a very generous man and I can honestly say that he really changed my life. Because of him I was able to learn how to colour-match and repair cars and this opened up many job opportunities in my life.

In 1959, Christos returned to Cyprus to see his father who was gravely ill.

Once again, fate stepped in to change the direction of his life. "When it was time for me to return to Australia. I went to visit the *Xormatis* travel agency in Varosi to arrange a stopover in England so I could visit my brother Nicholas who was living in London. Outside the agency was an old woman weeping. When I asked her what was wrong, she told me that she could not afford to pay for the postage to send a package to her daughter in England. I said, don't worry and gave her five pounds. Little did I know that my kind deed that day in Varosi would set in motion a series of events that would lead me to meet my future wife. You see the old woman's daughter Sofoulla worked at a cafe on Seven Sisters Road with her husband Fanos and when I arrived in England we became friends. I would visit their cafe for lunch almost every day and later, when we met at a seaside resort on Weston-super-Mare in North Somerset they introduced me to their friend, Eleni Pallourti.

After marrying Eleni in 1960, Christos decided to stay in England where he found work and raised his two children, Adam and Maria.

"Initially, my brother Nicos (Nicholas) helped me to find work at the Vaxhall Car Company on Russell Road in Wimbledon. I earned nine pounds in my first week which was a lot less than my salary in Australia."

Christos is an optimistic man who doesn't dwell of life's struggles. "You just have to get on with it," he tells me. "No point worrying about the past."

ACKNOWLEDGEMENTS

I would like to thank Christos (Chris) Georgallis for allowing me to publish his story of migration. Special thanks to his daughter, Maria Cormack and her husband Hamish for all their help and support.

PIERIS LOIZOU
PIERA

PASSENGER CARD

Name	PIERIS LOIZOU PIERA
Date of birth / Age	4.9.1930 / 21
Occupation	FARMER
Place of origin	KOMI KEBIR
Port of departure	LIMASSOL
Date of departure	17 DEC 1951
Date of arrival	4 FEB 1952

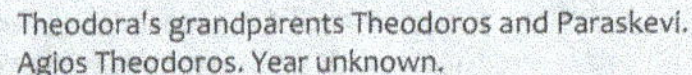
Theodora's grandparents Theodoros and Paraskevi. Agios Theodoros. Year unknown.

Pieris Loizou Piera was born on the 4th of September, 1930 in the village of Komi Kebir. His father was Loizou Piera and his mother was Florendia (Florenza) Petri. His siblings were Andriani, Kyriacou (Koulla) and Petros.

"I left primary school when I was ten years old and I went to work with my father in the fields," says Pieris. "We grew tobacco and cotton and wheat. I remember my father had these large oxen and I would help him to plough our fields. I used to wake up before the sun rose to collect *rodthi* (field herb) to feed our oxen.

When asked why he left Cyprus, Pieris smiles and says, "I wanted to leave. Everyone wanted to leave. Others were going to England but I chose Australia because I knew a man from our village who migrated there. His name was Vasilis Yerolemou. In fact, I offered to accompany Vasilis' father, Kyriacos to Melbourne as he was all alone in the village and wanted to be reunited with his three children. They had all migrated to Australia. I remember Kyriacos was around seventy-five years old."

"On the day of our departure we went to the Port of Limassol but the ship wasn't there so we had to spend a night in the town. My parents said goodbye and went back to the village. The next day we travelled on a barge to board the ship. I remember there was this crazy man who was climbing and walking all over all the suitcases. He wanted to be the first on the ship. I became angry with him and told him to stop."

Pieris was sent to the lower section of the ship where he slept in army-style bunks alongside many of the other male passengers. "When it became too hot for us to stay down below we would go up to the top deck and sleep in the life boats. No one saw us. We never got caught. There were three or four of us from Komi Kebir including Louis Kyriacou. Let me tell you a funny story. When we first climbed into the life boats we found all these tins of condensed milk. The Italian crew let us use their kitchen so we boiled some rice, added the milk and made *rizogalo* (Greek rice pudding) to eat. We would go back to the life boats and eat our *rizogalo*."

"I'll tell you another thing that I found disgusting on the ship," Pieris says boldly. "The toilets were blocked. There were people on this ship who came from villages and didn't want to flush the toilets. They just kept putting paper in the bowl and eventually there was so much paper that the toilets became blocked. It was terrible."

"I remember one day, they made an announcement on the ship that they were going to give us ice-cream. We all scrambled to find a container, a cup, anything for the crew to put the ice cream in. Well there was this man, I think he was from Strovolos, he snatched the old man Kyriacos' cup while he was drinking something and as he pulled it away, the old man's dentures fell out. It was funny at the time."

How did you pass the time on the ship I ask Pieris.

"What could we do. We just sat around all day talking to one another. I didn't play cards or *tavli* (backgammon). There was a swimming pool with no water in it. What could we do. Nothing. I remember meeting lots of Cypriots from the village Aradippou. We became friends and later after we arrived in Melbourne, I would have dinner with some of them at the Democritus Club in Melbourne. There was a man named Vangeli and he had a restaurant below the club and we would all meet there to eat. Others went to the Acropoli club. People used to gamble at these clubs. Imagine that! They came to Australia penniless, found jobs in factories and gambled their wages at these clubs."

When the Corsica docked at the Port of Djibouti Pieris went ashore with three or four other passengers to explore the town. "As we walked down the street, these men called out to us, 'hey, are you Greek?' Yes, we answered and then they invited us into their house and gave us cold beers. It was very hot in Djibouti. These men were Greeks and they worked for the large oil companies over there."

Pieris rented a room in Collingwood after he arrived to Melbourne. "This man had a house and was renting out rooms to new arrivals so I rented a room there and when my sister Kyriacou and her husband arrived, they rented another room. I worked at General Motors for a while and then I worked at the Jam Factory before moving to Gippsland for a while to work at the saw mills up there. It was hard in the

From left to right: Maria (friend), Theodora, Salomou (friend), Yianoulla (sister). Pieris' mother Florenzou is squatting up front. Komi Kebir, 1955.

Pieris at Station Pier in Port Melbourne. The buoy behind him reads HMAS LATROBE. Circa 1952.

beginning when I first came to Australia. Quite a few men went back to Cyprus. One man I knew, stayed five months but he missed his wife so much he went back."

After four years on his own Pieris' mother was worried about her son so far away from Cyprus and living on his own. She wanted him to settle down and marry a Cypriot girl and she knew just the girl. Her name was Theodora Elias from the village of Ayios Theodoros, which was only six miles from Komi Kebir.

"I was only seventeen when I found out that Pieris had agreed to marry me," Theodora tells me. "My mother didn't want me to go to Australia. She didn't want me to leave. She had tried to marry me to a man from Paphos and then another man from Limassol. At that time my Aunt had spoken with Pieris's mother and found out that Pieris was also looking for a wife. As soon as I heard that Pieris was in Australia, I wanted to go there to meet him. His mother jumped on a donkey and rode to my parent's house to meet me. 'Are you the girl your Aunt recommended for my son?' She said. 'My son will make you a queen.' Oh, she was so happy to see me. 'My son is very rich in Australia. He works for a company and he gets paid to do almost nothing.' Oh, she kept saying all these wonderful things about her son in Australia. I think she brainwashed me. She was hugging me and kissing me. I just told her that I wanted to see a recent photograph of her son. I had heard stories you see, about old men who had used younger photos of themselves to try and trap a young girl into marriage. I was only seventeen. I had to be careful."

Pieris laughs at his wife's recollection. "Back then I worked at the Jam Factory in Prahran. It's true. I did have an easy job. I would sit there with a long stick and when the cans got stuck on the conveyor belt, I would give them a gentle nudge to move them along."

"As I said, my mother did not want me to go to Australia," interrupts Theodora. 'I have five daughters,' she would say, 'and even if one was blind I would never send her to Australia.' No, my mother did not want me to leave so I decided to talk to my father. Please father, I said to him. Please say yes and I will go and send you money so you and mother can visit places all over Cyprus. Say yes and I will send you money so you can drink all the wine you want. Father send me to Australia and I will work for a few years and then come back to open up a cinema in the village just like we always dreamed about. My father finally agreed and I left by aeroplane to come to Australia. It took four days by the time I arrived."

"As soon as Theodora arrived we had to get married in the registry office," adds Pieris "We had a political wedding so that people wouldn't talk."

After their registry wedding on the 4th of December, 1956, Pieris and Theodora were married in the Evangelismos Greek Orthodox Church on the 15th of August, 1957. Two years later, their daughter Flora was born in July 1959.

Theodora speaks again. "I cried for weeks after I arrived as I remember the words of my mother. I cried on my own. I really regretted my decision to come to Australia. I was the first woman from our village to come to Australia. I was completely on my own. In the beginning it was so hard for me."

Pieris and Theodora bought a house on Park Street in South Melbourne before moving to Ferguson Street in East Brighton. Pieris eventually found a permanent job at Phillips in Clayton where he worked for twenty years.

"We lived next door to the Antoniou family," says Flora. "They were also Greek Cypriot. Across the road was the Withers family who were dinky-di Aussies. Barry Withers would come over every night with his bottle of VB beer to talk and drink with my dad. The Withers loved our Cypriot food, especially my mum's *koupepia* and *keftedes* (stuffed vine leaves and meatballs). Barry and his wife June became lifelong friends with my parents. Dad even tried surfing with Barry at Cape Patterson. June would take me to school and bring me home daily with her children. She encouraged me to play sports. Dad taught me to swim at Brighton Baths and we both loved the sea. Dad loved being close to the beach and he would go and collect mussels or go diving for abalone and sea urchins. In country Victoria he would go rabbit hunting, or foraging for wild mushrooms, or picking apples from the orchards. They were great years."

ACKNOWLEDGEMENTS

I would like to thank Pieris Piera for allowing me to publish his story of migration. Special thanks to his daughter, Flora Karitzis for all her help and support.

Pieris with his friend Louis Kyriacou near the Prince of Wales Hotel in St Kilda. Circa 1952.

Georgios and Augousta at Luna Park in Melbourne, 1957.

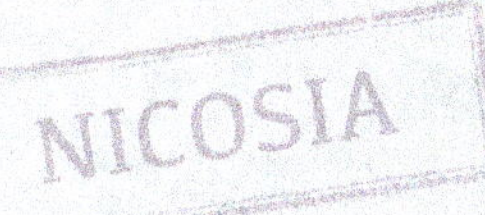

GEORGE
CHRISTOFI

Bearer
(Titulaire)

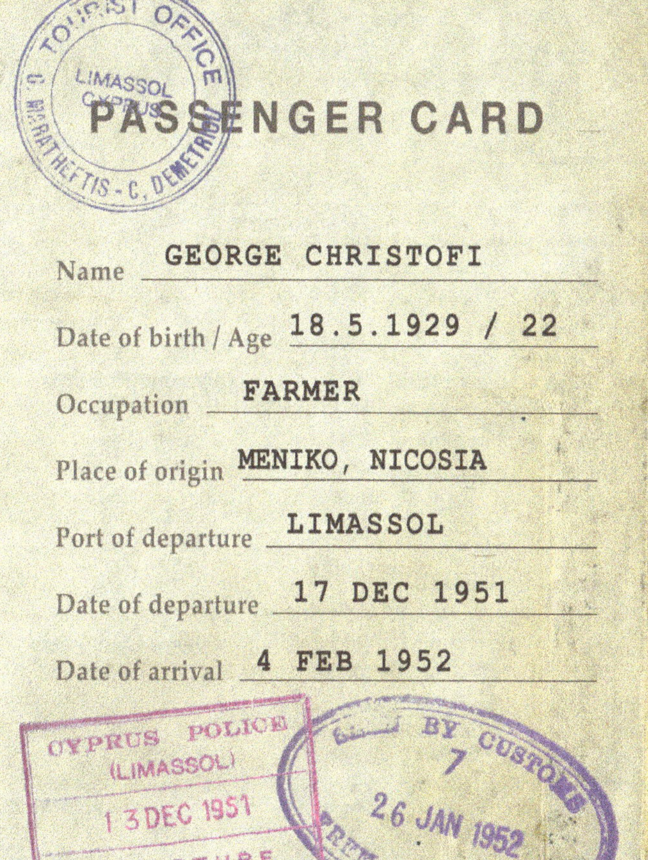

PASSENGER CARD

Name — GEORGE CHRISTOFI

Date of birth / Age — 18.5.1929 / 22

Occupation — FARMER

Place of origin — MENIKO, NICOSIA

Port of departure — LIMASSOL

Date of departure — 17 DEC 1951

Date of arrival — 4 FEB 1952

A Cypriot barbeque in the Australian bush, 1957.

G eorgios Haji Christofi was born on the 18th of May, 1929 in the village of Meniko. He was one of five children born to Christofi Hagi Pavli and Eleni Haji Christofi, including two older sisters named Charalambou and Anna and two younger brothers named Nikolas and Pavli. Georgios attended the local village school for about four years.

His father Christofi was a poor farmer who also worked the land for other farmers in order to make ends meet. When Georgios was eighteen, his father tragically died, ending his hope of gaining a trade as he desperately wanted. As the eldest son he took over the farming and agricultural duties, such as ploughing, to support his mother and siblings.

In 1951, Georgios left Cyprus to travel to Australia because he felt he could support his family while working abroad. Many young men left Meniko at that time to migrate to Australia and England. Upon his departure, Georgios told his mother that he would return to Cyprus after a few years, so she wouldn't be sad and cry. Instead he chose to stay in Australia and embraced the Australian way of life.

"Georgios came to Australia on the Corsica," remarks his wife Augousta. "The whole journey took a staggering two months. It was a very slow ship and there were many delays along the way. In fact, the ship was anchored in Limassol for about a week. No one knew why it was delayed there so long. One woman I know managed to climb onto the ship in Limassol and stayed with her husband in his cabin until it was time to depart. Georgios always talked about the sacks of potatoes and onions on the ship and how they became rotten because of the heat and had to be thrown into the sea. He talked about the awful stench on the ship and how he had to sleep outdoors, on the deck with many other passengers. To make matters worse, he was told that the Italian chefs on board the ship had cooked and fed the passengers cats. Some waiters told everyone that the meat was from rabbits but one Cypriot happened to see the cooked skull of one of the animals in the kitchen and noticed the teeth matched those of a cat".

Georgios often remarked that he was served spaghetti for breakfast, lunch and dinner as it was an Italian ship and that he had become sick to the stomach of it. Nevertheless, he was one of a few people who did not get seasick so he looked after the other passengers who were sick all over the deck.

In the port town of Djibouti, Georgios was curious about the large walnuts (coconuts) people were talking about. He paid one shilling and received ten large coconuts. Because he did not recognise or know what to do with all this strange fruit, he left them all behind and only took one on board the ship to try and eat.

When Georgios first arrived in Australia he lived and worked in the town of Yallourn in the Latrobe Valley, Gippsland. He worked for the State Electricity Commission of Victoria who operated the Yallourn Power Station. He initially worked 'pick and shovel' building train tracks in the coal mines. He later learnt to drive a truck and worked as a truck driver in the open mines transporting coal, all the while sending money home to his family in Cyprus. He stayed at Yallourn for five years earning ten and a half pounds a week.

When Georgios decided to get

Various photos from Georgios and Augousta's family album from the 1950s.

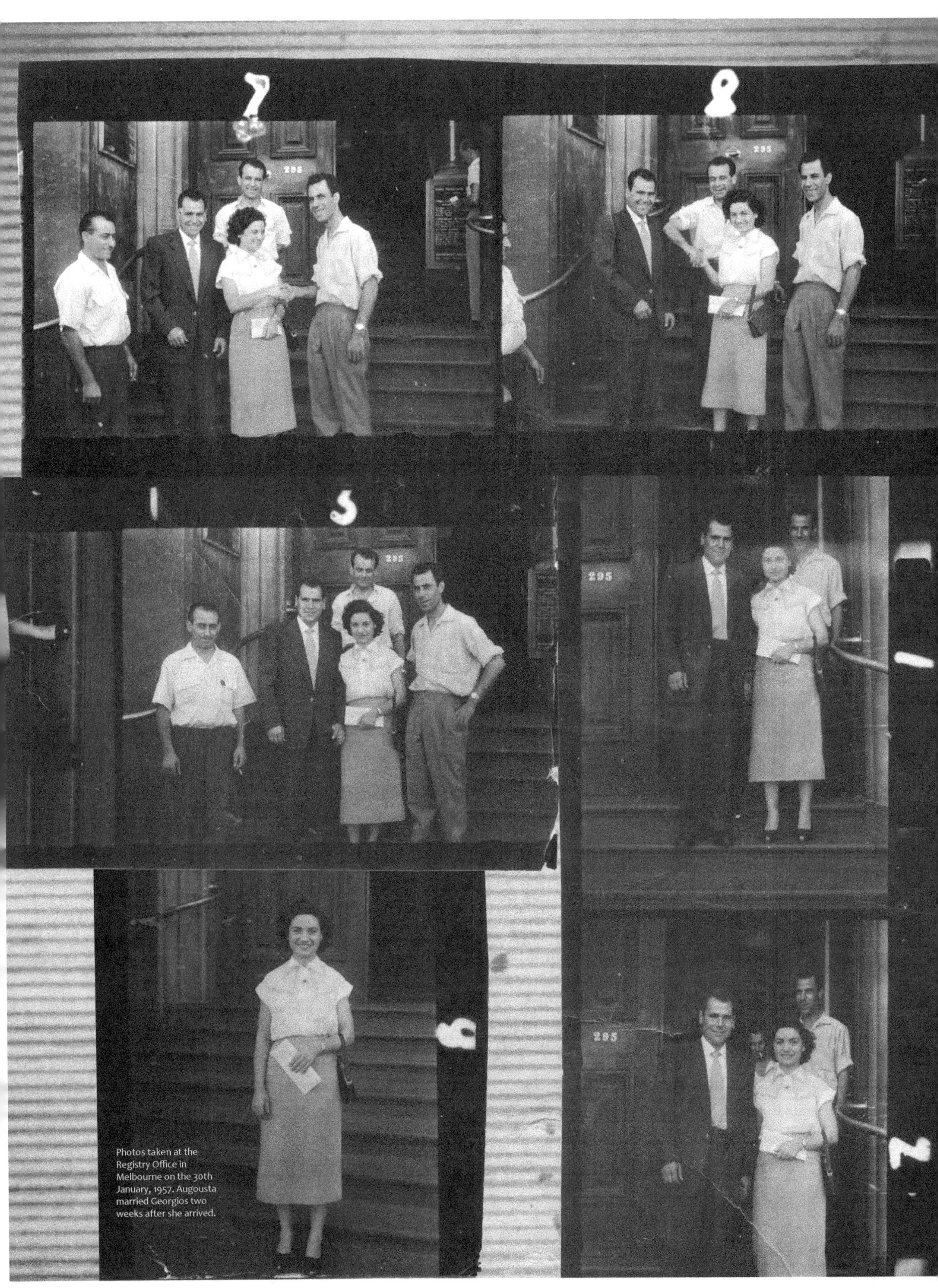

Photos taken at the Registry Office in Melbourne on the 30th January, 1957. Augousta married Georgios two weeks after she arrived.

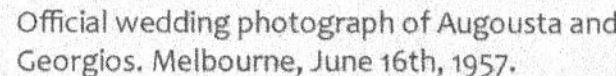
Official wedding photograph of Augousta and Georgios. Melbourne, June 16th, 1957.

married, he only thought about one girl – Augousta Alexandrou. He sent a number of letters to Augousta's parents announcing his intentions to marry their daughter. Eventually, they agreed. Having received her parent's approval, Georgios began writing to Augousta on a weekly basis until she finally arrived in Australia by aeroplane on the 18th of January, 1957.

Augousta was born in Meniko on the 24th of January, 1934. Her parents Alexandros Theodoulos and Vasiliki Hadjichtori had five daughters, Augousta, Athena, Anna, Maroula, Anthoula and four sons Andreas, Theodoulos, Ektora and Panayi.

As a young girl, Augousta was sent by her parents to learn sewing and to become a qualified seamstress . "I knew Georgios from school," she tells me. "He was always keen on me, even as a young boy. At our school there was only one teacher and around 130 students so our teacher instructed some of the older students to teach the younger ones. Georgios, who was around eleven years old at the time, was very keen to teach me. Of course, I was too young to notice his advances and was certainly not keen on him. I wanted my cousin to teach me, but Georgios insisted. Years later I asked him, 'why did you pursue me so much at school', and he said, 'you were the most beautiful and quiet girl there and I only had eyes for you.' I wasn't interested in him or any other boy for that matter."

By 1956, Georgios had saved enough money to put a deposit on a brand new house in Pascoe Vale. He returned to Melbourne and found work as a truck driver for the Board of Works. He was involved in water main maintenance all over Melbourne and its expanding areas for over thirty years. As a younger man he would say that he knew every water main in Melbourne.

Georgios bought his house for 3,000 pounds. The suburb of Pascoe Vale is located north-west of Melbourne, around seven miles from the city. "In the 1950s there were only a handful of houses built in the area," says Augousta, "and they were surrounded by muddy paddocks and pastures. I remember there were wild artichokes everywhere. Fields of wild artichokes."

After writing to each other for two to three years, Augousta finally arrived in Melbourne in 1957 from England. "Georgios was at Essendon Airport waiting for me. When he saw me he was so happy he jumped the security gate and whisked me away. We rode together in a taxi to his new house in Pascoe Vale. I was very shy and very scared. At the start I used to sleep in a room by myself with the door locked. It wasn't because I was scared of my husband. I was just very shy. Poor Georgios had to sleep in another room. I found out later that he would sometimes stand outside my bedroom window at night (standing in the garden) fearing that I wanted to escape."

Two weeks after she arrived, Georgios married Augousta at the Registry Office in Melbourne. It was the 30th of January, 1957. A few months later, on the 16th of June, they had a church wedding at the St George's Greek Orthodox Church in Carlton. "I remember it was a very cold day - but my heart was warm," Augousta says with a smile. "I was very happy to marry Georgios. I loved him so much."

In 1958, Georgios and Augousta welcomed the birth of their daughter Eleni (Helen). Four years later, in 1962, their son Andreas was born.

Georgios also helped Augousta's sisters and brother to migrate to Australia, allowing them to stay at their house until they were each married and able to move into their own homes. He later supported his own sister, Anna and her family to move from England to Australia.

Georgios became the beloved patriarch of his large family in Australia, supporting and guiding the local Cypriot diaspora to embrace Australia just as he did. He died in 2013 just a few weeks before his 84th birthday.

ACKNOWLEDGEMENTS

I would like to thank Augousta Christofi and her children, Helen and Andrew for allowing me to publish Georgios' story of migration and for their help and support.

Little Eleni and Andreas Christofi in front of their family car (a 1959 FC Holden), 1963.

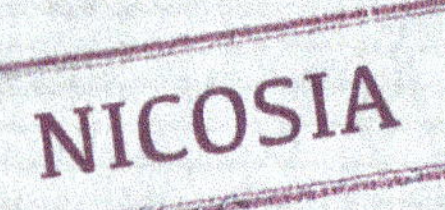

SEVIL HAKI ABDURAZAK

Sevil Abdurazak was born in Nicosia on the 26th of July, 1934 and is one of five children. Their names are Dincer, Suyev, Canev and Kivanc.

Sevil's father, Ismail Salih was a popular barber in Nicosia and her mother Suzan was a talented dressmaker. "My father's shop was opposite Hagia Sophia," explains Sevil. "He was a very friendly man and treated everyone with the same respect and care; rich and poor, Christian, Muslim, it didn't matter, he treated them all the same. My mother on the other hand was not a very caring or affectionate person. She was orphaned from the age of two and her troubled past had made her suspicious of others and somewhat over-protective. Even as I walked to school, my mother would walk behind me and constantly call out, 'be careful Sevil. Don't look at anyone Sevil. Don't speak to anyone.' I was so embarrassed."

After completing primary school, Sevil attended the American Academy in Nicosia where she studied English for three years before she was sent to learn dressmaking with *Kyria* Despou, a local Greek seamstress.

On the 26th of March, 1950, Sevil married Hakki Abdurazak. "I knew Hakki from when I was a little girl," she says. "He was my father's apprentice in the 1930s and was often invited to Sunday dinner at our house. He had to wait until I turned sixteen before I could marry him."

In 1951, Hakki and Sevil tried to buy a house in the new suburb of Neopoli, North Nicosia but the local Justice of the Peace sold the house to another buyer who was able to pay in cash. Feeling angry and dejected, Hakki decided to leave Cyprus and go to Australia where he was told he could make a lot of money in a short amount of time. "My plan was to work there for five years and then come back with enough money to buy a new house in Nicosia," he says. "I had to sell my barbershop business for 150 pounds to pay for my trip."

Hakki left Limassol in January 1951 on the ship SS Jenny. As soon as he arrived, he found work at the General Motors Holden plant in Port Melbourne where he was earning around eight pounds a week. "Once I had settled in Melbourne, I arranged to bring Sevil over here. I remember going to this travel agent on Collins Street to buy her ticket. He was a Cypriot travel agent. He showed me this picture of a beautiful white ship. It looked very clean. He told me it was a brand new English ship called Corsica and that every passenger gets a cabin. That's why I bought the ticket to send to Sevil in Cyprus. I bought two tickets, one for my wife and one for my brother Dervish."

Sevil laughs and shakes her head. "They lied to him. It was not a good ship. When it arrived in Limassol you could see that it was old. We had to go out in small boats with our luggage just to get on board. Then it just sat in the water, away from the port. We were waiting on the ship but it didn't move for five days. My uncle knew the reason it didn't move. He was a newspaper man and he knew, but he was too scared to tell my parents in case they rushed back to Limassol and tried to take me off the ship. I remember the crew were Italian and Greek. We always ate Italian food, spaghetti and we always had wine on the table. I remember we had fresh bread rolls for breakfast. That was nice. They told us it was a Greek ship and I think there were about fifty Turkish Cypriots passengers."

Like so many others, Sevil became quite sick on the Corsica. "I was very sick on this ship. I couldn't eat anything. I couldn't drink anything. It was the smell of the rotten potatoes but also ocean sickness. My brother-in-law Dervish was also very sick, but I didn't see him at all. He was in a different part of the ship. A family friend looked after Dervish. Did they have doctors on the ship? Who knew? I didn't see any. I just laid on my bed in my cabin all day and all night. I couldn't move. My friend would bring food to the cabin but I couldn't eat anything. We didn't even have any medicine. Nothing at all. It was hell. Such bad luck. Anyway, we got lost along the way. We ended up in Africa, in Djibouti. Never heard of this place before."

Sevil and Hakki at the spring in Lapithos with Sevil's brother Dinger and his family (on the left). Circa 1950.

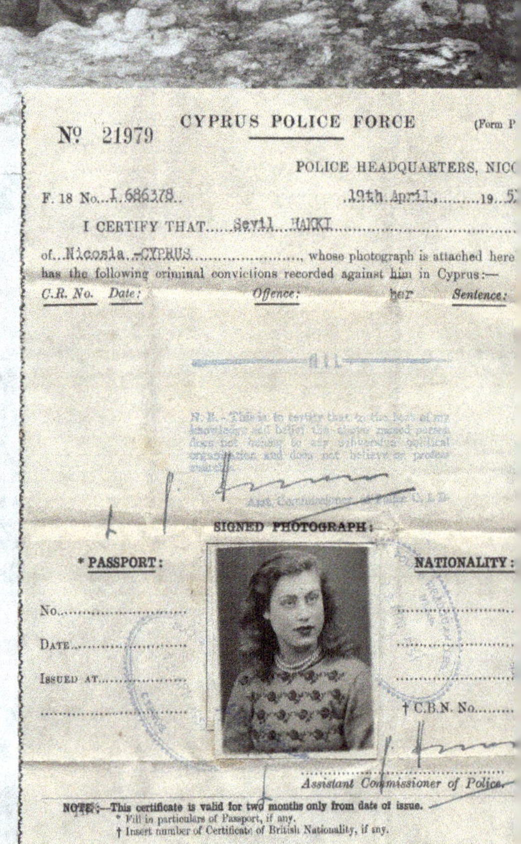

No. 21979   **CYPRUS POLICE FORCE**   (Form P

POLICE HEADQUARTERS, NIC

F. 18 No. I. 686378.   19th April, 19 5

I CERTIFY THAT Sevil HAKKI

of Nicosia – CYPRUS, whose photograph is attached here has the following criminal convictions recorded against him in Cyprus:—

C.R. No.	Date:	Offence:	her	Sentence

N.B.- This is to certify that to the best of my knowledge and belief the above named person does not belong to any subversive political organisation and does not believe or profess such.

Asst. Commissioner

SIGNED PHOTOGRAPH:

* PASSPORT: NATIONALITY

No.

Date

Issued at

† C.B.N. No.

Assistant Commissioner of Police

NOTE:— This certificate is valid for two months only from date of issue.
* Fill in particulars of Passport, if any.
† Insert number of Certificate of British Nationality, if any.

Sevil's police report required for immigration to Australia. April, 1951.

Hakki and Sevil (far right) entertaining friends and relatives in the back room of their Richmond house, 1952.

Despite her ordeal, Sevil recovered enough to socialise with her friends. "I became friends with these wonderful Greek and Turkish girls. We were all travelling to Melbourne to join our fiancées and husbands. My best friend was a Greek girl named Maria and we saw each other every day. I could speak perfect Greek back then. I shared a cabin with three other women but I cannot remember their names."

Once the Corsica reached Melbourne, the passengers were forced to remain on board for two further days until the immigration officials declared the ship fit to dock. "They wouldn't let us in," says Sevil. "They had to sanitise the ship first. That's how filthy the ship was. It was really terrible."

"I was getting worried," interrupts Hakki. "Sevil left Limassol in December and didn't get to Melbourne until February. I was checking the newspapers every day for news about the Corsica until she arrived. I went to the port and I could see the ship sitting there out in the bay. I had no idea why it took so long to arrive."

Sevil and Hakki rented a house in Richmond together with another migrant couple. "I remember we had to boil water on a log fire to cook our food or have a bath," laughs Sevil. "There was no gas or hot water in this house."

Unlike her husband, Sevil struggled to settle into Australia. "I didn't want to come here," she says softly. "To tell you the truth, I was so miserable in our little rented room in Richmond. Hakki would go off to work at six-thirty in the morning and he would come home late in the evening. I was at home all by myself. I didn't know anyone. It was hard for me in the beginning until our daughter Suzan (Sue) was born in December 1952.

The following year, Hakki and Sevil moved to Port Melbourne. "I bought a house there for 2,500 pounds," he says proudly. "This time we had gas and hot water. No more burning wooden logs to cook and clean. Then we sold this house and bought a new house in Keon Park. In March 1960, our son Serhat was born."

Hakki left General Motors Holden and bought himself a truck delivering soil to various building sites around Melbourne. Initially, he was earning very good money until the work contracts began to decrease. So he sold his truck and found work at a local foundry as a forklift driver.

Towards the end of 1963, Sevil received a letter from her father announcing that he had built her a new house in Neopoli. Before they left Australia to go to Cyprus, a family friend warned Hakki to stay away because the civil unrest was getting worse. Having sold everything, Hakki and Sevil decided to travel to London. "My two sisters were living over there," remarks Sevil. "Hakki bought a barbershop in Newington Green and we were living upstairs, above the shop. We stayed in London for three years and then we came back to Melbourne. Life was pretty good for us after that. Hakki bought another barbershop and we went on many lovely holidays together. We watched our children grow up, get married and have their own children. Praise God, Australia has been good to us."

ACKNOWLEDGEMENTS

I would like to thank Sevil Abdurazak for allowing me to publish her story of migration. Special thanks to her daughter Suzan and son Serhat for their support over the last few years.

Left: Hakki and Sevil in front of their rented house in Richmond. Sevil is nine months pregnant. September 23rd, 1952.

Right: Sevil and baby Suzan. Sevil was eighteen years old. January, 1953.

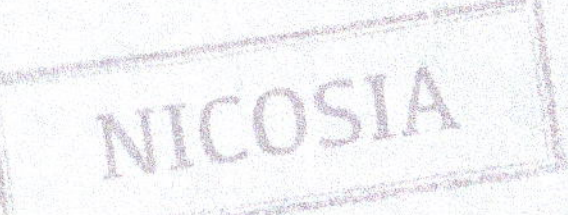

ANGELIKI
DEMETRIOU

PASSENGER CARD

Name ANGELIKI ERINI KYRIACOU

Date of birth / Age 10.5.1933 / 18

Occupation SEAMSTRESS

Place of origin NICOSIA

Port of departure LIMASSOL

Date of departure 17 DEC 1951

Date of arrival 4 FEB 1952

Bearer
(Titulaire)

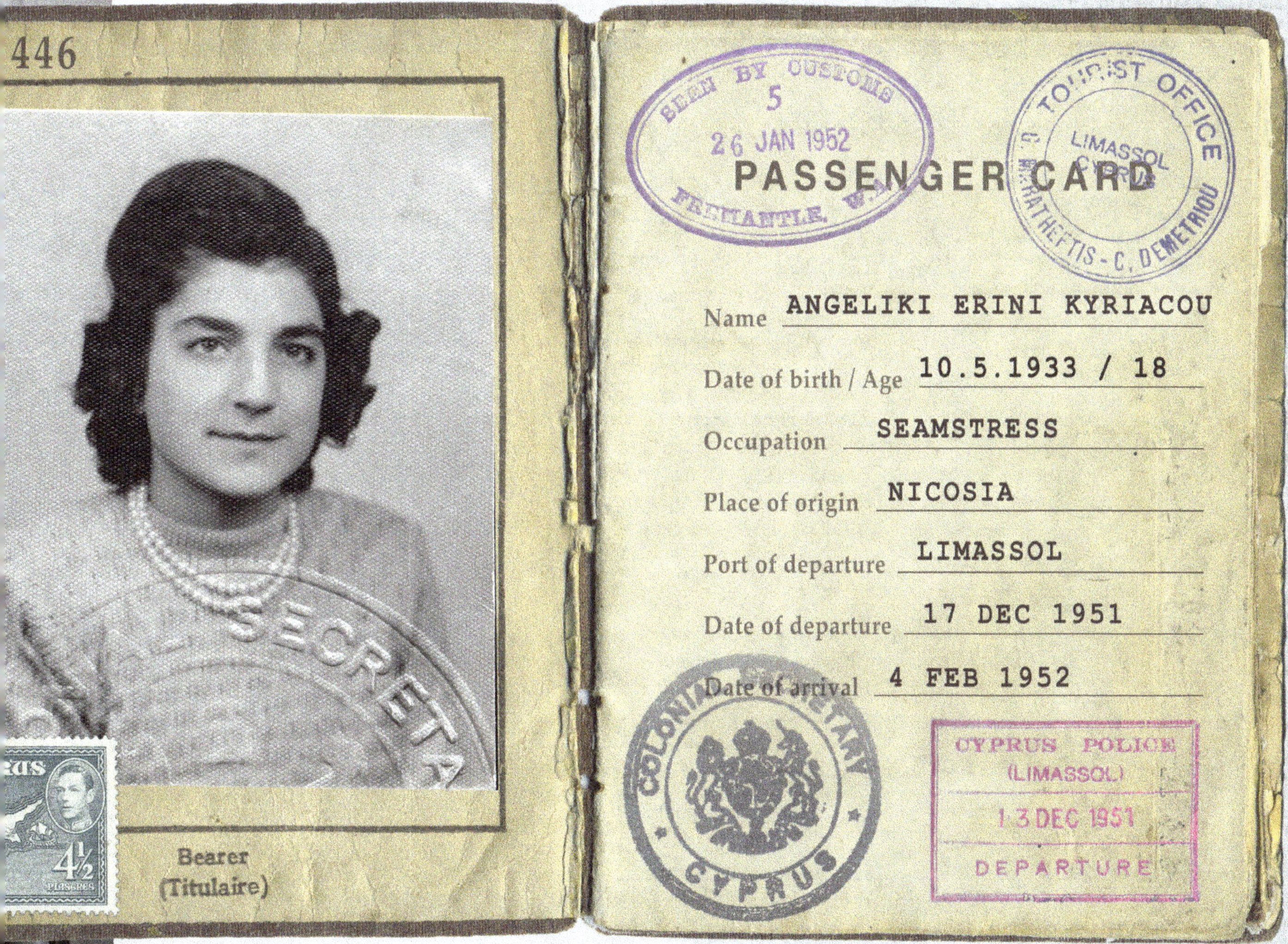

Andonis Demetriou on his motorbike in Nicosia, 1949.

Angeliki (Angela) Demetriou (nee Erini Kyriacou) was born in Nicosia on 10th of May, 1933. Her parents were Loizou Kyriacos and Haritini Agelidou. Her siblings were, Maroula, Takis, Andreas, Roberto, Olivia and Rena.

Angeliki's father was a carpenter who later became a baker, baking bread for the residents of his *mahallah* (neighbourhood) in Nicosia.

Like so many young Cypriot young girls at the time, Angeliki did not attend high school but instead was sent to a seamstress to learn how to sew. "The seamstress that I went to was one of the best in Nicosia. Her name was Mirianthi Karayianidou. Normally you would need to pay the seamstress to teach you how to sew, but because I was quite good at it, she did not charge my parents any fees."

Angeliki was eighteen when she left Cyprus on the Corsica. She was on her way to meet her fiancé Evripides Demetriou and was escorted by his brother Andonis.

Andonis was born in the village Vasa Kellakiou (Limassol) on the 18th of November, 1920. He took the opportunity to be Angeliki's chaperone but also to be reunited with his brother in Melbourne.

Evripides had migrated to Australia in June 1949 on the ship Cyrenia. "Evripides was seven years older than me," she tells me. "My sister Maroula and his sister were good friends. They were neighbours

Angeliki (left) with her Aunt Georgia (her mother's sister) and Uncle Michalakis Vasilakas, Nicosia. Circa 1948.

near the Kyrenia Gate in Nicosia. It was Evripides' mother who arranged for me to marry her son. She sent a letter to him stating that I was a decent girl from a good family and that he should marry me.

I personally wasn't that keen on getting married to him. After all, I didn't know him. Our parents arranged everything. I was only sixteen and I didn't really want to travel to Australia. My parents insisted that I should marry him, telling me he was a good man from a good family. Thankfully, it turned out to be true and everything was fine."

Unfortunately, on the day of her departure, a delay at the port meant that Angeliki and her family had to stay with her Uncle Stelios in Limassol for a few days until the Corsica was ready to leave.

"I'll never forget the tears my mother Haritini wept at the port when it was time to say goodbye. We both cried a lot. It was a cold winter's day. All my family were there. We all hugged and kissed. My mother was crying and wiping away her tears with a handkerchief. There were many other parents saying goodbye to their loved ones all around us. My mother gave me a medallion of St Nicholas. 'This saint is the saint for travellers,' she said. 'It will protect you on your journey'. At 3pm the ship's siren went off which meant we had to board the ship."

Angeliki shared a cabin on the Corsica with three other women. "I remember Kyriakou and Katina who were the same age as me. I can't remember the name of the other woman. The girls that shared my cabin were single as far as I remember. My brother-in-law Andonis stayed in separate quarters. I used to sit with my friends talking and singing songs. That's how we passed the time. There was a boy (around

seventeen) named Pavlos (Ttoulou) from Paphos who was related to one of the girls in my cabin. He took a liking to me. He even pretended to be sick in bed one day so I could go and visit him, but I didn't go. I could tell he really liked me, but I was promised to another man."

"I remember people used to complain about the food on the ship. Whenever they served us meat, some passengers would start to 'meow' like a cat, as if to say that they were serving us cat meat. I was lucky that Kyriacos (Christodoulou) was on this ship. He would bring food to our cabin for us to eat. I remember he brought *halloumi* and *loukaniko* (sausage). We were okay because of him."

Angeliki wore a pair of slacks (blue) on the ship, that her mother had sewn and given to her so she could hide her legs. "I remember when I was walking around Port Said with my friends, all the Arabs were staring at me and blowing me kisses. The same thing happened in Africa. The local men in Djibouti were all staring and

Andonis Demetriou at the Port of Limassol, December, 1951.

blowing me kisses. One morning a crew member came to my room to clean it. I said to him: 'I will clean my room myself, you don't have to do it.' He replied. 'You are a beautiful girl. I will call you Miss Corsica, after the ship.' He started calling me Miss Corsica every time he saw me and soon everyone started calling me Miss Corsica. Perhaps it was because of my appearance. I was very modern in my dress sense and fashionable."

In Djibouti, Angeliki attended the Greek Orthodox Church that was near the port along with many other passengers. "We stopped outside the church when we heard the liturgy. It was unexpected but

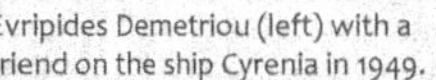
Evripides Demetriou (left) with a friend on the ship Cyrenia in 1949.

we were so happy. The priest was Cypriot. So many people went into the church that it was very crowded. I remember the black girls in Djibouti. When I walked past them, they would wave at me and blow me kisses. I'll never forget their beautiful smiles and their white teeth. They thought I was brave to wear slacks. I remember buying a necklace at the markets near the port. The man gave it to me cheaper because he said I was a beautiful girl."

Regarding the cargo of potatoes on the ship, Angeliki was under the impression that the potatoes were stored on the ship simply to feed the passengers and not for export. "I will never forget the smell. I knew that the potatoes had melted but I'm not sure why they melted. When we reached Colombo there was a long delay. They had to throw out all the rotten potatoes and clean the ship."

Angeliki visited the zoo in Colombo and even had a ride on an Asian elephant. "I wasn't scared to climb onto the elephant even though it was the first time I had seen this animal. I remember they let me ride the elephant for free. I didn't have to pay. I'll never forget the zoo. It had so many wonderful things to see. Colombo was a lovely place. Again, the local men started to stare at me and whistle and blow kisses to me when they saw me in my slacks."

"After we left Colombo we had no water. We used to buy our own water on the ship. That's when I began to cry on the ship. I was thinking, if my parents found out what had happened to me, to know how we all suffered on this ship, they would be devastated. I could hear other

people crying on the ship. People were complaining all the time."

When the Corsica finally arrived at Port Melbourne, Angeliki's future husband Evripides was there to greet her, together with his sister Anna and her husband Stellios Panagiotou. "I recognised Anna, because I knew her from Cyprus. Evripides gave me a hug. I was feeling very nervous and a little scared at first. Will he like me? But he treated me with so much kindness that I grew to like him. From Port Melbourne, Evripides took me to his house (by taxi) in Sunshine which was a new suburb in the west of Melbourne, around six miles from the city.

"After we arrived, we heard rumours that some people in Cyprus thought that the ship had sunk. A lot of parents in Cyprus wore black clothes because they thought they lost a loved one on the ship. I was very lucky my parents never heard these rumours. We also heard that after we arrived in Australia the Corsica travelled back to Cyprus with no passengers. They let it sink in the ocean. That was the end of Corsica."

On Wednesday the 16th of July, 1952, five months after she arrived, Angeliki married Evripides. She had just turned nineteen and he was twenty-six. Their sons Jimmy and Andrew were born in 1955, eleven months apart, followed by Fanos in 1958 and their daughter Mary in 1959.

Evripides worked as a painter for the Massey Ferguson company which was based on Devonshire Road in Sunshine. Massey Ferguson and Sunshine Harvester Works were two factories in the western suburbs that employed large numbers

of migrant workers in the 1950s. Most employees earned just over two pounds a week. Sunshine was once a thriving manufacturing hub that was an obvious destination for many newly arrived migrants.

According to many migrants, Sunshine was very primitive compared to their home country. Located ten kilometres out of Melbourne, there was no sewerage, electricity or access to fresh water. Some people paid a shilling for a bucket of fresh water. There was an absence of roads or footpaths. Children walked miles to go to school.

In 1962, Angeliki and her family moved to Darwin where they stayed until Cyclone Tracey devastated the town in December 1974. "I didn't like Darwin," Angeliki confesses. "My husband Evripides wanted to move there for work. We lost many things during the cyclone. Luckily we were able to escape with our lives and we moved back to Melbourne and back to Sunshine."

Two years after his migration, Andonis met Peritou Pantelli. They were married on the 4th of October, 1954 and settled in Sunshine West on Simmie Street, close to Angeliki and Evripides and close to his sister Anna and her husband Stelios Panagiotou.

Their house was only a few doors away from the Apostolos Andreas Greek Orthodox church and every Easter at the conclusion of the midnight mass, close relatives and friends would walk to their house where they would be welcomed with a large spread of traditional Cypriot Easter food, from pots of chicken soup to freshly baked *flaounes* and *koulourakia*.

Andonis and Peritou had no children of their own but were kind enough to raise and educate their niece Nikki from Cyprus who came to live with them at the age of ten. After Nicki completed her secretarial studies, she obtained a government role with the Ministry of Conservation. She returned to Cyprus in 1981. Two years later, Andonis and Peritou also decided to return to their homeland. Andonis passed away in 1987 at the age of sixty-nine.

ACKNOWLEDGEMENTS

I would like to thank Angeliki Demetriou for allowing me to publish her story of migration. Special thanks to her daughter Mary and son Andrew for their help and support over the years.

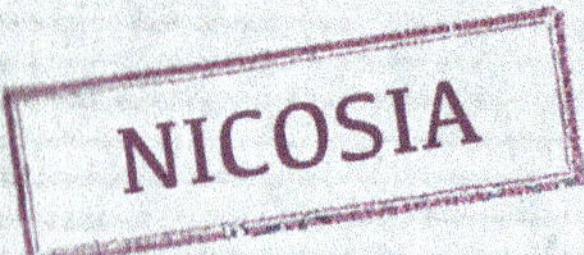

NICOSIA

EVDOKIA NIKIFOROU

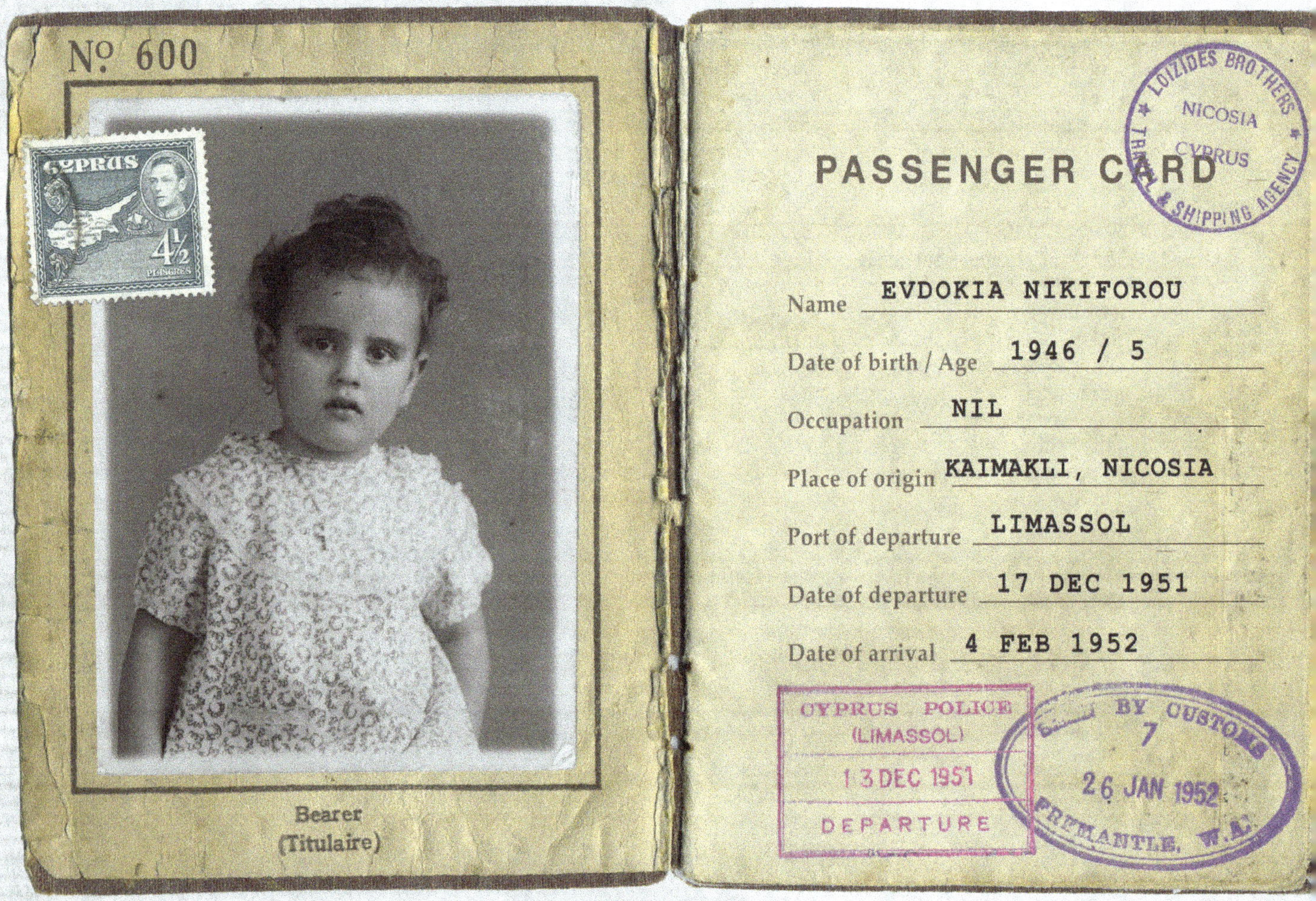

PASSENGER CARD

Name   EVDOKIA NIKIFOROU

Date of birth / Age   1946 / 5

Occupation   NIL

Place of origin   KAIMAKLI, NICOSIA

Port of departure   LIMASSOL

Date of departure   17 DEC 1951

Date of arrival   4 FEB 1952

E vdokia Nikiforou was born in Kaimakli, Nicosia in 1946. She was five years old when she travelled to Australia on the Corsica with her mother Eleni (aged forty) and her brother, Christakis (aged seven) and sister Kyriacou (aged nine).

"My father Savvas had flown out to Australia three years before we arrived," she tells me. "I remember arriving at Limassol harbour and seeing our ship anchored about a mile out to sea. In those days, they had to ferry all the passengers from the port out to the ship on small boats. My mother told me that the travel agents must have done this on purpose so that the passengers couldn't change their minds once they realised how disgusting the ship was. Anyway, we were given a cabin to stay in. There was a bunk bed for the four of us and another bunk bed for a woman with six children."

Evdokia clearly remembers hearing the ships engines blowing up as we were travelling along. "You'd hear these loud bangs and all of a sudden the ship would just be floating along, without its engines going. We could hear them trying to start the engines. It was the same noise that you hear when you're trying to start a car engine. That whining noise of an engine refusing to start. People were worried. You could feel the ship just floating around on the water."

Evdokia remembers when she first smelt the stench of rotten potatoes coming through the ship's ventilation. "My mum told us kids that a man named Louis went down to the hull to investigate where the smell was coming from. No one else wanted to go down there and so Louis went down and he slipped on the sludge and broke his leg. I'm not sure if that is true. We were also told that the passengers in First Class had a much better experience than everyone else. They were really looked after by the crew and staff of the Corsica. They had better food and service than the rest of us. With regards to the food, because it was an Italian ship with an Italian crew, we were getting mostly beans."

Aged only five, Evdokia found herself entertaining the other passengers from time to time. "They would give me a microphone and I would recite all these patriotic poems that I had learnt in kindergarten back in Cyprus. When we got to Melbourne the ship was quarantined by the Australia authorities. That was the word that mum kept using, quarantine. We got our suitcases and made our way to Sydney. We were placed on a train, like sheep. No one could speak English and we could only guess what was going on. My poor father had no idea that we had arrived and were on a train to Sydney. There was a lot of panic and drama when the train arrived at Central Station. The local Cypriots living nearby were notified to help the new emigrants and that was how my dad found where we were and he came as quick as he could. The Cypriots were a very tight knit community and always helped one another. When they heard new arrivals had arrived they would take sweets, food, wine and even clothes and blankets to welcome them and to help them settle in their new country. When my dad finally saw us, there were lots of tears. It was a very emotional reunion."

Settling into a new life in Australia was not easy for Evdokia and her family, especially when she attended school. "We were the only wogs at Darlington Public School and in the beginning, we would get punched by the Aussie kids every day. We looked so different to the other kids. They were all fair-haired or ginger-haired with freckles and we just looked so different to them. Eventually, we all managed to get along and respect one another."

ACKNOWLEDGEMENTS
I would like to thank Yvonne Symon for allowing me to publish her story of migration and for her kind help and support.

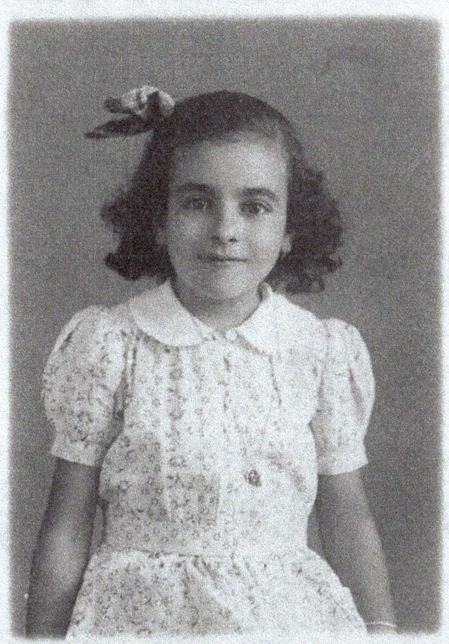

Passport photos from top to bottom: Eleni Nikiforou, her daughter Kyriacou and son Christakis. Evdokia's photo is shown on opposite page. Circa 1950.

Demetrious (sitting in car) with two friends in NSW. Circa 1957.

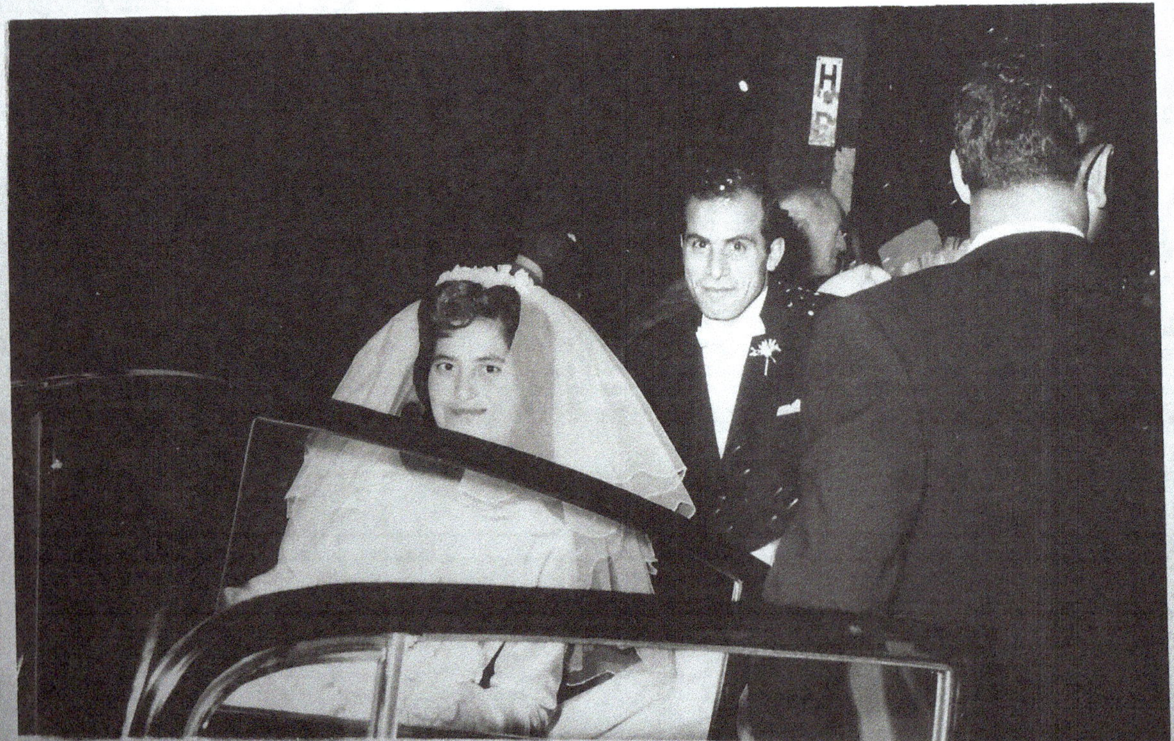

Demetrious and Foutoulla on their wedding day. Sydney, May 24th, 1964.

DEMETRIOUS GEORGIOU

D emetrious Georgiou was born in Geri near Nicosia on the 24th December, 1934. He was the youngest of five children. His siblings were; Costantinos, Eleni, Nicolas and Areti. Sadly, his father Georgios Havadjia died when he was only five years old pushing his family into deep financial crisis and poverty. As the eldest child, Costantinos (Costi) became the head of the family.

When he turned nine, Demetrious was forced to abandon his education to become a shepherd and look after the family's flock of sheep. Every afternoon, his mother Christalla would bring her son a piece of bread and a few olives to help sustain him during the long hours he would spend in the fields and mountains with his sheep. "He told me that the bread was so hard and stale at times he had soak it in sheep's milk so he could eat it," Demetrious' wife Fotoulla tells me. "Some days, his mother might bring him an orange or a tomato. He also told me that once a year, in the summer, he would take his sheep to the beach in Larnaca to wash them in the sea. The beach was about twenty-five miles from Geri. He would travel all day and night with the sheep to get there."

"Although his family were extremely poor," adds Fotoulla, "they managed to survive by selling sheep's milk to the village inhabitants in order to buy bare necessities such as flour and olive oil. When he was about fifteen, he was invited to play football with his village team against a team in Nicosia but he didn't have any shoes. That's how poor his family were. He put on his mother's shoes to play and he scored a goal wearing his mother's shoes. Oh boy, he was so happy that day. Two years later, when he was seventeen, his mother bought him his first pair of shoes when he was getting ready to come to Australia."

In 1949, Demetrious' brother Nicolas decided to migrate to Australia in the hope of finding work so he could help support his family. Once the people in the village heard that the son of Havadjias was going to Australia, they all exclaimed, 'Where on earth is he going to get the money for that?' The average cost was 120 pounds. But Nicolas was determined. He sold everything he owned, his lambs, his small parcels of land, everything.

Nicolas arrived in Melbourne on the ship SS Misr on the 21st of February, 1949 and went by train to Sydney. Two years later, Demetrious decided to join him there. "The day he was leaving, his family travelled by bus to the Port of Limassol. That was the first time his sister Areti had seen the ocean."

Areti gave the following account of the day her brother left Cyprus.

"When we got to Limassol, we needed to get onto a little boat to go into the sea. The ship was far away, we couldn't see the ship! When we were in the boat, a fair way out, the motor failed. We all panicked. I said, if we drown, what about Demetrious who is meant to go to Australia? I didn't even worry about the fact that I was going to drown! Finally, the man fixed it and we moved off again. That fear we felt that day stayed with us. It was very hard when my brothers left. No one went on holidays or moved away from the village back then. When Nicolas and Demetrious left, almost everyone from Geri came to farewell them. They gave them presents such as a singlet, a pair of socks, a shirt. They were one of the first to leave the village.

We were orphaned so young, and we were hungry, but we had so much love for each other. We loved our mother. We were always by her side. Whenever she would go to sleep, we would sleep next to her. When Demetrious was due to leave for Australia, he wanted to sleep next to his mother. 'I just can't (sleep), I need you next to me,' he said. 'Come, let's sleep next to each other.' It was winter and we set up a bed on the floor. After our father died, our bond with our mother grew even stronger. When Dimitris was leaving, I would sing him songs and he would sing me songs. The songs were about how much we loved each other. When he went to Australia, he would write to me and he would write all of these songs in his letters."

The journey on the Corsica was full of new experiences for this young boy from the village. Demetrious would see toothpaste for the first time. He would often recall the smell of the foods that were served. In fact, one of the first meals served on the ship was tinned salmon. "He didn't recognise the food on the ship," his Fotoulla tells me. "It looked so different so he wouldn't eat it. He and others on the ship would bribe the kitchen staff to cook them up some chips. Thankfully, he had some friends on the ship (including someone named Savvi) from Geri. He told me it took them three months to get to Australia. All the way, he was very, very sick. It was a very, very old ship. It was full of potatoes and the potatoes got rotten."

Demetrious had told his family, that after leaving Cyprus, the Corsica lost an engine and that is why it took so long to get to Australia. The ship had to stop at Colombo in Ceylon for repairs and to remove the rotten potatoes. "Apparently, when the captain of the ship asked for volunteers, many passengers refused due to the stench, so the captain had to volunteer and during the process, he slipped and broke his leg."

When he arrived to Melbourne, Demetrious caught the train to Sydney where his brother Nicolas was waiting for him at Central Station. His brother helped him to find accommodation in Woolloomooloo where he shared a room with five other migrants. "Demetrious didn't stay there too long," says Fotoulla with a laugh. "He couldn't sleep because all the men in the room were snoring. One night he got up, packed his bag and went to a Greek club. It was just before 1am. 'What are you doing here?' The man at the club asked him. 'We are just about to close.' Anyway, this man let Demetrious sleep at the club that night, on a couple of chairs, and the next morning he helped him find a new place to live."

By all accounts, Demetrious had a good time as a single young migrant

Demetrious (right) walking down George Street in Sydney with a friend. Circa 1956.

in Sydney. He was a confident dancer and enjoyed visiting the dance halls and meeting the young local women who went there. He enjoyed spending time with his friends at the beach and going on picnics at various parks. From time to time, he would experience a bit of racism from some of the locals. If he was speaking in Greek to a friend on a train, he was often abused and told to 'go back to his bloody country.'

Soon after he arrived in Sydney, Demetrious found a job at a milk bar in the heart of the city. "I think this milk bar was owned by a Greek man named Andreas," says Fotoulla. "At the start, Demetrious only knew a few words in English, yes and no and words like that, but he was very smart and he soon picked up the language. He did attend a few English classes at night and that is how he was able to read and write. Anyway, he didn't like this job much so one day, with a friend, they took the train to Wollongong where they found work at the Port Kembla Steelworks."

Demetrious worked at the steelworks for around eight months before returning to Sydney where he moved in with his brother Nicolas and his new wife. "This was about 1955, or 1956," Fotoulla recalls. "That's when he went into business with his brother. They opened up a small sandwich shop in Elizabeth Street. In those days, most of the customers were factory workers because on top of the shop were textile and clothing factories. They would open early in the morning and close around 9 o'clock at night. They worked together in this shop for twenty-five years. That's where I met Demetrious. I used to work around the corner from his shop in a factory sewing dresses."

Twelve years after Demetrious arrived to Australia, he met and married Fotoulla Stassi. Fotoulla was born in the village of Aradippou in 1944. Her parents were Georgios and Kaliopi Stassi and her siblings were Zinou, Pantelis, Myrofora, Christalla, Stavroulla, Panayiota, and Haralambos.

Fotoulla laughs, "Okay, I will tell you. My two sisters Myrofora and Stavroulla were married to two men that were on the Corsica with my Demetrious. My sister Myrofora was sent from Cyprus to marry Kyriacos Constanti. It was arranged before she left Aradippou, our village. Then my sister Stavroulla came out as a single woman and she was introduced to George Antoniou. Later on, my other

sister Panayiota came to Sydney and she married a man named Kypros. Anyway, there was this man who would go around Sydney selling halloumi and stuff like that. Well one day, he said to Demetrious' sister Eleni, 'I have a lovely girl for your brother.' So, they took me to meet Demetrious at his sister's house and then I also went to see him at his shop. I was nineteen and Demetrious was twenty-nine but that doesn't matter, he was a lovely man. And let me tell you another thing. He always said to me, I never wanted to get married until I had my own house. The girl I marry, I have to take her to my own house, and that's what he did."

Demetrious and Fotoulla were married on the 24th of May, 1964 and they lived in Ashfield where they raised their four children; Christalla, (born in 1964), Andrew (born in 1967), Kaliopi (born in 1968) and Georgina (born in 1976).

At one time, Demetrious opened a sandwich bar near Central Station which he operated for about six months but it was not very successful. For the first time since arriving in Australia in 1952 he found himself unemployed with four children and a wife to support. He had a very strong work ethic and energy about him and while looking to purchase another business, he applied for a job as a kitchen hand at the Kirribilli Ex-Services Club. Within a week of starting, he was promoted to assistant chef as his experience in food preparation was evident. He would spend nine months there before selling their business in Elizabeth Street and purchasing a milk bar in Hornsby with a house at the rear.

In Australia, Demetrious would later add Havadjia to his surname (after his father) since there were many Cypriot migrants with the name Demetrious (or Demetri) Georgiou. In those days, migrants moved around a lot so their mail from Cyprus would be sent to the Greek Club for collection. Given there were so many men with the same name, Demetrious added Havadjia to help avoid the confusion as did his brother, Nicolas.

Demetrious did not see his mother again. By the time he returned to Cyprus, (forty years later) his mother and so many of his relatives had all passed away. "When I married Demetrious I made sure that he would send his mother five pounds a month," says Fotoulla. "After we worked for a few years in the milk bar

Demetrious in his Elizabeth Street shop, Sydney. Circa 1975.

business I said, 'you have to go back to Cyprus to see your mother before it's too late,' but he was so busy working in the shop with his brother Nicolas, and besides, we didn't have a lot of money back then. When he was told that his mother was in poor health, he made plans to visit Cyprus with our son Andrew. They even started packing their bags, however, the talk of war breaking out in addition to the financial strain and the business meant they had to cancel their plans. After his mother died, Demetrious felt so bad. He would regret not seeing her for the rest of his life."

Although in the early days Demetrious felt terribly homesick and wanted to return to Cyprus, the memory of the abject poverty he endured as a young boy helped him to commit to his new life in Australia. Demetrious had a determination to succeed, energy and an entrepreneurial spirit. His strong work ethic was something that his wife and children always admired about him. Demetrious was driven to ensure that his children were university educated. This made him proud and thankful. His love of sport, wonderful sense of humour and charisma endeared him to all those he met. All these qualities saw Demetrious not only survive but thrive in his adopted country.

ACKNOWLEDGEMENTS

I would like to thank Fotoulla Georgiou and Georgina Stamatopoulos for allowing me to publish Demetrious' story of migration for their kind help and support.

EVDOKIA
HARALAMBOUS

Name **EVDOKIA HARALAMBOUS**

Date of birth / Age **7.9.1933 / 18**

Occupation **SEAMSTRESS**

Place of origin **MORPHOU, NICOSIA**

Port of departure **LIMASSOL**

Date of departure **17 DEC 1951**

Date of arrival **4 FEB 1952**

On board the Corsica, en route to Australia. January, 1952. The man standing with his leg on the bench is Yiannis Kalonas. The woman standing on the bench is Dimitra Phillipou (aged twenty-one). The four men at the back from left to right: Nicos Michali (aged twenty-four), Andreas, unknown, Polycarpos (Polis) Stylianou (aged thirty-four). In the centre is Georgia Kefala. Front row: Evthokia Haralambous, Elenitsa Ioannou (aged fourteen) and her sister Anthoula Ioannou (aged eighteen).

Evdokia Haralambous (later Ladomatos) was born in Morphou on the 7th of September, 1933. She was the fourth of nine children born to Haralambous Papandoni and Panayiota Foundaji. Her siblings were Christakis, Neophitou, Andoni, Michali, Maria, Stavros, Revekka and Yiakovos.

Evdokia's parents were successful farmers in Morphou. They grew seasonal fruits and vegetables including oranges, mandarins, lemons and figs. They would sell their fruit and vegetables at the local markets in and around Morphou. Sometimes they would travel together with other farmers to sell their produce and therefore share all the costs.

At home, Evdokia's mother Panayiota would use a loom to make her own bed linen, table cloths and tea towels. Evdokia remembers coming home from school at midday to feed the silk worms some mulberry leaves. The silk worms would spin their silk cocoon in a ball and then her mother would sell the balls to another person to be processed into raw silk.

Like most Cypriot children during the 1930s and 40s Evdokia would make her own toys. She would fasten together two sticks and use cotton off cuts to make a doll. She attended school in Morphou until the fourth grade before abandoning her education to help her parents on their farm and to look after her younger brothers and sisters. Once a week she would wake early to bake enough loaves of bread to last the whole week. "My parents had a very large stone *forno* (wood-fire oven) in the courtyard of our house," she explains. "Many of our neighbours who did not have a *forno* would come to our house to bake their bread and family meals. My mother was very kind and accommodating with other people. Everyone was welcomed. I remember the whole neighbourhood would gather at our house to make halloumi whenever our goats had plenty of milk to spare. The halloumi would be shared with everyone. My life in Morphou was a happy one. I enjoyed playing with the neighbourhood children and helping my mother and father."

After the Second World War, the Australian Government was actively encouraging Cypriots to migrate to Australia. They began advertising in local cinemas and in the Cypriot newspapers. When Evdokia's oldest brother Christaki, saw these advertisements, he pleaded with his parents to allow him to migrate to Australia. At first they were very concerned about their oldest son leaving them however they could see that he was looking for better opportunities.

Christakis left Morphou in 1949 by aeroplane. There were other Cypriots on the same plane including Andreas Ladomatos. Andreas' father and uncle were co-owners of the Pantheon Cinema in Morphou. After they arrived in Australia, Christakis and Andreas shared a house together in the inner-city Sydney suburb of Surry Hills. As fate would have it, Christakis would one day introduce Andreas to his younger sister Evdokia and he would become her husband.

Back row, left to right: Michalis, Andoni, Neophytos and Evdokia.
Front row: Stavris, Haralambous Papandoniou, Panayiota Foundajis, Iakovos, Revekka and Maria in Cyprus. Circa 1950. Evdokia's eldest brother Christakis is absent having migrated to Australia in 1949.

1950, Evdokia's brother Andoni, seeking the same opportunities as Christakis, also migrated to Australia. The two brothers, Andreas Ladomatos and other Cypriots all lived together in the same house in Surry Hills. They worked hard in various jobs and travelled around Sydney by train and tram as no one owned a motor vehicle. The new arrivals from Cyprus found the cost of living in Sydney very high. Apart from paying someone to do their laundry, they found it increasingly

His parents agreed, as they trusted their eldest son. Evdokia remembers being very excited about coming to Australia as lots of others her age had already migrated. Her mother packed some hand made bed sheets and also small silver dessert forks to take with her, which she has treasured all her life.

When the time came, Evdokia's father Haralambous paid 130 pounds for a general class ticket on the Corsica. "When we arrived at the port in Limassol my

cabin with Marianna Georgiou and her three children, Katina (aged twelve), Christos (aged ten) and Antonis (aged two).

Marianna was on her way to be reunited with her husband George who was already in Australia and was also a friend of Evdokia's brother Christaki. Her daughter Katina would later become a bridesmaid at Evdokia's wedding.

According to Evdokia, her Corsica voyage began without any real concern or

On the deck of the Corsica at Port Said, Egypt. December, 1951. Front left to right: Evthokia Haralambous, Dimitra Phillipou and Georgia Kefela. The two men at the back were both named Andreas.

difficult to work during the day and then come home to cook, clean and look after the household. That was when Christaki sent a letter to his parents requesting that his sister, Evdokia, should be sent to Australia to help them. He wrote that it would be a better life for his sister.

father discovered that general class meant that I would be sleeping in a large area with strangers. He didn't like this so he paid an extra ten pounds so I could have a cabin."

Once on board the Corsica, Evdokia discovered that she would be sharing a

incident. "The ship did sway consistently but I thought this was normal for a ship as I had never been on one before. Then later, there was a terrible smell, which I discovered came from the rotten potatoes and onions down below. I remember how one passenger slipped on the rotten sludge and broke his arm. Luckily there was a doctor on board to plaster his arm. When we reached Ceylon, the ruined potatoes and onions were all thrown overboard and the decks on the ship were washed and cleaned. The smell was now not as bad. I passed my time by walking around the ship and spending time with other girls from Cyprus."

At each port, a bus was organised for the passengers to go on day trips to the main cities however Evdokia and her friends preferred to stay at the port and have lunch. "We were worried that we would miss the boat if we went too far away," she explains. "When we docked at Fremantle, a bus was organised to take us to see Perth. I was very excited that we had reached Australia. I loved Perth and remember how clean the city looked. After leaving Fremantle we all noticed that the ship was now swaying a lot however we did not realise that there were problems with the ship's engines. When we arrived in Melbourne, we were told that the ship was unseaworthy and therefore could not travel to Sydney. The ship's company organised train tickets for all the passengers who were heading to Sydney. We then caught the interstate train to Sydney. In those days you had to change trains at a border town called Albury due to the different train tracks."

Evdokia's brothers Christakis and Andoni were waiting for her in Albury (on the border of Victoria and NSW). Reunited at last, the three siblings travelled by train to Central Station in Sydney and then to their rented house in Surry Hills. That's when she met Andreas Ladomatos. "We liked each other from our first meeting," she confesses.

As expected, Evdokia helped with running the household in Surry Hills. This included washing and ironing everybody's clothes, cooking the daily meals and doing the weekly shopping. Eventually, she found a job at a nearby sewing factory doing the finishing work.

Evdokia loved Sydney. "It was such a beautiful city with lovely buildings," she says. "I especially remember how beautiful the Australian ladies were. They were tall, slim and wore hats, gloves and had these beautiful handbags. I had never seen anything like it. My English language was very limited however if I needed something at the shops I would just point to it. In those days you weren't allowed the handle the fruit, only the fruit shop worker could. I remember I had to travel to a special delicatessen to purchase olive oil. In those days, we mixed a lot with the other migrants from Morphou. We would have picnics at the national parks and go by tram to visit different parts of Sydney. I loved Sydney."

Soon after Evdokia met Andreas Ladomatos, their parents met in Morphou to discuss their engagement. After receiving their parents' approval and blessing from afar, Evdokia and Andreas were married on the 5th of October, 1952 at Saint Sophia Greek Orthodox Church in Surry Hills. They spent their

Andreas and Evdokia in Sydney, 1952.

Andreas Ladomatos and Andoni Papandoniou at the Bluebird Cafe, Windsor, 1955.

honeymoon in Katoomba. They continued to live in Cleveland Street, Surry Hills for approximately two years, where they were renting and sharing their house with Evdokia's brothers, Christakis and Antoni.

In 1954, Andreas, Christakis and Antoni opened a cafe at Windsor named The Blue Bird Cafe. They knew that the local Australians loved their food. The favourite item on their menu was the Blue Bird Special which consisted of a piece of steak, chips, grilled tomato, peas, beans and a fried egg. They also provided fish cocktails to a nearby club.

In 1954, Evdokia and Andreas welcomed the birth their first child John, followed by Harry three years later in 1957. They then left the cafe and bought a fish shop at Haberfield. After a couple of years, they decided to move back to Windsor. There was a fruit shop in the main street that was up for rent and there was accommodation for the family

to live in at the back of the shop. In 1959 their first daughter Penny was born and then in 1960 their second daughter Roulla (Eva) was born. The fruit shop was very successful and Andreas would drive all the way to Haymarket for fruit supplies. After seven years they decided to move closer to Sydney and they bought a grocery/delicatessen shop in Belmore, again with accommodation at the back. They worked hard and built up the business. There were many factories in the area and many customers requested them to make sandwiches for their lunch and this was now included in the shop. They also started to sell many Greek, Italian and Lebanese products so many customers would travel from far away to shop with them. The shop was open seven days a week and twelve hours a day.

After seven long and exhausting years they sold their business. Andreas found work as a delivery driver for Red Tulip

chocolates and Evdokia went to work at the R.J. Brodie Lighting factory. In 1973 they purchased a house in Roselands. The children were growing up and their first grandchild arrived in 1980. Evdokia and Andreas both worked hard until they retired in their sixties. They were blessed with eleven grandchildren and twenty-one great-grandchildren. Andreas passed away in 2008 and Evdokia still lives in her house in Roselands.

ACKNOWLEDGEMENTS

I would like to thank Evdokia Haralambous for allowing me to publish her story of migration. Special thanks to her daughters Roulla (Eva) and Penny and sons John and Harry, for their kind help and support along the way.

CLOCKWISE
- Maria Sotiriou, aged sixteen. Cyprus, 1954.
- Maria Sotiriou (right) with her cousins Xanthoulla, Kostakis and Anastasia on an expedition in the mountains of Cyprus. Year unknown.
- Kyriacos Christodoulou, aged sixteen in Cyprus. Circa 1948.
- Kyriacos Christodoulou (left) aged fourteen, as a child worker in Nicosia with another young worker and his sister (names unknown). Circa 1944.

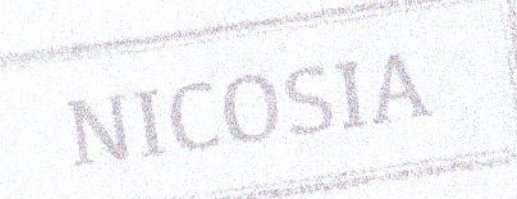

KYRIACOS CHRISTODOULOU

Bearer
(Titulaire)

yriacos Christodoulou was born in the village of Lagoudera, near Troodos, on the 2nd of November, 1932. He was the eldest of six children born to Christodoulos and Paraskevi Irakli. His siblings were Theonitsa, Melanie, Yianni, Nikos and Andreas. After completing primary school in his village, he attended secondary school in Agros for a few years. Paraskevi's family was from Agros so Kyriacos stayed with his aunt.

In his teenage years, Kyriacos performed various agricultural duties but his family still struggled to earn a living. His father sent him to work for local farmers, performing various tasks such as deliveries of goods and agricultural work, for room and board. Christodoulos soon realised that the nature of the work his son had to endure was very taxing so he arranged for him to come home.

Kyriacos however concluded that staying in Cyprus was not an option for him, if he wanted a better future. In 1951, he applied for a visa to travel to America, where his uncle lived, and also to Australia where his cousin Stelios Panagiotou lived. As fate would have it, the approval for Australia was granted first so he packed his bags and booked a place on the Corsica. In fact, it was Stelios who sponsored his immigration.

Regarding the journey on the Corsica, his wife Maria explains that Kyriacos didn't say too much about the trip other than it took seventy-four days and they had to dump the rotten potatoes and onions in the Indian Ocean. "He did mention the smell," she tells me, "and that there was a woman with three children on board the ship and he would watch over her and help her with the children at times. Her name was Melanie Nathanael."

When Kyriacos stepped off the Corsica at Station Pier, there was no one there to greet him. "It was late at night and his cousin Stelios wasn't able to meet him," Maria explains. "So he was taken to the Democritus Club on Russell Street along with some other newly arrived migrants. They were given a hot meal and a chair to sleep on. Kyricaos told me that he didn't sleep at all that night but thankfully, the next day, his cousin Stelios arrived and took him to Sunshine where he had organised a house for him to stay."

Kyriacos soon found a job at a slaughter house in Footscray. "It was a dirty and smelly job," says Maria. "They would bring in these dead animals, dead dogs and all that and cook them in large ovens to make food for other animals. It was very dirty and smelly and he had to have a hot shower and get changed into fresh clothes before he could go home."

Sometime in 1955, Kyriacos left the slaughter house and purchased a fruit and vegetable cart. During the day he would operate his cart in the city centre of Melbourne and at night he would work as a waiter at the Old Menzies Hotel, together with another compatriot named Nicos Jonis. In 1956, he sold his fruit cart and purchased a restaurant in Moonee

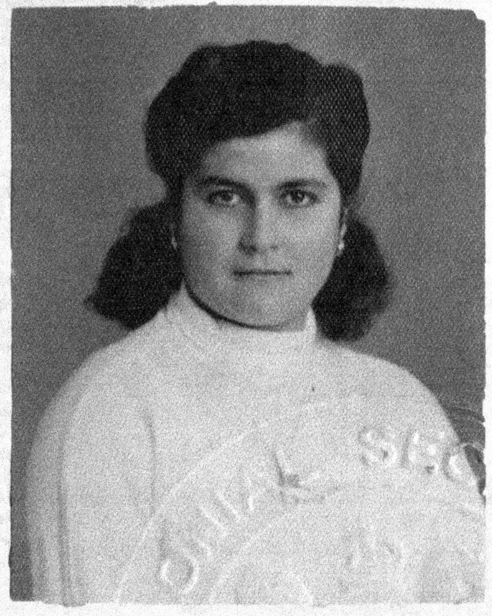

Maria Sotiriou's British Passport. She arrived in Melbourne in September 1956.

Ponds. He was renting a room at a house on Lygon Street, Carlton at that time.

In September 1956, Kyriacos met Maria Sotiriou. She was from Karmi tis Kyrenia and had left Cyprus to escape an arranged marriage. "I was desperate to leave Cyprus," she tells me shaking her head. "I was working in the mines trying to earn enough money to pay for my fare to Australia. My older sister Nifodora and her husband Kypros were already living in Melbourne. Can you imagine a young girl of fifteen or sixteen carrying these big heavy blocks of limestone to a gravel making machine? It was such back breaking work but I was earning ten shillings a day and I managed to save enough money to pay for my ship fare which cost 150 pounds."

Five days after Maria arrived in Melbourne she was introduced to Kyriacos. Maria laughs as she recalls their introduction. "I arrived on Monday the 18th of September and the following Saturday we met and agreed to get married. I remember it was the day that the Olympic Games opened in Melbourne. My sister Nifodora knew Kyriacos and was keen for me to meet him. She worked at his restaurant in Moonee Ponds with her husband. Anyway, I went there to meet him with my friend Yianoulla. When I first saw him, I said to myself, 'I've seen this man in my dreams.' You see in Cyprus, young girls were told to place sweets under our pillows if they wished to see their future husband in their dreams. To tell you the truth, I wasn't that keen to marry Kyriacos but my friends and family convinced me that he was a good man."

Kyriacos and Maria were married on the 10th of February, 1957. In September that year, their daughter Skevi was born, followed by two sons, Terry (born in 1961) and Andrew (born in 1962).

After Skevi was born, Kyriacos and Maria bought a grocery store on Rathdowne Street in Carlton (next to the Kent Hotel). The shop had accommodation on the upper level. "We had the best summers in Carlton," says Skevi. "Dad had an old FJ Ute and we would all pile into the back and he would drive us to the beach. Everyone was so inclusive in Carlton in those days and we all got along without any problems."

"That's right," adds Maria. "Especially the Jewish community. They helped me to learn English. There was this older Jewish woman who would walk me around the shop pointing at various goods, 'this is called butter and this is called beans,' she would say, teaching me the names of each product in English. She also told me to read the newspaper every day. That's how I learnt to read and write. Oh yes, everyone was so kind and lovely to us new migrants."

Skevi also remembers how on Saturdays, her father would fill up the back of his Ute with customer orders and deliver them to their door in Sunshine. "Before he bought the car, he had a Malvern Star bicycle with a basket up front. When he didn't have any deliveries, he would put me in that basket and take me for rides."

Over the years, Kyriacos and Maria were actively involved with the Cypriot diaspora and with many local community-

Christodoulou family portrait taken in Cyprus in 1960. Kyriacos was in Australia.

grateful that she was able to spend so much time with my parents because of the family business. "They kept the grocery store running until 1981," she says. "We had lots of conversations during the quiet moments inbetween serving customers. I learnt so much just by being around my parents. I have always admired their single minded work ethic and their love for family, not just their own family but also the families they left behind. I appreciated the long hours they put in to make a better life for us all and to create a firm foundation that supported us as we grew older. This all happened because of the sacrifice and courage of my dad – who as a teenager - decided to leave his homeland, with no language and minimal education and travel halfway around the world for a better life."

"My parents were glad that they migrated to Australia," adds Skevi. "I remember asking my father. 'Are you happy that you came to Australia,' and he replied. 'Why wouldn't I be happy. It's the first time in our lives that our stomachs were full. If life was good in Cyprus we would have stayed."

based events. "My parents were active members of the Cypriot Senior Citizens Council and they helped to organise lunches every Wednesday. Dad would source the produce for the lunch of the week and mum and the other ladies would go in early to cook and set up for the day. It was a special place for them both to be actively involved with their community but also be able to catch up with their friends, to share a meal or a glass of wine and play a few games of Bingo. They were also involved in the annual Cypriot Wine Festival. Mum would make her delicious *koupes* (fried bulgur pastries) and *shamishi* (fried sweet pie) while dad would help set-up and sell tickets at the door."

Today, Skevi feels fortunate and

ACKNOWLEDGEMENTS
I would like to thank Maria Christodoulou and Skevi Argyrides for allowing me to publish Kyriacos' story of migration and for their kind help and support.

Anastasia outside her first family home in South Yarra, 1954.

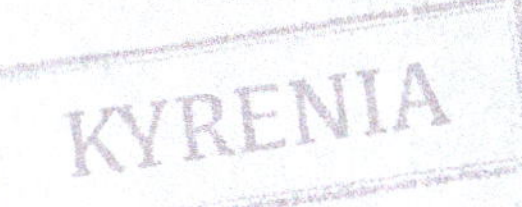

ANASTASIA IOANNOU

Name ANASTASIA IOANNOU

Date of birth / Age 9.2.1928 / 23

Occupation -

Place of origin LARNAKA TIS LAPITHOU

Port of departure LIMASSOL

Date of departure 17 DEC 1951

Date of arrival 4 FEB 1952

Anastasia Ioannou was born in the village of Larnaka tis Lapithou near the town of Lapithos, on the 9th of February, 1928. She was the youngest of five children born to Yianni Tofi-Abraham and Katerina Zysimou.

Her siblings were Andreas, Pavlos, Elizabeth and Eleni. Andreas was eleven years older than Anastasia. Sadly, her sister Elizabeth died when she was only sixteen during a Pneumonia related illness.

Like most young girls from that era, Anastasia's education was cut short in order for her to stay at home and learn how to sew as well as undertake a range of domestic duties. During her teenage years she worked as a seamstress, making clothes for anyone in the village who required her services. She was also trained to use the family loom and together with her sister Eleni, they would weave fabrics for Anastasia to use in her dressmaking. There was not an abundance of fabric to use. Her brothers Andreas and Pavlos became jewellers and the sisters would help them with various jewellery tasks when required.

Anastasia aged around twenty-two in Cyprus. Circa 1950.

Anastasia's family were quite self sufficient. They raised goats and pigs and even kept silkworms to create their own silk (*metaxi*) for their fabric making business. They also had a wide variety of crops and vegetables including, tomatoes, eggplants, potatoes, olive trees and fruit trees. They even made their own wine, *zivania* (alcohol) halloumi cheese and olive oil. Their house was located at the edge of the village with a magnificent view of the mountains from the rear. By all accounts, she enjoyed her childhood and was always in the company of family, friends and relatives. She was never alone.

When her brother Andreas decided to emigrate to Australia with his wife Marianthi and their daughter Eleni (Helen), Anastasia decided to join them with the hope of a new world of opportunity and freedom. Their application process included a medical examination (x-rays and Smallpox injection) together with a police report that was sent to the Australian Immigration Office for approval.

Because of her failing memory, Anastasia cannot recall too much about the Corsica or the voyage itself. According to her daughter Kathy, there was a story often told about how a Cypriot passenger named Sotiris Charalambous, a carpenter, was asked to patch a large hole on the side of the ship. As the story goes, the ship's captain was asking skilled passengers to work on the ship during the voyage as they were short staffed. They were looking for carpenters, repair men, kitchen staff, cleaners etc. Sotiris volunteered and he was required to temporarily mend a hole in the side of the ship until they reached the Port of Colombo. They tied ropes around his waist as a harness and dangled him over the side of the ship to complete the task. He used wooden boards and concrete to seal the hole."

After Anastasia arrived in Melbourne, she initially rented a room with a cousin in inner Melbourne. Her brother Andreas moved to Geelong with his family to live. In fact, it was at a Greek club in Geelong where Andreas would meet Georgios (George) Constantinou and become close friends.

Georgios was working as a carpenter at the Shell refinery in Geelong.

At the end of December 1953, when Andreas and his family decided to move back to Melbourne, Georgios offered to help. They were moving into a house in North Melbourne where Anastasia was also living and renting a room. Upon their arrival, Andreas introduced Georgios to his sister and six months later, on the 11th of June, 1954, they were married.

Prior to their wedding, they had bought their first house in South Yarra, just off Commercial Road. They had borrowed the money from friends and a female money lender in Chapel Street. The only way they could afford to make the repayments was to rent out as many rooms as possible, which they did. Georgios also built a bungalow in the backyard to rent as another source of income. It wasn't long before every bedroom, apart from their own, plus the bungalow were occupied by new tenants. Unfortunately, the house had only one bathroom and the toilet and laundry was located outside. As crowded as it was, everyone in the house somehow managed to get along and make ends meet. Some of the tenants became lifelong friends and *koumbari* (groomsmen).

Soon after she arrived to Melbourne, Anastasia went to work at a tobacco/cigarette factory in Richmond named George Dobie & Son Australia Ltd. She worked in the stemmery building sorting the tobacco leaves. At the end of the week, each worker was given two packets of cigarettes for free. Anastasia worked there until her daughter Despina was born in 1955. Three years later, in 1958, Anastasia and Georgios welcomed the arrival of their second child Kathy followed by Christina in 1965. Later, Anastasia went back to work, this time part-time at the AJC Jam factory on Chapel Street in Prahran, Melbourne.

ACKNOWLEDGEMENTS

I would like to thank George Constantinou for allowing me to publish his wife's story of migration and for Kathy Constantinou-Dunster's kind help and support.

Anastasia Ioannou's engagement photograph taken at a park in North Melbourne, 1953.

OTHER PASSENGERS CYPRIOT

Apart from the fifty-six passengers who feature in this book, there are a number of others who were not included for various reasons. I would like to acknowledge them here.

VASILIOS MICHAEL

Place of Origin: ....Odhou
District: ....Larnaca
Year of Birth: 1925
Age on ship: 26
Listed Occupation: ....Shoemaker

OLGA SOUVERTZI

Place of Origin: ....Scala
District: ....Larnaca
Year of Birth:.............1920
Age on ship:..............31
Listed Occupation: ....Housewife

ERACLIS NISIPHOROU

Place of Origin: ....Paralimni
District: ....Famagusta
Date of Birth: ....23 July 1928
Age on ship:..............23
Listed Occupation: ....Gardener

CHARALAMBOS GREGORI (GREGORY)

Place of Origin: ....Nata
District: ....Paphos
Date of Birth: ....25 February 1923
Age on ship:..............28
Listed Occupation: ....Farmer

STRATI (STATHIS) CHARALAMBOS

Place of Origin: ....Tochni
District: ....Larnaca
Date of Birth: ....12 June 1914
Age on ship:..............37
Listed Occupation: ....Farmer

Vasilios Michael (left) with a fellow passenger on the deck of the Corsica, January, 1952.

Many of the passengers listed on this page had passed away by the time I began my research. Those whom I did meet were able to share a few of their memories of the Corsica.

For example, Zoe Pavlou told me that her mother was very sick and stayed in bed for most of the trip and that the water was so dirty and smelly that no one dared to have a shower. She does recall some happy occasions when the crew decorated a large Christmas tree and gave the children cake and chocolates to eat. She also remembers her mother tripping on the gangway and falling into the water at the Port of Colombo as they were disembarking from the ship. Thankfully, her mother was unhurt.

Varnavas Varnava remembers how one passenger had his watch stolen in Massawa and how in Colombo he was talked into getting a tattoo on his arm.

I only wish I had time to meet more passengers and conduct more interviews.

ANDREAS HARALAMBOUS
Place of Origin: ....Neo Chorio
District: ....Paphos
Date of Birth: ....18 February 1928
Age on ship: 23
Listed Occupation: ....Mason

RENOS ANASTASIOU
Place of Origin: ....Yerani
District: ....Famagusta
Year of Birth:.............1942
Age on ship: 9
Listed Occupation: ....Student

SOFIA THEODOSIOU
Place of Origin: ....Kellaki
District: ....Limassol
Year of Birth:.............1930
Age on ship: 21
Listed Occupation: ....Not listed

ZOE PAVLOU
Place of Origin: ....Anogyra
District: ....Limassol
Year of Birth:.............1937
Age on ship: 14
Listed Occupation: ....Housewife

SOTIRIS CHARALAMBOUS
Place of Origin: ....Pyla
District: ....Larnaca
Year of Birth:.............1926
Age on ship: 25
Listed Occupation: ....Carpenter

PETROS PETRIDES
Place of Origin: ....Unknown
District: ....Unknown
Year of Birth:.............1931
Age on ship: 20
Listed Occupation: ....Clerk

HUSSEIN DJEMIL
Place of Origin: ....Anogyra
District: ....Limassol
Year of Birth:.............1931
Age on ship: 20
Listed Occupation: ....Farmer

ANDREAS PHILIPOU (PHILIPPOU)
Place of Origin: ....Athienou
District: ....Larnaca
Year of Birth:.............1927
Age on ship: 24
Listed Occupation: ....Farmer

MICHAEL NEOFYTOU
Place of Origin: ....Konia
District: ....Paphos
Year of Birth:.............1919
Age on ship: 32
Listed Occupation: ....Waiter

VASSOS KATSIAMIS
Place of Origin: ....Xeros
District: ....Nicosia
Year of Birth:.............1930
Age on ship: 21
Listed Occupation: ....Oxygen Welder

DEMETRIS YEROLEMOU
Place of Origin: ....Ayios Ioannis
District: ....Limassol
Year of Birth:.............1924
Age on ship: 27
Listed Occupation: ....Mechanic

NEOKLIS GREGORI
Place of Origin: ....Neo Chorio
District: ....Paphos
Year of Birth:.............1925
Age on ship: 26
Listed Occupation: ....Farmer

DEMETRA ZANNETTOU
Place of Origin: ....Trikomo
District: ....Famagusta
Year of Birth:.............1930
Age on ship: 21
Listed Occupation: ....Seamstress

HARALAMBOS (HARRY) GREGORIOU
Place of Origin: ....Agia Varvara
District: ....Nicosia
Year of Birth:.............1929
Age on ship: 22
Listed Occupation: ....Mechanic

NICOS SAVVA
Place of Origin: ....Neo Chorio
District: ....Paphos
Year of Birth:.............1923
Age on ship: 28
Listed Occupation: ....Farmer

VARNAVAS VARNAVA
Place of Origin: ....Frenaros
District: ....Famagusta
Year of Birth:.............1932
Age on ship: 20
Listed Occupation: ....Farmer

COSTAS THEOCHARI
Place of Origin: ....Limassol
District: ....Limassol
Year of Birth:.............1930
Age on ship: 21
Listed Occupation: ....Labourer

ACKNOWLEDGEMENTS
I would like to thank the following people for their help and support: Effie Thomas, Lina Pandeli, Christina Turner, Harry Neokleous, Freida Stylianou, Elli Ioannides, Margaret Read, Kim Souvertzi, Anne Koutrouzas, Ifigenia Gerolemou, Kathy and Charlie Charalambos, Andrekos Varnava, Sally Michael and Yesh Djemil.

OTHER PASSENGERS

GREEK

MANOLIS (EMMANUEL) MITRAKAS

Place of Origin: ....Lesbos, Greece
Date of Birth: ....2 January 1913
Age on ship: 38
Listed Occupation: ....Farmer

GEORGIOS DOUKAKAROS

Place of Origin: ....Lesbos, Greece
Year of Birth:..............1906
Age on ship: 45
Listed Occupation: ....Farmer

GEORGIOS VOGATZIS

Place of Origin: ....Lesbos, Greece
Year of Birth:..............1911
Age on ship: 41
Listed Occupation: ....Carpenter

In early December 1951, Manolis (Emmanuel) Mitrakas, Georgios Doukakaros and Georgios Bougatzis (Vogatzis) left their village, Anemotia on the island of Lesbos, to go to the Port of Piraeus in Athens to find any ship that would take them to Australia. The three friends decided it was safer to leave Greece than face persecution for their political beliefs (or perhaps even execution at the hands of the local Greek authorities). As fate would have it, the ship they found in Piraeus was the Corsica. One can only imagine that the Greeks in the port were working frantically to make the ship seaworthy before it embarked on its fateful journey to Cyprus to collect over 780 Cypriots who were waiting anxiously at the Port of Limassol.

Manolis Mitrakas was born on the 2nd of January, 1913. After completing his secondary school education in Mytilene, he had ambitions to go to university to study law, however his affiliations with the Greek Communist Party (KKE) would later squash his career plans. In fact, his political views would also threaten his life.

Last drinks and final goodbyes at a well-known Greek *kafenion* (coffee house) in Omonia Square, Athens. On the left is Georgios Doukakaros next to his brother Panayiotis Doukakaros and Panayiotis' wife Aspasia. Georgios Boyiatzis is fourth from the right and Manolis Mitrakas is second from the right. This photo was taken a few hours before boarding the Corsica. Early December, 1951.

ΚΑΦΕΝΕΙΟΝ
Η ΣΥΝΑΝΤΗΣΙΣ
Μ. ΚΟΡΔΩΝΗ

In 1943, Manolis married Stella Styliani and together they were blessed with three children, Athena, Dimitrios and Eugenia.

"I remember the day my father left Greece," his daughter Eugenia tells me. "I was only three but I can recall it clearly. My family accompanied him to Athens where we spent the day sightseeing and visiting the Acropolis. When it was time for my father to leave, we went to the Port of Piraeus where the Corsica was waiting. I remember he turned to me and said. 'Don't worry. I am just going to buy you some karaméles (lollies) and I will return home soon.' Then he left. We returned to

Manolis Mitrakas aged twenty-one. Lesbos, Greece, 1934.

Newly engaged, Manolis Mitrakas and Stella Styliani, Anemotia, Lesbos, 1942.

did not want to leave Lesbos. Every time he would sponsor our application to immigrate, she would let it lapse on purpose. That is why it took us a few years before we were finally reunited with our father. We left Greece in 1955 on the ship Skaugum and we arrived in Melbourne

on the 22nd of August. My brother Peter was born in Australia."

Initially, Manolis found work at various places in and around Melbourne. He rented rooms in various houses in South Melbourne except when he worked as a fruit picker in Mildura or for the State Electricity Board in Traralgon in country Victoria.

When his family arrived from Greece, Manolis rented accommodation above a fruit shop in Clarendon Street in South Melbourne. Nine months later, he bought his first house on Dorcas Street and two years later he bought a fish and chip shop on Montague Street in Albert Park which had accommodation on the second storey. In 1964 the family moved to a new house on Kerferd Road in Albert Park. While his wife Stella and daughters Athena and Eugenia were working at the fish and chip shop, Manolis was working at the Victorian Railways where he stayed until his retirement.

George Doukakaros was born in the village of Anemotia, Lesbos in 1906. He was married to Irini and they had three

Lesbos and every morning I would race down to the village square to wait for the eight o'clock bus from Mytilene in the hope that he had returned with the bag of lollies that he promised me. But he was never on the bus and I would always return home heartbroken. It was only after I tripped one day and cut my forehead that my mother finally told me the truth."

According to Eugenia, her father Manolis had decided to leave Greece for good. "He had no intentions of coming back," she says. "Especially after being persecuted for his pro-Communist views and ideology and becoming a fugitive in his own country. His plan was to go to Australia, get settled and then arrange for the rest of us to join him. My mother

A group of young men from Anemotia, Lesbos celebrating May Day. Georgios Doukakaros, who was a logistics manager for the Communist Party, is squatting near the centre and wearing a light-coloured suit. Circa 1945.

"My father was the first from our village to organise immigration papers to go to Australia," says Louis. "Initially, he wanted to take me with him but they wouldn't let me go so he decided it was better for me to stay and finish my primary school education. One of the conditions on my father's application to come to Australia was that he had to work on the land to help develop agriculture and viticulture in country Victoria. They wanted him to cut down the bushland to plant orchards, orange trees, apples, apricots and things like that. So that's what he did after he arrived. He worked on farms in Mildura and eventually bought his own farm in Kyabram and later a dairy farm in Shepparton. We arrived in Melbourne in 1954 on a ship called the Seven Seas. My father set us up in a house in Melbourne, while he stayed and worked on the farm. He didn't want us to live on the farm. We eventually moved to North Carlton which was an inner-city suburb, inhabited by Jews, Italians and Greeks. I remember we played football in the streets because there was very little traffic in those days."

ACKNOWLEDGEMENTS
I would like to thank Eugenia Mitrakas and Louis Doukas for allowing me to publish their fathers' story of migration and for all their help and support.

Georgios Doukakaros wearing a fez in Port Said, Egypt, en route to Australia on the Corsica. December 19th, 1951.

sons, Elias, Theophanes and Panagiotis. Louis was eleven years old when his father left Greece on the Corsica. "You have to understand, that life in Lesbos was difficult due to the poverty and lack of infrastructure," he says. The main source of income for my family came from the production of oil and grapes. There was also a lot of fear in Greece at that time, because of politics and the civil war. My father was branded a communist and accused of supplying the rebels. He was arrested many times and tortured. We rarely saw him. When he was in Athens in 1947, someone advised him to go to Australia because there was no future for him and his family in Greece. My father told me that the Corsica was a very bad ship. It was filthy. There were rats everywhere and many people got sick. Two or three people died on that ship and they had to throw their bodies in the sea. That's what my father told me. They got sick and died and they threw their bodies from the deck into the sea."

According to Louis, it took his father three attempts before he was granted permission to immigrate to Australia.

Manolis Mitrakas with his wife and children in Melbourne soon after they arrived from Greece. From left to right: Athina, Jimmy (Dimitri) Stella, Eugenia and Manolis. September, 1955.

This Passport contains
32 pages.

Ce passeport contient
32 pages.

CLOCKWISE
- On board the SS Florentia. Back row: Manoli, Evelyn Semini, unknown. Front row: Godfrey Semini (young boy), unknown and Marcel Cheles, 1951.
- Joseph and Annie Doggett-Williams at the Melbourne Show, soon after arrival in Melbourne. September, 1949.
- Evelyn Semini's passport photo, 1951.
- The SS Florentia, 1951.
- Emmanuel Mallia's immigration photograph, 1953.
- Annie and Joseph Doggett-Williams with their three children (left to right): Dolores, Carmen and Josephine, near Customs House in Valletta, Malta, waiting for the ferry to take them to their ship to go to Australia. April 26th, 1949.

ISLAND OF MALTA AND ITS DEPENDENCIES
ÎLE DE MALTE ET SES DÉPENDANCES

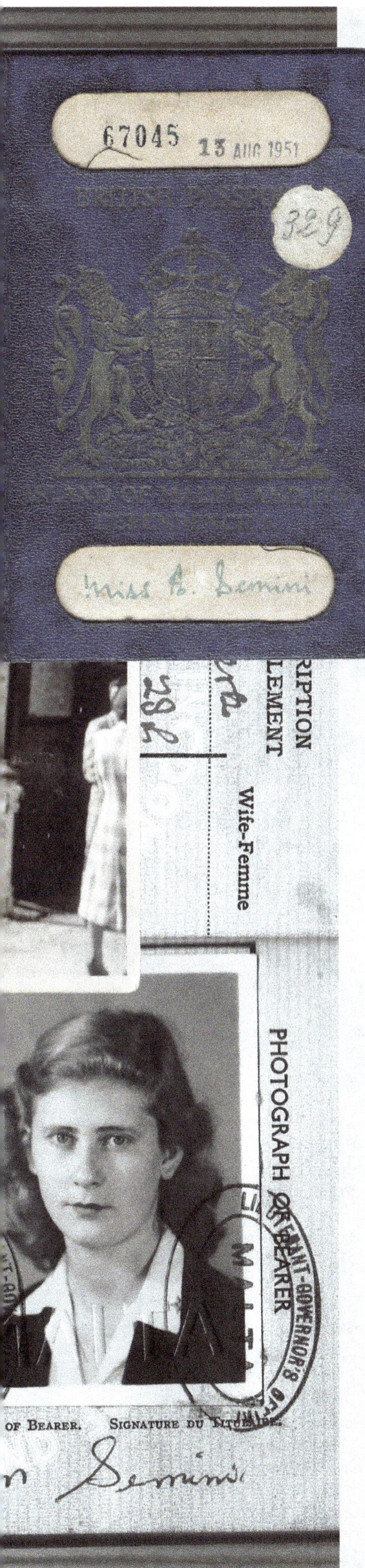

A QUICK LOOK AT MALTESE MIGRANTS

When I began to document the stories of Cypriot migration to Australia, it occurred to me that I should also look at Maltese migrants, who were also British subjects, to compare their immigration experience.

After the Second World War, 33,317 people had migrated to Australia from Malta (up to 1955). Almost 70% of these migrants were accepted under the Assisted Passage Migration Agreement.

In 2022, I was fortunate to meet a few Maltese migrants, who travelled to Australia during this time period and discover a few remarkable differences between the Cypriot and Maltese immigration experience.

The first major difference was that most Maltese migrants came to Australia under the Assisted Passage Agreement that was signed between Australia and Malta in 1948. This meant they only had to pay ten pounds for their trip and children under nineteen years of age travelled for free. Cyprus did not have an Assisted Passage Agreement with Australia, despite being a member of the Commonwealth. Cypriots wishing to emigrate to Australia had to pay their own passage, which was anywhere between 120 and 150 pounds one way. Most Cypriot migrants were forced to sell property or to borrow the money at high interest rates to afford the passage to Australia, which was a great disadvantage to them.

The second major difference was that Cypriot migrants needed a sponsor residing in Australia to support their application for migration and secure their passage. Assisted Maltese migrants did not need sponsors resident in Australia. Their accommodation and employment needs were also looked after by the Australian Government, providing they stayed and worked for two years. The person who sponsored a Cypriot migrant had to agree to provide accommodation and to help them find work before their application for a permit to enter Australia was approved.

I also found it remarkable, that most Maltese migrants could speak English (even Italian and French). By comparison, most Cypriot migrants knew little to no English upon arrival. Furthermore, it appears that Maltese migrants arrived with more disposable income compared to their Cypriot counterparts. Most of the Cypriot migrants I interviewed for this book arrived with less than five pounds in their pocket.

What follows are the recollections of three wonderful Maltese people who agreed to share their stories of migration.

EVELYN SPITERI

Evelyn Spiteri (nee Semini) was born in Malta on the 28th of July, 1933. She was eighteen and working as a bank clerk in Casal Pawla when her father decided to move her family to Australia. They left in August 1951 on the Italian migrant ship SS Florentia. "I was excited about leaving Malta to go to Australia," Evelyn tells me. "I left with my father, step-mother, my younger brother and two half siblings and we all travelled for free. My father was a police inspector in Malta and he knew the owner of the ship Antonio Ghidoli, and that's how we got free passage. I heard that other Maltese migrants paid ten pounds, but they had to stay down below in the steerage section of the ship. If they wanted a cabin, they had to pay more."

According to Evelyn, the journey to Australia took forty days. "We stopped first at Port Said where we took on more migrants. Then we stopped at Colombo before reaching Fremantle and Melbourne, where we disembarked. The ship then continued to Sydney. I remember making friends with some young Italian men who I met at Port Said. When we got to Melbourne there were doctors that came onto the ship and they checked all the passengers. I think they looked at my skin and that's all."

Once settled in Melbourne, Evelyn worked as a typist with Australian National Airways. She met her husband Charles

Spiteri in Melbourne. "He worked as a flight steward for Qantas. He used to work for the air force in Malta as a bell boy and he migrated to Australia in 1948. A friend of my father arranged a meeting between me and Charles and it was love at first sight. By this time, Charles was based in Sydney and used to come to Melbourne to visit me. We were married in 1955 and I then moved to Sydney. I remember we had to switch trains in Albury because the railway tracks in NSW were a different width to the tracks in Victoria." In 1957, Charles accepted a job as Catering Officer at Qantas House, Sydney.

Evelyn and Charles settled in the southern Sydney suburb of Gymea and that is where their children (Jane, Linda, Anne and Andrew) were born and raised.

When asked if she was pleased that she migrated to Australia, Evelyn stated that there were more opportunities for her and her family in Australia. "I liked that Australia was more egalitarian than Malta. Australia gave my family a lot more opportunities, especially with regards to work, than we would have received back home."

EMMANUEL MALLIA
Emmanuel Mallia came to Australia in 1954 on board the ship Surriento. "The Surriento was once an American carrier and the Italians bought it after the war and fixed it up as a passenger ship. It was a big ship, maybe four levels. We left on the 21st of April, and we arrived on the 21st of May. It took us one month. There was another ship named Sydney that left at the same time as we did from Malta but arrived a week earlier. That was a very fast ship." Emmanuel shared a cabin with his fiancé Mary Borg and her family. "I was only seventeen but I had to look after my fiancé, her mother, her two sisters and four brothers. Her father was in Australia. We only paid ten pounds and we had to stay two years. That was the condition of our immigration. Mary's brothers were underage so they didn't have to pay."

Emmanuel recalls a strict upbringing in Malta. "In those days, parents in Malta were very strict with their children. They would beat you with a belt if they caught you lying or if they thought you were secretly seeing a girl. You weren't supposed to have a girlfriend. You were meant to be in church. Discipline was number one back then. But I tell you

something, I thank God I grew up during those times. Because of the way I was brought up, I was able to avoid getting in trouble later in life.

According to Emmanuel, a young bride in Malta was given a glory box by her parents containing clothes, linen and sometimes a pram for her married life. The groom did not receive any gifts or rewards. "Most men were expected to have a job before they could get married," says Emmanuel. "But not the women. If they wanted to work, they had to ask their husbands for permission and most men would have said no. We would give them whatever they want so they would stay home to look after the family. In my time women had to dress respectable and not show any skin. They couldn't even wear lipstick. If a woman wore make-up you knew that she was a woman of the road."

Emmanuel left primary school and became a carpenter. By the time he left Malta, he could speak three languages; Maltese, Italian and English.

"I remember when I applied to come to Australia I had to get a medical check-up. They check your teeth, lungs, everything. Then I had an appointment with the Australian Immigration Officer in Valletta who told me to get a haircut and shave off my moustache because he thought I looked like a Bodgie. You see in those days, Australia had Widgies and Bodgies. The Widgies were young rebellious girls and the Bodgies were young rebellious boys. I remember the Immigration Officer said to me, 'Mr Mallia, I like you. You have a trade and you are a church boy. I know this. You have scored a 100 out of 100 with your application, but I warn you. You look like one of these Bodgies and when you see the next immigration officer he will turn you away. My advice to you is go to the barber shop and get a short, back and sides and make yourself look respectable.' I can understand that at the time, they wanted to get the best people to come to Australia but back then, I was angry because I had to change the way I looked. I wasn't a Bodgie. I used to go to church every day."

After the Second World War, most of the buildings in Malta were destroyed. "Malta was the most bombed place on earth at that time," says Emmanuel. "Everyone wanted to leave. Every fortnight a ship would leave Valletta for

Australia with 800 people on board.

Our cabin was right down the bottom of the ship, in steerage. You could see the water from the port-hole. I mean we were under the water. As far as I know, the cabins at the bottom of the ship were larger than the cabins on the upper levels. I think they put us there because there was nine of us travelling together.

The best advice I got before leaving Malta was to buy these cigarettes called Rummy and bring them on the ship. One penny, you can buy three cigarettes. I bought three boxes, around 100 cigarettes. Every time an Italian crew member would bring us food to the cabin, I would offer them a few cigarettes. I would do this so they could like us. After a while they brought us whatever we asked for. The cigarettes helped us to get friendly with the crew so they could do us special favours.

I remember we stopped at Port Said, Colombo and then Fremantle. I got off the ship at Fremantle and there was a park nearby and I saw these local boys playing soccer so I went over and joined them. I went crazy with joy and I just kept playing with them and sweating so much. My poor mother-in-law was calling out to me, 'Lelle! Come back Lelle, the ship is leaving.' I was playing soccer with the Aussies and having so much fun. I could speak English you see, so it was no trouble playing with them.

When we arrived to Melbourne, I remember there were two tug boats dragging our ship to the port. We got all our bags ready but we had to wait for the Immigration people to check our papers and all that, before we were allowed to leave the ship and step onto the pier."

Three days after he arrived, Emmanuel found work in a factory called Service Industries in Port Melbourne but unfortunately sliced off two fingers on a buzzer saw. "I had to go to court and the judge awarded me 100 guineas compensation which in those days was a lot of money. One guinea was 21 shillings. I was earning eight guineas a week back then. It took me three months before I could work again."

Emmanuel believes that the British Subjects such as the Maltese migrants were treated better than the non-British Subjects. "The Italian migrants for instance were sent to work on the roads or the sugar plantations. The Italians were a gold mine for the Australian people because they were hard working and experienced. Let me tell you something else. When I used to go to the butcher's shop with my mother-in-law to buy meat, we were shocked to find out that the Aussie butchers would throw out the meat that we would pay money for back in Malta. Meat such as cow hearts, liver and all that. Yes, migrants really taught the Aussies a lot."

Emmanuel and Mary were married in Melbourne on the 21st of May, 1955, one year exactly after they arrived from Malta.

ANNIE DOGGETT-WILLIAMS

Annie Doggett-Williams was born on the 7th of February, 1922 in Valletta, Malta. "My father Peter Grima, was Greek," she tells me proudly. "He was from Corfu. They say that he ran away from home when he was sixteen and he came to Valletta. That's where he met my mother, Lorenza Ciantar."

Annie met her husband Joseph in Valletta when she was fourteen. "We met on the 7th of August, 1936," says Annie. "He was fifteen and five months. Joe's mother died after he was born and he was adopted by a close friend of his father. We used to meet in a park when we were teenagers. It was the Upper Barrakka in Valletta. It was wonderful. There was music, violin and mouth organ. Beautiful Italian songs. I wasn't allowed to go with boys in those days. You had to sneak out. Everything was in secret. Joe was mad about football. He became a goalkeeper for Malta after the war."

Annie and Joseph were married during the Second World War in 1941. "When the war started most of the schools closed down. We stayed in Mdina for five years during the war. My husband Joe was in the police force. He used to help remove the rubble from the bombed buildings to save our people."

"Malta was bombed continuously during the war," adds Annie. "The island was in ruins. So many buildings destroyed. We heard the bombs coming down. We heard them, and heard them and heard them. They dropped hundreds of bombs that can cut you into pieces. Most of the time, there were three air raids a night. It was frightening and exhausting. Going up and down from the bomb shelters all night. We lost everything. They bombed our house. I had my two baby daughters with me in the shelters. Dolores was born

in 1942 and Carmel in March 1943. Later my daughter Josephine was born in 1945."

After the war, many Maltese families decided to accept Australia's Assisted Passage Scheme and leave their homeland. When Joseph's sister Elizabeth (Lizzie) migrated to Australia with her family in 1947, he decided to do the same.

"We left Malta on the 26th of April, 1949 on an Egyptian ship named Misr," Annie recalls. "We arrived in Melbourne on the 29th of May, 1949. I remember we stopped at Port Said, Colombo, Perth and then Melbourne. It took us 35 days. It was me and Joseph and our three kids and Joseph's mother, Guiseppa. Joseph and I had our own cabin because I was eight months pregnant and our kids were downstairs with Guiseppa. We were separated. All we needed was a Maltese passport. We paid ten pounds each but Joseph's mother had to pay 100 ponds because she was an older woman. My son Peter was born a month after we arrived. It was a good trip. Beautiful weather, good food. We brought over 2000 pounds with us from Malta because we sold everything before we left. I remember we arrived on a Sunday and everything was closed. There were no cars. It was so quiet and so empty. I didn't like it at first. It was so different to Malta. I missed the weather and the atmosphere of Valletta."

Eight days after they arrived, Joseph bought a shop, (a mixed business) on Adderley Street in West Melbourne with a large house attached. "There were twelve rooms which we would rent to other people," says Annie. "The boarders would pay one pound each a week. Joseph bought the shop because he could make more money than working as a bank clerk. The bank grabbed him, and they offered

Annie Doggett-Williams aged 100, in 2022.

him a job. He could speak seven languages you see, so they wanted him but they could only pay him seven pounds a week. It wasn't a lot of money for our growing family so that's why he bought the shop."

Annie explained that in the early years, her family did experience some racism. "We were always considered to be New Australian," she says firmly. "We suffered a lot in those days, especially the kids at school. When my daughter Dolores went to primary school, the teacher made her stand on a desk and turn around so the other kids could see what a little foreign girl looked like. Even when we would go to catch the bus, the locals would push us. It was very difficult in the beginning."

ACKNOWLEDGEMENTS

I would like to thank Emmanuel Mallia, Evelyn Spiteri and Annie Doggett-Williams for allowing me to publish their stories of migration. Special thanks to Lenard Ciantar, Michelle and Sophia Hanger and Evelyn's daughters Anne and Jane for their kind help and support along the way.

Just over one million people migrated to Australia between 1945 and 1955, almost half of which were British. The number of migrants had increased to two and a half million by 1977.

Almost 7,000 Cypriots migrated to Australia between 1947 and 1955 (4,670 had arrived by 1952).

Over 2,800 migrant voyages to Australia took place after the Second World War, between 1945 and 1977. In that time two and a half million people migrated to Australia.

The population of Australia in December 1945 was 7,430,197. This increased to 9,311,825 by December 1955.

In the years between 1947 and 1966, the total Australian workforce increased by almost one million, of which fifty-nine per cent were born overseas.

Sixty-five percent of the workers employed at the General Motors Holden plant at Fishermans Bend in Melbourne were migrants.

The Australian Steel Industry workforce increased by seventy-five percent between 1945 and 1955 due to migration. This resulted in significant increases in local production, boosting the economy by reducing the reliance on imported goods.

In 1955, a third of the workforce at McKay Massey Harris were migrants which resulted in the production and export of agricultural machinery worth one million pounds.

At one point during the war, Australia had a shortage of around 200,000 houses. No fewer that 41,000 building tradesmen were brought to Australia between 1947 and 1955, helping to overcome the shortage of housing.

Most of the early development work on the Snowy Mountain Scheme was dependant on the employment of 100,000 migrant workers.

Over seventy percent of the workforce employed in harvesting fruit crops and sugar cane during the 1950s were migrants.

THE LIGURIA AT WHARF WITH THE SHIP'S CAPTAIN. 1951

PASSENGERS ON THE DECK OF THE LIGURIA. 1951

VIEW ALONG LOWER ESPLANADE, PORT MELBOURNE, VIC.

Constantinos (Costas) Emmanuelle is an Australian-born Cypriot artist living in Melbourne. This is the second book in his Tales of Cyprus series. His first book *Tales of Cyprus. A Tribute to a Bygone Era* (published in 2018) was a sell-out success, embraced by lovers of Cypriot culture from around the world.

Over the past thirty years Costas has taught art and design at various tertiary institutions both in Australia and overseas. He has enjoyed a celebrated career working as an illustrator, graphic designer, visual artist and photographer. His culturally inspired art has been exhibited in a number of successful group and solo shows.

Costas is married to Dr. Christina Pavlides, an archaeologist and London-born Cypriot. He has four children and a cat called Stampy.

conemmanuelle@talesofcyprus.com
www.talesofcyprus.com
www.facebook.com/talesofcyprus

ETIQUETA DE EQUIPAJE DEL PASAJERO
CORSICA
CIA NAV DARU - PANAMA
NOMBRE
NAME Elpida Loizou
DESTINO
DESTINATION
PER SS/MS
HUT Nº 469PP
d.d. 13
CA
GRAND HÔTEL DE LA POSTE
PORT SAÏD
Egypte
HUT Nº 469PP
CABIN
NOMBRE
NAME Elpida Loizou
DESTINO
DESTINATION
PER SS/MS
CORSICA
CIA NAV DARU - PANAMA
d.d. 13 DEC. 1951
469
LOUIS
Tourist Agency Ltd.
HORN OF AFRICA
DJIBOUTI
CYP
PORT OF LIMASSOL
CYPRUS
MASSAWA
CEYLON
GALLE FACE HOTEL
COLOMBO
GRAND
PORT SA
Egypte
GALLE FACE H
COLOMB
CEY